-KINETICS-
-In Search of Willow-

-ARBOR WINTER BARROW-

The people, some locations, and most incidents in this book are fictional,
any resemblance in name or appearance is probably coincidental.

Chapter quotes (by real people) belong to the person who spoke them and
no infringement is intended.

Cover Art/Fire Bump Emblem: Arbor Winter Barrow

ISBN-13: 978-1505579437
ISBN-10: 1505579430

DEDICATED TO:

All of those people who encouraged me, discouraged me, lifted me up, and tore me down. You have made me stronger than you will ever know.

<3

TABLE OF CONTENTS

PROLOGUE

Rage.

Without knowing what I was doing I lunged forward and released a blast of fire from my fingertips. It was bigger than anything I could have imagined possible. The ground itself seemed to set on fire in front of me. In seconds I was on the ground, Grey had tackled me and the fire I had produced was raging out of control. My clothes were setting on fire as were the clothes of Grey. I struggled under his scarily strong grip and the fire continued to rage.

Grey was unaffected by the fire I was blasting out. It was out of control now. I didn't have any more control over it than an ant has over the weather. I started to get scared. I couldn't stop it. Grey slammed his hand into my head.

STOP. I felt his voice in every crevasse of my brain. His telepathic voice shuddered all the way down my spine.

My muscles locked and I stared wide-eyed into his face. But something else was happening in my chest. Tears started flowing out of my eyes and the pain in my chest started to grow. I curled in on myself and clenched my chest. I felt a fire like none other burning a hole. I looked down and saw a bright light coming from where my heart was. And suddenly everything went dark.

I should have prepared myself for this. I should have known that I wasn't strong enough. But one month ago failure

was the furthest thing from my mind.
   I'm so sorry.

PART 1:
WHEN NIGHTMARES BECOME REALITY

CHAPTER 1

*"Destiny is no matter of chance. It is a matter of choice.
It is not a thing to be waited for, it is a thing to be
achieved."* - William Jennings Bryan. American Politician.

ONE MONTH EARLIER

If I'd known that the last normal day of my life would be spent pining over a girl, I might have made some different choices. I probably would have been a little smarter about my time, a little nicer to my mother, a little more forgiving of my father. But, hindsight is like a wolf in sheep's clothing, ready to bite you the moment you turn your back.

To say the least, I was not ready for what was to come.

Instead, the last day of my normal life began with a phone call to my friend Nick as I rode the bus on the way to school one morning.

"Willow is the love of my life," I declared to him. The loud conversations and shouts from the other kids on the bus nearly drowned me out.

"You're fifteen, Eugene," Nick said. *"I don't think you can make that kind of statement."*

"But it's true. Who says you have to be, I dunno, *twenty-four*," I said, taking a stab at his age, "to know what it means to have a 'love-of-your-life'?"

I glanced out the bus window and pressed the phone close to my ear to hear over the road noise and the other kids shouting. Houses passed in blurs, coming into focus only when the bus stopped to pick up another kid standing on a street corner. I still hadn't gotten used to riding the bus alone.

Willow lived within biking distance of the school, so she never rode the bus anymore. When we were younger, we lived on the same block and went to and from school together every day. Before the Pattersons moved a couple years ago, I had never been more than a mile from her at all times.

"She's mine, and that's all there is to it," I said, sighing. "I really can't imagine going on without her."

Nick laughed.

Nick was originally my brother's best friend. They were the same age, and had gone to school together most of their lives. They parted ways when Jacob joined the Peace Corps at nineteen.

I was twelve years old when Jacob left, and Nick had quickly inserted himself into my life as sort of a substitute older brother. It didn't hurt that Nick was close enough to my parents to come and go as he pleased.

The time after my brother left wasn't an easy one. I thought I could never be as good as he was in my parents' eyes. I felt the weight of my parents' high expectations pressing on me. Jacob was good at everything. He excelled in school, and decided to skip college entirely to start working with the Peace Corps.

Having an older-brother figure like Nick eased some of the tension. When I was thirteen, an argument with my parents had made me decide to run away, but Nick talked me into spending a few days with him on a trip to some universities in New York instead. When we returned I wasn't angry with my parents anymore and running away was the last thing on my mind.

Nick was the first one to teach me how to play basketball. When he wasn't off on a business trip, he came over every Saturday and played one-on-one with me, talking to me about school and life in general. He listened to my frustrations and my successes with an open ear and calm replies.

When I was fifteen I failed an exam and after beating myself up over it for hours, Nick sat me down and went over the whole thing with me. "You can't change a failure, but you can learn from it and do better next time," he said.

He was usually the one I went to when I had really important things to talk about, but he was out of town that day, so I had to settle for the phone today.

My feelings for Willow didn't come out of nowhere. I had known her for most of my life, and I'd recently started to get the "warm fuzzies," as Nick liked to call them.

"Sure, E-man," he said, still laughing. *"I'm sure that will last about a week, kinda like the period you're having right now."*

"Nick!" I knew I was whining, but I didn't care. I hunched into a ball and tried to avoid the sideways glances my classmates were giving me.

Nick was having a great time at my expense. He was treating my life-changing realization like a skit on a comedy-hour show.

It frustrated me, but he was the only person I really felt like talking to about it. The only other person I would talk to about stuff like this was Willow, but since Willow was the subject...Well, I had few options.

"All right. Let's say that, hypothetically, she's the love of your life. Then what? What's your game plan?"

He was still laughing, and I really wanted to reach through the phone and sock him in the jaw.

I scratched at a bit of gunk on the window, taking my frustrations out on many years' worth of grime and who knows what else.

Finally, I replied, "I don't know. She's been hanging out with that senior, Harry."

"The nerdy football player?"

"Yeah," I said.

I'd forgotten that I'd told him about Harry. He had been at our school only a year, but already he was popular, good with football, good with the teachers, good with classes, and apparently good with Willow.

She'd had nothing but googly eyes for him since the honors club had gone on a camping trip over spring break a few weeks before.

"What? Did he sing her mathematical sonnets in the

bleachers or something?" Nick asked.

"I don't know. I don't really see the attraction."

"Of course you don't. You're about as attractive as a doorknob."

I ignored him and continued to scratch the bits of crusty dust off the window. My fingernail dug deeper into the gunk.

Before spring break, I had a planned to tell her, to let her know that I was...well, that I really liked her. Nick had always said that sometimes it's better to go slow with things like that. Telling her she was the "love of my life" might scare her off.

Nick chuckled. *"You gotta admit it, though, girl's got some class going after that oxymoron."*

"Moron is right," I muttered.

"Since when did you get straight As in all *the AP classes?"*

I finally erupted. "Nick, I love this girl and she's my best friend, and *I don't know what to do!"* I flung my one free arm out, hitting the seat in front of me with my fingers.

I got more stares and a few snickers. I knew I was making a massive fool of myself.

"Tell her. What is she gonna say? 'No, thanks'?"

"Yes." I said flatly. "I can see that happening."

And I really could. Willow could be irritatingly flippant about the most serious things. I could see her laughing at my confession of love.

"Well, you'll never know unless you ask."

"I already know," I said.

I didn't know what else I could say to that, but I knew that telling her right now wasn't an option. She was practically hip-to-hip with Harry every day. They had three classes together and a club together, and she spent a lot of time at his place every few days out of the week to study.

I didn't think a lot of studying was going on.

I was, at that point, facing inevitable rejection. I was more willing to let the warm fuzzies quietly stew than to face Willow and get the "no" that I knew was waiting for me.

The bus jostled roughly as it turned into the school parking lot, and I let out a breath of air.

I was ready to stop talking about it.

"We're at the school now. I'll catch you later."

"Don't stress, dude," Nick said, reassuringly.

Easier said than done. Willow was taking up more of my head space than I could deal with at the moment.

Nick said goodbye and hung up, and I shoved my cellphone into my pocket.

"Trying," I said to no one in particular.

I walked off the bus into the morning sunlight and into the last normal day of my life.

***

I found Willow sitting outside our first class. It was the one class we shared all semester, and it was usually the best part of my day. She was always early, reading a book or jotting down notes in her journal. And she always sat in the same place with her back to one of the big windows in the hallway.

Today, the sun was out enough to catch the red strands of hair escaping from her braids. She had a cloud of light around her head brightening up her already pale skin. It was beautiful. She was beautiful.

The hallway was buzzing with kids catching up on last night's television show or talking about video games. There was even a crowd of girls bickering loudly in a corner, but all I could see was Willow.

How could I not love her?

She looked up from her book and smiled at me. "Hey," she said.

I grinned. "Hi."

I plopped down on the bench next to her, shooing away any betraying feelings and putting on my poker face. "Whatcha reading?"

She chuckled. "Something incredibly dry by an author you'll forget the second I tell you."

I frowned playfully, bumped her shoulder with mine, and leaned over her shoulder to look at the page she was on. "Try me."

She gave me a pitying smile. "*Nicomachean Ethics*, by Aristotle."

"You've read that before," I said, glancing at the words on the page like I knew what the hell they meant.

"Yeah. I'm thinking of doing my next English paper on it." She put her bookmark into the pages and closed the book.

"Ugh. How do you do it? AP English?"

She laughed. "You know I like a challenge. Besides, it's fun."

"I don't know if I'd use that word for it." I leaned against the window pane and the heat from outside seeped into my back.

"Of course you wouldn't. And that's okay." She rested her head against the window and smiled at me.

I shrugged and smiled back. "What can I say? With your brains and my brawn we could take over the world."

"Brawn?" She shook her head and grinned. "Are you hiding it under your hat?" She lifted my cap and ruffled my hair. "No brawn here."

I swatted away her hand and tucked the runaway strands of black hair back under the brim of my hat.

"Cut your hair, you bum," she said, tugging teasingly at the back of my hair. "You could compete in the Rapunzel Olympics and probably win"

"What about you, Little Mermaid Einstein?" I shot back.

She lifted her nose at me and smiled. She always said that she hated her wild, frizzy, red hair. If her mother wasn't one hundred percent against it, Willow probably would have already dyed it brown and cut it short.

"I'd give you a piece of my mind, but class is about to start and we both know it would take too long." She rolled her eyes comically at me and tightened her braid.

"Noted, you pretentious ass." I shoved her arm.

She stuck out her tongue and laughed. As we stood up to enter our classroom, one of the bickering girls in the corner pushed out and ran past us. All I saw was a blonde head flash by and disappear into the throng of students making their way to class.

I looked at Willow, but she just shrugged. Neither of us knew the girl.

We took our seats in our first class, and the teacher began his instruction.

"Monday, as you all know, is the start of Career Week. On a piece of paper, I want you guys to tell me about your plans after high school, be it college or traveling the world, anything. We'll discuss them when you guys come back on Monday."

Mr. Grant walked around the room as papers rustled.

I tapped the piece of paper with my pencil, but nothing was coming to mind. It's not that I didn't have plans, but the empty space on the paper was daunting. I knew anything I wrote wouldn't determine my whole life, but not a lot interested me besides hanging out with my friends and talking with Willow.

I wasn't good enough at basketball to think about pursuing a scholarship or a career.   My second best class was math, but I really didn't want to be a mathematician. What did they even do? Write equations on a dusty chalkboard and stare at it for hours? Yeah, not for me.

"Two more minutes, guys," Mr. Grant said, tapping his watch.

I copped out in the last second.

Go to college, get a degree in math, play basketball on scholarship, I wrote.

I glanced over at Willow, who was smiling over her notebook. She'd filled an entire page with her plans.

What was I thinking? Trying to even get to her level was impossible. I looked down at my meager sentence and sighed.

***

I walked with Willow out into the hallway and to our next classes. Mine was another hallway past hers, so our route worked out well. I hated that since high school began, Willow had been taking all the advanced and honors classes. We had few classes together. Meanwhile, she was set to graduate high school with enough college credits to graduate college in just two years.

"What did your folks say about taking classes at the community college?" I asked, bringing up the tail end of a conversation we'd had on the phone the night before.

As if high school wasn't enough, she was gearing up to start taking actual college classes. It wasn't hard to feel dwarfed.

"They think it's a great idea. I'm probably going to start next semester." She hugged her books to her chest and skipped a few feet with a smile.

"Pre-med still?"

"Yup." She sighed wistfully and picked at a loose strand of hair.

"What's that about?" I asked, frowning. "Don't you still want to be a doctor?"

For as long as I'd known Willow, she'd aspired to be a doctor. Sure, we went through the fireman and policeman stages together as children, but when the doctor stage hit, she stayed there while I moved on to action star and astronaut.

She knew the Hippocratic Oath before she ever memorized her own address.

If anyone was going to be a doctor, it was going to be her.

"Of course." Her expression brightened, and she smiled at me. "It's nothing. Had another thought. Don't worry about it."

"Hey!" another voice interjected before I could reply to her.

Harry, the nerdy football player, ran up to Willow and tugged on her braid. I looked away to hide my scowl. He could have been the poster child for tall, dark and handsome with his suntanned skin and brown hair that seemed to always look perfect.

I hated his guts and the way Willow looked at him with something akin to adoration. Heck, every girl in school looked at him with adoration, but he only had eyes for Willow.

Damnit.

"'Sup, Red?" asked Harry. He didn't really acknowledge

me. Not that I expected him to.

"Harry!" Willow grinned up at him.

I clenched my teeth to keep from making any remarks I would regret.

"I'll catch you later," I said.

I moved to leave, but Willow caught my shirt sleeve.

"Hey," she said. She smiled, but her eyes were serious. She seemed to sense that something was wrong. "Still want to meet up after extracurriculars?"

I nodded and waved as I started to walk away.

I had to leave before I heard any of their conversation. I didn't want to know how much of a fool I was for feeling the way I did. She paired well with Harry, the too-smart, nerdy, football player; not me, the directionless idiot.

I continued to my next class. Alone.

CHAPTER 2

"In everyone's life, at some time, our inner fire goes out. It is then burst into flame by an encounter with another human being. We should all be thankful for those people who rekindle the inner spirit."
~ Albert Schweitzer. German philosopher and theologian.

My last extracurricular class of the day was basketball practice.

Every Tuesday and Friday, the team met up in the gym to play a few games while our coach tried to teach us new plays.

"Dude! Pass it!" Pete yelled to me from the other side of the court.

I dodged around some of the other guys, dribbling fast. I faked a throw toward Jerry, but caught the eye of Tim the center and passed it to him instead. Tim swerved with the ball and spun in a tight half-circle around an opponent. He threw the ball, and it spun around the rim of the net before finally falling in.

I high-fived a couple of the guys.

"Alright, guys!" Coach Greene clapped his hands and blew his whistle. "Good try. Form up again!"

When I think back on it, I don't remember that much of the game or exactly what happened. But between the shouts and cheers, something was being drowned out.

One of the other guys had just scored and the few kids sitting in the bleachers cheered. It wasn't until we formed up to start again and the gym quieted that we heard it.

Screams.

They weren't the shouts of spectators, which normally accompanied our games and occasionally our practices.

They were screams of terror.

The other team's center stopped with the ball in his hands and looked around. Others also stopped and began to listen. Within seconds, everyone was looking toward the double-doors that led into the school.

"What's happening?" Pete asked, wiping at the sheen of sweat on his forehead.

"Everyone stay back," yelled Coach Greene as he waved us back. He peered through the doors' small windows.

"Coach, what is it?" someone asked from the back of the room.

Coach Greene's face paled, and his eyes darted back and forth.

"Outside! Go outside," he yelled, pointing to gym's back door, which led out into the parking lot.

The others looked at each other, waiting for someone to take charge. I sucked in a breath, not fully sure of what to do, and ran for the back door. I slammed my hands on the bar latch. It swung open, hitting the brick wall adjacent to it.

I stopped in my tracks.

About twenty feet in front of me on the grass, a pillar of fire blasted up from the ground. From a single point on the ground fire shot up, spread out and began circling the school. A wall of fire now stood between us and the outside.

I couldn't move. I wanted to get away from the wall of fire, but my legs would not budge. In my head I was screaming at myself to back up, close the door and hide. But every muscle in my body was locked. I couldn't feel any heat coming off the fire, but it didn't matter. It was too close, heat or not.

Tim had followed me out. He shook off his shock before I could.

"Fire!" he yelled.

He grabbed the back of my shirt and pulled me inside, yanking the door shut behind us. I tumbled back and hit the floor hard.

I gasped, not realizing that I had been holding my breath, and looked down at my hands. They were shaking violently. I pushed through the shakes and got to my feet, deliberately not looking behind me at the door standing between us and a raging fire.

My friends, teammates and I gathered around Coach Greene, looking for some explanation for the chaos rising around us. The screams from inside the school were getting louder. We were trapped.

And then it hit me: Willow was still in the school.

She could be in trouble.

"I have to go in there. Willow's in there," I said.

The adrenaline that had taken over while I stared at the wall of fire rushed back through my limbs. I ignored the protests from my friends and sprinted for the door, ducking under Coach Greene's hand when he tried to catch me.

I slammed the doors open and tumbled through. My legs locked when I saw what lay beyond the doors.

Students and teachers alike were writhing and screaming in pain on the floor of the hallway, blindly lashing out at things only they could see. Screams echoed down the hallway from every corner of the school. The ceiling lights were flickering in and out and whole sections of hallway were doused in darkness.

I hesitated for only a second before I took a breath and started to job down the hall toward the classroom where I knew Willow should have been.

I carefully stepped over people lying on the linoleum floors. Some were muttering under their breaths, and others were outright screaming.

One of the janitors was crawling across the floor shouting, "Bodies! *The bodies.*"

I inched around him, trying to stay away from his grasping hands. He saw me and held out his hands. "Save me. Save me!"

I jumped away from his grasp. He rolled over and hugged the wall, slamming his fists into the concrete and drawing blood.

21

Shaking, I crept down the hall, careful not to step on anyone.

They were all the same. All the students and teachers in the halls were caught in the same hallucination, and a sinking feeling in my gut told me it was only a matter of time before it would also happen to me.

Not before I find Willow, I scolded myself.

Willow had to be safe.

I ran past a wall of windows which should have offered a view of the schoolyard and skidded to a halt.

The fire that we had seen from the back door of the gym was outside these windows too, and I felt myself start to shut down again.

Willow, I reminded myself. *I have to keep going.*

The fire was at least three stories high, but as I sprinted past the windows, I noticed that the fire had no source other than the grass. What was feeding it? Was it surrounding the whole school?

I looked away, determined to make it to Willow's classroom before the fire or whatever was afflicting the others could get to me.

Finally, I reached her classroom, but she wasn't there.

I shouted her name over the chaos of voices and screams. I searched the faces of people sprawled in the hallways and into the classrooms, but I saw no sign of her.

I began running from room to room, kicking doors open and repeatedly shouting her name. I skidded into the main hallway and stumbled to a stop.

Willow was standing across the expanse of the hallway staring at another girl whose back was facing me.

The other girl was unaffected by the insanity around us. I couldn't see her face, but I saw messy blond hair. Her shoulders rose and fell harshly as she breathed.

I slid behind an overturned table and watched the silent, staring battle between the two girls. Willow took a step forward. The other girl, who I vaguely recognized as a transfer from a few weeks ago, stood her ground but clenched her fists.

Willow took another step forward. Her eyes never

blinked, never wavered. Beads of sweat trailed down her brow. Her expression was more intense than I'd ever seen.

I shifted behind the table, and my foot knocked into a jar and it rattled across the floor. The other girl's head snapped in my direction, and fierce blue eyes found me.

Suddenly, I wasn't in the school anymore. Instead I was surrounded by a hurricane of fire. It roared and hot winds circled around me, whipping my clothes.

"Stop!" I shouted, but the fire closed in. The heat was nearly unbearable. I wanted to close my eyes but they wouldn't close.

"It's all your fault, Eugene," whispered a familiar voice in my mind, resonating through my skull and into my bones. As I heard the words, a face protruded from the fire and a flame shot out at me.

"You should never have been born," said another voice, louder this time. Another face. Another flame.

"You could have killed us all," shouted a third voice. A third face appeared, and the three joined together, whispering and shouting their hatred.

The voices. They were the voices and the faces of my mother, my father and my brother. All rolled into one judgmental, three-headed fire beast. From the waves of flame, licking at my heels and my face, the beast circled me, growling angrily. My family stared down at me, their faces reflecting the hatred in their words.

"You killed, us Eugene," it said, the faces bobbing. *"You made us die because you were too weak."*

Their voices had merged, creating an entirely new one.

"No," I said. "No, I didn't mean to! I'm sorry!"

I shielded my eyes against the hot glare of the fire beast.

"TOO LATE!" it screeched, and the monster rose up like a snake preparing to strike.

I covered my head with my arms, yelling, "I'm sorry!"

The monster struck, but when it did, the fire exploded around me and dissipated, leaving me in total darkness.

I spun around, reaching with my hands to find something, anything. The darkness was so absolute that I couldn't see my hands in front of my face. My breath sounded loudly in the silence.

I reached down in the darkness to touch the floor, but there was nothing there.

I was standing on air.

My heart beat faster. What if I fell? What would I fall into?

Something sparked in the distance. A light. I ran forward, not entirely sure that I wouldn't fall into nothingness. I could feel a heat at my back. The fire beast was bubbling back up from the darkness. I could hear its vicious whispers rising.

The closer I got to the light, the more I realized it wasn't just a light. It was a person. It was Willow. She stood reaching her arm out toward me. She glowed.

-*Be strong,*- echoed her voice in my mind. -*It's an illusion. It can't hurt you.*-

"Willow," I gasped, clasping her outstretched hand.

The darkness evaporated, and I was in the hallway again, standing in front of Willow and clasping her hand.

Willow was on her knees, but she was looking past me at the other girl. She let go of my hand.

The girl gritted her teeth and screamed in frustration.

"You need to stop," Willow said to her. "You don't need to do this."

"Who are you to tell me what I need to do?" the girl shouted. The others still stuck in illusions gasped and screamed.

"You're hurting people, Laura!" Willow pushed herself to her feet, never letting her gaze waver from the girl.

The girl, Laura, sobbed.

"They hurt me first. It's my turn." She stamped her foot, and the whole school shuddered.

Suddenly, all around us monsters made of black slime, glistening like an oil slick, began welling up from cracks in the floor.

They were huge salamander-like, with bulbous limbs and dripping claws. Their teeth and eyes were molten red, glowing with the light of a waking volcano.

The kids on the floor began emerging from their personal nightmares only to enter the one we were all sharing.

Willow didn't break eye contact with Laura, but instead reached out and grabbed my hand again.

Her fingers were slick with sweat. I squeezed them tightly, hoping some of the strength she had given me would pass back to her.

"Willow, what is this?" I whispered.

I could see tears forming at the corners of her eyes.

"When this is all over, Eugene, I'll explain everything. But for now, trust that I know what I'm doing."

I had never seen her serious about anything but her schoolwork. Everything else was a joke or a game.

"What can I do?" I asked.

"Don't let go," she whispered, squeezing my hand. She closed her eyes.

Cries from the slime monsters pierced the air as they crawled out of the floor, joining the shouts and screams of the students on the floor. The monsters filled the entire space of the hallway within seconds.

Willow squeezed my hand, and she suddenly began dragging me away from Laura, through an emergency exit and out into what should have been the front lawn of the school.

The wall of fire surrounding the school burned even taller and brighter. It roared and reached toward us like grasping hands. Dark smoke spilled upwards.

Willow didn't let me stand there long before she was dragging me toward the fire.

I screamed in protest.

"It's not real!" she shouted before dragging me with her into the fire.

I expected heat. I expected to feel the pain of my skin burning off.

But I felt neither.

We landed hard on the other side, rolling across the grass. I touched my chest and hair, expecting them to be on fire, but I was fine.

Willow scrambled up and pulled me to my feet.

The fire was gone and the school looked like it did every other day. No fire or slime monsters trawling every surface. The blue sky wasn't tainted with smoke, but instead lazy white clouds passed overhead.

"Where'd it go?" I asked, shocked.

"You can only see it from inside her sphere."

Willow turned to look back at the school.

"Um...Sphere?"

"It's the area she can influence."

I had more questions than answers, and my whole perception of Willow was beginning to change.

She clutched at her hair, loosening it from the braid that had come partially undone.

"I know this is all confusing, but I promise I'll explain later. Come on." She took my hand and led me quickly across the lawn.

"Who is she?" I asked, breathless, as we ran.

"Her name is Laura," she replied. We stopped on the side of the school where the gym was. "She's a sophomore, just transferred in from a school in Indianapolis."

"How is she doing this?"

"Somehow she's taking people's fears and nightmares and turning them into hallucinations."

"What do we do now?" I expected her to say we should go for help, but I should have known better.

Willow clung tighter to my hand.

"We have to find the source."

"The source?"

"Yes." She pulled and we plunged back into what Willow called the sphere.

Fire surrounded us again, but it was now even higher and louder. From somewhere above us, ash began to fall and coat the ground in a fine, gray blanket.

"Laura made a decoy. That's what I was facing in the hallway. She's actually somewhere else."

"I really don't get how you know all this," I said as Willow let go of my hand to open the back door of the gym.

My teammates inside had succumbed to Laura's

26

illusions and were screaming and shouting.

"Eugene, the second you feel her trying to make you see illusions, tell me," she said.

We skirted around the edge of the gym to get to the door. As we stepped out into the hallway, which now stood eerily empty, she reached her hand out again and smiled at me. I took it and nodded.

We ran hand-in-hand through the school. Willow seemed to know where she was going, so I let her lead me through each hallway. I didn't know what was going on or why this was happening.

Willow was so focused on finding the real version of Laura that I was sure any questions I had would go unanswered.

We turned a corner, still running, and collided with someone.

We fell to the floor, but I scrambled to my feet and stared at the person we had run into.

"Harry." Willow smiled and got to her feet.

Harry, the nerdy football player stood in front of us.

CHAPTER 3

"I believe that we are at a precipice. A middle ground of sorts. We are confronted with a great leap into darkness from the relative safety of light and familiarity. The question is: Are we truly ready to take the leap that on one hand could lead us into a time of prosperity and increased safety but on the other hand could herald the beginning of our certain end?"
~ Former Chief Minister of the Anyan's Alliance Thomas Reddinger in a speech to the Council of Six.

"Are you okay?" he asked.

She nodded.

I picked myself up and eyed Harry.

"Have you seen Laura anywhere?" she asked him, but he just shook his head.

"Not yet. I was coming to find you to make sure you were safe."

Willow flicked some stray hair out of her face.

"Thanks, Harry. But I can keep myself out of trouble."

"Obviously." Harry quirked an eyebrow and glanced behind us.

I glanced back and there were about a dozen people with glazed-over eyes and dull expressions on their faces walking toward us.

"They're sleepwalking," Willow said. "We should go."

"I think she's in the eighth-grade-English classroom," Harry said.

"How do you know that?" I asked fueling every syllable with mistrust.

Why wasn't he affected by the illusions?

"All the people under her influence are collecting in the area," said Harry. "It's like there's something drawing them there."

Willow turned on a heel and sprinted down the hall. She didn't get far.

The double-doors in front of us slammed open, and people writhing in pain and shouting incoherently tumbled through.

They saw us and ran toward us.

"Your fault! Your fault!" they shouted as they ran.

The sleepwalking people collecting behind us began shouting in unison with the people in front of us.

Laura's nightmare monsters began oozing out of the cracks again, joining the sleepwalkers in tightening the circle around us.

A loud crash sounded behind us, and a boy in a blue hoodie jumped through a broken window. Water pooled at his feet, and then in a move that would resonate with me the rest of the day, he lifted his arms in an arc and the water slammed upwards and over the sleepwalkers.

The rushing water pushed them away from us, but the water parted around us, not getting a drop of it on Willow, Harry or myself.

The kid, hoodie pulled tight around his head, didn't give us a second glance before jumping back through the window, taking the majority of the sleepwalkers with him.

The slime monsters were unaffected by the water, though, and continued to close in.

"Who was that?" I asked.

"Not sure. But I'm not looking a gift horse in the mouth," Willow replied, pushing forward.

The slime monsters didn't move out of her way, but reacted like oil to water as she passed through them.

I glanced at Harry, who merely shrugged and followed after her.

"C'mon, Eugene. They can't hurt you, they're just illusions," she said.

"So you keep saying," I muttered before running through the clutch of nightmare monsters.

I looked over my shoulder and saw the monsters re-form to continue following us. I tried to ignore the fact that they were beginning to light up like candles around me.

"Eugene!" Willow was now down the hall. I jumped, not realizing that they had gotten so far ahead of me already. I turned on a heel and ran after them.

But I was too late. They were gone. The hallway stretched out in front of me, empty and dark. Behind me the nightmare monsters came closer with their heatless flame. I shuddered to look at them.

"Willow!" I shouted down the hall, but Willow and the nerdy football player were gone. I was alone.

Alone.

Alone with monsters on fire.

I ran down the hall, repeatedly screaming Willow's name.

They can't have gotten far. They wouldn't leave me, would they?

The hallway seemed to stretch on and on. Finally I burst through a set of double-doors only to see a strange vision of myself bursting through another set of doors in front of me and disappearing.

"What's happening?" I asked out loud. My voice was small and muffled.

I ran through the double-doors again, and again I saw myself burst through and disappear.

I gasped, suddenly realizing I had been holding my breath. This was impossible. I tried again, but with the same results. I was stuck.

"No, no, no," I whispered. I opened the door behind me and went through and watched myself do the same on the other side. I was in some kind of loop.

The monsters oozed through the cracks in the door and began filling the small space. I stepped into the center of the hallway, where I was furthest from the walls. But at my feet, fire was growing. I sucked in a breath.

The fire was eating through my shoes. It spread up my legs and over my stomach. It was taking over my whole body. The monsters now fully on fire leapt from the walls and joined the fire already taking over on my body. It was turning me into fire itself.

I screamed as it reached my face.

It's an illusion... An echo of something Willow had said resonated through my mind.

Oh...

Oh.

Oh!

It's not real, it's an illusion!

I was losing myself. What had happened to the teachers and students had begun to happen to me. I was losing my grasp on reality. I looked around at the monsters circling me and at my limbs on fire. How do you escape an illusion?

I closed my eyes tightly.

"It's not real. It's not real. It's not real." I made it a mantra and walked toward the double-doors. I opened my eyes and pushed through, half expecting to come out on the other side seeing another illusion of myself. But instead I was in a bedroom.

It was a room I could only remember from pictures. My bedroom from when I was a baby.

I turned around to try opening the door, but it was locked.

Everything was weird in this illusion. I could see my hands moving before I moved them. It was like I was seeing a ghost of myself moving before I did. And unlike before, there was no sound. I couldn't even hear my own breath.

I turned back toward the room and looked around.

It was nighttime in this illusion. Through the window I could see a sliver of the moon between the branches of a distant tree. A baby's crib sat in the middle of the room, an orange glow emanating from inside.

I hesitated for only a moment before walking over to the crib and looking inside. There was a baby sitting in the middle of the crib, its blanket was pushed back and little stuffed animals were scattered at its feet. The baby was me. I was little more than a year old.

The baby me was on fire.

He looked at me and screamed a scream that made no noise. He seemed frightened, but who wouldn't be if they were on fire?

The door burst open and a young boy ran in. I recognized this boy, too. He was my brother--a much, much younger version of him, but unmistakably him. The illusion slowed as my illusion-brother reached my crib. His mouth was shouting in slow motion.

Then suddenly the world was spinning. The illusion blurred, and we were back in the room I grew up in. It was the same place but a different time. The decorations in the room had changed and there was a small toddler bed in the corner. And there I was, sitting on the floor playing with blocks, a couple years older than the baby I had seen in the crib.

And then it happened again. Fire shot from my small hand and set the blocks on fire. First the blocks, then the floor, and soon the curtains and the walls themselves were on fire.

The younger version of me was standing in a ring of fire, crying and screaming. The illusion slowed again as a woman, my mother, came through and grabbed me from the fire. Her clothes and her hair caught the flame. I shut my eyes trying to shut the illusion out, but there it was, under the darkness of my eyelids, forcing me to watch my mother burn alive.

I screamed, trying to force the vision from my mind. And then it was gone.

I could feel heat around me. I let my eyes flicker open and saw flame again, but this time it was mere embers on the fringes of papers, billboards and the walls around me. It was dying out and I could feel the heat coming off it. I looked around and saw that it had made a perfect charred circle around me.

There was no one around and the monsters were gone. I sucked in a breath and jumped out of the circle.

I ran, not caring what direction I was going in. I had to get away from the fire. I only stopped when I was tripped by a fallen chair that had been strewn haphazardly across the hallway.

Only then did I realize hot tears were leaking from my eyes. I jammed the heels of my hands against my eyes and stopped myself from sobbing.

I had to be strong for Willow. I had to always be strong.

I pushed myself up and tried to find my bearings. I was near the media lab, close to the front of the school. In the distance, under the distant screams and shouts, I could hear someone speaking.

A girl.

I followed the muffled voice to a classroom. And inside was the girl, Laura.

She stood in the center of the classroom with her hair falling over her face in blond waves. With her hands clutching a chair and her face hidden and shadowed, she looked more like someone deep in thought or prayer than someone wreaking havoc throughout the school.

"It's okay. It will all be okay. They can't hurt me here," she muttered to herself.

"Laura?" I called out.

She looked up at me. Her eyes were red-rimmed and bloodshot. Her mouth was set in a frown.

"Laura, whatever you are doing, you... you need to stop." I stepped forward, holding up my hands to show that I was no danger.

"They've hurt me enough!" she screamed, throwing the chair she had been clutching. "It's my turn!"

I was breathing hard, trying to figure out what I could say to her to stop the screams filling the school.

"No one's going to hurt you," I tried to assure her, stepping around the chairs and tables.

"Too late." I felt the invasion into my mind the second it happened. At the corners of my vision, I saw fiery monsters rising from the depths of my subconscious. She was trying to frighten me.

"Stop!" I shouted, pushing away the vision. I could feel heat at my fingers and didn't dare speculate what was happening.

She grabbed two clumps of her own hair and sobbed. "No!"

I forced myself to step toward her.

"Look, I don't know about anyone else in this school, but I won't hurt you. I'll help you," I said.

She glared at me with clenched teeth and tears flowed from her eyes in streams.

"It's too late," she said softly and looked away. "I can't go back."

"Yes, you can." I said. I wracked my brain trying to think what Willow would do in this situation. She was ten times smarter than I was and she probably would have known what to do here seconds ago.

Laura shook her head, her eyes dull and distant.

"Tell me what I can do to help you." I didn't know what I was saying. But she needed to stop this terror.

"Make it stop," she cried, looking at her hands. "I can't make it stop. It's too late."

Suddenly, Willow was beside me. I didn't know where she came from or how long she'd been standing there. I never heard her approach.

She touched my shoulder and smiled.

"It's okay," she said. "I'll take over from here."

Willow walked to Laura. Not like she was afraid of her or about to fight, but like she was a friend.

"I want you to look me in the eye, Laura," she said, holding her arms open wide. "It's not the end. It's never the end. You can always come back."

"No...It's impossible." Laura looked at Willow in the eye and shook her head. "I'm tired."

"I know." Willow reached Laura, wrapped her arms around the sobbing girl and held her.

"I'm so sorry!" Laura said into Willow's hair.

"It's okay."

Willow had turned slightly, and I could see a soft smile on her face and tears in her eyes.

I saw her whisper something into Laura's ear, and

almost instantly the firewall that I could see through the classroom windows flickered out, and the lawn returned back to normal. The screams echoing through the halls receded into sobs.

But that all seemed unimportant compared to the sight in front of me.

Willow was glowing. Every strand of her red hair was bathed in a white light coming from under her skin. The girl in her embrace was soaking in the glow, and for the first time since I'd seen her with red eyes and an unhappy face, she looked content.

Willow let go of Laura and the glow faded.

I was so stunned that I didn't notice Harry had come up behind me.

"Did you see it?" I asked.

"See what?"

"The glow."

Harry shook his head.

"The illusions are gone," he said.

CHAPTER 4

"Sometimes the best course of action is to hide in plain sight." ~ Marian Powell. A Kinetic who helped American Kinetics recover from the Salem witch trials. 1693.

If I thought the past hour with Laura's nightmares hell on Earth, I was not prepared for the next two hours.

Stoic men and women in tan jackets and black slacks had surrounded the school within moments of the firewall disappearing. No one was allowed in or out. They herded all the kids and teachers into the gym before leading them out, one by one. They ignored everyone's protests and questions with an overly practiced routine that none of us could decipher.

Laura was nowhere to be seen. Last I saw, she had been carted off by one of the guys in jackets toward the front of the school, but the effects of her actions remained. The gym was loud with students and teachers talking about the shared nightmare. Some were still huddled together, crying over what they had seen. One of the teachers was sitting at the back of the gym staring at the ceiling blankly.

No one had come out of this unscathed.

Willow, Harry, and I were all at the back of the gym.

Willow had dragged Harry aside, out of my earshot and was talking frantically to him. I was only slightly miffed that she hadn't wanted to include me, but I settled with sulking by myself and kicking imaginary holes in the gym floor. With every passing minute, the crowd of confused people grew smaller and smaller.

Willow popped back up beside me and touched my arm. I looked down at her and smiled. "You okay?"

She nodded and smiled back. "I will be."

"Who're they?" I asked, tilting my head at the people corralling everyone.

"InfoCon," she muttered, looking around.

"Info...?"

"I told you earlier, let's get through this, Eugene, and when we get home I'll explain everything. I promise, but please, for right now..."

Her eyes were half-lidded. She looked more tired and worn out than I had ever seen her. No piano recital, no soccer game, no late-night movies had ever sapped her as hard as today had.

She pinched some of the fabric on my shirtsleeve and dragged me into the crowd.

"Let's get this over with. I need to sit down," she said.

I closed my mouth against the billion questions trying to push their way out and instead followed quietly. We reached the door, and she pushed me into the hands of one of the "InfoCon" reaching for a new body to move out. The guy who grabbed me pushed me in front of a woman who looked ready to fall asleep from boredom. She touched my head and took one of my wrists. A sharp feeling like an ice pick spearing from one temple to another startled me.

"Vunjika. Registered. Alliance. No power noted," she said to the guy behind her before pulling my wrist and sending me off into the hands of another woman who pushed me down the hall.

I touched my smarting temples, confused.

"Go to the auditorium and nowhere else," the second woman said before turning back around.

I blinked in shock, walking forward with no argument. Her voice had too much authority to allow any room for it. I was dazed, trying to process the words the first woman had said.

Vunjika? What was that? Registered? With whom? What

Alliance? What kind of power?

I stepped into the auditorium, where a few other students and teachers were sitting making idle conversation with each other. They glanced up at me, but quickly returned to talking. What little of it I cared to listen in on didn't make any more sense than the rest of the day.

"...didn't know she was a Kinetic..."

"...tired of hiding..."

"...probably deserves whatever's coming to her..."

I stopped listening after that because Willow stepped into the room and slid into the seat next to mine. She rested her head on my shoulder and appeared to fall asleep.

I didn't dare move for fear of waking her.

It was rare times like this that I let myself stare at her. Her lashes weren't long, she had a small nose covered with freckles and the space between her eyebrows always creased in a funny 'W' when she was tired. I hated that she hated her hair because I loved it. It was wild, like her, wild and free, untamed by the outside world.

I reached out to touch a strand, but stopped when she adjusted her head a little. I closed the offending hand under the other and chastised myself for being so daring. She was my friend. My best friend. Those were our roles. I wasn't boyfriend material. None of the other girls in school interested me, so I hadn't even tried to be that for anyone.

My hope lay firmly in the fact that I wanted to be Willow's and Willow to be mine.

So corny. So stupid.

"I'm so glad it's the weekend," Willow said, her voice muffled by my shirt.

"Me, too," I said.

We became silent after that, and I let my mind wander. I looked at all the faces of the people in the auditorium, but I'd had little to do with most of them. What was so different about these people that we had to be segregated? And then I realized that I hadn't seen Harry.

"Where's the nerdy football player?" I asked.

"I wish you wouldn't call him that." Willow sat up and

gave me a stern look.

I shrugged and grinned. The nickname bothered her, and I loved it.

She rolled her eyes and sat back with her head tilted back.

"He's not one of us, so he'll be with the other group."

"Ah, is that something you'll explain later?"

"Yup." She popped the last letter with her lips and closed her eyes again.

I sighed and closed my eyes, too, waiting for the end of this day to come.

Almost two hours after the illusions ended, the InfoCon guy guarding the door to the auditorium ushered in the kids' parents and told the adults they could leave.

I was surprised to see my parents appear next to all the other parents. My father's black hair and my mother's brown hair bobbed through the crowd. Dad was in his grey suit and tie. I cringed inwardly. They had called him from work. Mom was in jeans and t-shirt from the high school she went to in California.

Dad grasped my shoulder. "Doing okay?"

His grip was firm and his lips pulled tight into a thin line. He was stressed about something.

"I've had better days, but I'm sure it's not the worst I'll ever have," I said, trying to keep my attitude light and not let them see how close to tears I was at seeing them.

Willow's parents had her in a tight group hug, so I wasn't able to wave goodbye before Mom pushed me out into her waiting car, my dad only a few steps behind us.

***

"I'm sorry you had to find out this way." Mom gently put a cup of tea in front of me with a reassuring smile. I frowned into the steaming cup. Mom still didn't get the idea that tea wasn't my... well, cup of tea.

I pushed the undissolved sugar in circles at the bottom of the cup with a spoon. Mom had a calm expression on her face, but the fact that she had put too much sugar in my tea told me otherwise. She seemed to think putting extra sugar in things was like a spell that could make bad situations less hard on people.

"What *is* going on?" I asked after a few minutes.

Dad was standing at the sink and staring blankly out the window. "It's hard to know where to start."

"Well, start somewhere," I snapped. After all the events at school, my temper was frayed and it was beginning to show.

"Eugene." My dad glared at me.

"Sorry." I stared into the cup, continuing to spin the spoon around the edge. Maybe the rotating drink would give me quicker answers.

Dad sat down next to me and took the spoon out of my fingers. The tea slowed to a bob instead of a rotate.

"You are part of a people who have no official name in the world that you know. You would know us by the pseudoscientific names of psychics, clairvoyants, users of ESP, magicians, wizards, witches, and many others. Among our people, we go by the common name of Kinetic."

"Like, telekinetic?" I asked. I'd heard the word 'kinetic' a couple times during the day, but it had made no sense.

"Yes, but let me finish before you ask any questions. There are approximately 63 million Kinetics in the world. And each of those Kinetics is bound to the rules set forth in our society before people knew to begin recording history. No Kinetic may intentionally reveal his or her powers to those who are not Kinetics. Anyone who breaks this rule is stopped and arrested by the InfoCon."

"The tan and black jacket guys at the school?" I asked.

Dad nodded and continued speaking.

"You were kept in the dark because of an incident when you were a child. There was an accident that kept you from expressing your powers correctly. You're what we call a Vunjika: an untrainable."

"Untrainable?" That didn't sound good at all.

"Since you are a Vunjika, you are inherently, naturally, blocked from being able to use your powers. If we can't find a way to release the block, then there is no way for you to use, much less learn your powers."

"Why am I blocked?" I asked. I couldn't remember ever feeling like I had strange abilities. But what kid doesn't feel like if he tries hard enough he can get a pencil to move across the table?

"We're not sure." Dad crossed his arms and leaned back in the chair. "Sometimes it's due to a lack of training, but yours is more complicated. It happened when you were barely a few years old. It shouldn't have happened. We were going to wait until you turned sixteen to throw any of this at you."

"I turn sixteen in like...eight months."

Dad nodded again.

"Like your mother said, you were never supposed to find out this way."

Mom rubbed my shoulder and smiled encouragingly. I smiled back, but looked at Dad, hoping he would keep going.

"I had hoped to do this a little more prepared...There is much to do between now and when you turn sixteen."

"Wait," I said, as a realization began to dawn on me. "This means I have a power?"

Dad nodded.

"Can I move things with my mind... like Yoda or something?"

Dad pursed his lips.

"Telekinesis is a common power to have, but we won't know what your specialty is until we've gone through a few tests."

"Do you guys have powers?"

"I do," Dad said. "Your mother isn't a Kinetic."

"You're not?" I asked, looking at her.

She sat down and smiled at me. "I am a Non. A Non-Kinetic, that is."

"Can't you learn?"

"It's not something that can be trained. It's genetic," Dad responded.

"Oh." I thought about that for a few minutes. "Is that why I'm this...Vunjika, thing?"

Dad shook his head. "No, when you were a child you displayed all the traits of a perfectly normal Kinetic child. You went through the normal power displays, shifting from one power to another while your mind developed. We're not sure why your powers became unstable. By the time you were seven, your powers should have solidified on one thing but they kept shifting. And then you had another accident and they just quit shifting altogether until you weren't displaying any powers at all. Our Healers determined that you blocked yourself due to the psychological trauma of unstable powers."

"Wow." I wasn't sure I understood everything that he was saying, but I didn't know what questions to ask to make it better.

"In the end, we are faced with a decision. We can have the InfoCon change your memory of the events at your school like those who are not Kinetics, or I can begin your training into the Anyan's Alliance Corps."

"Anyan's Alliance?" I asked. It was another word I had heard.

"Our group is called the Anyan's Alliance Corps." Dad puffed out his chest ever so slightly. He was proud of it, whatever it was.

"Are there other groups?" Something about the way Dad had said "our group" made me think that it wasn't the only one.

"Some. But they aren't important to know right now." He looked down at the table, breaking eye contact.

"Oh, okay." Dad was a terrible liar, and he was definitely leaving something out. I let it go, and he continued to speak.

"Do you know what you want to do?" Dad asked and stared at me. "Thoughts?"

I shook my head, but really I was thinking about Willow. "Is Willow...a...a Kinetic too?"

"Yes, as are her parents."

"So she's also in the dark? Or..." She'd known too much today. That the illusions weren't real and that Laura was the cause...Willow had to know.

"She knows." Mom supplied, taking the now-cold tea from in front of me and sticking it in the microwave to warm.

"She'll be going through some of the early stages of training starting this summer. Greg and Moira were just going to tell everyone that she was going to community college for a pre-Med program."

I bit the inside of my cheek. I was already a recipient of that lie. It hurt that she lied to me, but I wondered if she had much of a choice.

"I guess I'll train, but can I have a few days to think about it?" I said after a moment. Wherever I was, I wanted to be with Willow. If she was training, then I should too.

Dad nodded and exchanged a glance with Mom. She picked up her cellphone and disappeared into the living room.

"It will be the right choice, Eugene." Dad reached over and grasped my shoulder giving me something that was and wasn't a smile.

"Thanks, Dad." I felt a momentary surge of pride. I hadn't heard those words come out of my father's mouth in ages. I was pretty sure he thought I was an overwhelming failure in all things. It wasn't hard to see why. If I was part of these Kinetic people and I should have had a power from an early age, how wasn't I failure? I was a disappointment from childhood.

I tried to soak in that feeling of pride for as long as I could. Who knew when I would get it again?

CHAPTER 5

"We are the movers of fate. We are the kinetics that will ultimately decide how this war will end and that which will join our world together in harmony and shun those who would seek to do us harm." ~ Chief Minister Ashraf bin Saqib Al-Fulani in a speech to the members of Anyan's Alliance on the restoration of Anyan societies. Cairo, Egypt. 1832.

────────────────────────

My moment with my father was interrupted by a knock at the door. Willow didn't wait for any of us to answer and came on in, kicking her shoes off at the door. "Hey, how's it going?"

"Good." I smiled at her, relieved to see her face. "I think I'm going to train."

"Oh!" She sat down across from me and grinned between me and Dad. "That's a relief. I was worried you wouldn't want to get involved." Her eyelids were almost half lidded, and her grin was a little forced. Her back wasn't quite as straight as it usually was. The fatigue from earlier was still in her face, but she seemed less worn out than when we had been at the gym.

"How long have you known?" I asked.

She pressed her lips together and looked up as if trying to find the right words in the ceiling.

"My whole life."

"And you never told me?" I ignored the audible scoff from my father.

"If I did, the InfoCon wouldn't have let you keep the knowledge if they found out." Willow smiled apologetically. I wanted to press her on it, but a look from Dad stopped the words before they could leave my mouth.

I crossed my arms across my chest and begrudgingly decided to change topics. "Speaking of the InfoCon, what are they going to do to Laura?"

Willow shrugged, but Dad spoke up. "She's not yet 16, so she can't be offered training. They will relocate her and her family to a new and safer location that will be accommodating to an emerging Kinetic."

"Oh," I said. I would probably never see her again. And for that I was glad. I shuddered to think about the nightmares she had awoken in the school. "What happens to me now?"

"They are going to send someone here with the contract," Mom said, walking back into the room and setting her cellphone on the table. She sat next to Dad and grasped his hand. They smiled at each other.

"Once you have all the paperwork out of the way we will have to work with a specialist to construct a training plan for you. You will be a little different than someone like Willow," Dad supplied.

"Why?"

"Because you are a Vunjika," Dad said curtly.

"It's something we will have to work through, Eugene. You don't have to worry about it right now." Mom reached across the table and patted my hand.

Willow flicked my arm.

"I could probably try to teach you a thing or two. I'm a Healer Kinetic, so I don't know how much I could pass on. Depends on your power, but I can try."

"Thanks." I said with a smile.

I didn't have much time to think about what I was going to do when the front door creaked open and someone came in. This time it wasn't someone I expected to see. My brother stepped through the door and smirked at me from the doorway. I took a deep breath.

"Jacob!" Mom grinned and got up to hug him. Dad also got up, but instead of hugging him he shook Jacob's hand and patted his shoulder like a politician greeting a voter.

"Mom, I know it's a bit unusual but I intercepted the

contract request. I figured this should stay in the family." Jacob shook the manila envelope in his hands.

"How did you get here so quickly?" I asked, surprised. Last I heard he was still in Switzerland and had no plans to visit for at least another few months.

Jacob smirked at me. "One of the things you're going to learn very quickly, Eugene. We have methods of transportation far faster than anything you could have imagined living your provincial little life."

"Jacob!" Mom swatted his arm and shook her head disapprovingly.

"Sorry, Mom, just a bit of brotherly humor." He grinned. The grin never quite reached his eyes.

My brother hadn't visited us in almost six months. He talked to my mother on the phone every few days or so, and I'm sure that he conversed with Dad over email, but I hadn't actually talked to him since he left for some university in Switzerland last November, a few days after my fifteenth birthday.

"So I take it you're a Kinetic, too?" I asked.

"Of course," Jacob said, and laughed as if I had just asked the stupidest question of all time.

He looked menacing in what looked like a military suit. He had three silver triangles on his left breast above a circular crest that I vaguely recognized and a black line on his collar. The crest was a framed picture of the Earth with an upside down triangle underneath it. I'm pretty sure I'd seen the crest on some of my dad's paperwork before.

Jacob was seven years older and was always considerably taller than I was. But I think the last six months had given him a few more inches and the height of his closely cropped hair only added to it.

When did he enter the military? Or was it some version of the Swiss ROTC? Or was it something to do with the Alliance my parents were a part of? Was he part of it too?

I don't recall Mom or Dad talking about it, and usually they were pretty open about what Jake was up to, besides the whole Kinetic thing, of course. But now that I think about it, I had heard nothing about his activities or academics in months.

My brother still hadn't made eye contact with me. Like Dad, it always seemed like he was perpetually disappointed in me. He had never let me play with him and his friends when we were younger. Mom always claimed it was because there was such an age difference between us. I always assumed it was because he hated me.

I was not looking forward to this sudden visit.

"Sorry to be so...impromptu. I figured the sooner the better." Jacob yanked on his tie, loosening it. He slid into the seat across from me at the table.

"It's alright," Dad said. "I can understand the need for brevity."

"Hello, Willow," Jacob said pointedly. He still hadn't even looked at me.

"Jacob." She smiled at him and a tinge of red stained her cheeks. I bit the inside of my cheek. This again. At least I had been given six clean months of no flowery looks from her to him.

I sighed behind my hand and glared between the two of them. First it was Jacob and then Harry and now my brother again. I wasn't ever going to escape the fact that I wasn't on Willow's radar in the slightest.

I tried to ignore them both and watched as Mom put a glass of water in front of my brother. He sipped it without looking at anyone. The atmosphere had completely changed with him in the kitchen. Whatever tenseness had been building up was now focused through Jacob. My mother stood in front of the sink, wringing her hands. Whatever worries she had couldn't be washed down the sink. Dad stood at the kitchen door. He clutched the edges of the door; a frown pierced his face, and he stared only at my brother's back.

This silence, while my brother took in deep breaths, preparing to speak, was frightening. The only time this had ever happened was when my brother had been tasked with telling me that my dog had been hit by a car when I was ten. Our parents had been out of town at the time and he was the only one who could relay the terrible news to me.

Back then he hadn't seemed to know what to say. He stumbled over his words, and when I broke down over the death of my dog, he had to call Mom to figure out how to calm me down. But now he sat with a straight back and a chin held high, boasting a solid confidence that had developed since he had left home. If his height made me feel dwarfed, his confidence made me feel like a grain of sand in front of a tsunami.

Jacob looked at Dad and nodded his head. Dad left and returned moments later with his laptop. He set it on the table. Jacob opened it up and slipped a disk into the CD drive. He tapped an icon on the desktop and a video file started to play. Jacob turned the screen all the way in my direction.

"Hello, citizen. For the first time, you are entering a part of human society little seen by most people. In the upcoming days after your sixteenth birthday you will be introduced to various concepts and ideas that may be hard to handle. If at any time you are confused or stressed by what you are seeing, there will always be someone around to help you understand. The first thing you will do is read the contract of Anyan. "

Jacob opened the Manila envelope and pulled out five slips of paper. He pushed them toward me and finally looked me in the eye. The intensity there shook me. I paused and then took a gulp of air.

The video continued: *"Next you will be taken to a facility where Kinetics are trained, and there you will be paired with a mentor who can train you in your specific abilities.*

At the age of seven, your memories were suppressed because of your inability to develop properly during the Prime. According to Anyan Alliance Codes, this means that the last opportunity for you to fulfill your proper heritage as a Kinetic and as a functioning member of Kinetic society will be presented to you upon your sixteenth birthday.

Upon review of the corresponding letter, you must agree to Anyan's Contract to serve and support the cause of Anyan's Mission (see Page 2) and protect the Honored People against enemies of the Mission. Else, you must agree to a full wipe of your mind.

In Respect and Loyalty for the Cause of Anyan."

The video flickered off, and Jacob snapped the laptop closed.

"Eugene, in these papers you will find a choice. What choice you make will determine the rest of your life. I hope you choose the right one, because you will be needed." Jacob stared at me as he crossed his arms over his chest.

I grasped the papers and let my eyes slide down to the words at the top of the page.

The Contract with Anyan's Alliance.
Re: Eugene P. Yoshida
DOB: November 10, 1998
Mr. Yoshida, this letter is a notification of your current status. Please read the following information carefully. After signing the Contract your status as a Vunjika will change to Initiate. You will be given a mentor and tasked with remedial training. If you do not sign this contract you will have to submit to a mandatory mind wipe, memory alteration and ability augmentation in the form of medication.

I kept reading, but the more I read, the more distressed I felt. I glanced up at Willow then and back at the page. Her gaze was locked on me. It was like she was trying to read my mind. If she hadn't already told me she was a Healer I would have thought she was succeeding.

I know my parents had mentioned that something big was going to happen on my sixteenth birthday, but this wasn't it. I expected a big party or maybe my first car. Even sending me to a boarding school in England would have made more sense than the straight-up insane letter I was reading. What the heck kind of fantasy was my family bringing me into?

If I hadn't watched my whole school go batshit crazy, I would probably have thrown the papers back at my brother and demanded they not make a fool of me. Part of me wanted to believe that this was some kind of elaborate joke they were playing.

But Jacob wasn't a joker. Jacob wasn't much fun at all, actually.

My hands were shaking by the time I read the last page.

I wanted to laugh and cry at the same time. It was absurd. Everything from the last day was sinking in and hitting me like a ton of bricks.

"What's this 'Isiro' it talks about? Who was Anyan?" I started parroting back the strange words in the document at Jacob.

"There will be time to explain all that later, Eugene. But first we need to talk about the contract." Jacob sat up even straighter. If he went much further, I'd start to think he was going to shoot through the roof.

I looked down at the papers in my hands. The last page was a contract.

"It's a standard contract with Anyan's Alliance." Jacob said when he saw the page. "All Alliance Kinetics sign these when they start training."

"Even I will when I start official training in the summer." Willow said.

I read over the contract. And then I read over it again.

I looked to Willow for some support.

Her eyes dilated for a split second and her voice filled the inside of my head. *-Just sign it.-*

I fell out of my seat as a confusing swath of emotions and whispering thoughts trailed with the loud words in my head. "What the..."

"Eugene!" Mom reached out for me and grasped my arm. I saw so much concern there it almost hurt.

"Sorry, I 'Pathed him." Willow tapped her head.

Mom clutched her chest. "A little warning next time, Willow."

"Sorry, Mrs. Y." She smiled at me bashfully. *Don't worry, this is natural.*

"I, you, how, what..." I stared at the four of them. These people were suddenly strangers. I knew my family was strange, but I'd thought maybe they were illegal aliens or secret government spies or something else a little less crazy. This science fiction crap coming out of left-field...What the hell?

My brother looked back at my dad. Something passed between them, an unsaid agreement or acknowledgment.

This was insane. My family was pulling something out of their asses, and Willow was happily playing along. It had to be that. I couldn't really be this...this Kinetic thing. I would know if I had ESP or whatever these abilities were called. Wouldn't I?

"You guys are making a fool out of me," I said. I tried to ignore the soundless words that Willow kept throwing at me. I was going batshit. I was going certifiable, and they were not helping. "I need...I... Fuck it."

I stood up and walked out the kitchen door into the backyard. I didn't stop when Mom called out to me frantically or when my dad ordered me back into the kitchen. I did stop when I heard Willow's voice in my mind. *-Please, come back.-*

Under the words filling my head, there was an emotion that I can only describe as abject pleading. These were Willow's emotions; she was calling me back. Honestly, I didn't know where I was going when I headed out the door, but I knew that I needed to get away and think. Willow and her pleading emotions turned me around.

She spoke to my father and then walked toward me. She grabbed my arm and led me out into the alleyway behind our house.

We walked arm-in-arm past my neighbors and their neighbors until we were almost three blocks away. Willow turned to me then and grasped my fingers.

"Your dad and Jacob were probably hoping that you would react better than that." Her gentle smile stirred the butterflies in my stomach.

"How can you handle all this?" I let go of her fingers and trapped my hands behind my back to hide the cold sweat breaking out there.

"It was just the way cards fell, I guess. You would know, too, if you hadn't turned into a Vunjika."

"I still don't understand this Vunjika thing."

Her grin got impossibly wider. "Let's keep walking."

We walked, this time at arm's length, down the street toward the high school. "So you know we're called Kinetics, right?"

I nodded. "Weird word for people, but I got it."

"Kinetic is a term given to us...there's some history behind the word, but you don't need to know that. A Vunjika is a Kinetic who can't use his or her powers. Each Kinetic is born with two powers. The first is always the ability to talk through the mind." She took a deep breath. *Like this.*

In the words, I saw and felt undercurrents of ideas and emotions. These were strong and intentional, unlike before. She sent me confidence and happiness in her words.

"The second power varies from person to person. I am a healer." She touched the slight scabbed-over cut on my arm where I had hit the bleachers in basketball practice two days before. It swelled with a strange inner light and then faded to nothing but a clean layer of skin.

"Each person develops his or her abilities around the age of five or six. Vunjika, which is what you are, never develop their abilities, either from lack of training or from lack of will to train. I don't know the circumstances of your situation, but usually when no powers manifest by the age of seven, the child is labeled a risk and their memory of ever having powers is suppressed until a later date, when the child is old enough to accept remedial training. Usually that happens when the child is sixteen. At that point, they are given the contract and they have two options: train or..."

"Forced amnesia?" I supplied.

"Essentially. It's okay, Eugene. Things will get easier as we go along."

"I hope so. I don't even know if I believe it."

-It's hard to ignore hard facts.- I was starting to get used to Willow's voice in my mind.

"So can you talk to anyone with that?" I asked.

"I could." Willow replied, aloud.

"What about normal people? Can they hear telepathy?"

"Yeah, they can hear if you are specifically sending them thoughts, but they can't respond."

She smiled. "You'll want to be careful though, telepathy is one of those things that..." she considered her words for a moment. "It's personal. You're not just sending words, like a text message, you're sending a piece of yourself, of your feelings and memories."

She sucked in a breath, and I felt her words enter my mind. -*Do you remember when we were children and we would play hide-and-go-seek in the field behind our school?*-

In those words I saw flitters of memories of golden grass as tall as we were, hiding us from each other. I could hear echoes of our childish laughter and feelings of something like contentment.

"Wow."

She smiled. "Yeah."

***

At some point we turned around and headed back to my house. I tried to grapple with the new concepts and names floating in my head, but they only seemed to encourage a headache to blossom at my temples.

When we reached home, I trudged up to my room. Willow trailed behind. Jacob had left at some point, and the only evidence of his visit was a half-empty glass of water, beaded with perspiration, and the papers spread out like a fan at my empty kitchen seat.

I ignored my parents, for the sake of my own sanity more than anything, and buried my head under my pillow.

I kept my eyes closed the whole time. Trying in some way to visualize what my power would be. How would I even know how to use it if I found out? How is something like that trained? I wasn't sure how much time passed.

Willow sat at my computer and played video games, occasionally telepathically sending me little words of encouragement. Right before she sent something, I could always feel a glimmer of something at the back of my mind.

"That's my link. I have to create one with you before I can send you thoughts," she said after I asked her about it. "If you could 'path,' then you would have to create one with me to send thoughts my way."

"How would I make one?"

"I don't know how it works with Vunjikas, but my mom

told me it's sort of like redirecting a stream. If you can find the stream of your thoughts then you can try to redirect them toward the person you are trying to 'path.'"

I opened my eyes and watched her play games for a while. She was focused, her eyes set on the screen and her eyebrows knitted tight. I was glad it was the weekend. I don't think I could have handled school at the moment, especially not the constant reminders of what went on there today. Willow, despite how tired she was after it all, seemed like she took it in stride. But I guess for her this was normal, everyday.

I let my eyes close again. I know I should have been up and talking with Willow or playing games with her, but my head felt too full. I guess I should have been excited to learn I have powers. Who hasn't read comics about superheroes? Who wouldn't want to be one or at least have their abilities? I think if I could choose, I would want to fly. I tried to imagine it. I could see myself flying through the clouds, going wherever I wanted to, as far as I wanted to.

Eventually, I heard Willow say that she needed to go home, and I only barely acknowledged her as she left. I could still sense her link flitting at the back of my mind. It was a small bird, and I was a loser with a broken net.

At dinner, my parents spoke quietly in Japanese.

My dad was originally from Japan but had moved to the United States for work. They had met while my mom was on a university study abroad program in Tokyo. They liked to joke that she stood out like a sore thumb when he met her. She was the only white woman in a whole room full of Japanese students trying desperately to learn how to ask where the bathroom was. Though now that I knew there was more to my father's "work," I questioned the story of their meeting. I would have to ask again when I didn't feel like I was growing a brain tumor.

My parents would revert to his native language when they were trying to keep something from me. I didn't even try to listen in. Most time if I really wanted to I could get the idea of what they were saying, but right now I didn't care. My head hurt, and everything involving concentration made it worse. It even took a second for me to realize when my mom switched to English that she was asking me a question.

"What?"

"I hope you don't have any plans for tomorrow," she said.

I shook my head. Willow and I had initially planned to go to laser tag, but I really didn't think that was going to happen now.

"Good. You're going to come with us to the Conference."

I had known about the Conference for years. I used to go before I entered elementary school, but after that, whatever went on there was a big secret between my parents and my brother. My vague memories of the time offered no clues. I had always thought that it had something to do with Dad's college fraternity.

"Why do I have to go?"

"A woman will be there, and she will discuss more of the contract with you." Dad said between bites of his chicken. "And if you agree to it, then she will sign you up for some remedial lessons and find you a specialist to help you find your powers."

I wanted to ask what these remedial lessons were all about, but Dad wasn't looking up from his plate. He was unhappy about something.

"Ok," I said and didn't speak of it again for the rest of the night.

***

That night, I dreamed that a man dressed in fire walked toward me.

His face was too bright to see, but I knew he was someone I should know. He walked in a circle around my room, and everything that his fiery clothes touched burned. I was surrounded by the bars of a prison, and I couldn't escape. The smoke stifled all my screams.

I think I died.

CHAPTER 6

"The world in which we live is full of suffering. No one person can go through life without experiencing some kind of pain, emotional or physical. We as Kinetics are surrounded by hardship. The men and women we lose every day are each someone's lover, parent, or child. But we have a great hope. No Kinetic is truly alone, for we are connected in a way our non-Kinetic peers are not. We have telepathy. We have a connection that defies all borders and all languages. No one has to suffer alone." ~ Jordan Vanderwaal. Anyan's Alliance member. Excerpt from The Writings of Jordan Vanderwaal on the State of the World and Its People. 1956.

A red and green banner with a white crest fluttered in the midday wind.

According to my parents, most people associated the Anyan's Alliance crest with a super-exclusive fraternity. My parents had told me it was used as one of the fronts for the Alliance, among others that they had yet to reveal to me.

Hundreds of Kinetics filed into the huge convention center. My parents kept me squarely between them as we walked with the flow of the crowd. It felt like they were trying to guard me from something, but the people going into the convention center looked just as normal as anyone else on the street.

We reached the entrance, where a man in a tan and grey coat, an InfoCon officer, stood pressing two fingers to each person's temple. He would nod, stamp something on the person's hand and wave them inside.

First Dad went through, and then Mom tapped my

shoulder to go next. I stood in front of the man as he pressed his icy fingertips to my temple. His eyes narrowed, and he studied me. "Vunjika?" he asked.

I nodded.

His lips pressed into a thin line, and he took a red marker from his coat pocket. He grabbed my hand and slashed an *X* on the back of my hand. A couple people around us saw it and whispered under their breaths to each other and stared at me. Mom went in with much the same process as mine, but her *X* was black.

I ignored the stares and a few pointing fingers and followed my parents into a conference room where a man stood on a podium adjusting his tie. My mother and father walked ahead of me and bee-lined toward the front.

Outside the conference center, life moved about normally. Normal people went about their lives, completely unaware that the people congregating inside the center were capable of powers beyond their wildest imaginations. I desperately wanted to be out there with them. I barely understood the world that was opening up to me, and I craved some kind of normality.

We took seats in the second row from the front. There were names and job titles on the seats. Mom and I just had our names, but Dad's had 'Chief of Intelligence' under his name.

"So are you like...the Kinetic CIA or something?" I asked Dad.

He had his notebook open and was reading some papers, so he didn't look up. "Yes."

"Nice." I sat back and looked around at the room filling up with people. I wondered what powers each of these people had. In the distance I caught a flash of red hair, and Willow appeared from between a couple groups of people. Her parents followed closely behind.

I waved at her.

"Hey!" She smiled as she and her parents approached. "It's *so* weird seeing you here."

"It's weird *being* here," I said under my breath.

"I wish you were coming on a better day. It's all silly

political stuff this year," Willow said as she plopped down into the seats directly behind us. Her parents were both Intelligence Analysts, according to their seats.

"Is it different other times?"

"Yeah, some summers they have more of a county fair sort of feel. That's when the Regional Chiefs travel around the world to each of the conferences and 'spread culture.'" She chuckled.

I nodded and looked at the people standing on the podium. The man who had been adjusting his tie was now looking out at the crowd and waiting for people to finish getting seated.

"So...what's gonna happen now?" I asked no one in particular.

-I'll explain,- said Willow's voice in my head. I sensed lots of bubbly humor flowing through her link. It was almost infectious. I smiled while facing the podium so she couldn't see my face.

Dad apparently hadn't heard Willow's telepathy.

"The Conference is made so that we in the governing sectors of the Alliance can keep up to date with other regions. It is also a way for the Council of Anyan to notify us of new rulings or decisions," he replied.

"Council of Anyan?"

"They are six people chosen to make the decisions to guide our people. They tell the Chief Minister, and the Chief Minister tells the Regional Chiefs and on down," he said.

A man tapped the microphone and cleared his throat. The Conference had begun.

-Ok.- Willow began. -The guy up there now is Jon Perry. He's originally from the Eastern Canadian Region, but he transferred down here to work directly with the North American office in Columbus. He's also the de-facto spokesperson for North America. He goes to all the conferences.-

After he had introduced himself and the topics for the conference, Jon Perry motioned for the next person to come up. It was an elderly man with enough hair on his face to make a blanket.

-That's the Chief of War, Idelfons Heilbronner.- Willow nodded her head in the direction of the man sauntering onto stage. *-Your brother is his second in command.-*

The man spoke for a while with a painfully thick German accent about something called the Pendulum Initiative. I understood nothing of what he was saying about it, so I stopped listening. I felt Willow's link at the back of my mind, and I tried grasping at it. She must have sensed it and responded.

-Want to practice?-

I nodded my head.

-Okay, can you find my link?-

I nodded again.

-Alright, try to imagine your thoughts as a stream and push that stream to my link. Think of the stream going between speech and thought.-

I tried as she said, but I felt no response from her.

-Remember, try to find the in-between. If you have to, close your eyes and visualize.-

I did as she instructed and closed my eyes. How do I find the place, the idea between thought and speech? I tried to think about speaking, but I got no response. I tried to speak without moving my mouth, but still nothing.

I went back and forth for a little bit with myself. I thought about Willow and what she had meant to me my whole life. We had been the best of buds for longer than I could even recall. I don't think I had spent more than a month outside her company. As I felt around in my head for the intangible link between our minds, I envisioned her face, her hair, and the little blue hairpins she always wore. I reached for that image, the sound her voice, the way her hair looked in the sun, the touch of her fingertips on my face.

Can you hear me?

-Oh, look. It's Jacob!- Willow said without answering.

Jacob stepped out onto the stage. He stood out like a sore thumb with no suit jacket, no tie and rolled up sleeves. His mentor stood next to him on the stage and patted his back encouragingly. I was still grappling with the link from Willow, so I almost didn't catch that he was getting ready to speak.

I shook my head, as though that would get rid of a mind link.

Jacob took the podium and cleared his throat.

"Ladies and gentlemen, I am here to present to you a new plan that my mentor and I are developing. If you look here," Jacob pointed a clicker at the projector, and the screen behind him changed from a rotating Alliance Insignia to a map of the world, "you can see the clear territories between Anyan's Alliance and the Isiroan Legion. Over the course of the last hundred years, they have taken territories in the mountainous regions in nearly every continent. In the past two years they have begun taking over well-forested regions."

He changed the screen again. This time to a grainy picture of a compound filled with oddly shaped buildings. The picture showed some kind of construction work around a circular building.

"It has become clear to me and the Chief of War, Idelfons Heilbronner," he pointed to his mentor, "that the Legion is taking key territories around the planet. As you all should know, Isiro is a very old being. His access to vast banks of alien technology is becoming increasingly used in Isiroan defenses. This is clear because sensory-field Kinetics cannot penetrate the electromagnetic barriers set up around each and every one of the Isiroan Legion bases. Our researchers have no idea what kind of technology he is using or even how to begin reverse-engineering it."

I glanced back at Willow who was staring at Jacob. She wasn't blinking. Her face was so still as she concentrated on his words that I felt a little uncomfortable.

I turned around and crossed my arms. I wondered if she was still holding a torch for him. Could she not decide between my brother and Harry? I suddenly hoped Willow's link didn't pick up on my train of thought. I wasn't sure if it could work like that. I tried to imagine a brick wall and only a brick wall, willing the disappointment to go away.

My brother went on to talk about changing key policies in the Alliance laws. I stopped listening and doodled basketball defenses on the back of my hand, covering up the red *X* with little circles and smaller *X*s.

Dad raised his eyebrows at me. "Eugene."

I clicked the pen and shoved it into my coat pocket.

Another hour passed and then the large group of adults split off into smaller groups and went to different specialized sessions. Dad went off with the Intelligence people. They didn't have a non-Kinetic room, so Mom sat with Willow and I at a table near the back of the large conference room with all the other under-sixteen Kinetics. Mom stood out, and sometimes the others stared at her, but she ignored them with patient indifference.

Mom smiled at Willow. "Just think, next year you'll be joining the Healers."

Willow stretched her arms and grinned. "I knoooow. I can't wait to find out what they all do."

I laughed. "Heal people?"

She frowned at me. "Well obviously, but I'm talking about the kind of training and stuff. You know, I'm only a Level One right now and I heard that they try to get you up to Level Three in under two years."

"Levels?" I asked.

"I'll explain later." Willow waved her hand nonchalantly.

"On top of everything else you said you would explain," I said, annoyed.

"Fine. Here's the skinny of it. There are three levels of Kinetics. Each level is kind of a milestone for your sphere of influence. Your Sphere is what you can affect with your powers. In my case, Level One is direct contact. I have to actually touch someone to heal them. Level Two would be a small extended sphere that doesn't require contact but is limited by distance. Level Three would be the ability to directly target individuals at long distance. Within reason, of course."

"So... you could heal someone across the room at Level Three?"

"Exactly."

Mom smiled at the two of us. "I remember how excited Jacob was when he had his initiation. I couldn't even imagine—

" Mom's cell phone rang. I cringed at the *Walk Like an Egyptian* ringtone. She was not bashful about letting everyone know about her love of 80s music.

"Yes? Yes. Ok. The usual place. See you soon. Love you." She flipped the cell phone closed and smiled. "Jacob's on his way. He wants to talk to you."

"Me?" I asked. The last time he wanted to talk to me, he told me about that stupid contract. What other mind-blowing things did he still have to shove me into?

Willow cupped her hands around her face and grinned impishly at me. "I think I know what he's gonna say."

"What?"

"He's going to say that he's sorry for being a jerk and that you're the best brother in the world."

"As if," I said out of the corner of my mouth.

Jacob stepped into the hall and approached the table.

"Hey, Mom." He pecked her cheek. He was always so affectionate toward Mom. Compared to the very not-gonna-take-your-shit attitude that he saved for everyone else, he was downright cuddly.

"Eugene." Jacob nodded at me.

"Hey, Jake." I unenthusiastically waved.

"Come with me." He jerked his chin toward the foyer. I hesitated enough to see Willow give me a thumbs-up sign and grin impishly. I shook my head at her and followed my brother out.

Jacob stepped into a small room off the side of the larger conference room. The wall was lined with tall ceiling to floor windows. The light outside was beginning to dim into late afternoon.

"Eugene, do you know what you are planning to do yet?"

"With what?"

"The contract."

"Oh. I don't know." I looked away suddenly, wanting to be very far away from here.

"I want an answer." He crossed his arms and stared down at me. I hated that he had almost four inches over me and could stare down at me condescendingly.

"I don't know yet, Jacob." I shrugged. "Up until yesterday, I was planning to go to college to be a... a mathematician." I wasn't too sure about the mathematician part, but it was better than telling him I didn't know what the heck I was doing with myself. "You can't expect me to flip my life around on a dime."

"Unfortunately, Eugene, you don't have much time to be indecisive. If you don't make a choice soon *they* will make the choice for you." Jacob leaned in close, glaring down at me.

I frowned. "Who will?"

"The Council of Anyan. There are so few people like you that the Council deals with it directly. So unless you want to end up a useless peon of non-Kinetic society, you'd better make a decision before the day is out." Jacob turned on his heel and swept out of the room.

I growled under my breath and went back to where Mom and Willow were sitting. Jacob thought he could order me around, but I wasn't going to be bullied into making a decision.

I got back to the table, but Willow was sitting by herself drawing on a napkin with a permanent marker.

"Hey." I said when I sat down.

Her mouth opened to speak, but before she made a sound, a rumble shook the building.

Everyone in the building went silent and looked around for the source of the sound.

KrrrrrrraaaBOOM!

Screams rose as debris began to fall from a shattering ceiling. Shafts of light broke through the falling roof. The building was caving in around us.

CHAPTER 7

"We never understand how little we need in this world until we know the loss of it" ~ James Matthew Barrie. Scottish Novelist.

Large chunks of ceiling, glass, and insulation rained down around us, hitting people too stunned to move out of the way.

Willow stepped back, but it wasn't enough. I grabbed her arm and pulled her back just as a large piece of metal broke free from above us and hit the floor.

I heard the crackle of energy before I saw it. Lightning shot down from the new skylight and hit dead center in the middle of a crowd. The people scattered like dominoes as more bolts shot down, charring and shattering everything in their paths.

A series of popping noises filled the room. Dozens of men and women appeared in the middle of the rising tide of voices crying out in shock and anger. They looked like any other men or women on the street, except they were wearing orange armbands with a strange symbol.

"Isiroans!" someone shouted. "Isiroans are attacking!"

The crowd dispersed toward the walls, leaving the Isiroans in the center, exposed among the debris. Orders were quickly called out, and Kinetics lined up around the intruders. In the chaos it was hard to distinguish who or what was fighting. Brilliant lights, colors, energy and chunks of building shot back and forth around the conference room. The sound of screams and shouts and crackling power deafened my ears.

Willow tugged my shirt and led me to a large piece of

wall that had fallen over. She motioned for me to get down next to her. I knelt just enough that I could still look over the wall and watch the unfolding disaster. The fight, while scary, was amazing to behold.

The Alliance fighters moved in elegantly coordinated groups. They kept a tight perimeter around the attackers, blocking and deflecting anything that came their way. The attackers--the 'Isiroans,'—were less organized, splitting off from each other and running in chaotic circles around the groups of Alliance. They didn't seem fazed by the ease with which the Alliance rebuffed their attacks.

"Why are they fighting?" I asked as a large chunk of wall blasted across the room hitting the opposing wall.

"I don't know." Willow looked back and forth across the room, her eyes searching for something.

"What is it?"

"Where are our parents?"

I shook my head. I didn't see them anywhere either. All the faces in the sudden battlefield were unfamiliar to me. But one face in particular drew me in, even though I didn't know who it was. A man was standing just on the outside of the chaos, watching with an expressionless face. He had the orange armband of the attackers, but he was different somehow. His long hair hung down his face and across his shoulders in grimy clumps and dreads. His skin was a sickly yellow color that looked like it hadn't seen a decent dose of sun in ages. Veins on his face and neck protruded, purple and blue.

In the middle of all the people fighting, he was calm. His eyes were the only thing that moved; they were tracking from person to person and barely blinked.

Then, I saw my brother. He stood back a ways and watched everything with a cool gaze and crossed arms. I almost sat back to speak to Willow but my brother moved from his spot and ran through the crowd. I watched him move like a serpent through the fray and target a woman who was standing stationary inside of a brilliant circular forcefield. Every object or power thrown at it ricocheted away at sharp angles.

The surrealism that made up this entire event didn't come close to making what I saw next any easier. The woman was deflecting so many blows that the inelegant ballet of destruction swirled around her, but as my brother ran at her it seemed as if he was spearing through it all, avoiding objects and powers effortlessly.

Jacob skidded to a stop in front of the woman and held out his hands. Her eyes widened and she exploded from an inner fire. The forcefield collapsed and Jacob slipped away. The attackers saw the woman fall and the frenzy intensified.

I blinked, unsure of what I had just witnessed. It replayed in my head, skipping back and forth like a corrupted video file. Jacob stopping, hands held high. The woman's face revealed seconds of abject terror just before her entire body went supernova.

I think my brother had just killed someone.

That's when the entire fight degraded. There was no order, no elegance left to the fight at all. Instead I saw raw, chaotic, adrenaline-driven battle of wills. Two men, not far from us traded blows, one was throwing objects with what I assumed was telekinesis and the other I wasn't sure. He melted into the walls or into the floor and would appear behind the telekinetic and swing at him with a strange looking blade holstered at his back.

Others threw impossibly immense waves of energy at each other, causing the air around us to scream with sound. Shockwaves rattled everything and everyone around us. I held tight to Willow's arm, readying myself in the event that we would have to start running.

I searched the beaten and bloody faces of the fighters for my father and mother. I saw neither of them, only people and faces racked with anger and pain as they desperately tried to tear each other apart.

The greasy haired man, still standing in one place, reached a hand out toward the crowd and let out a bellow. Jacob was running through the fighters again, this time toward the man. "Grey!" He shouted. "You'll pay for this!"

"Yoshida! You will die!" The man clenched his fists and

two bolts of highly charged electricity sprang from the ground and arced over the other fighters toward my brother. Jacob jumped out of the way and waved his hand at the man. Around him, dozens of chunks of wall, glass, tables, and chairs began exploding with brilliant light.

The man was unfazed. From the lights and a power socket on a pole near him he pulled massive branches of electricity that crackled and blinded like lightning. Each one was thrown at my brother, but he dodged and sprang away with ease.

"Eugene," Willow grasped my hand, startling me for a moment. She pulled me away from the battle. "I have something I need to show you. I know you don't understand much about Kinetic culture right now, but one day you will."

I stumbled after her. The screams and cries around me tore through my ears and I blinked away the dust that was thick in the air. What the heck was going on?

She ran through the room, between fighters on either side until we burst through a set of double doors into an untouched hallway. The lights had gone out and we moved by the dim light of tinted windows. Only the muffled screams and cries of the people beyond could be heard in the distance.

Willow took my head in her hands and rested her forehead to mine. She closed her eyes and breathed. I felt something open inside my mind. The link. I concentrated like Willow taught me and grasped at it. Like a river flowing through a backed up dam I found myself drowned in thoughts, emotions, ideas, convictions, colors, images, imagination, and above all else the sense that I should *know something.*

I couldn't figure out what that thing was, as I reached for it, Willow's head and hands pulled away abruptly. I hadn't been aware that I had closed my eyes, but when she was gone I was surrounded by the darkness of my eyelids. I opened them only to see the greasy haired man from earlier with an arm around Willow's neck. His other hand was a rolling ball of compressed electricity.

"Willow!" I stepped forward ready to-- to do what? My hands shook and even though these people said somewhere under my skin was a power; I didn't know what it was or even how to begin to use it.

"Move and she loses her pretty face." The man smirked and dragged Willow back a few more steps.

"Eugene, don't worry." Willow said. Her face was going red, and tears were starting to leak from her eyes. Her link was wide open, filling me with reassurance. I brushed it aside.

But my legs were frozen. Even as the building rocked from explosions and screams, I couldn't move. I didn't know what to do. My mind was a roaring chasm of nothingness. The link that Willow had worked hard to teach me was the only thing I could sense. Her mind was terrified, but she didn't want me to get hurt, and she wanted me to not worry.

A woman appeared with whoosh of outward air out of nowhere and sprinted toward the man. "Grey!" She screamed. At first I thought she was going to attack him, but she leaped onto his back and wrapped her arms around his neck. Instead, as her grip on him tightened, they literally vanished with a snap of inward rushing air and a rapidly fading glow.

"No!" I cried out and stumbled forward. The instant that Willow disappeared I felt her ever-present link get ripped away. It hadn't been there just from when she started to teach me this link; it had been there with every laugh and every dream. She had always been there for me in the silent dark nights when I thought I was alone. I had never noticed before just how present in my mind she had been. And now that it was gone, there was a hole, a jagged, biting hole in the fabric of my mind.

I rushed to where they had vanished, but it was no use. They were gone. The questions running through my head outnumbered the answers. Why her? Why take Willow? As little as I understood about this place and these people, why take her?

I knelt to the ground where one of Willow's hairclips had fallen and picked it up. The little blue flower shook with my hand. I clasped my fist around it and searched the room frantically for an answer. This quiet hallway had been a sanctuary for whatever Willow had impressed on my mind through the link, but she was now gone and I couldn't save her.

But I wasn't alone. I jolted up to my feet and sprinted out of the empty hall. Mom, Dad, they would help me. They would help Willow.

I stumbled out the door, stepping on something soft. A body. I lurched back and stared into the lifeless eyes of an old man. Blood covered his face and back where slender gashes made crisscrossed markings all over.

I coughed and looked up to see people limp on the floor or crawling over debris. The hole in the ceiling let in the false joy of a sunny day.

"Willow!" I heard someone scream. Willow's mother came running through the bleeding and sobbing throng with tears rolling down her red face. "Eugene! My baby, have you seen my baby?"

Words lodged in my throat and I couldn't speak. She grasped my arms and squeezed till it hurt. "Where is she?"

"They took her." I croaked.

Mrs. Patterson wailed and fell to the ground. "No! No!"

I shuddered and knelt next to her. "I'm sorry, I'm sorry." I said, as she weakly pounded her fists on my chest. I felt my insides crumbling. Willow was gone. Gone because of who?

Because of me, whispered some angry part of my mind.

"Eugene!" Mom screamed and skidded to the floor next to me. She pulled me into her arms and kissed my head and my forehead. "You're safe. Oh, you're safe. My boy, my little boy."

"Mom. Mom. Mom." I could barely speak. "They took her Mom. They took Willow."

Mrs. Patterson was still on the floor sobbing. Mom took one look at her and then held onto her like she was a child. Moira Patterson's cries took over my entire world, mimicking the raging battle inside my own soul.

Mom, Dad, Mr. and Mrs. Patterson and I sat together at the back of the destroyed conference center. Jacob had left with few words to our parents. As he left, the image of the woman exploding under whatever power my brother had shook me. I didn't dare look him in the eye.

Through a window I saw a line of InfoCon officers

surrounding the conference center. "They're going to remove the memories of this incident from the minds of the Non's before it gets out." He said, following my gaze and came to sit next to me at the table, pulling his chair close.

Willow's mom was leaning against her husband's shoulder with his arm around her. Her eyes were closed and she shook with silent hiccups.

"Dad, what was that? Who were they?"

Mom, Dad and Mr. Patterson exchanged unreadable looks.

"Eugene," Mom started. "There's something we didn't tell you."

Dad crossed his fingers, and held my gaze. "We are in the middle of a war."

CHAPTER 8

"I don't mind living with Kinetics. They're human after all. And, yes: sometimes I get jealous that I can't do what my wife or my children can do, but I love them, so it's easy to forget that I'm different." ~ George Matheson. A 34-year-old non-Kinetic who married a Kinetic. How Nons Live with Kinetics by Ralph Legend. 1992.

"A war?" I asked.

"Yes." Dad's face held no emotion. He was watching for my response, I guess.

I felt a headache forming. "With who?"

"Not a who, Eugene, but a what." He loosened his hands and splayed them flat on the table. He seemed deep in thought, and stared down at his hands. He swallowed as if unsure that the words that wanted to come out of his mouth were the right ones.

"A...what?" I asked.

"We, that is, our people, have been involved in a war longer than humanity has been recording history." Dad sat back and watched my face. I couldn't tell you what was on my face because of all the absurd things I had experienced in the past couple days. This was just the cherry on top. "We are the Anyan's Alliance. They are the Isiroan Legion. We have been fighting for humanity's future."

I glanced between my Dad and Mom's faces. Dad was serious. Mom was biting her bottom lip and rubbing her arms like she was cold.

"What, are... You said we were fighting a 'what?'"

Dad nodded. "The Isiroan Legion is led by..." Dad didn't seem to know if he wanted to tell me, but he pushed the words out. "It's led by an alien we know only as Isiro."

"An...alien?" First we have superpowers and now aliens?

"He came to Earth many thousands of years ago, and the Alliance has been battling his efforts to enslave the whole planet."

"Why?"

"Why, what?"

"Why does he want to enslave us?"

"Well, that's what's under a lot of... debate. The most common opinion is that he is raising an army from us to continue a reign of terror across the galaxy. It is said that he was initially banished here for that very reason."

"But, it's been thousands of years. How is he still alive?"

Dad shook his head, "To be honest no one really knows why he has managed to keep living so long. There are speculations but... we can't say for certain."

I took in a breath, trying to understand this new concept. "How does Willow fit into all of this?"

"She... well, it may not be my place." Dad stood and tugged at my shirt. "Come along. There is someone you need to speak to."

"Dad, what does Willow have to do with this?" I asked again, pushing my way out of the chair.

Dad pursed his lips and avoided eye contact. "I'm not the one who should explain."

The Pattersons stayed at the table. Dad said someone was coming to talk with them about their options. Mom gave me a reassuring smile and a shoulder hug as we left them behind, but it did little to alleviate the worry filling my mind.

We left the destroyed conference center, cleared by the InfoCon to continue on without being 'wiped.' I had to look away when I saw a young mother and her small son staring dazedly up at the InfoCon officer.

Behind us, dozens of Kinetics were converging on the center where the building appeared to rebuild itself. The walls

and wood were clasping together in a 3D puzzle worked by
people with powers. We passed the threshold of the street and
the air around the building shimmered. A perfect image of the
building appeared behind us. I stopped and stared at it.

Dad looked back. "It's only an illusion until they can
rebuild."

"Weird." It was strange that something so terrible had
happened behind that illusion. People walked the streets with
no cares, no worries, and no idea that they were mere feet
away from some kind of battlefield.

We headed to our car that was parked a few streets
away from the convention center. A couple hours ago I had
stepped out onto the sidewalk not knowing what the day had
in store for me. I stepped up into the back of my parents car
wishing this day have never even started.

We drove toward home in near silence. Mom flipped the
radio from station to station, never quite deciding what she
was in the mood for. I wanted to ask them more questions, and
I really should have been writing them all down.

Dad stopped at the house to drop Mom off. I sat in the
car while they stood in the doorway of our house and spoke. I
couldn't look at them. They had each other always, but I had
just lost my best friend.

I closed my eyes against the sun that was just beginning
to fall. In the quiet of the car, all alone, my thoughts became
louder. I kept feeling something nagging at the back of my
mind. A thought that I couldn't capture, perhaps? But it felt like
Willow. Not just a thought about Willow, but some part of
Willow herself.

After feeling her mental presence stripped away, I
didn't think I would feel something like it again. But there it
was, a sensation at the back of my mind that I couldn't quite
grab ahold of.

I closed my eyes and reached out for Willow's link. But
the sensation of Willow in my mind was not the same as the
telepathic link. Perhaps it was my lack of training, or because I
was this Vunjika thing, but it felt like I was trapped behind a
mental wall. Where before, when Willow had her link open for

me, there was the feeling of wings flying free, but now there was no such thing. I tried to visualize what the link might look like if it were physical, like a cable connecting minds. For a moment I thought I found it, but instead I was met only with my own mind bricking me in.

I opened my eyes when Dad got back in the car. He started up the engine and we drove off leaving the house on a quiet street. Dad didn't turn on the radio and we spent much of the drive in silence. I realized though, that I hadn't really had the chance to talk to my father about this whole situation. I didn't even know what his power was.

"Dad?" I looked over at him.

"Hm?"

"What... uh... What's your power? Ability?"

Dad didn't say anything at first. He changed lanes to pass a slow driver and only then did he glance at me. "Invisibility."

"Really? Cool."

The corner of his mouth twitched and he fell silent.

"And mom's a... a Non-Kinetic?"

"Yeah."

"But... I thought people who weren't... Non-Kinetics, couldn't know about all this?"

"They can't. But sometimes exceptions are made. And your mother deserves that exception. It's a story I'll tell you when we have more time."

I looked at my hands where the marker of a red X still stained the skin announcing me as a Vunjika. "What am I?"

He considered it for a moment. "Not sure. You switched between a few when you were younger, I don't think..." He paused and I saw a thought pass over his eyes but not manifest. "Either way, they will test you for your power when you receive training."

"Oh." I covered the marking with my other hand and looked out the window. Another thought occurred to me. Flashes of memory from just an hour ago made me shudder. "What about Jacob?"

At first I thought Dad wasn't going to say anything. He

was silent for so long I began to think he hadn't heard me. He adjusted his shoulders and glanced at me. "Your brother has a rare power, rare enough that it doesn't really have a proper name. You will learn this when you train, but each power has a proper name and then a common name. It's listed in textbooks as Hutor's Will. But its common name is just...Fission."

I didn't ask any more questions after that. I let it all sink in and let myself ponder what my power might be. I didn't know what all of them were, or what I had seen before Willow got kidnapped. I could only really understand the ones that were common in regular movies and games. Like telekinesis, and Willow's healing ability. Jacob's powers... the images from the conference where he straight up made a woman explode... Jacob's power was frightening. I couldn't imagine having a power like that. What could you do with a power that destroys and kills except destroy and kill?

We drove all the way through town until we reached an office park near the airport. The office park was labeled only with a sign for Intent Securities. This was the work I had thought Dad did. "I thought you worked for a corporate security contractor?"

"It's a front for the intelligence sector of the Alliance." Dad replied.

"Oh, what do you do then?"

"We have agents everywhere in the world who feed us reports and intel on the activities of the Isiroans. I lead and manage their activities." Dad parked the car and we got out. The Intent Securities building was made of some weird brown concrete with a straight line of glass wrapping around the whole complex. The majority of the doors and windows were unmarked and darkly tinted. There wasn't really any way to tell which of the dozen or so doors I could see would give entrance into the building.

We entered through one of the doors, and I'm not sure how Dad knew which to pick. They all looked the same to me. What little stenciling there was on the door gave no hours-- only a cramped "Intent Securities" over the door handle.

The reception area was clean and bland. A single desk

and a couple fake plants decorated the room. Two fold-out chairs sat along the wall.

The woman at the desk was unfazed by us entering. She greeted Dad like she had done it every day of her life. She pushed a button on the desk and a door along the back wall clicked open. Her brightly colored fingernails waved us along.

We passed through the door which locked behind us firmly and entered a hallway filled with endless doors. Dad knew the route through the featureless halls, with only numbers to indicate a change in location. I tried keeping track of the twists and turns but after a while I lost where we were.

Finally, after going down two flights of stairs and going around blank walls and through unmarked doors we reached a set of doors made out of some kind of dark, expensive looking wood. Dad pushed open the door and inside was no average office but a huge auditorium-sized room with rows of monitors going down tiered platforms. At the very back of the room was an enormous screen taking up a whole wall. On it was projected a map of the world with little multi-colored dots freckled everywhere.

Dad didn't let me stare at the whole thing for long, before dragging me off toward the side of the room where we pushed through another set of doors into a conference room. The room was adorned with a long table and lots of empty chairs. At the head of the table sat a blond-headed, pale-as-death woman. Her fingers were lightly steepled over her lap.

A man stood behind her chair watching us with intense dark eyes.

Dad sat me down at a chair not far from the woman's and then bowed politely at her. He squeezed my shoulder firmly and then stepped to the other side of the room with his back against the wall. The woman leaned forward slightly and smiled at me.

"How are you feeling, Mr. Yoshida?" The smile on her mouth wasn't reflected in her eyes. I had to resist the urge to look away.

"I've been better." I muttered.

She chuckled. "I'm sure that you have. I heard about

76

your friend Willow. I am very sorry that happened. We are doing everything we can."

"You can save her?" I asked. Hope fluttered in my chest.

She sat back and shook her head. "Eugene--may I call you Eugene?" She didn't wait for my answer and continued. "At this point saving her may not be possible. Few people have ever be found after the Isiroans have taken them."

"Why?"

"The Isiroans are cowards, and cowards are the best at hiding." Her soft voice never faltered.

"There must be something..."

"There is, actually. But first, I seem to have neglected to introduce myself and my colleague." She stood up and touched the shoulder of the man. "This is Joseph Carmichael, and I am Miriam Lancaster. I am the Chief Minister of the Anyan's Alliance, second only to the Council of Anyan. Mr. Carmichael is *my* second-in-command."

"Uh, nice to meet you, I guess." I followed her with my gaze as she began pacing from one side of her end of the table to the other.

"Yes, I wish we would have met under better circumstances, but what is done, is done. You were brought here because it is time for you to decide if you will take the remedial training, or if you want to live out the rest of your life as a Non."

I considered for a moment. I didn't really know what would happen with either, but Lancaster appeared to be willing to answer that for me.

"Choose carefully. If you decide to give up Kinetic life, then you will forfeit not only future access to your powers, but also all knowledge of our society."

"I was told you could tell me why Willow was taken?" I forced the question out, my forehead was sweating and the seat was increasingly uncomfortable. I fidgeted as Lancaster considered the question.

"What we know is that Willow is one of the few people left in the world that Isiro can bond with. And unfortunately, if what we know is true, then your friend will not be herself after a month's time."

"What do you mean?"

"The Isiroans will be making her one of their own in the worst way possible. She will become the host of an alien parasite. Has anyone explained what Isiro is?"

"A little."

"In order for Isiro to influence people, he requires a host to live through. He has no physical body and has to make a parasitic bond with a human. He has been doing this for thousands of years. As one host begins to die, he seeks another. And unfortunately, Willow is the next on his list."

"You can't let that happen!" I stood up. Lancaster's second-in-command, Carmichael stepped forward and uncrossed his arms from his chest.

Lancaster held her hand out to stop him.

"In war, sacrifices have to be made." She said quietly and looked down at her hands.

"But..." I sucked in a breath to protest.

"But, nothing." She frowned. "Your friend is no more important than the operatives I would have to send in after her. It's far too dangerous, especially when it comes to Isiro's personal security. They are highly trained Kinetics with no qualms about killing."

"But I..."

She shook her head. "...could do little. The amount of time it would take for you to learn the basics of your powers exceed the time limit before the girl is lost to us completely."

"But there's still a chance!" I cried. "She's not gone yet! You said so yourself. We could--we could still save her!"

She shook her head. "Impossible."

"Then I'm not training." I said, nearly spitting out the last word. "I'll go after her now!"

"Mr. Yoshida, you haven't been out of Ohio for most of your life and you are a *Vunjika*. What makes you think you know anything about where she is or how you could save her?"

"Well I better at least try! It's my duty as a friend."

"I'm sorry," Her eyes narrowed. "If you refuse the training, then we have no choice."

I stood up ready to begin yelling but Dad came up behind me and clenched my shoulder. "It has been a hectic day, Chief Lancaster. Let me take my son home and we will return in a few days with our decision."

"Very well." She clasped her fingers together and smirked at me as we left.

I refused to speak to Dad the whole ride home.

CHAPTER 9

"It's better to act and to regret / Than to regret not to have acted." ~ Mellin de Saint-Gelais

A single light from my iguana's terrarium illuminated my room. The darkness was comforting in some small way, but it made the hole in my heart where Willow should have been feel that much larger.

It was a whole day later since Willow had been stolen away from all of us. Her parents had been by, but I hadn't left my room to see them, despite the prompting from my mother. I was in no mood to be around anyone else.

I stared at the picture of Willow on my wall. It was of us, smiling on a soccer field in a happier time, a time I couldn't feel anymore. She was gone, and the people around me couldn't, or wouldn't, do anything to save her. How bad could this Isiro person be that she was unreachable? All these people with abilities beyond anything I ever could have imagined and she was truly gone?

Impossible.

But what could I do? I was fifteen, gifted with average grades and average friends. Anything I could do was limited by my severe lack of... ability. I traced the faded outline of the X on the back of my hand. I had nothing to offer a rescue if I could even start one myself. Whatever power I was supposed to possess was out of my reach for the time being, even if I knew what it was.

I couldn't see myself returning to school like nothing was wrong. I couldn't see myself letting her go. I couldn't see myself taking another step outside my bedroom door that didn't include some thought of her.

I buried my face in my hands and imagined the faces of everyone I knew. My parents were adamant that what this Chief Lancaster said was rule and law; Jacob would probably be no better. All my friends were... well, kids. They were involved in sports or clubs but nothing that could possibly benefit a crackpot rescue plan. If Nick were in town right now, I could probably go to him for help, but he was thousands of miles away in Amsterdam on some job thing.

I let out a laugh. I was actually considering going after her with no knowledge, no powers, no money, nothing but me, myself, and I. Hell, I wasn't even that smart. Not as smart as people like Nick or Harry, the nerdy football player.

Harry? Harry knew Willow. Harry was smart. Even I had to admit he was probably genius level. Could Harry make sense of the crazy that was happening to me right now? Could Harry figure out a way to save Willow that wouldn't get us killed? I didn't know him well, and I certainly didn't consider him a friend, but Willow called him her friend. I wanted to trust her judgment.

I waited until I was certain my parents were asleep and then I slipped out into the night. I remembered passing by his house one day with Willow. She had pointed it out not long after her and Harry had become friends. He was the only hope I could think of right now, and if he wasn't able to help me, then I... I didn't know what I could do.

I yanked my bike out of the garage and, as silently as possible, I pushed it out into the night. The night was stuffy. The last bits of the cool months were about to start fading away. The hot night air of summer was well on its way in. I huffed the thick air all the way to Harry's house, riding as fast as I could. It wasn't that far from the school and I couldn't help but remember the incident at school with Laura and her nightmares. I had really hoped to go a few more days without thinking about those things again.

I rolled the bike to a halt in the driveway and stared toward the single lit window on the first floor facing the house next to Harry's. It was late, and I didn't know what Harry's folks did, so it could very well have been them awake, but I took a chance and crept up to the window. The room was obviously inhabited by a teenager. A few gaming posters and a stack of textbooks from our school were scattered around the room. I didn't see anyone asleep on the bed or sitting at the desk. I was only moments away from calling defeat when the door opened and Harry stepped in. He was typing something on his cellphone and didn't look up.

I tapped on the glass.

Harry's head shot up and he squinted at me through the window, confusion contorting his face. He popped the latch on the window and slid it open. Cold air-conditioned air washed over my face. "Eugene? Why are you here?"

"I need your help." I said. I was mildly surprised he even remembered my name.

He stared at me for a moment, the confusion on his face suddenly turning to realization. "Does this have to do with Willow?"

"Yeah," I said, surprised. "How'd you know?"

"She was supposed to call me today and hasn't answered any of my texts or calls."

"Yeah... she... she was kidnapped." I swallowed. It felt a little awkward standing at his window.

"Kidnapped?" Harry's eyebrows nearly shot up to his hairline.

"It's a long story." I said, not really wanting to explain from the outside of his window. Harry seemed to realize that at the same moment.

"Come to the front door," he said, and pushed the window closed.

He let me in and tapped the couch in his living room. I looked around at the sparsely decorated house. There were a few photos on the walls of a kid who was probably Harry in various stages of childhood on up. "We're not going to wake your parents?" I asked in a low voice, taking a seat on the couch.

"It's just my dad, and no, he's out of town on a business trip."

"You're... all by yourself?" I was a little shocked.

Harry shrugged, and changed the subject. "Willow?"

"Yeah... uhm, I don't know where to start..."

"Well, how about who kidnapped her for starters."

Harry sat down in the chair across from me and eyed me.

I took a deep breath. "Some guy named Isiro."

Harry's eyes narrowed. "Isiro?"

"Yeah."

He frowned, "What kind of name is that?"

I shook my head. "I don't know, all I know is that he took her from this conference we were at with our parents, and..."

"Why did he take her?"

"They said that he wanted her to be a host."

"They?" Harry's eyes got even more narrow and I'm pretty sure he hadn't blinked since I started talking.

"My parents... the lady my Dad works for. Apparently they want her to be the host for some kind of parasitic alien."

"Wait, she was taken to be a *host*... for an alien?"

"I know it sounds crazy..."

"It's more than crazy, Eugene. It's absurd."

I sighed, frustrated. "I know. But I don't know who else to go to, Harry."

"Alright, day of the body snatchers aside, what's stopping you from going to the police?"

"Well... nothing really... but Harry these people are powerful. If I went to the cops *my* people would send this InfoCon organization in to wipe everyone's memories. "

"Wait...InfoCon?"

"Oh, my god, Harry. I don't even know how to tell you all this stuff. Look, there are two organizations of Kinetics. I'm what's called a Kinetic. Supposedly, I've got powers or something and so does every other Kinetic. Willow has powers! She can heal people.

"Anyway, one organization is the A...Anyan's Alliance? And the other is led by this alien guy Isiro, the Isiroans. The Alliance and the Isiroans have been in a war for centuries. Willow was taken to be a host by the alien guy, and the Alliance thinks she's a lost cause."

Harry considered me for a moment. His face was serious, but there was something being worked behind his eyes. Finally he said, "What do you want me to do?"

I licked my lips. I felt dry all too suddenly. "I can't let her be taken like that. They, Lancaster, the lady my dad works for say there's nothing they can do. I... refuse, *refuse* to believe that she can't be saved. Help me make a plan or something, anything that I can do that will let me make sure she gets home safe."

Harry let out a sign. "Tell me... tell me everything you know."

So I started. I figured he would call me out, call me crazy, and tell me I was imagining things, but he was blissfully silent while I began from the moment in school where Laura loosed the nightmares on us all. "Wait," Harry said. "When did all this, these nightmares, happen?"

I blinked, surprised. "You were there. It was just a couple days ago."

Harry frowned at me and searched my face with his eyes. "Are you sure? I don't remember anything. Last time you were in school, there was a late fire drill, but no nightmares."

"Oh." Then it clicked. "I forgot. That's because you're not a Kinetic. They wiped the memories of all the Non-Kinetics there."

Harry shook his head. "That's strange. Knowing that you should know something, but it's just not there."

I shrugged. "It's all very new to me, too."

I continued and told him about the InfoCon. How they had piled us all into the gym and one-by-one had sorted us between Kinetic and Non-Kinetic. I talked about the contract they wanted me to sign, the conference yesterday morning that now seemed too far away. I explained in as much detail as I could about the attack and Willow's kidnapping.

"This woman called him Grey?" he finally asked, referring to the woman who had pounced on Grey right before they had disappeared. I barely dared to look him in the face for fear he was laughing at me, but his voice was merely curious.

84

"Yeah."

He smiled at me. "That's your first clue. And I think I have an idea."

Harry and I continued talking through the night. I answered what questions I could for him. At this point, though, he knew just about as much as I did. Up until today I hadn't exchanged more than a greeting with Harry. This leap of faith had been more beneficial to me and to Willow then all the conversations with my parents, my brother, and that Lancaster woman combined.

We were probably being stupid. I was probably being a massive idiot just thinking I could save her. But at this point in time, I didn't know how hard the next few days and weeks would be.

It was nearing dawn. We had spent the better part of the night planning. Harry had picked my brain clean of all the information I could remember about my father's workplace.

I had even gone so far as to draw a messy map of the route we had taken in and out.

We were going to break into my dad's workplace and raid the bank of computers I had seen. Surely they would have tons of information about the Isiroan named Grey. I could still see his greasy hair and face in my mind. I refused to forget it for the rest of my life.

As I said goodbye, I hesitated to ask about how wise it was to try and break into a facility with people who had who-knows-what powers, but kept my mouth shut. If Harry was half as smart as he was in school and a tenth as smart as he was acting now, then I had to hope that he knew what he was getting us into because I certainly didn't.

***

The next night, Harry had brought along a small toolset, and once we reached my dad's office, he seemed fairly confident that he could crack open the door. With Harry working away at the lock on the door, I kept a lookout for any wandering eyes. Having been here only once, I wasn't sure what to expect, but when Harry clapped his hands and the door popped open, I set my worries to rest.

We slipped in the door, letting it close behind us with a soft click. We made quick ground after that. I worked us through the halls until we found the room where all the monitors were laid out. Up at the front of the room there were only a few people at computers. One looked half asleep at his monitor.

Harry motioned for me to follow him and we snuck around the back of the room until we were hidden behind a bank of computers and a huge black board.

He sat himself in front of a computer and started opening files and programs.

Harry typed quickly and within moments had what looked like intelligence reports. Harry's keywords of Isiro, Grey and Willow Patterson pulled up a dozen or so pages of something. Harry pushed his flash drive into the computer and was saving report after report, picture after picture.

What little I was seeing was enough to make me feel sick. Someone had been tailing Willow. They had distant, grainy photos of her walking to school, talking to teachers or classmates, myself and Harry included, even some of her with her parents at dinner.

How Grey fit into all this wasn't clear to me yet. Harry kept going. He was getting into stuff that I didn't recognize from an over the shoulder glance.

Harry pulled the flash drive out and nodded to me. We began working our way out of the room. But it was not to be without trouble.

"Hey!" someone in an Alliance uniform shouted from down the line of computers.

"Shit!" Harry ducked down and pulled me down with him.

"Stop! Come out!"

We crawled along the floor, barely avoiding being seen a second time.

"Run!" Harry hissed, shot from his hiding spot, and sprinted toward the door.

I tried to go after him but my shirt caught on a chair and I fell down. I saw the back of Harry's head disappear behind a corner and then adults in black and tan uniforms closed in around me.

I jerked away from the chair and ran toward the door, dodging around the grasping fingers of the people in uniform. My fingers brushed the door handle seconds before something sharp seared through my brain. I tumbled to the floor and grabbed my temples. "Ahhg!"

For a brief moment the image of a set of angry hazel eyes flashed before me but was gone before I even realized it was there.

My nose met hard carpet and tears leaked out my eyes. My brain was shuddering with what felt like shards of glass. I felt like the inside of my head was bleeding.

I took one look up, just in time to see the man that had stood at Lancaster's back, Carmichael, stepping toward me, and everything went dark.

***

Joseph Carmichael looked down at the boy lying on the floor. His body twitched as if it couldn't come to terms with unconsciousness. Carmichael leaned and touched two fingers to the top of the boy's head. He felt the synapses of the child firing in a confused dance. It was unusual to say the least, most people would be completely down by now.

This boy was fighting it.

Carmichael stepped away and motioned to two guards outside the door. "Take him to..."

"Sir!" one of the guards pointed at the boy.

Carmichael looked back and saw the boy push himself to his feet. Carmichael readied his powers to strike the boy down again, that is until he saw the boy's eyes. The whites were bloodshot and the pupils were fully dilated. Sweat poured down the boy's forehead and he breathed roughly.

Carmichael could feel power rising from somewhere in the boy's mind. A wild and ferocious power.

"You will stop now," the boy said, but his voice was strange. It sounded mixed with a woman's voice.

He wasn't prepared for the boy's next move. A jolt of fire blasted past his face and he barely moved out of the way.

Carmichael reached out and tried to take command of the boy again, but his mind was closed tighter than the jaws of a pit bull.

Flames manifested all around the boy in a swirling tornado, charring everything in the hallway. The two guards took positions on either side of Carmichael and wielded their powers. The first one tried to tie the boy in metal vines from the water pipes in the floor. The other was making shields around the boy to prevent his wielded fires from attacking them.

This seemed to anger the boy even more.

The furious flames filled the circumference of the guard's shield and then exploded outward, dousing everyone in fire.

At the last minute Carmichael used all his strength of will and shut the boy's brain down into a coma that would last for hours.

The boy fell to the ground, completely still this time, but his handiwork of fire still ate at the walls.

Miriam Lancaster came up behind him and stared down at the boy. "No Vunjika could do that. Find out who trained him."

CHAPTER 10

"Three hundred years ago a prisoner condemned to the Tower of London carved on the wall of his cell this sentiment to keep up his spirits during his long imprisonment: 'It is not adversity that kills, but the impatience with which we bear adversity." - James Keller

My body was on fire. My skin burned as my muscles felt like they tried to eat their way through my skin. I rolled over and fell out of a hard cot and onto a cold floor. I scrambled up and rubbed my limbs of the prickling sensation. It hurt like nothing I had ever felt before. What had that guy done to me?

"Rubbing it won't help." A voice close to my ear chuckled.

I fell backward while trying to turn around. A bent over old man grinned down at me, his teeth cracked and broken, and his nose was crooked as if he'd been punched in the face one too many times. He chuckled once again and limped over to a small metal desk and chair off to the side. I looked around and tried to anchor down reality. The cell--that's what it obviously was--was made entirely of metal, interspersed with large rounded off bolts in vertical lines like bars through the walls. The only door in the room was flat against the wall with not enough space in the frame to fit a credit card. How they opened it was beyond me.

Harry was nowhere to be seen.

"The feeling will pass in time. Not to worry." The old man returned and leaned over me. He patted my chest and I felt a sharp pain in my chest. I clutched at the area that he touched and tried to take deep breaths.

"What did you do to me?"

I looked up at the man, but he was back at the desk flipping through some sheets of paper.

"Who are you?" I gasped.

He didn't answer me but came and knelt at my side. He touched my chest again and I felt a searing pain near my heart. The old man sucked in a deep breath and clenched his fist, pulling his arm back like he was about to strike. Instead I saw a bright light at my chest and from it a little metallic ball the size of a golf ball emerged. I gasped as the pain subsided and the little ball fell out onto the floor.

"It's been there for a good bit, yes?" The old man smiled and plucked it from the floor. He stood and studied it for a moment. I didn't take the time to ponder this because suddenly my limbs were burning again. I curled up into a little ball and rested my forehead on the cool floor. My chest, my arms, my legs--they all hurt so much. I felt water slide down my face, but I couldn't tell if it was sweat or tears. Maybe it was both.

The pain subsided and I gained enough energy to sit myself back up. The old man was crouched in front of me still studying the little ball. After a few minutes he dropped it in my lap. With aching arms and fingers I picked it up and studied the little metallic ball. It was split into sections and each of the sections moved. The ball was not a smooth sphere. It had triangles and square knobs on each subsection of the ball. Even with my nonexistent powers, I could feel a strange energy pulsating from it, causing the nerves in my hand to buzz.

I used my fingernail to move a couple of the sections around and it clicked, with each section moving.

"It will help you." The old man said happily.

"Who... who are you?" I rubbed my arms more, dropping the ball to my lap again, and massaged the burning skin.

"Ah, the question of the ages. Who am I?" He grinned at me, plucking thoughtfully at his short white beard. "I am a prisoner without keys to free myself. A prisoner to life. A prisoner to my own choices."

His cryptic words sailed over my head and I couldn't

help but stare at him, confused.

"Ah, but you are young, what would you know of such things." He let out a belly laugh and sat all the way down on the floor, crossing his legs. "My name is Benjamin Sujit Ashwater. Father of two. Grandfather of three. Isiroan Technologist. Enemy to all things Alliance." He laughed with his last sentence, apparently highly amused with himself.

Isiroan Technologist? This old man, this Ashwater, was an Isiroan?

"Why am I here?"

"Why are we all here?" I almost expected him to start saying cryptic things again, but he merely smiled and looked up at the ceiling dreamily. "We all have done something another believes that we should not have. You have ignored rules that are to be kept, I stole something important. Your next question will be 'where are we,' hmm?"

I nodded, staring at the man across the room.

"We are still in Ohio, United States, Earth, Solar System, Milky Way, and the Universe." His constant grin never faltered. "The real question is?"

I never got that question, because a split second later I was staring up at the ceiling again feeling my body spasming out of control. I felt my lungs contract and expand roughly and my heart beat like a jackhammer inside my chest. I cried out involuntarily and could do nothing but flail helplessly when the old man came to sit on his knees at my side. He grabbed the sides of my head in an unyielding grip. It was almost impossible in my mind that this old man could possess such strength. But I had little time, or patience, with my fevered brain to consider it. I felt my body calm as though a stream of ice water were flowing from my temples down every vein in my body, stretching through my arms and fingers and all the way down to my toes. It felt good for only a moment, because in the next second I was freezing. My blood felt like ice. I grasped out at Ashwater's arm as he held me down and saw how unnaturally blue my skin had become.

"Wha? What are you—what are you doing?" I gasped out.

Before the Ashwater could answer I felt the heat from earlier begin to take hold again. My body warmed slowly and I stayed an exhausted heap on the floor. The man pushed back and sat against the wall, tinkering with what looked like a paper airplane. *Crazy old man*, was my last thought before I passed out.

I woke up later with a pounding headache. An unfamiliar man stood over me and grabbed my shirt almost as soon as my eyes opened. He pulled me out of the cell and dragged me down an unfamiliar hall.

He pushed me into a well adorned room.

"Sit and do not move." He frowned at me, and shut the door firmly behind him. I tested the door, but it didn't budge, so I did the only thing that my throbbing head wanted to do and that was sit down for a bit.

The hands on the clock at the back of the room ticked by slowly. Seconds were passing like hours, minutes like days. I picked at a loose thread in the armrest of my chair and tried to not go crazy as my muscles burned.

Stuck in this room I knew I was probably going to some kind of prison for Kinetics. I highly doubted that they were going to let me and Harry's attempt at information theft go unpunished. Speaking of Harry, I hadn't seen him at all. Had he escaped?

The door opened and three people entered. The man who had dragged me in here came in first followed by Lancaster and Carmichael. Lancaster took a seat across from me and smiled.

"You caused a bit of trouble." She shook her head.

"Sorry," I replied, flippantly.

"Hmm, I wonder. We couldn't tell what you and your friend were looking up. Would you mind telling me?"

"We were looking up information on how to save Willow."

She sat back and smiled. "You are looking for information that doesn't exist."

I ground my teeth together and narrowed my eyes at her. "I refuse to believe that you people can't save her."

"I told you once before that we have had people in her situation before. It is not possible to save her. The people who have taken her are not to be messed with. They are evil people with nothing but harm to cause. She is lost, and we cannot let someone like you endanger our society with delusions of heroism. You must think of her as dead, because the girl you knew a few days ago is gone."

I shook my head. "I can't... I can't."

"Listen." Her voice softened. "You have an opportunity to get trained, right here, right now. You could be like your brother, powerful, respected in our community. Don't you want to be respected?"

"I want Willow saved!" I shouted.

"Then get trained." Her voice was stern again. "Then you can go after the Isiroans who took her. She may be gone to us now, but you can get the retribution you want with a little patience."

I didn't want retribution. I didn't want to get trained. I REALLY didn't want to be like my brother. I barely knew what he did except kill. I shuddered away the memory of his kill at the Conference.

"Let me...add to my argument." She said slowly and pulled a large photo out of an envelope in her hands. She slid the photo across the table and smiled warmly when I made brief eye-contact over the glossy picture of a man.

"Is this the man you saw at the convention center?"

I studied the image. He had greasy dark hair, with a few grey streaks running along his temples and out over his forehead. I didn't have to look at it long before I saw the very clear resemblance to the man who had grabbed Willow. That moment was seared onto the back of my eyeballs. "Yes."

"His name is Marcus Grey. He's a former, high-ranking admiral in the Isiroan ranks and now teaches their new recruits. He's very close to Isiro himself, so it's no surprise that he was the one tasked with capturing your friend to be his new host."

I swallowed, a lump forming in my throat.

"He was in charge of their special operations around the

93

world and was a major force behind the Second Great Kinetic War. He was Reginald Cook's adviser!" Lancaster sat back and studied me. "Although you likely have no knowledge of Cook and his war... a part of history that has eluded you due to your "disability."

"I don't really..."

"This," she interrupted, "is the caliber of man they have capturing a little girl from her home. A girl who couldn't hurt them if she tried. I don't think you realize the gravity of what we are facing if we even try to attempt a rescue. Now: training. If you are trained by the best of the best in the Alliance then you can be powerful, and someday great. If your brother is any indication of what you could be, then I think we could easily win this war."

"But if I go through the training then..."

"You have to let Willow be taken."

"No thanks." I shook my head vehemently.

Lancaster shrugged and looked at me with an intense gaze. "Your loss, my dear boy. Do you feel your abilities are where they need to be? You seem relatively well trained."

I was confused. "I... haven't been trained?" It came out more a question than a statement.

"You display abilities beyond what someone in your position should have." Lancaster eyed me with what could only have been suspicion. "You must have been trained a little."

"I mean... Willow tried to show me how to use telepathy, but... I don't even know what my other power is supposed to be."

Her eyes narrowed, "I don't like being lied to. We will talk later when you feel like being more truthful."

She waved her hand and the guy from before grabbed my shirt and pushed me toward the door.

They threw me back in the cell. I hit the floor hard and didn't try to pick myself up as he closed the door. But there was no Ashwater. The old man was gone.

I clutched my arms as the spasms returned and I felt only pain coursing through my whole body. What was happening to me? Why was this hurting so much? I opened my eyes only to see Ashwater sitting cross-legged on the floor flipping through a magazine. If I hadn't been in so much pain I would have been a little more surprised. A second ago I was alone in this cell.

I pushed myself up. "What the heck is going on?" The ball that Ashwater had... had *pulled* out of my chest was clutched tightly in my palm.

Ashwater put the magazine down and walked over to me. "It's almost time."

"What?"

He plucked the ball from my fingers and examined it. His fingers nimbly moved the pieces, too fast for me to follow, and then closed his hand around it. I saw an intense orange glow come from the ball and then without warning Ashwater punched out--fast for an old man--and hit my chest. The little ball had vanished from his palm.

I doubled over and coughed. "What the heck, man!"

He smiled, pleased with himself. "That's much better."

I wanted to ask what was better, but I felt my heart shudder and had to stop. My hands shook as I reached through my shirt to feel my heart beating. I had never before felt my heart like this. If I had been running at a full sprint for five minutes I would not have felt this much intense beating. At first I thought that I was having a heart attack, but then I felt something not unlike cool water streaming from my heart all the way through my extremities.

"What...did... you do?" I grasped my chest where it felt like a weight was on my heart. What did he do with that ball?

"What needed to be done." He began to back up, watching me intently. He pressed his back to the wall but the wall didn't stop him. It gave way and he melted into the wall, disappearing, leaving no trace that he had ever been pressed up against it.

The door to the cell opened, and as I turned around to see who had entered, the entire world around me bleached white. I felt my body disintegrating. I was dying!

I wanted to close my eyes, but they no longer existed. All that 'was' was bright white mist. Cold to the point of being hot, stuffy to the point of drowning.

The brightness receded and I found myself staring up at the sky. Clouds moved across the sun, lazily strolling across the sky on a warm midday. I pushed on my bruised fingers and stumbled to my feet.

I'm not in Kansas anymore, Toto.

For miles around me all I saw was sand and tiny dry bushes that probably needed more rain than sun. The horizon line shimmered with heatwaves blurring my view of anything more than a few hundred feet out from me. I turned around in a circle but the only thing I could see was a small structure, distorted by the heat in the distance.

I touched my chest where there was no more pain and gasped. "What the..."

CHAPTER 11

People can surprise you. But it's not because we aren't observant enough or even lacking as people. It's because there's more to a person than can be seen by the naked eye. You can't know your friend or neighbor like they know themselves. You can't know when a person will be a Healer or a murderer. You can't know when your own children will choose to take or leave your advice. You can't know when the person you share your home will turn to darkness. - Mavis Day. Alliance Politician. On the rise of Reginald Cook.

I started walking toward the structure. Nothing was familiar. Whatever Ashwater had done with that ball it had sent me to another place. I wondered, briefly, if it was an illusion. My experience with the things hadn't been too good so far, but the further I walked the more I was becoming certain I was not in an illusion. "Hello?" I called out, even though there were no people to be seen at all. My limbs were still trembling from whatever it was that was burning my body. The heat had subsided but the sun that was now beating down on me from the sparsely clouded sky more than compensated.

I reached the structure only to see that it was a building made of wood and concrete bricks. There was a door and a couple windows but I didn't see any immediate signs of life.

"Hello?" I called out again.

No answer. I stumbled around the building looking for anyone who could help me. I called out a couple more times to the same lack of answer. There was a clothesline out back with a few shirts hanging off it, twisting in the light wind, the only sure sign I had that someone inhabited this place.

Around the side of the building I found an old bathtub filled with dirty water and some clothes that had seen better days. I touched the edge of the tub and looked over at my reflection in the water. My hair was stringy and damp with sweat. My face was weird. My eyes were sunken in, and they looked like I felt: that I hadn't slept in days. I splashed my hand into my reflection and kept walking.

I got around to the front of the building again and stood in front of the door. I raised my fist to knock on the door when I heard a shout behind me. I turned just in time to see an Asian girl with ripped and scuffed jeans heading toward me. She spoke in quick Chinese and I shook my head. "I don't understand."

The ground beneath me flashed and everything went white. In seconds I found myself back in the cell. A klaxon was going off and there was a man unconscious on the floor. I gasped for air and then saw the door open. I took one look at it, one look at the man and then sprinted for the door. I skidded out past two guards who yelled in surprise at me, and I didn't dare think about where I was going. I had a fifty-fifty chance of going deeper into the compound or finding a way out.

I didn't stop for anyone or anything. My body and my lungs burned and my heart hammered through my chest. I pushed until my eyes burned. I pushed until my hands stung from blasting through doors and slamming into walls. My shirt was torn from slipping through the hands of guards.

I rolled into an open room, a storage room of some kind, and saw my way out. It was nighttime, dark, and raining but it was freedom. Pure unadulterated freedom. I jumped out of a trailer port and twisted my ankle on the pavement. I didn't let that stop me as voices and shouts punctured the hallways behind me. I limped into the rain and didn't stop until I was surrounded by people. Within seconds I was soaked head to toe.

I wrapped my arms around my chest and stared at the people running through the rain, fleeing to their homes and cars, to their safe places. They were running from the rain and cold. I was running from pursuers who I couldn't even see anymore.

The sky that had been threatening rain for days had finally followed through on its threat and had opened up a torrent of bitter cold droplets on the whole city.

At first my only thought was to run. I didn't think about where I was going, taking random turns down streets I only vaguely knew, trying to lose myself more than to lose my pursuers. Down every turn, past every streetlight, a realization was dawning on me. I didn't know what I was doing. I didn't know where I was going. I didn't know who to trust. I didn't know where Willow was. I didn't know how to find her. I didn't even know how or where to begin.

I let the rain soak through my skin and willed it to cool the burn in my body. Other than a small glimpse of his face, that was all I had on my best friend's kidnapper. The sound of rain pouring down from the sky in torrents filled the world around me with static. But his name reverberated through my skull like a drum. The rain was white sound blotting out the city streets around me while I ran with soaked shoes toward some uncertain future. Streetlights and passerby tried to escape the clouds cracking open with bright lightning to pour its harvested moisture everywhere.

Marcus Grey.

This name was the one thing keeping me going despite the cold water seeping up my legs. I repeated it over and over in my head, in time with the unsteady beat of my footfalls on wet sidewalk.

Marcus Grey.

A fire was building in my chest. A fire that was sure to fuel a rage for months to come. At this point in time I didn't think about the future beyond finding Willow. I didn't think about what I would do when I found Marcus Grey. I didn't think about what he would have in store for me when I finally came face to face. Every thought was consumed with the hunt, the hunt for the man who had stolen the love of my life.

The steady drizzle of the rain chilled my mind and I reached out with my mind trying to tap the telepathy that I knew was in there somewhere. I called out to Willow. I called out to my parents.

No one answered back.

No one answered...

No one...

It wasn't long before I had run out of breath. I was athletic, but not enough to maintain a constant run, especially with a twisted ankle, for as long as I was trying. I stumbled through a small park with a fountain and fell to a seat on the edge of the fountain. The drone of the rain and the loud bubbling of the fountain that that gushed brown water, bloated with rainwater drowned out my raging confused thoughts for a few blissful moments.

I opened my eyes, only to get my eyes full of rain-irrigated sweat. I wiped at my eyes and squinted through the rain at the passing headlights. There was one person and one person alone who I could possibly trust. Nick. He was the person who became my surrogate brother after Jacob had left. He was the one who taught me how to ride a bike. He was the person who stuck with me when I was sick with appendicitis. In the absence of Willow, the first person I would have gone to in this situation, Nick was all I had. I didn't know if Harry was safe or not, I didn't know if our plan was completely bust. My parents were at the whim of these Alliance people, I had a few other friends, but they were so far away from any of this. They were normal students, probably sleeping by now, getting ready for another day.

Nick was the only hope I had left if I was to even begin to know how to save Willow from whatever fate these "Isiroans" have in store for her. He was probably still out of town, but I knew where he kept the spare key to his house.

I picked myself up and shook off the chill that had settled over my skin and sunk deep into my bones. Nick's house was far, but not far enough that I couldn't make it. And so I walked.

People ran in slick coats, trying to escape from the rain under awnings and umbrellas. Cars passed, sloshing water out of the ditches and potholes. It was all so ordinary in contrast to the things I had seen in the past week. They were enough to make anyone question reality and normality. All these things that people were doing, something as ordinary as protecting themselves from rain, made me ache with a strange nostalgia. What I was seeing now was the end of my normal life. Whatever I did from here on out was the beginning of a new life.

I let the rain wash away my regrets. I had to be strong, strong for Willow and myself. Once I had everything explained to Nick, I'm sure he would have some kind of plan.

It was five A.M. by the time I reached Nick's place. I shuffled up to his doorstep, soaked through, cold and utterly worn out. I didn't see him open the door. I didn't hear him call my name. I didn't really experience much of anything after that. For four days I slept, and it was the best peace I would have for months.

**

I should have been feeling Deja Vu by now. Blacking out and waking up again in unfamiliar places. But I was too tired to protest this new place. It was quiet, and faint sunlight lit the room from thin curtains.

I didn't recognize it, but I was feeling better than anything. My heart ached but didn't pound. My body tingled but didn't burn. More than anything, I felt weak. I touched my chest where I thought I could feel the strange little metallic ball residing, but it was just a phantom feeling that passed as soon as I paid attention to it.

I didn't move for a while but listened to the sounds of the house, and I was fairly positive that it was a house. I could hear the subtle sounds of a neighborhood. Children laughing. Dogs barking. Cars driving past.

After what seemed an eternity lying prone, I pushed myself out of the bed. Actually I fell out, but fortunately no one witnessed the embarrassing fall. I desperately wanted to laugh about it, but the second that laughter climbed up my throat,

Willow's face flashed in my mind.

How could I laugh when she was out there? Under the hands of some enemy I had only just found out about. How could I allow myself to rest when her future was still uncertain? I pushed myself up, no-- FORCED myself up and dared my legs to buckle under me.

Something in the force of standing up triggered a flaring burn in my body again. I collapsed. "Dammit... Dammit," I said under my breath and pounded my fist on the ground.

I tried again and again, but my body wouldn't cooperate. I sat back against the bed and tugged at my hair. It was only then that I gave the room a second look, and I realized I was in Nick's house. Nick's guest room to be exact. The walls were bare, but I would recognize those New Orleans Saints curtains anywhere.

The door opened and I looked up the see Nick standing at the threshold. "Hey, how are you feeling?"

"Like boiled shit." I said into my hands.

"Heh, creative," he said. He looked much the same as he had the last time I'd seen him face to face a month ago. Hipster glasses with dishwater blond hair sticking in all directions and a stupid cockeyed smile on his face.

I pushed myself up as much as I dared and groaned under the sudden strain my muscles were feeling. "Oh, god, Nick, I'm in a lot of pain. I don't know what I did. How long have I been asleep?"

"About four days, I think. Haven't really been keeping track." He stepped into the room and sat on the bed patting my shoulder.

I nearly choked. "Four days?"

"You really needed sleep, so I didn't bug you. The EOS will do that to you."

I wanted to stand and pace, or move or something, but my body was perfectly content to let me do none of them. "Willow's been gone for almost a whole week and a half." I rubbed my face and searched every corner of my brain for an answer or a way.

I didn't know anything. I didn't even know where she

was, where to find her or how to start.

"Hey, you okay?"

I pinched my nose, trying to get the pain that was quickly rising in all my limbs and organs to go away with the willpower of my mind alone. I was not successful.

"EOS?" I asked, trying to not think about the fact that Willow was one week in on some hellish kidnapping. It hurt my mind to think about what she was probably going through. "You said earlier, 'The EOS will do that to you.' What's the EOS?"

"Energy Overload Syndrome. It's most common in people who are learning their powers. Seeing how you used your powers in such an explosive way, it's not unusual that you got it."

Powers...?

"You're a Kinetic, too?" I gasped, forgetting for a moment that my lungs hurt like I'd been inhaling glass.

"Yeah." Nick grinned.

I tried to wrap my brain around that. How many of the people I knew were going to turn out to be Kinetics?

"Yeah, jeez, it was hard not talking or doing things around you when you were little. Your Dad threatened to turn me and Jacob over to the InfoCon if we ever revealed ourselves to you. I'm glad you know now, kind of lets a little stress off the old shoulders. What all have they told you?"

"A little bit here and there. Vunjikas, powers," I swallowed. "The war."

"Ah, yeah. The war. Isiro, too?"

I nodded. The effort for that alone was enough to cut off the desire to field anymore questions.

Nick started chatting about random things while I pushed myself into my own head and tried to come to terms with the burn shuddering through my limbs.

"When Jacob and I were training we had all these big dreams of being bigger than the system, of finding a way to end the war. We thought we knew it all." Nick sighed wistfully, "It's funny how things change. Jacob and I had a falling out not long after we graduated high school. I guess you could say that we disagreed on certain vital points. He went to work for Heilbronner in Switzerland and I joined Intel in Paris. Actually came back because your dad picked me up to work under him."

I remembered Nick's brief vacation to Paris. He had returned with a thumb sized replica of the Eiffel Tower and it still sat on my desk at home. I didn't let myself dwell much on home. I wanted nothing more than to be back in my own room, my own bed, not dealing with this crazy... but Willow was worth it.

Putting Nick's version of the story in context was strange but the more he talked, the more things made sense. Jacob and Nick used to hang out all the time, back when Jacob seemed like a semi-normal teenager.

Jacob's other two friends Napoli and Joe I never really connected with. They wanted nothing to do with a pipsqueak like me. Nick on the other hand took to me like double sided tape.

He even came to my fourteenth birthday party and gave me a present not long after my brother went to Switzerland. But then he left for France and I hadn't expected to ever see him again.

When he returned and inserted himself in my life, even without Jake being around, it was like I had acquired a new brother. He came over almost every weekend and played video games with me, talked me through my troubles and frustrations.

I should have gone to Nick first. Nick was one of the few people I should have considered first. Not that Harry—jeez, as soon as I could move without feeling my muscles burn with pain, I was going to have to find him and get the information he had gathered on Marcus Grey.

"Hey, you said you worked for my dad in Intel?"

"Still do, actually."

"Do you know anything about Harry?"

"Harry? The nerdy footballer?"

"Yeah."

"Was he the one with you the other night?"

I nodded.

"They weren't able to get any information about him, none of the cameras or guys were able to catch a glimpse of his face."

"Good, then whatever info he got is safe."

"What did you guys find?"

"Stuff on Marcus Grey. He's the one who took Willow."

"Marcus Grey?"

"Yeah, you know the name?"

"Know it? Anyone in the Alliance that doesn't know his name must have been living under a rock. No offense."

"None taken."

"He was responsible for a lot of the guerilla activity in the Isiroans in the 70's and 80's. He was the friend of the guy who started the Second Great Kinetic War."

"I don't know what that is."

"Don't worry about it now. I'll give you some reading materials."

I moved my leg and a spike of pain shot up it. "Jeez, what the hell."

"What do you expect, a Vunjika using his powers like that?"

"You said that earlier. I haven't used my powers. I don't even know what they are. Willow tried to teach me telepathy but..."

"Not telepathy, Eugene. Your Pyrokinesis."

"Py-what?"

"Do you really not know? That's... rare."

I shook my head. "I really don't."

"Well, no point in trying to talk about it. I'll show you. Come here." He pushed himself out of the chair and held out an arm for me to use if I needed it. I felt a little unstable on my feet, but when the room quit tilting, I was comfortable enough to follow Nick on my own. The pain coursing through my whole body subsided to a dull ache.

Nick led me to a room with a ton of monitors. He tapped a keyboard and on the largest of the screens I saw words on the screen say: "File Footage." The date was the day that Harry and I had broken in to the headquarters.

On the screen I saw myself fall. Then I saw myself stand back up and what came next made my blood run cold. The fire. The fire engulfed everything. I pushed the chair back and tried to leave. The EOS or whatever the heck was disabling my body, made me fall to my knees. Nick tried to help me up but I waved him away.

I glanced back at the screen where Nick had paused the video. All I could see was a blurry image of me surrounded by fire. I held onto the chair in front of the desk and pushed myself up. It was strange seeing that other me in video form. I had no memory of that.

The last think I could remember was hitting the carpet and the deadening darkness that followed.

"It's really amazing." Nick said while looking at the screen. "Your power is Pyrokinesis. I never thought a Vunjika would be able to do what you did just then."

"No, I don't... I don't want that." The air in my chest constricted and I forced myself to breathe.

"Hey." Nick's voice was the last thing I heard before my forehead hit the corner of a desk.

PART 2:
A JOURNEY OF A THOUSAND MILES…

CHAPTER 12

"A journey of a thousand miles begins with a single step." ~ Confucius.

I spent the next three days recovering. The bump on the head was nothing, but the residual effects of the EOS were turning me into paraplegic dodo bird. I spent a lot of time on Nick's laptop reading some of the history of the Kinetics. It was just about as dry and dull as most history I had ever read in school.

We weren't talking about the thing with the Pyrokinesis. Every time I thought about it, my head hurt, like something deeper than my subconscious was trying to prevent me from thinking about it. The one time I did try to really delve into what it meant to be a Pyrokinetic, flashes of incoherent memories and feelings rose up out of a long-forgotten part of my mind, and all I felt was sorrow. So I pushed it away.

"Don't worry. You're safe here from Trackers." Nick had assured me when I had asked how safe I was here. "You have something running in your system right now called the A.D." He pulled a small bag out from under the chair and opened it to show me a series of quarter sized patches.

"These are kind of like nicotine patches, ya know? They inhibit the chemicals in your brain that allow access to your powers. It also has the added effect of cancelling out a tracker's abilities, so they don't see you." He snapped his fingers trying to think of something.

"You know how the Stealth works? Normal radar doesn't see it. Kinda like that. You, my friend, are essentially invisible."

I wasn't sure how we were going to get there yet. I didn't have a lot of money and what I did was in a pickle jar under my bed at home. Nick was quick to advise me not to go home. That was the first place they would look for me. There was no doubt that the Alliance would have the house under constant surveillance.

"I don't know what to do. I don't want to do nothing..." I had said to Nick one day.

"It's all about resources, kiddo." He leaned back and crossed his arms.

"What resources?"

"Right in front of you." Nick aimed his thumbs at his chest and grinned. "I'm a first class Tracker!"

"Can't you find Willow then?"

"Well, see, here's when being a Tracker fails. The Isiroans have Technologists. They have developed tech with the ability to block Trackers."

"Then... you guys can't do much?"

"Well there's the thing. The tech creates an 'emptiness' or "Zero Zones" and we can sense that too. There are only so many locations that have ZZ's around them, and there are only so many locations where they would take a prisoner like Willow."

"So, it's narrowed down."

"Exactly."

"So?"

"Wait." He stood up and went into his work room. He came back with a laptop.

Nick set the laptop down in front of me and pulled his chair up close. On the screen was a map of the world. Six blue dots were scattered around. "These are the ZZs, and these..." he clicked a button. "These are the places where they take high profile prisoners." Three of the blue dots flashed red and then turned purple.

He touched a finger to the screen. "This is probably the first place they took her after they left Columbus." The point was in the western United States.

"What is that? Colorado?"

"Wyoming. Your best bet is to start there. After that, well, she could be anywhere. Once an Isiroan or their prisoners of war are in a ZZ they could be moved to any of the ZZs around the world and no one on the outside would know any better."

I touched a finger to the point on the screen. Willow might be there. "But what if she's not there?"

"That's always a risk, isn't it? You can always start there, though. Otherwise you're welcome to start in Argentina."

"So, when do we go?"

Nick frowned. "It won't be 'we,' kiddo."

"What? Why?"

"I have too many responsibilities here. They would know if I went missing."

"But I can't go by myself. I don't know anything, anyone!"

"Well, I don't know what to tell you, Eugene. I can give you tons of information and tell you where you need to go, but I have to stay here. I'm due back at the Saudi Arabian office in less than three days for an internal review."

"What do I do then?"

"Find someone to go with you."

Nick took his laptop and disappeared back into his office. I leaned back and stared at the ceiling. The room was swimming a bit, and all I wanted to do was close my eyes and sleep for a month. The thought that Willow was out there somewhere stopped any and all thoughts of rest from taking hold.

I wish she could be here now. She always knew what to say to help me think things through. If I was chasing anyone else, my first choice for a companion would have been Willow. She was goofy and acted stupid at times, but I knew she was far more intelligent then she let on. She also knew this Kinetic society way better than I did.

I wasn't going to let my limitations hold me back. I may have no usable powers and I may not be able to do it on my own, but with Nick's information I would save Willow. I just hoped that I could get Harry's help. As much as I didn't want to take Harry, the Nerdy Football Player with me, he had helped me once. He could probably help me again.

The last day of my recovery I tugged on a borrowed and ratty Pink Floyd t-shirt and a pair of one-size-too-large cargo pants. Nick didn't have much at this house. Most of his life was now in Amsterdam.

Nick had left to do work at the Alliance HQ, so I was on my own for the rest of the day. I pushed out the back door of Nick's house and hiked through backyards and back streets. Harry's house was almost five miles away.

Nick had informed me that the less I showed my face the better off I would be. So taking the city bus was a legit no-no. I don't know how much time passed by the time I got to Harry's house, but I knew it was just as school was letting out. I saw Harry walking with his backpack slung over one shoulder. A friend of his walked next to him talking up a storm. Harry seemed only mildly interested.

I waited until they split off from each other and Harry walked by himself to his front doorstep. Just as he was about to open his door I threw a rock at his feet. He pondered the rock for a moment then with only a moment's pause he casually moved from the door to the flower bed to the bushes where I hid. He acted as if he had done that every day of his life.

"Eugene," he said when he saw me. "I was wondering when you would show up."

CHAPTER 13

"The best laid plans of mice and men often go awry." –
Robert Burns. Scottish poet and lyricist. 1785.

"You made it out safe?" I asked, coming to stand next to him.

"Yeah, uh, after a bit of a hold up. I thought you were dead for sure." His eyes watched the passing traffic as he came to stand next to me.

"Fortunately no. What's been going on?" I grinned. I was immensely relieved to see him. He hadn't been captured by the Alliance people, which means that all the information that he had gotten off the computers was still intact.

"I take it you haven't been watching the news then." He said.

"Been a bit preoccupied." I replied. What in the world was going on in the news?

"Hmm, c'mon inside. My dad's still out at work." Harry hiked his backpack up onto his shoulder and strode inside. I shook my head in amazement. From my short interaction with Harry I was quickly realizing that Harry was never one to get phased by anything and this should be no surprise. I'm sure he was take it pretty calmly if I told him I was the Buddha and was here to claim my place as king of KFC.

"I think it would be better for you to just watch it and see." Harry said, grabbing the remote on the way to the living room couch.

I sat down to the early evening news where my face was tattooed in the tiny boxes at the shoulder of the newscasters. At first it didn't compute that I was seeing my face on the screen, but after seeing my face on the security cameras at the Alliance HQ, I thought that I would take it better.

"Yoshida is still wanted for questioning in connection with a large military-grade stockpile of weaponry found at Briggs High School earlier this week. Police say that the suspect is still at large but they are following up on leads."

"I never took you for a terrorist." Harry said, not even looking up from his fingernails.

"I'm... not?" I stared at the pictures of my alleged crime. "This is bullshit. I'm no terrorist."

"They seem pretty convinced." Harry raised an eyebrow at me and jerked his chin toward the TV.

"Yeah, well, what do they know?"

"That's what I said." Harry shook his head and muted the TV. "I would peg you for roadside axe murders, not some overly complicated Columbine-esque affair."

"Uh, not helping." I frowned.

"What happened after you got caught?" Harry asked, grinning.

"That's kind of why I'm here." I took in a deep breath.

"By the way, the school said Willow was sent on an impromptu vacation with family in Ireland or something. They really need to work on their cover stories. 'Cause really, who leaves this close to the end of the term? And the fact that the both of you stop coming to school the same day, I mean, really. The connection is screaming. There's a rumor that you two eloped." He had a quirky half smile on his face.

"No kidding?" I squeaked, and then coughed.

Harry chuckled. "Yeah, the guys at school are crying foul. You know how much they like her."

"I wish it was that simple." I whispered and shook my head.

"Anyway, by the time I realized you weren't behind me I was too far away to be of any help."

"It's okay. It worked out. I was put into this weird looking cell..." I explained what happened after we were caught, and about the strange interaction with the old man, intentionally avoiding the topic of my "powers." Harry's expression was one of curiosity the whole time I explained the cell, the little ball that he took out and then put back into my chest, and the teleportation to the desert and shack.

"This guy's name was... Ashwater?" Harry finally asked. Harry had pulled a notebook from somewhere and was taking notes with a fascinated expression on his face.

"Yeah, he was a little strange, talked strange, too." I chuckled a little.

"So... is this thing, this metal ball still in your chest? Can you feel it?" Harry leaned forward and looked at my chest as if the ball would magically appear if he stared at it long enough.

"I dunno. I thought I did right when it teleported me, but the feeling is gone." I patted my chest where I thought the thing would be.

Harry scratched his chin. "Hmm. I wonder if that's exactly what he put in you. A teleporter or something."

I shrugged. "I really don't know. Nick suggested I get an x-ray to see if it's still there. Oh yeah, what were you able to pull off their computers?"

"Mostly the information on Marcus Grey. I still have it on my flash drive. They have an interesting Intelligence report on it. It shows the route he took from here to some place in Wyoming."

"Laramie?"

"Yeah." Harry's eyebrows raised in surprise. He pulled his laptop out from his backpack and showed me a few of the files he had managed to get. One was a profile of Marcus Grey. I took it from him and read over the details.

"I'm going to introduce you to my friend Nick. He's a Kinetic, too. Knows scads of stuff about them."

"I almost think we should follow the same route. It seems strange to me, that people who have the ability to teleport long distances would choose to take a recently kidnapped girl on a road trip."

I scratched my head. "That does seem strange. I'll have to ask Nick about it."

Harry's phone began ringing. "Hold on a second, it's my Dad." He got up off the seat and disappeared into the kitchen. I could hear the low tones of him speaking to someone. I switched files and looked at the map that showed Grey's route. There were pictures notated on the document too. Harry had been only able to get a couple of them but from the two he was able to get, I was able to see a couple pictures of Willow just after her kidnapping. Their backs were facing the camera, and Willow was standing between a man who I assumed was Grey and a woman who was pointing at something off camera.

I touched the screen and felt my heart ache.

"Hey, sorry about that." Harry came back in and I dropped my hand. "That was my dad asking what I wanted for dinner."

"Ah, cool." I sighed. I didn't know when I would get to have dinner with my family again. Mom and Dad were only a dozen blocks away but I wouldn't be seeing the inside of my house for some time.

"It's a good thing it's just me and Dad." Harry said, smiling. "It means we know when someone is going to be here."

"I guess." I said, looking around at the living room once again.

"What's the plan now?" Harry sat back down and glanced at the picture on the screen I had been looking at. "Are you sure you want to go cross country?"

"Well, I don't really know what else to do. If I go back to the Alliance, then they're going to wipe my memories or force me into training that's not going to let me go after her anyway." I handed the laptop back to Harry. "I know it's insane, but I really don't have any other options. I don't want Willow to become a mindless host to whatever that thing is. I'm going after her, end of story."

Harry nodded, uncharacteristically quiet, while he considered. I sat back and stared at the silent pictures moving across the muted TV.

"I'll help you the whole way," he said finally.

"Yes." I sighed with relief.

"Give me tomorrow to finish up the rest of my school work and I'll be ready to go." Harry stood up and closed the laptop with a firm click.

"Aren't finals in a week?" I stood up too and stared at him incredulously.

"I would think you would want more time..." Harry raised his eyebrows.

"I do, but how-"

"I'm going to ask my teachers to give me all the required work and I will finish it up within in a few hours." Harry smiled. "My only reasoning to be in school is so that my dad won't make me get a job, and at this point the teachers are okay with letting me do whatever because I always turn everything in on time, or *early* when I want to do something else."

"Serious?" I stared at him in surprise. I knew he was smart but not that smart.

Harry grinned. "That's right."

I wrote down Nick's address for him and waved goodbye. "I'll see you tomorrow."

As I headed back to Nick's house on a bike borrowed from Harry, I felt a small weight lift from my shoulders. I wasn't in on this alone. But I could still feel the suffocating weight of the task ahead of us.

Tomorrow after Harry was done with school he would come to Nick's house and we would begin our mission plan. *Soon, Willow. Soon, we are going to find you.*

CHAPTER 14

"Distance? What's that?" ~ Gareth Cypress. A teleporter
noted for his travels of the world. 1909.

"To be perfectly honest, I'm as stumped as you are."
Nick was reading over the stuff we had grabbed off the Alliance
computers. "In all my years as an Intel Operative, I've never
seen a kidnapper take his quarry on a joyride across the States.
It just defies logic and most of all safety. I don't see why we
couldn't have jumped on this and gone after her. He's pretty
much taunting us."

"That's what I thought, too." Harry interjected.

"I knew Lancaster was lying." I pushed my chair up
closer to Nick's desk. "She told me it was impossible."

"It could be they are attempting a new form of
brainwashing." Nick scratched his chin.

"Brainwashing?" Harry asked, incredulously.

"Yeah, they have this way of getting perfectly sane
individuals to turn to their cause and believe it." Nick replied
shaking his head.

"What is that anyway?" I asked. "Their cause?"

"I've heard a couple different stories, depends on who
you talk to, but the general consensus is that they are trying to
raise an army to take over Earth and any other habitable planet
they can find."

"Why would they do that?" I shook my head.

"Why does any dictator or pathological villain do what
they do? Power." Nick shuffled some papers in front of him and
frowned.

"Hmm, are you sure there aren't some other reasons?"

Harry didn't seem convinced.

"Look, I only know what I've been told and what we can see from external reports." Nick looked over at Harry. "We know for a fact that the majority of the bases and facilities the Isiroans possess are dedicated to military training and tech development." I saw Nick grind his teeth, his bad habit when he was frustrated.

"Sorry man," Harry laughed, and patted Nick's shoulder. "I like to play the devil's advocate."

"It's alright." Nick shook his hands dismissively and looked back.

I shook my head at them. Over the past few hours Nick and Harry had been at odds. I guess that's what you get with two really smart people in the room. I felt out of place as I tried to keep up with them and listen to as much as they were saying. They were covering the reports and info we had gathered from the Alliance HQ, and added in some of the higher security stuff that Nick could access.

What we--and I say 'we' lightly--were finding was a picture of Marcus Grey. Marcus Grey wasn't even his real name. He had been born in a small town in China around 1933 and had been adopted by Catholic missionaries in 1945 who changed his name.

He had once been a bold military leader in the Second Great Kinetic War, the equivalent of one of the Non-Kinetic World Wars. There were about a dozen registered Kinetic groups around the world. Grey and an unnamed brother had run one of them before the war. And then somewhere in the middle of it, they had incorporated themselves into the Isiroans and then the war ended with an unsteady truce that was probably all but violated with Willow's kidnapping.

The fact that the Alliance wasn't jumping into war over Willow's kidnapping was frustrating. The fact that it was so clear that the Isiroans were in the wrong was even more so.

We took the information on Grey's journey across the state and made a detailed map. What little we could gather from the reports, he had Willow and another woman with him. The woman was likely extra help to watch over Willow, according to Nick.

Harry was deep in thought, studying the map. "Why St. Louis? You said this isn't a location terribly important to either the Alliance or the Isiroans?"

Nick nodded. "Undoubtedly, Kinetics of either side live there, but what possible use could a man like Marcus Grey have with it? But Grey has been off the grid for some time. Your guess would be as good as mine as to what's changed. "

I plucked the small printout of Willow's trek across the states with Marcus out of Harry's fingers. "My question is, why here?" I pointed to the Alliance facility in New Mexico. "You said it's Alliance, what's there that Grey needed?"

Nick shook his head. "The only thing I know about it is that it's a temporary housing for first-gens."

"First-Gens? Those are...?" I asked.

"First generation Kinetics. Means their parents have no abilities or knowledge and their kids are suddenly sprouting powers. Usually causes a pain in the neck for the InfoCon. First-gen emergence is not a pretty job responsibility."

"Maybe Grey came here to pick up some new recruits?" I said.

"Unlikely. He was outrageously stupid for attacking an Alliance member like Willow in the first place, but that's because she's been pinned to be Isiro's next host. While you can't completely discount the idea, it wouldn't have the same payoff."

"So... What say we just follow this path?" I traced my finger along the highlighted line that showed their trek across the states.

"Their first stop was at this place just outside of Columbus." Nick tapped the map.

"What's there?" Harry asked.

"Nothing as far as I know. A Non-Kinetic warehouse district." Nick shrugged, and then frowned. "Unless..."

Nick scooted his chair back and pulled a folder from one of his shelves. He flipped through the pages quickly and then stopped on one page in particular.

"What is it?" Harry asked me.

"I don't know." I shrugged.

"Aha!" Nick stood up and began pacing. "It used to be the location of an Alliance research and development group. It burned down about thirteen years ago."

"Why would they need to visit there?" Harry stood and looked at the folder in Nick's hands.

"I'm not sure, but it's not far away."

"I don't understand why we can't just go straight to Laramie." I said.

Nick scratched at his chin. "I need time to go through the information that we have been gathering on him. Plus there is a reason he's taken Willow on this joyride. I think you should take the opportunity to understand who it is that you're going after. Grey isn't the kind of person to do things on a whim. He's deliberate. And this deliberate journey is something that you need to understand. Even I don't know why, and if I didn't have serious responsibilities here, I would be going with you. Plus, our people are still looking for you and they know the first place you'll probably go is Laramie. They will be looking for you."

"Gives them some time to cool their heels." Harry laughed.

"Yeah, exactly." Nick smiled. "Smart friend you have, Eugene."

"Heh." I frowned. Even though I was getting Harry to help me, I still didn't know if he could be called my friend.

"Anyway, I've got you two new IDs. As long as you guys don't make any big scenes, you should be alright." Nick handed over two fresh IDs. Our fakes said we were from Florida.

∗∗∗

"What's this?" Jacob Yoshida looked down at a flash drive that one of his assistants just placed on his desk.

"Uhm, it's about your brother, sir." The assistant was nervous around him and Jacob knew it. He hadn't gotten to this position in the Alliance by being nice and most people below and even some above him treated him with a healthy sense of fear and respect. That's just the way he liked it.

Jacob picked up the flash drive and nodded to the assistant releasing him from having to stand next to the desk anymore.

He twirled the drive in his fingers wondering what his brother had done now that prompted someone to send him a flashdrive over it. Eugene was not exactly the biggest thing on anyone's radar, so this was almost alarming.

The incident at Eugene's school was not anything the Alliance hadn't dealt with before, a first generation Kinetic manifesting powers was almost every day, nothing the InfoCon couldn't handle. But now that his brother was involved, Jacob had taken the time to investigate the issue. Fairly standard issue event, the girl in question was a little emotionally unstable, but her psyche eval from the last time came back mostly normal. Eugene's friend Willow had really been the key player in the whole mess. But now that she was in Isiro's clutches and Eugene was facing his decision to train or be permanently removed from Kinetic society, he shouldn't have been a trouble.

Jacob took one look around the office, where a few people worked on computers, but most were at a table in the center of the room working on a layout. His direct supervisor and mentor, the War Chief Heilbronner, was seated at his desk falling asleep to cat videos on the internet.

Jacob shook his head and then with one smooth move pushed the drive into the port on the side of his laptop.

There was one file on the drive. Jacob clicked on it and watched a video compilation of his brother's actions from the past few days.

He had broken into the Alliance facility where their father worked, and at first Jacob didn't know why this was interesting but then--

His brother produced fire. A known Vunjika manifested his powers brilliantly.

Eugene had spent time in one of the brigs but not before...

Then he saw Eugene run.

Jacob smiled.

***

We piled into Nick's car the next afternoon. While Nick couldn't go with us out of state, he could at the very least take us to the first stop on Grey's journey.

The warehouse district was mostly empty, so when we got to the burned out husk that was once an Alliance facility, it was about as eerie as the beginning of a horror movie. Sounds of traffic on the freeway echoed from the distance, but the area around the gutted building was hushed. The few trees that surrounded the area wavered in the light winds but didn't bring a single sound with them.

We stepped out of Nick's car and onto charred remains.

It had been burned. What was left of the facility lay in scraps and shambles. We walked the perimeter of the large warehouse, not so much looking for a way in as we were gauging the place. At our feet small plants were erupting from the cracks in the pavement. Fallen leaves and branches covered a layer of charred wood, brick and other bits of building. A few of the concrete walls still stood high, casting long shadows across the debris.

"It used to be a research facility?" I asked as we hopped over fallen steel beams.

"What were they researching?" Harry asked.

"Tech. I think this was the primary facility for backward engineering of Isiroan tech." Nick supplied.

"Why haven't they done anything with this land?" Harry asked Nick. "I assume they still own it."

"I'm not entirely sure." Nick shrugged and leaned down to pick up a stick off the ground.

I walked into what was left of the structure and looked at what Willow would have seen when she was here. Why did Marcus Grey bring her here? What about this building was so important?

"Why did it burn down?" I asked aloud.

Nick used the stick to poke at piles of dirt and grass.

"Thirteen years ago there was a battle here. It was one of the last before we made a temporary truce with the Isiroans. Now that I think about it, the reason that Alliance don't want to come back here is that our leader at the time, Chief Reddinger, was killed here. A lot of Alliance people loved him. I've been told that what he did during his term was the single most reason why we aren't still fighting the Isiroans daily. But when the battle happened, it took down the whole place and killed a dozen scientists in the process."

We found traces of other people having been here with empty beer cans scattered in a corner and graffiti on the remaining walls. But none of it could explain why Grey had brought Willow here.

We stepped out into a large open area with no ceiling and exposed to the sky where a large tree had burst up from the center of the concrete flooring. Chunks of the floor were ripped up and surrounded the tree trunk in concentric circles.

Harry touched the trunk. "Are you sure this place was burned down thirteen years ago? This tree... it's too big."

Nick pursed his lips. "It's probably a tree created by a florakinetic."

"A *flower*kinetic?" I asked and stepped on top of a large chunk of concrete to look over the whole area.

"No, *flora*. It means plants in general. Florakinetics can create and grow all types of plants." Nick shook his head at me. "I can see that I need to get you a book on Kinetic powers."

"Sure." I said absently, my attention was caught by one of the walls where there was an eye and the words: *"The Eye Knows. The Mind Sees"* spray painted onto the surface.

"Anyway, is there anything else here?" Nick asked, looking around.

"I guess not." I said. "I don't understand why Marcus Grey brought Willow here. What's there to see?"

"I'll do a little digging and see if I can find any more information about the place." Nick said, pushing concrete chunks around with his foot.

We waited around a little more. There was literally nothing for us here that helped. I was more than a little sad. I felt strange here, like part of me had been here before, but going through all my memories I couldn't find anything that tied back to this place. I wanted to leave, and I said as much to Nick.

Harry on the other hand seemed morbidly fascinated with every detail of the place. His face was a constant mask of wonder and awe.

The return to Nick's home was quiet. Tomorrow Harry and I would be leaving Ohio to follow the track of Marcus Grey and Willow across the states.

Harry left for home and promised to return bright and early after spending one more night with his dad. He had told his dad that he was leaving to go to a Math Camp of all things, and apparently his dad was more than okay with that.

I was sitting in the living room half watching some movie about a Roman gladiator when Nick came in with a huge smile.

"One more thing to take care of before you leave." he said. Nick reached into back pocket and pulled out a pair of scissors. Then without warning he grabbed a thick lock of my hair and chopped it off.

I scooted sideways on the couch and cried out. "What the hell!"

"Hah, been wanting to do that for months!" He laughed.

I hopped off the couch and ran for the bathroom to look at my destroyed hair. It was all lopsided now, one half reaching my shoulders and the other frayed and cropped close to my ear.

"We have to change your appearance." Nick said from behind me, taking another hand full of hair and snipping it in half.

"What? Why?" I turned around and frowned at him.

Nick gave me a sour look. "Your face is all over the news."

"Oh." I hadn't thought about that yet.

"Eugene, trust me." He smirked. "I won't harm that pretty head of yours. I'll make you look like a rock star."

"I don't want to look like a rock star." I muttered, but let him do his work.

By the time he was finished, Nick had chopped my six-inch-long hair down to about one. Nick swept away the cut hairs from the back of my neck and told me to look at myself in the bathroom mirror. I did look different without the hair covering my face, but it felt weird. I touched the back of my head and ran my fingers through the prickly hair.

"Here." He pressed a pair of glasses into my hands when I turned to talk to him.

"I don't need glasses." I said looking up at him.

"You do now." Nick crossed his arms, waiting for me.

I shrugged and slipped the glasses onto my face. I looked in the mirror. I didn't look the same. The short hair and the glasses didn't make me look like a rock star but made me look like-- I wasn't sure. That wasn't Eugene Yoshida in the mirror. I didn't know that person one bit. I didn't know my own self.

"Not bad." Nick said with pride.

***

The bus station was full of people. Conversation was loud in the crowded terminals as people transferred buses, reached their final destination or started their trips. The clicks and clacks of the buses gearing up and gearing down filled the void between the conversing public. We dropped what little luggage we had at the bus destined for Cincinnati.

"Be right back, *Toshi*." Harry chuckled, using the fake name on my new ID, and dug through his bag for something. "I have to go pick up the tickets."

"Alright, *Oliver*. I think I'm going to head over to that convenience store next door and buy something for lunch." I pointed at the crowded store off in the corner.

"Okay. We'll meet back here in a few minutes?"

"Yeah." Absently, I rubbed my temple where the glasses had been rubbing against the skin. The glasses felt obnoxious and ungainly. I browsed the convenience store for a second or two and finally grabbed some chips and a couple small bottles of soda. Not long after that, I was back in the station and walking toward our bus terminal.

Then, I saw him. He stood not a hundred feet away holding a map up to his eyes as if he were any other tourist. But his gaze was anywhere but at the map. He was scanning the crowd with a sharp predatory stare, pausing on a person, blinking, then moving on to the next and repeating the process all over again. I started to back up and get away from him, but his gaze found me quicker than if I had a bright orange banner above my head pointing out my exact position.

Napoli Stewart was an average looking man with pale skin and didn't have any remarkable features other than a pair of piercing blue eyes.

Split seconds after I saw him we made eye contact. He grinned maliciously and started walking toward me. The crowded station seemed to part before him as he glided smoothly over to me. I did not have the same skills to part the crowd, so I bumped into people and got yelled at multiple times in a matter of seconds. Once I was clear of the crowd, I took off at a run. I knew he was following me. I could hear the shouts behind me as his uncanny skill to part crowds failed him as he ran not far behind.

Napoli was one of my brother's best friends. Nick had already told me that my brother's other two friends were also Kinetics. Part of the Military Corps just like Jacob. Nick had gone ahead and told me their powers, too. Napoli had some kind of copying power called Mirror that let him mimic anyone's power for about an hour or two. Joe was something called a Solid Shifter. He could literally break apart the atoms in his body and move through solid objects.

I had to find Harry. It looked like we wouldn't be leaving Columbus unhindered. I skidded around a corner but found myself trapped in an alcove with a dozen or so pay phones.

"Trapped yourself, Eugene?" Napoli chuckled from behind me.

I turned and backed up a few steps. He stood in the center of the opening to the rest of the station with a grin on his face and peered over his glasses.

"You should just give yourself up. There is no point in running."

I chose not to answer and instead looked around the small alcove and the spaces between Napoli and the wall and backed up a step more.

"Your brother wants to talk to you, Eugene. Why don't you come with me without argument and we can get this whole thing resolved like rational human beings." He took a step forward to compensate for the increasing distance between us.

"Back off," I snarled.

"Tsk tsk, is that how you treat an old friend?"

"You're not my friend!" I had reached the wall and bumped up against the long metal table sticking out of the wall. My hand found the spine of a phone book and I flung it at Napoli, aiming for his face. He tried to duck under it and grab me, but I dove out of the way and scrambled toward the exit. The phone book only clipped his shoulder and Napoli recovered faster than I was able to escape. He seized my arm and held on tight.

He grinned viciously and I felt my skin tingle unpleasantly where his fingernails dug into my skin.

"Let go!" I shouted.

Napoli laughed and shouted back, "Got it!"

He let go.

His hand burst into flames and he lunged at me. I tripped over my feet and fell to the ground.

"Never seen my powers before, have you?" Napoli's fiery hand got close to my face. "I can copy any power I want and now yours is mine."

I rolled away, more afraid of the fire than of him.

Before Napoli could readjust to my new position, a speeding ball of water came from behind me and slammed into his face, knocking him against the wall and unhinging the phones from their rests. He slumped to the ground, unconscious.

A fire alarm started to go off and I flipped around to see someone in a blue hoodie surrounded by streams of water. The water was flowing out of a fountain that had been violently ripped from the wall. It was then that I heard the screams and shouts of the other patrons in the station. Most were running away from the hoodie person as the water flowed in elegant circles around him to reenter the pipes of the water fountain. Others were standing in shock around him. He flicked his wrists and fingers and the water froze in a cap around the fountain.

"GO!" he called and sprinted into the muddled crowd. I lurched to my feet, uncertain. Harry peeked his head out from behind an arrivals bulletin board just as the blue hoodie and its wearer disappeared into the crowd.

"Who was that?" he shouted at me over the fire alarm.

"I don't know!" The floor quaked and I saw two Kinetics teleport in. They split off into different directions and I heard a huge tone sound over the crowd.

Harry grabbed my shirt and yanked me into the crowd. Everyone around us stopped and with glazed eyes looked up. Harry didn't stop pulling until we exited through a service door where we passed through some kind of barrier made with thick air.

Behind us was a slight shimmer, only there if you were really looking for it. And, impossibly we had just walked through a sign that said: *Sorry for the inconvenience. Under Renovations.*

Through the doors it just looked like a building under construction. I moved forward a bit till my head passed the threshold of the door and the sign and the people still staring at the ceiling reappeared.

Harry looked too and sighed. "An illusion. That's amazing. Is this the InfoCon?"

"Yeah. I think so."

"Then we better move quick. We don't want to cause any suspicion."

Only a small portion of the bus station was shut down because of "renovations." Even though it had just happened, everyone believed it to be truth. Compared to the chaos that had destroyed part of the bus station, the Nons that wandered the station went about their business with no worries.

We found our bus and crouched down in the seats when people passed by the windows, some of whom were looking for someone. Me. I didn't let myself breathe any relief until the bus roared to a start and rolled out of the garage. Sunlight hit my face and I sat back with a sigh.

CHAPTER 15

"As a single footstep will not make a path on the earth, so a single thought will not make a pathway in the mind. To make a deep physical path, we walk again and again. To make a deep mental path, we must think over and over the kind of thoughts we wish to dominate our lives." - Henry David Thoreau.

"—That, anyway?" Harry's voice pierced through my thoughts.

"What?" I asked, turning away from the window. I was so zoned out I didn't realize that Harry was talking to me.

"I was just wondering who that guy was. The one who attacked you." Harry flipped through a notebook of his own writing. They looked like dozens of math equations.

"Oh. That was Napoli." I said.

"Who?" He tilted his head to the side, looking at me.

"Napoli Stewart. He's one of my brother's best friends. He's in the Alliance, too. Nick told me that he and Joe, the other guy, all joined the Corps together."

"Oh." Harry looked slightly disturbed. "I wonder..." He started to say something but stopped mid-sentence.

"What? What do you wonder?"

He just shook his head. "Never mind."

"No, what?"

"Well, that guy, the one with the water powers. Who do you think he was?"

"I don't know. I saw him once before...back at the school, when Laura went crazy, he was there too. I don't know who he is. He's not anyone I recognize from school."

"That's really odd." Harry frowned. "At least he's

helping us."

"Yeah."

"But how did he know we were there?"

I just shrugged and turned my head to watch the wavelengths of the power lines go up and down as they passed. "What are we going to do about transportation after St. Louis?" I asked.

"I say we cross that bridge when we get to it. But I'm confident that we'll be okay. What all did Nick give you?"

I reached into my pack and pulled out the zippered binder. Inside was a cellphone and copied files of information about the Laramie compound. Among them were some maps and diagrams of the Laramie base, all of which had been updated almost 8 years before.

"They're old." Nick had said. "We haven't been able to take any pictures of the place because of their new securities."

There were also some small reports of possible entries into the compound. However, all the reports said that entry was inadvisable. The location was considered a Level Two area, whatever that meant. But I assumed that Level Two was supposed to be dangerous.

Whatever the heck we were going into was dangerous either way. At least I wasn't going in alone.

I glanced at Harry who was reading what I had opened. "Level Two, huh?" I was happy that I wasn't alone on this mission, but part of me was also worried that we wouldn't be enough to save Willow.

"I don't know what that means." I said, shrugging.

"Beats me." Harry pinched a map from my hands and looked over it with a keen eye. "Old maps, huh?"

"Yeah. Nick said that the place has got some serious safeguards against photos and snoopers."

"Then I guess we are going in half-blind."

"Better than nothing." I grinned at him.

"Yup." Harry moved his finger around the map and then tapped at a small road labeled "service." "This will probably be our way in. I guarantee you it will be guarded, but they will have shipments or something coming in. Why else would they have a service road?" Harry marked the place on the map with a blue pen.

"Where do you think they would keep Willow?"

He looked over the map. "I don't see anything labeled lockdown or prisons."

"Huh."

"Look at this though." Harry pointed at a small building on the map. "It says records. That's probably your best bet for more up-to-date information."

He marked that too and then we spent the rest of the journey going over all the other information. When I was putting it all back in the binder I saw a small Ziploc bag with four nearly fluorescent pills inside. There was a small folded note on the inside. I pulled it out to see a hand written note from Nick.

A lot of our information is out of date, but what I do know is that their security is heat sensitive. Take the blue ones when you are about to get to through security, one for each of you. Don't forget to take the red set when you are through.

"Useful." Harry read the note over my shoulder.

We rode in silence after that. I put everything away and held onto it tight. These things, what little they were, these would help me save her. These would help me get Willow away from these people.

I wasn't going to let them win.

***

The ride from Columbus to St. Louis seemed like nothing. When we arrived at the station it felt like everything was finally looking up. We had successfully traversed the first leg of this probably foolhardy mission. But I was sure I could see the light at the end of the tunnel. Willow was worth it.

From the bus station we walked the ten blocks to the location where Marcus Grey and Willow had stopped.

It wasn't what I expected.

Instead it was a house, old looking, but obviously taken care of. The neighborhood was fairly peaceful despite being in the middle of a big city like St. Louis. I wasn't sure what to do at first, and Harry seemed content to sit on the sidewalk across the street and watch the few people who were working in their yards.

"You decide, Eugene." Harry said, watching the passing traffic.

"I don't know what to do." I said, tightening my hands around the straps of my backpack.

"This isn't my mission, Eugene. I'm here to help, but I can't hold your hand the whole way." Harry shrugged.

Before I could work up the courage to go and knock on the door, an old man came out and started watering the flowers outside his door. He was black with super white hair. He was plainly dressed with a blue plaid robe and grey slippers. He glanced at us, and at first it didn't seem odd, but then he kept looking at us. I made eye contact a few times, and each time I did he smiled and nodded his head.

When he had watered the last flower he came down to the edge of his small yard and opened the mail box. He grabbed a single envelope and looked up at us again.

"I have tea and water inside if you would like to join me," he said.

I felt my heart jump into my throat. Why was he talking to us? Were we suspicious?

Harry stood up and grabbed my shirt. "C'mon, he's invited us inside."

He pulled me along until we got to the doorstep and nodded to the old man who was holding the door open for us.

"Sit," the old man said and pointed to a couch under the large living room window.

The old man's house was full of books. Every bit of wall was covered in bookshelves stuffed to the brim. The coffee table in front of the couch had three very large stacks of books.

He shuffled around in the kitchen and brought out two glasses of water. "The tea is heating up."

I grabbed a glass out of his hand and held onto it with shaky fingers. I didn't know why we were in this house. Why did we come in? Marcus Grey had been here with Willow. For all we knew this man was a friend of Grey's, and we had just let ourselves be invited into a death trap.

"I know you have questions, and I will gladly answer them. But first tell me something about yourselves." The old man sat himself down in a chair across the coffee table. He clasped his hands in his lap and smiled warmly at us both.

I glanced at Harry. He seemed intrigued by the old man. "What's your name?"

"My name is unimportant. Tell me your name." The old man deflected.

"Uh... Oliver."

"No. Your real name."

Harry blinked in surprise. "How did you know that's not my real name?"

The old man smiled, "I know a lot of things. Now, your name."

"Uhm, my name is Harry. Harrison Gleeson."

"Your middle name?"

"Frederick."

"Tell me about your mother."

I saw Harry pale at that. He stumbled over a few words and then with wide eyes he asked, "What do you want to know?"

"Why do you think she left?"

Harry glanced at me nervously, then swallowed. "She... she is an important woman in her company. She didn't have time to raise a child."

He nodded. "And do you think she will ever come back?"

Harry took a large gulp from the glass of water, "Well, I mean she and my dad didn't really leave on good terms. I always hoped that... that she would come back, but... but Dad says she probably won't ever try. Just... too busy."

I know that I had only known Harry for a little bit of time, but I had never seen him as shaken as this man's questions were making him. He was filling the empty spaces between words with sips from his water. He had scooted to the very back of his chair and looked like he was ready to sink into the cushions.

The old man nodded and then looked at me. "And you, your name... your *real* name."

"Eugene Preston Yoshida." I answered quietly.

"Tell me about the dream."

"What dream?" I whispered. I already knew which one. It was the dream that had been visiting me every night since the encounter with Laura in the school.

The dream of fire encapsulating my whole world.

"You know." He smiled and cocked his head. I suddenly wanted to join Harry in sinking deep into the couch.

"It's me... I'm a baby and my room is on fire. I can't stop it. It's just taking over everything."

"But... is it really a dream?" the old man asked.

"I don't know. It feels..."

"Real?"

I nodded.

"Describe the events."

"I'm sitting on the floor, playing with blocks. And suddenly, everything I'm touching is setting on fire. The floor is on fire and the curtains are lighting up, and then my... my mother comes in and she's not safe from the flames. Her clothes catch on fire and she's... screaming. I think I burned her. I think she's dying."

My eyes are closed. I can see the images so clearly, but I'm afraid if I open them I will start crying. What self-respecting fifteen-year-old starts crying at a stupid dream?

"What do you think it means?" The man asks.

I open my eyes. "Does it have to mean anything? It's just a dream."

"Thank you." The old man gets up just as a tea kettle from the kitchen starts to whistle. He goes to the kitchen, and in the few moments that he's gone Harry and I did not speak.

He returns with two steaming cups of tea. "It's chamomile. Try it."

I take a sip and it feels good on my constricted throat.

"I will tell you this. It may not be what you want to know, but it is what you need to know," the old man began, and sat in his chair again. He clasped his hands in his lap and smiled at us.

"You are beginning something that will not be ended easily. Marcus Grey is only the beginning and Willow Patterson is not the end. There is more to this journey that you are on than what seems. Take note of even the unimportant details, because those will decide how you handle the events to come.

"The ghosts of the past will haunt you for years and the certainties of the future will elude you until you take command of your lives. Don't be afraid of failure. Embrace it and overcome."

The old man stood and nodded at us. "Drink up. You have a long way to go." He disappeared into a back room and left Harry and I sitting there in silence.

I didn't know how to take what he was telling us. None of it made sense, and how could this possibly be what I needed to hear?

Harry and I finished the tea, and when the old man returned he came back with two books, one for each of us.

"These will help you on your journey," he said as he ushered us to the door. Before I could step over the threshold, he touched my shoulder. "You have a long path ahead of you. Just know that there is always a way to climb out of the deepest pits, and there is always a light to lead the way. Just know how to find it."

He patted my back and pushed me out the door.

"When you feel the time is right, come back to me and tell me your stories," he said before closing the door between us.

Harry led the way back through the city. Neither of us did much talking, but I knew eventually we would have to start talking about what to do from here on out. Our next destination was way off in Oklahoma. What little money Nick had given me wouldn't get us another set of bus tickets.

"I'm going to call Nick," I said to Harry. When he nodded, I fell back a bit and called Nick from the little prepaid cellphone he had given me.

"Hello?"

"Hey, it's Eugene."

"Hey! You made it to St. Louis ok?"

"Yeah. We went to the address where Grey stopped and it was just this house. This old guy lives there." I explained the old man's questions and what he had told us at the end.

"Interesting. Any clues to who he was?"

"No. But it was strange. We never told him we were looking for information about Grey. He knew their names and everything."

"I wonder if he's some kind of mind reading Kinetic."

"I hope not. I don't want anyone like that in my head."

"Either way, what's the plan now?"

"Not sure. I guess we need to find some way of getting to Oklahoma."

"Be careful."

"We will. Uhm...hey, do you know how my parents are?"

"Your Dad hasn't been at work for a few days. They said he's out on some assignment. I checked up at the university. Your mom took a leave of absence because of reporters harassing her at the school."

"Oh."

"I'm sure they're worried to heck about you, Eugene. But you gotta understand at this point their kid is being accused of domestic terrorism. They have to be pretty low key."

"Yeah, I guess."

"Hey, I'll let you know if anything changes. I gotta go now, okay? Talk to you later."

"You too."

I hung up the phone and caught back up with Harry. We were only a block away from the bus station.

"Let's stop inside for a bit and reassess, huh?" Harry said. His eyes looked tired.

"Sounds good."

We sat in the waiting area watching people pass by for about an hour while we discussed options. Harry kept trying to find some way of suggesting we dupe the bus drivers into letting us on the bus.

"I just don't know if that's a risk we should take. I don't want to get arrested."

"I doubt they'll arrest us. Just kick us to the curb."

"Still."

We went back and forth for almost an hour before a rumble in my stomach loudly announced the fact that all we had consumed today had been the old man's water and tea.

"Food?" Harry asked.

"Food." I replied.

A quick survey of the bus station revealed a couple tiny fast food places but none of it was all that appealing. Harry took charge and went to the front desk to ask directions to some other restaurants."

We had barely exited the bus station when I heard a call over the parking lot. "Hey! Stop!" someone shouted.

"Eugene, run!" Harry grabbed my shirt and dragged me after him just in time as a car came hurling at us from around a corner. Some of the people waiting by the bus station were shouting and yelling obscenities at the car when it nearly hit them.

I recognized the driver immediately. Napoli. I also recognized the person in the passenger seat. Joe Barrett was my brother's other best friend. This wasn't good.

"Crap!"

We ran down a narrow alley way to get away from the car, but I heard a door slam followed by footsteps. I turned back for only a second and saw Joe charging after us.

"Don't stop!" Harry yelled back at me, and kicked over a trashcan full of rainwater. I skidded past him just in time for a great wall of water to rise up and solidify into ice blocking the way through the alley. The guy in the hoodie was behind us. He shouted, "Go!"

Harry didn't stop to see if the guy would keep Joe forever but instead sprinted out of the alley past a parking garage underneath a large office building. I had no choice but to follow him.

"How could they have found us?" I gasped.

"I don't know, but we have to run." Harry looked over the edge of a concrete divider and pointed toward the parking garage. "Do you know how to drive, Eugene?"

I glanced between the direction he was pointing and the absolute seriousness on his face. "A little, why?"

"We're stealing a car!" He was suddenly running across the empty road toward the parking garage.

"Harry! Wait!" I chased after him, checking back to make sure Napoli or Joe hadn't discovered us yet. I followed him all the way down the lines of parked cars until he reached a car that looked like it had seen better days. "We can't steal a car!"

"If you have a better idea, then shoot, but for now we're getting the heck out of here!"

"Then why are we stealing this one?" The color of the car doors didn't even match the rest of the car, not to mention the hood was smashed slightly on the corner. It looked ready to fall apart at any moment.

"No security alarms."

"How can you tell?"

"Trust me," Harry huffed. "I know what I'm doing." He pulled out a shirt from his duffel bag and handed it me. "Be right back." He came back a second later with a rock in his hand and took the shirt from me. Harry proceeded to wrap the shirt around the rock and then slammed it into the driver side window of the car. The glass broke into a spider web pattern but didn't fall out of the window. He hit the glass again a couple more times and then peeled the shards away, using the shirt as a protective mitt.

"I can't believe this! We don't even have the keys!"

"I know how to wire cars," Harry said bluntly.

I laughed nervously, looking around for any suspicious eyes watching us. "What is this, a freaking movie? You're a little too good at this. Is there something you're not telling me?"

Harry had just taken out the last shards of glass and popped open the locks. "Just get into the car, Eugene. Do you want to get caught by those two?"

"Fine, but if the cops come after us for this, it's not my fault." I pushed past him to sit in the passenger side.

Harry just answered with a roll of his eyes, and started

messing with the wires under the steering wheel. He took a small bag out of his duffel and I saw a small array of screwdrivers and small, sharp objects. He worked diligently for a good fifteen minutes under the dash while I kept an eye out for Napoli or Joe.

"Done!" Harry cried out and the car rattled to life seconds later. It sounded even worse than it looked. "Hmm, sounds like a belt is loose." He commented as he finished his work under the steering wheel.

"A what?"

Harry ignored me again and slid into the driver's seat shutting the door after him. He looked behind us as he steered the car out of its parking place. "Oh, crap!"

Joe was right behind us phasing out of a concrete support beam. He was talking frantically into a cell phone, and not far behind him, three other people were running toward us. Harry hit the gas and the car backed up rapidly right toward Joe. His face registered some shock, but I didn't have time to dwell on it before Harry changed gears and we were speeding toward the opposite side of the parking garage.

"Look out!" I shouted. A car with no driver had just careened out of its parking spot blocking us.

"One of them is a telekinetic!" Harry hissed as he swerved to avoid the car, and careened around the corner that led out onto the street. He didn't even stop for the long yellow board with the word 'STOP' stenciled over it. It was supposed to keep people from driving past and not paying but we slammed through it and the shattered board cracked the windshield in about five places.

"They're following us!" Harry cursed. Joe, Napoli and the three others were now in a car that was much better than ours and were tailgating us dangerously close.

"Should have risked an alarm going off to get us a *fast* car." I muttered under my breath.

Either Harry just ignored my comment or didn't hear it and just kept swerving through traffic, swearing. I had no idea eloquent-big-words Harry was able to curse like that. And before I could digest the fact that this rickety car was going over 90 miles an hour through city traffic, we were in the middle of the city itself. I watched behind us as Harry jutted through traffic like a madman drawing honks and flipped birdies from every direction.

One of the guys in the SUV reached his hands out and something came shooting toward us. It hit the roof and tore a jagged line through the metal.

Trashcans scattered as our skidding vehicle rounded a corner. Harry swore vehemently and jerked the steering wheel away from the sidewalk where pale-faced pedestrians were diving out of the way of the small, grungy car.

"Please don't hit anyone." I pleaded through gritted teeth as we threaded between oncoming traffic.

"Eugene, have some faith!" Harry didn't even take his eyes off the road. "I drive all the time!"

"At what, an arcade?" I grasped the seat as we cut a turn that should have flipped the car.

"Your screeching is going to *make* me hit someone!"

"Well forgive me if I don't want to add *murder* to the stolen car you're driving!" I grabbed onto the door and hung on as Harry cut a sharp corner. Behind us, the car giving chase trailed only a few yards back. The glare-hidden driver sped up and rammed us in the back. I jerked forward, the frayed seat belt the only thing keeping me from marrying my face to the windshield.

Napoli was following us. Only he would be crazy enough to follow this close *and* try and knock us off the road with his own car.

"Shit."

"What?"

"Cops!" Harry hit the gas. We catapulted down a one way street—in the wrong direction. I looked back again, this time seeing blue lights flanking Napoli's car along with two helicopters roaring in circles above us. The police probably thought we were with Napoli's crew.

"Helicopters, too!" I yelled.

Harry looked up through the sun roof and let out a string of curses. When the street entrance to a small neighborhood appeared, he waited until the last second. He nearly flipped the car making the turn.

"We gotta shake 'em." Harry hissed through his teeth.

"How? The helicopters won't lose us, even if the cars do."

Something hit the roof and we looked up to see a dent in the roof. "That's what you think," a voice shouted out there. "Drive straight!" The hoodie guy peered through our new sunroof.

Water started following us. From birdbaths to pools to puddles on the ground, Hoodie was gathering whatever water and moisture that he could. In one hand he controlled the massive, amorphous, airborne globule of water trailing after our car, and with the other he took slivers of water from the globule and formed ice spikes the size of my arm.

The helicopters were hovering above us nearly side-by-side. Hoodie jabbed his hand out and the spikes followed his command, striking the helicopters. One of the choppers spiraled out, crashing into someone's back yard. The pilots had jumped out at the last minute. One tumbled down the roof taking a leaf-filled gutter with him, the other dove into a tall tree.

Harry grinned. "One down!"

The other chopper started to pull back but Hoodie wasn't letting it get away. "Not so fast, sucker!"

The spikes hit it in the tail section. It started spinning midair, smoke spewing from the engine. Napoli's car slowed abruptly, the cop cars were forced to slow with him. The chopper was between us in the air when it finally plummeted to the ground. In the rear view mirror I saw a tower of smoke rising from burning wreckage. I could see the pilots running away from the fire, barely escaping with their lives. My heart beat jumped a notch.

"He almost killed them." I whispered.

Harry didn't reply but focused intently on the road in front of him. I looked up but Hoodie was gone.

"At least we're safe."

I stared at him as we pulled onto one of the interstate

on-ramps. He was breathing deeply and looked a perfect picture of calmness. He glanced at me and smiled, "Stop staring and see if the radio works.

I leaned forward and tuned the radio on. It was going to be a long ride. With the sun sinking into the horizon in front of us we sped toward the west.

CHAPTER 16

"A real friend is one who walks in when the rest of the world walks out." - Walter Winchell

---

"Well, this is what we get for stealing a crappy car." I bit out and chucked a rock into the hedge. I pressed my weight against the passenger side door and tilted my head slightly so that I could see Harry's face as he fiddled with the car parts under the hood.

Not an hour into our getaway the crappy car had up and died. Apparently it wasn't made to go at 90 miles per hour for any extended length of time. Harry didn't know what was wrong with the thing, and the more and more time that passed I came to the realization that the car wasn't going to get fixed. We would probably end up hitchhiking the rest of the way to Oklahoma and beyond.

"Oh, stop complaining," Harry's muffled voice drifted up. He was trying, and the key word here was trying, to get the car running again. So far he was having no luck and the sky was getting darker and darker by the moment, and here we were stuck in the middle of Nowhere, Missouri, about five miles west of some town called Rolla. A few cars had passed us but none of them had stopped.

The darkening sky was cupped by steel gray clouds. It was well west of us and it was hard to tell from this vantage point where the storm was heading. The clouds looked strangely unnatural against the brilliant pink and orange of the sky to the east. Dark blue was slowly overtaking the sky but all that would be gone if the storm passed over us.

"How far is Springfield?" Harry asked and dropped the

hood of the car with a huff. He wiped his grease-smeared hands absently on his shirt and came to stand next to me while I flipped through the ancient road atlas we had found in the trunk of the car. I stopped on the map of southern Missouri and located the road that had taken us out of St. Louis and led us straight into the boonies.

"About forty or fifty miles, it looks like." I used my index finger to gauge the distance between Rolla and Springfield. Harry started to rub the bridge of his nose, then belatedly realized that he still had a bit of car grease on his fingers and scowled at his hands irritably. "So what now?"

He started wiping his hands on his shirt again, leaving little black trails on the red fabric. "I don't know. I think we're better off walking."

"Maaaan." I felt like chucking the yellowed road map into the hedge after the multitude of rocks that had been thrown into the ditch during my idle time after the car had broken down.

"There should be a gas station or a motel or *something* nearby."

"But fifty miles?"

"It's shouldn't take too long."

"Harry we are *not* made of magic or these Kinetic teleporters, whatever they are called. We have to *walk*. That is going to take us *hours*." Harry was being far too optimistic.

Harry pushed off the edge of the car and pushed around me to open the door. I moved out of the way and he grabbed his duffel bag. He started walking along the road and it took me a moment to grab my own bag and run after him.

"There's bound to be someone passing by here in a car, Eugene. We can hitchhike."

I frowned at the back of his sandy blond head and rolled my eyes. "Oh, great, then if we get picked up by an axe murderer, it'll be just as dandy as rain."

"People are more likely to think *we're* the axe murderers." Harry looked back and laughed over his shoulder at the expression of distaste that I let twist my face. Harry picked up his pace and *sauntered* as if we were only taking a stroll, not walking 50 freaking miles to Springfield, and, despite his cheerful walk, dark blue began staining the sky behind us like a bad omen. I knew that if we didn't make it to someplace soon, we would be out in the dark by ourselves in no time at all. We passed a little Inn but Harry was really against stopping since we still had a long way to go.

"We could get another car, I guess," I said to him as we walked away from the place.

"Naw, we can't leave a trail. Besides I thought you were against car thievery."

"I am. But we don't have a lot of time to dilly-dally."

"If we are caught leaving a trail, more than one of the people chasing you are going to know the direction you are going."

"They won't know by where we left the clunker?"

"They will, but at the same time the more we do something like that, the more likely there are to want to catch us. Besides that whole thing was to get us out of St. Louis quick and fast. It wasn't supposed to be that permanent. It just turns out that it wasn't as useful as I had originally planned."

We continued in silence, but all too soon, Harry's pace slowed to a steady walk. The only sounds were the wind in the trees, and our feet scraping against the gravel alongside the road. Darkness overcame us and the amount of cars passing us on the road went from a steady flow to a slow trickle until finally there were no cars at all. We had tried sticking our thumbs out to get a ride, but no one even hesitated. By the time no cars graced us with their presence we were ready to stand in the middle of the road and make someone stop. But no one came anymore.

"What do we do?" I asked at the night sky. We were taking a breather, perched under an overpass just in case it started to rain.

"Well, I figure we're just going to have to keep going. These little exits we are passing don't really seem to have lots of traveler's accommodations, but for now I think we should stop in one of them and see if any locals will help us out."

"Right."

"Let's rest for a bit first."

Harry scooted a distance away and called his Dad on his phone. Harry had told him he had taken up an internship at a camp to explain away his absence. Harry's dad was surprisingly cool with it all.

I closed my eyes and listened to the faint sounds of the trees between the rushes of wind as cars passed under the overpass. I let my mind wander. Things had been so strange. I don't think a few weeks ago that I could have predicted that I would be sitting under an overpass with the nerdy football player.

I went back to what the old man in St. Louis had said to me. *"Marcus Grey was only the beginning, and Willow was not the end."* But Willow had to be at the "end" of this journey. She was the whole reason I was running out here into the unknown. I wasn't about to let her become the host of some deranged alien.

Nick was probably right. The old man had probably read our minds and spouted out what he thought we wanted to hear. That was the only thing I could think of that would explain away his questions and his answers.

It disturbed me that he went right for that dream. The dream I tried to not think about when I was awake even though it visited me every night. I didn't want to think about what it meant, and I certainly didn't want to believe that it was anything more than a nightmare.

But the truth was seeping through the cracks in my delusions. I knew that our first house when I was nothing more than a baby had burned to the ground in a freak accident. My parents had always said it was an electrical fire. But the contents of my dream said otherwise. It was me. My fault. And now that I knew that the latent power that I couldn't use was the power over fire how could I not believe that I was somehow responsible for the fire that destroyed our home and in the process had hurt my mother.

I wiped away a sudden wetness on my cheek and heard Harry say goodbye to his dad.

I opened my phone and stared at the contacts list. Since

this was the phone Nick had given me, I didn't have any of my old numbers, but I knew one number by heart. Willow's cell phone.

I called it. I didn't expect her to pick up and my expectation was true. But the brief message on her voicemail was what I wanted to hear.

"Hey guys, this is Willow, the one and only. Tell me your name and number and I'll get back to you as soon as I find my phone. Love you!"

I hung up and redialed the number.

"Hey guys, this is Willow, the one and only. Tell me your name and number and I'll get back to you as soon as I find my phone. Love you!"

I buried my face between my knees and listened one more time.

"Hey guys, this is Willow, the one and only. Tell me your name and number and I'll get back to you as soon as I find my phone. Love you!"

"Love you." I said into the phone and closed it.

I let my eyes rest and counted my breaths in and out, but my peace was short lived. My entire mind suddenly became filled with an unfamiliar presence. It was like feeling hot shards of glass slicing through my thoughts followed by the whisper of a voice. *–Let me out!-*

And then it was gone. I was so shocked I dropped my phone, and it skittered down the concrete slope hitting the tiny patch of grass between the overpass and the freeway.

"Eugene? What happened?" Harry scrambled over and stared in concern at my face.

"I don't know." I said, gasping, trying to organize the sudden chaos in my head.

I waved him off and told him I had just lost my balance. He frowned at me. I knew he didn't believe me, but he didn't press and went back to his spot.

I closed my eyes but didn't dare to explore the strange feeling.

Briefly I wondered if my brother and his friends were the cause.

It was a good thing it was so silent, because I might not have heard the indistinct rumble of an engine. I stopped and looked in both directions. Harry sat up and opened his mouth to speak but I held up my hand and tapped my ear.

He cocked his head to the side and did as I did and looked in either direction for the cause of the noise.

It was only a second later that I saw the source of it. Through the darkness of night I saw the unevenly lit headlights of a red pickup truck speeding toward us from the west. The truck roared noisily toward us like a chugging missile.

"I think we should hide." I said. Something about the contact with the unfamiliar presence, and now this, had me worried. There was no way that they could be related but at the same time something was wrong.

Harry grinned at me and jumped down to the road to stick his hitchhiker's thumb out. I followed and tried to push his hand down, but the decision to do so didn't come fast enough. The truck slowed impossibly quickly and came to a rolling halt in front of us. The guy driving shifted the gears and rolled down the window.

"Hey, you guys need a lift?" The guy couldn't have been more than twenty-five but didn't look too dangerous. But if what I was learning about Kinetics, what was on the surface didn't tell you anything about what kind of powers they had or even if they were a Kinetic in the first place. There was no telling if this guy was the cause of the strange presence in my mind, but I wasn't going to trust it.

Before I could even think of responding to the guy, Harry jumped up close to the truck window. "Yes! You're a godsend! We thought we were going to be walking forever!"

You didn't seem worried at all. I let my inner dialogue take over for my lack of ability to speak aloud.

"Man, I've been there! I hitched across the States when I was seventeen. I know how it can be sometimes. I just so happened to be out for a ride.   You guys are lucky!"

"Oh, that's awesome." Harry didn't seem at all concerned about that. But I knew otherwise.

"Well, I sure don't mind taking you where you need to

go. Where are you headed?"

"Ultimately, Wyoming," Harry supplied. I balked at him. Why was he being so forthcoming? Especially after his 'we can't leave a trail' bit.

"We just need to get to Springfield for now," I interrupted and caught Harry's eyes, out of the sight of the driver, and gave him a meaningful glare. He grinned and said quickly, "yeah, we sort of got in a little trouble with our car."

"How long have you been walking? From over there?" He poked his thumb out in the direction of the decrepit car.

Harry nodded. "We've been walking for, what, five hours?"

"Six." I snipped. I didn't know what his deal was right now, but we were going to have to have a talk about this later. I just hoped that he knew what the heck he was doing.

"Really, now?" The guy chuckled and waved us into the cramped front seat of the truck. "Hang on tight! I can be a bit of a crazy driver sometimes!"

The guy who introduced himself as Chris yammered to us about fate and circumstance and that he just knew he wanted to be out for a ride tonight.

"Been feeling a need for speed for a whole day. Thought that I was going cray cray, if you know what I mean."

I pressed myself into the door and tried to tune out Harry striking up a conversation with the guy.

He drove us all the way to Springfield and dropped us off at a truck stop on the outskirts of town.

We sat in the 24 hour fast food place attached to the gas station and looked over the route. "The next place is this town just inside Oklahoma. I'd say we're only about a couple hundred or so miles away from it." Harry tapped the map.

"Think we can sneak onto one of these trucks." I tilted my chin at the window where we could see a whole line of trucks idling in the parking lot. One of them had to be heading in the same direction.

"We could try. I guess it depends on the truck and how easy it is to break in."

I was beginning to feel the lack of sleep setting in. As

much as I wanted to keep going, I think I needed sleep more than anything. I sighed and rested my head on the table. Out of the corner of my eye I saw Harry watch me for a moment before pulling the book the old man in St. Louis had given him.

He read quietly and I drifted in and out of sleep.

A few hours later we set out to find a truck headed toward Oklahoma. A few short conversations with some of the drivers revealed a few options. One of the trucks was transporting what the guy said was farm equipment and his truck was the one we were able to crack the lock and sneak inside. We sat huddled between a few very large things of metal that I had no earthly idea the use for.

We sat in quiet for a few moments and then listened with anticipation as the truck rumbled to a start and began moving. The farm equipment creaked and for a moment I realized if this stuff moved wrong we could end up getting crushed. That would bring a swift end to this journey.

After I was sure that we were on the freeway I settled back into a cramped and semi-comfortable nook between two parts that looked unlikely to move. Harry sat opposite with his arms around his knees. There was so little light that I could barely see him at all.

I sighed and opened the phone, dialing Willow's number. It went straight to voicemail as always.

"Hey guys, this is Willow, the one and only. Tell me your name and number and I'll get back to you as soon as I find my phone. Love you!"

When I closed the phone I saw Harry in the glow of his own cell phone looking at me with a soft smile on his face.

"You really love her." Harry said.

"Yeah," I swallowed the lump in my throat.

"Why didn't you tell her?"

I pinched the tips of my fingers. It was all I had to keep myself from getting sad.

"Because I'm an idiot. A scared stupid idiot. I don't know why I screwed it up."

Harry chuckled. "Man, you are just a teenager. It's completely normal."

"You say that like you're not a teenager."

Harry shrugged. "No, I'm just smarter than most."

"Humble, too."

"Obviously." Harry quipped. "No, look. I'm sure she feels the same way."

"I'm pretty sure she has a thing for you actually." I curled in tighter around myself. The cold aluminum of the floor was beginning to sink into my bones.

"Me?" Harry laughed. "Dude, you have no idea."

"Why?"

"Willow is great, and beautiful, but not my type." Harry smiled.

"I thought everyone loved redheads." I chuckled.

"Yeah, man... but... I kinda... play for the other side." His face was full of amusement as he spoke.

"Other side?" I blinked.

"Yeah, you know." His grin grew wider.

"Oh. OH. You like guys?"

Harry nodded, his eyes full of amusement.

"Sorry." I didn't know why I was apologizing.

"Don't be. It's not a big deal. But listen, when me and Willow hung out she talked about this guy she liked. Aaaand I think she was talking about you." He nodded his head toward me.

"She never said." I looked down at my hands.

Harry shook his head. "You can't expect her to know how any more than you did."

I curled in on myself a bit. "I'm going to make it right, Harry. I'm going to save her and I'm going to tell her I love her."

"I'm with you all the way, man." He smiled and rested his head on the equipment behind him.

"Thanks." I laughed.

***

"We've lost them for the moment but we've figured out who the other kid is." Napoli said over the phone.

Jacob took his cellphone off his desk and pushed the speaker phone button off. Best to not let anyone listen in on

152

this.

"Send me a report later. To the secured email." He said.

"Right," Napoli said. Jacob could hear the frustration in his voice.

"What is it now?" Jacob asked.

"Jake, this isn't right. There's more going on than your kid brother wandering across the states. This route they are following... Joe seems to think--"

"Nap, I understand your concern, but right now is not the time. Find their trail again, they can't have gone far. I'll meet up with you in a few days to go over the plans for H-ville."

"Ok, but Jake, you owe me big for this."

"Got it."

Jacob hung up the phone and shook his head. This all better be worth it.

CHAPTER 17

"As a Neutral, I don't think it's right for either the Alliance or the Isiroans to interfere in our lives. We want nothing to do with the war, so why should either of them pay any attention to us? We only want to live our lives in peace." ~ Martha Macha in an open letter to the Isiroans and the Alliance from the Council of Neutral Kinetic Societies. 1992.

I was startled awake by a loud crash and a bright light shining in my eyes. I pushed up back against the farm equipment and saw Harry groggily looking at the source of the light. A man was shining a light into the trailer and was glaring at us.

"Step out! Get out here!" He shouted at us.

We slid out from the equipment and jumped out onto the ground. We were pulled off to the side of the freeway. On one side was a stretch of fields off to the right. It was almost dawn. We had been in the truck for a few hours already.

"I told you, Bill, that lock looked sketch." A second guy said.

"Shoulda said somethin' earlier!" the first guy said.

"I did! You said I was drunk!" the second guy said.

"Man, I can never tell with you."

The two continued to bicker and Harry caught my eye. He jerked his chin toward the wheat field off to the right. I nodded.

Harry mouthed the words: *On three.*

I nodded again.

One.

Two.

"Three!" We bolted toward the field and enveloped ourselves in the prickly strands of wheat. I heard them shouting behind us and heard their pursuit, but they were not nearly as young or as athletic as Harry and I were. Harry pointed in the direction of a rusty water tower surrounded by equipment. We skidded behind some large barrels. I pressed my back to the barrel and strained my ear for the sound of the two guys. I could hear them off in the distance shouting at each other, but their voices were receding.

Harry laughed and swung his backpack around to set it in his lap. "Well, that was close."

"Yeah, let's not do that again."

We waited until we heard the truck pull off before coming out from behind the barrels. "Where are we anyway?"

"Not sure. It's only 5:30 A.M. Hold on." Harry tapped his phone and pulled up a map. "Let's get back to the road. Maybe we can hitch a ride to the nearest town."

"Hitchhiking again?"

"You got a better idea?"

"Not really."

Harry shrugged and led the way back through the wheat field. For the next few miles people passed our outstretched thumbs without stopping. I guess we didn't look like the trustworthy type. We were covered in dirt and dust. Neither of us had showered in at least a couple days, and now there were bits of wheat I kept finding in my hair.

Harry's phone wasn't getting any signal out here so he couldn't pull up the GPS and get us directions. About three miles later we passed a sign that confirmed we were in Oklahoma. From the mile markers and the signs we had to be about 60 miles from our next destination.

It was a small town called Quinn just off the freeway. I opened my phone but I was also getting no signal. There was no chance of calling Nick right now.

"Do you remember what the town was supposed to be?" I asked Harry.

"Not really. Though I do remember Nick saying

something about it being a town with a high population of Kinetics. Wouldn't something like that stand out?"

We walked another four miles before someone finally stopped and offered to drop us off at the nearest town. Once there Harry took it upon himself to ask a bunch of people if they could get us a ride to Quinn.

"No takers." Harry said after almost two hours of wandering around the gas station.

I sat down on the edge of the sidewalk around the gas station with a huff. "Well, maybe we ought to keep walking."

"Uhg." Harry came and sat next to me. "It's the middle of the day and I think we would probably die of heat stroke."

"Hey guys." We turned and there were two police officers coming up to us.

"We heard you guys have been looking for rides." The first officer said.

"Got any ID?" the second asked.

We pulled out the fakes that Nick had given us.

They looked between the IDs and us for a moment and then one stepped away to talk into his walkie. The one who stayed with us smiled and said, "You guys far from home?"

I exchanged a glance with Harry, "Yeah, kinda."

"Where you headed?"

"Quinn."

The guy laughed. "That Podunk town?"

Harry and I chuckled. I wasn't sure exactly what we were laughing at though.

The second cop came over and talked to the first in low tones. They looked at us and then handed us our IDs.

"Florida IDs, huh? Far from home, aren't ya?" The second guy asked.

"A bit." Harry replied. I could see the gears in his head turning. He was trying to figure out how to get out of this, I hoped.

"You guys can't just be asking for rides around here." The first officer said.

"Yeah, where are your parents or guardians?" The second one said.

"Uh..." A few lies passed through my head but none of the preparing that Harry and I had done had prepared us for this.

"Boys!" An unfamiliar voice called out to us.

We turned and saw a woman coming toward us. She looked between Harry and me like we were long lost family.

-I'm sorry for the intrusion. But act like I am your Aunt Josephine!- a telepathic voice rang through my head. It was coming from the woman. I hadn't ever felt a telepathic voice besides Willow's before now and the sensation was unsettling. It was like an alien had just left a message in my brain. It didn't feel right.

Harry jumped at the same time but acted faster to the telepathic voice than I did. "Aunt Josephine! You found us!"

I kicked myself into gear a second later. "Our cellphones are dead! We couldn't call you to tell you we missed the bus."

'Aunt' Josephine played right along. "As soon as you didn't show, we knew something was wrong. Oh, Officers, thank you for looking after my boys. We were sure something had happened to them."

"It's alright, Ma'am. Just be sure that next time you boys keep a full charge on your phones. We can't have hitchhikers out here. It's not safe for them or you."

She smiled at them. "Thanks."

"Sorry," Harry said, grinning at the two officers.

The cops walked back to their cars and took off. Josephine patted our backs. "I overheard you boys are headed to Quinn?"

"Yeah." We exchanged glances.

"My husband and I live in Quinn, and I would be glad to take you there."

"That would be awesome."

Quinn was one of the few openly Isiroan towns. Nick had said it was mostly populated with elderly people who were much too old to fight in the war anymore.

Josephine and her husband, Theo, were not terribly old, but still lived in the quiet little town. Josephine was quick to tell us her life story, trusting us with a transparency I had only witnessed in little kids.

She drove us to her place and offered us dinner.

"My children have long left the nest so it's always nice to see young Kinetics out and about in the world. Did you know that it was once regular practice for young Isiroans to travel the world at your age?"

That was another thing. Because we were headed into Quinn she believed us to be Isiroans. Harry and I were comfortable letting her believe whatever she wanted to.

Theo was a little more cautious of us and had a never ending list of questions.

"How long have you been traveling?"

"A few days." I said.

"What are you kids in Quinn for?" Theo had another question waiting as soon as I answered the first.

"We're looking for information about someone." Harry said, equally ready to answer any and all questions.

"Who?"

"A man named Marcus Grey."

"Why?"

"He has something we need." I interjected. I was less sure about this guy. He seemed a bit shady.

"Marcus Grey was here not too long ago." Theo watched us carefully. "He had a young girl and a woman with him if I recall the gossip."

"That would be Willow." I nodded.

"Mr. Grey stopped in only briefly," Theo said. "I believe he visited the little clinic on Tyson Street."

Josephine chipped in. "He went to visit his son."

"He has a son?" Harry asked in surprise.

"As much as a vegetable can be a son," Theo shook his head.

"I want to go visit him." I said.

The clinic was small. More of a nursing home for the elderly, but Marcus Grey's 35 year old son lay in a bed just as comatose as many of the other residents.

"He wakes sometimes. But he does not know who he is, or where he is," the nurse was saying to us as Harry and I stood over his bed.

"His father comes to visit every couple weeks to check on him, but I'm afraid that there is little hope of recovery."

"What about Healers?" Harry asked.

The nurse, like the vast majority of the town was an Isiroan, and Harry took the opportunity to ask questions that would seem strange to most Non-Kinetics.

"I'm afraid that Healers can only fix the body. The mind is a battlefield that none have been able to conquer. And his injuries are on a very mental level," the nurse shook her head sadly.

"How did it happen?" I asked.

"The rumors say that he got into a fight with a Kinetic who could rip a person's mind apart."

"Jeez." I let out a breath. Harry and I exchanged a glance.

"When you're done, sign out on the register, will you?" The nurse smiled at us both and left, closing the door behind her.

We sat in a couple chairs and looked at the man who had been in an on-and-off coma for close to ten years. The nurse couldn't tell us much about Grey's visit here; only that it was much like all the other visits he made. But with the red-haired girl in tow, the visit had been strange and morose.

"I wonder who did this to him?" Harry asked after a few minutes of silence.

"I don't know. But the fact that there's a Kinetic out there who can do this to someone... It's kind of scary." I replied. "Wouldn't want to get on their bad side."

Harry reached out and touched the man's wrist. "I guess his visit here had nothing to do with Willow, but still, it raises the question why he would bring her nonetheless."

I shook my head.

"I really don't think there's anything for us here, Eugene. Grey has a son who can't tell us anything and this town is a viper pit if they find out why you're chasing after him." Harry stood up, nervously.

"Yeah." I shook my head and we turned to leave. I looked back once more at the man, and for a brief moment I thought I saw his eyes open.

We decided to spend one more night with Josephine and Theo before heading to the next place, a town called Hooverville in New Mexico.

I opened my phone and began pressing numbers before thinking about what number I was dialing.

It rang and instead of Nick's voice I heard my mother's voice. I gasped and looked at the number I had dialed. I had called home.

"Hello?" she said again.

I didn't dare say anything, but suddenly there was a constriction in my throat.

"Hello? Eugene? Is that you?"

It hurt to not say anything, I couldn't. I bit my lip.

"Eugene, baby, I love you. Please come home. We're not mad, we just want you safe..."

I clicked the phone closed and buried the heels of my hands into my eyes.

Once I felt like I could talk without wavering, I dialed Nick's number.

"Hey, Eugene."

"Hey, Nick. Just wanted to let you know we are in Quinn."

I told him about meeting Josephine and Theo and about Grey's son.

"What's the son's name?"

"Rainey Sheng Grey."

"Huh. Feel bad for the guy."

"Yeah."

"I'll research it and see if I can find anything. Though I'm beginning to have a disturbing idea about why Grey's been taking Willow on this journey."

"Why?"

"That guy you visited? The guy in St. Louis."

"Yeah."

"His name's Timothy Frank. He's a Kinetic who has affiliations with a group called the Corpus."

"What are they?"

"Not entirely sure. Very secretive group, but they are known for playing very decisive parts in national and global conflicts. The last time the Corpus showed up was about a year or two before Thomas Reddinger was killed."

"Reddinger? Remind me who that is again."

"The old Alliance Chief."

"Oh, the guy who was before Lancaster?"

"Yup. The Corpus apparently had something to do with the end of the last Great Kinetic War. What I'm finding is that they probably had a great deal of influence in ending the war, and the fact that so few people know about them... well it's like having a shadow group behind the scenes."

"I see. And this old guy was part of them?"

"Yeah, but we have no records on their members or anything. There's no telling who or what he was to the group, or even Marcus Grey."

"I almost feel like I've jumped in too deep," I laughed.

"You are in too deep. But hey, you can always turn back."

"I suppose," I said, but I knew there was no turning back now. I wouldn't let myself.

"Listen, I'm going to do some research on Grey's son.   Call me back when you get to Hooverville."

"Will do."

I hung up the phone and sat outside, staring at the dark sky, full of bright stars. 'In too deep' was right. Here I was, a newly minted Alliance member, neck deep in an Isiroan town. Harry was handling it well. I could hear him inside now joking around with Theo. The man was apparently an avid reader and had a library in an extra room. Harry was soaking up as much information about Kinetics from the "Isiroan Perspective" as he could.

I joined them inside and briefly let myself be part of the jokes and conversation. Tomorrow we would be off again into another long journey to yet another town, the last before Marcus Grey had gone to Laramie and disappeared with Willow in tow.

I woke up with a start at something moving outside the guest room, where Harry and I were splayed out on couches.

I could see through the open door a light coming from the kitchen, and I could hear a single voice talking. I pushed up off the couch and peered through the door. Theo was standing in the kitchen with a phone in his hands.

"No record of these boys at all. ... Yes. ... Yes. ... I think so. I even checked it against what we have from the Alliance. Still nothing, but at this point I'm sure they are fake IDs. ... Yes, they were asking after Marcus Grey."

I wasn't sure who he was talking to, but it didn't sound good for us. I rushed over and shook Harry awake.

I shushed his protests and dragged him to the door where we heard the tail end of Theo having someone come pick us up for questioning.

"Just wipe their memories if nothing is suspicious and no one is the wiser," Theo said, and then said good bye to the person on the other side.

He headed toward the room where we were, and Harry pushed me back to my couch and rushed to his. Taking the hint, we faked asleep. I tried to regulate my rapid breathing, and when I was sure he was gone to his and Josephine's room, I rolled off the couch and quickly changed. Harry stuffed our things in our bags and within minutes we were out the door.

"Over here," Harry whispered and dangled Josephine's car keys in my face.

"Oh, no, not again." I stopped in my tracks.

"We have no choice. Do you want them to find out who we are?"

"N...no."

"Let's go, then." He waved for me to follow him.

Harry got in the driver's seat and put it into neutral. We pushed the car a whole block before Harry felt like we were okay to start driving.

Harry didn't stop driving except to put some gas in. We used up the last of our money on it, but Harry said we just had to bite the bullet. The drive across Oklahoma was a lonely one. Sure there was traffic, and sure Harry and I were in the car together, but we barely uttered a word in between the abject silences. The radio in Josephine's car didn't work, so each mile marker was passed with quiet concentration. Despite all we had done since leaving Columbus, I still didn't really know a lot about Harry.

But despite how much I felt the curiosity rising, I kept my mouth shut. Part of me was still wary about making him any more than just help on this journey.

So instead of talking to him, I opened my pack and looked through all the reading materials that Nick had sent along. Packed between two folders was the book that the guy in St. Louis had given me. Harry had already read through his multiple times, but I had yet to touch the one he had given me.

I pulled it out.

The Future of the Alliance by Thomas Reddinger

There is something to be said about an organization such as ours that has managed to survive from the earliest annals of history to modern day. We have survived multiple wars, fracturing conflicts, poor decision makers, and many internal battles. The fight with Isiro alone has not sustained us as an organization but rather our struggle with our identity as a people in a world where we are merely myth and superstition.

I flipped a few pages.

I do not see how we can continue on the course that we have maintained. The fractured nature of our relationship with other groups of Kinetics does not bode well for a future where we as humans can exist. If it is indeed true that Isiro is here to raise an army to, what one scholar put succinctly, 'bring into being the first great galactic empire' with Kinetic humans as its power force, then we will not be able to fight it with what few kinetics we have spread across so many allegiances.

I flipped a few more.

We will never truly be able to enter the future until we can understand and respect our past.

I sighed and closed the book. Why in the world would that guy give me this book? I put it back in my pack and looked around at our surroundings. It was late morning a day after we had left Quinn and we were already reaching the border of Oklahoma and Texas.

"Once we get to Amarillo, we have to head south into

Lubbock," Harry supplied. I pulled out the map and looked at what he was talking about.

"Hooverville is in New Mexico though, right? Why aren't we headed straight in?"

"It's southwest of a town called Artesia."

I looked at the map but didn't see Hooverville anywhere near Artesia. "Where?"

"It's not on any official maps. Look at the map Nick gave us."

I pulled out Nick's map and compared the roads and towns.

"Neither the town nor the road are even on the regular maps."

"Yeah. I guess they don't want any tourists."

"Tourists?"

"Yeah, look, it's not that far from Roswell."

The drive through Amarillo was uneventful. We stopped for a bit and tried to find some way to get some food and gas. Harry was continuing to surprise me with his resourcefulness. What would have taken me a whole day to do he was doing in a matter of hours. He not only got us a full tank of gas an hour into Amarillo, but before we left, he got some lady to buy us some food enough for the journey through Lubbock and then on into Hooverville.

We were smooth sailing after Amarillo. It seemed nothing could go bad. How wrong I was.

CHAPTER 18

"Entrances are always better than exits, except when it comes to death." ~ Lucia Oberman, a rogue Neutral who was a key player in the Third Kinetic War. 1829.

We were stopped at a deserted exit just inside the state line of New Mexico on highway 380. The road was dark and in the distance we could see a small airport. A plane or two made its way across the sky, and those were the only sounds to accompany our naptime. For a while after Harry had fallen asleep I stared out the window at the stars. How many days had it been since Willow had been taken? How long did she have until she was turned into a host for Isiro?

I closed my eyes and willed myself to sleep. I would save no one if I was sleep deprived, and we were so close to the second-to-last place on Marcus Grey's journey across the States. The places that we were going... The people we were meeting... What did it all mean in the big picture?

I don't know when I dozed off, but I awoke to a loud crash. I jolted up and stared out the front windshield. The whole front of the car was on fire. I looked to Harry, but his door was already open and he was standing outside. A huge wave of water flashed past him and hit the fire.

"Eugene! Get out of the car!" He yelled to me.

I tumbled out and stared at the fire. I could feel a cold sweat crawling down my back. In front of the car I saw the guy hoodie standing in front of the car pulling water from behind him in the ditch and putting out the fire. Behind him I saw two people I had hoped to never see again. Napoli and Joe.

They were standing back admiring their handiwork and

watching Hoodie put out the fire. Napoli reached out for hoodie but stopped. His eyes widened and he looked back at Joe.

Harry grabbed my arm and pulled me along with him down into the ditch. We tumbled into wet grass and the light from the fire couldn't find us. I looked up but Harry pushed my head down.

"Don't move," he whispered.

What I could see from our spot in the ditch, Hoodie was having an all-out fight with Napoli and Joe. Water was flying everywhere and Napoli and Joe were yelling obscenities at Hoodie.

Suddenly it was quiet.

I looked up again and they were all gone.

"Where..." I began.

"Shh." Harry pushed himself up and looked around.

He waved at me and we crawled up the ditch onto the road. The pavement was soaked and the car was charred.

"How did they find us?" I asked.

Harry shook his head.

"Good thing Hoodie found us, too." I said.

"Yeah, good thing," Harry murmured. He popped open the back seat of the car to get our bags out.

"I guess we're walking again." I said.

"Yup," Harry said quietly.

I frowned. "Are you okay?"

"Later," he said and grabbed his bag. I grabbed mine, but Harry was already walking down the road with speed in his step.

I ran after him and caught up to him.

"What's the matter?"

"They shouldn't have been able to find us," he said.

"Well yeah, but..."

"I don't think we should stop again, Eugene. I think they're playing with us."

"Why?"

"Haven't you felt it?"

"What?"

"The whole way, we've been followed. They know

where we are and they are just messing with us." He didn't look anywhere but forward, his eyes were angry. "They're just slowing us down. They could have taken us out already if they really wanted to."

I looked around at the dark sky and the tiny lights of the airport down the road. "Why would they do that?"

"I don't know. This journey hasn't made a lot of sense, Eugene. When we get to Hooverville, maybe we can get some answers."

"What's different about Hooverville?"

"Other than the burned out husk of a building in Columbus, this will be the first place that's actually run by the Alliance." Harry's face was a mask of fury, but that didn't scare me. What scared me was that I didn't know why he was so mad. Yes, we just lost our transportation... again. But usually he was so ready to just keep going. Now he just looked furious.

***

We were about thirty miles outside Roswell. It was hot and the road in front of us swam in heatwaves. The sky was cloudless and there wasn't a single square foot of shade to keep us from burning alive. Summer was in full force. The tiny towns and businesses we passed on the way offered nothing and even Harry's uncanny luck had run out.

I was about to call it and ask if we could sit on the side of the road for a bit when an ugly looking RV pulled up beside us. The guy inside was an older guy with stringy white and brown hair sticking out in every direction. He offered to get us as far as Roswell and then we were on our own.

I was too tired to object to Harry's quick acceptance and just followed along. We sat at the little table that rocked every time the RV hit a bump.

The guy was quiet for a bit but then began speaking to Harry. "You boys all alone out here?"

"Just had some car trouble," Harry replied, giving me a look I couldn't read.

"Seem a bit young to be out travelling alone," the guy

continued.

"Uh, I'm older than I look," Harry lied. "Turned 19 just last May."

The guy grunted and was silent again. Harry gave me another look but this time shook his head.

What is it? I mouthed.

Harry was about to say something when the guy spoke up again.

"Hitchhiking is dangerous 'round these parts."

Harry chuckled. "We've been alright so far."

"Heh heh." The guy turned back to look at us. "Lucky boys."

One of his eyes didn't move with the other one. He grinned at us, flashing a set of blackened teeth and then turned back to the road.

"You know, I lost my eye to hitchhiking," he said, and put one of his hands up to his face. It came away with a shiny glass eye pinched between his fingers.

I looked at Harry with wide eyes. He pressed his lips together and reached into his pack.

"Couple boys just like you if I remember correctly." The hand with the fake eye pressed back up to the guy's face and he turned to look back right at me. "Kids sure are dicks these days."

"If you say so," I said, not sure what to say to the stare from him.

The guy went silent and the drive was quiet for almost twenty minutes. Then the RV pulled off to the side of the road and the guy turned it off.

Harry scooted out from behind the table and stood up. The guy got out of his chair slowly and stood blocking the door out. "It really is dangerous to hitchhike. Didn't your parents teach you better?"

"Look we can just go now," Harry said. I started to get out of the seat when the guy shot forward and pushed me back down.

"How about you stay awhile," he hissed, hitting me with the smell of rot on his teeth.

"Uh..." I pushed him away just as Harry pulled a flip knife from his pack and pointed it at him.

"Back off," Harry growled.

"Oo, you brought a toy!" The guy cackled and swiped out at the knife grabbing the blade with his hand. I saw drops of red running down his arm. "I can play, too."

He reached back with his other hand and pulled out a freaking *machete* from behind the driver's seat. I saw it a split second before Harry and reared back, kicking at the guy with my feet. Harry let go of the knife and spun around to uppercut the guy under the chin. The guy stumbled backward.

"Move!" Harry said, and I jumped out of the seat, grabbing my pack. Harry jumped over the guy's legs and plowed through the door. It broke away, filling the RV with the hot outside air.

I started to jump over the guy like Harry had but the guy grabbed my leg making me trip on the steps out the door. My chest hit the steps hard and suddenly I felt something burn right next to my heart.

The guy, machete in hand, drew his hand back to strike with the blade but without warning my outstretched hands lit up with fire, exploding in the guy's face. Harry grabbed me under the armpits and dragged me back.

-*No!*- a voice inside my head screamed. I was too startled by the fire to realize that it didn't come from anyone around us.

The guy began screaming, his hair and face were on fire. He had dropped the machete. He stumbled out of the RV and let out a howl. He started coming at us with searching hands. I felt the burn in my chest again, and reached my hands out toward the man. He was right in front of me when my hands exploded again and a hot jet of fire engulfed the man.

He tumbled over and rolled to a stop, writhing in pain on the ground. Even at this distance I could feel the heat coming off his burning body. I started breathing hard, hyperventilating. I hadn't meant to hurt him.

"Oh shit," Harry said, looking past me. I followed his gaze. The RV was beginning to burn. It had begun eating at the front of the RV, catching the floor, the curtains, the seat, all of it on fire.

"We gotta go before it gets to the gas tank!" Harry pulled me up and pushed me to start running.

Cars began slowing down, watching the RV glow brighter and brighter with fire. We didn't stop running until we got to the sign that said Roswell City Limits no more than a mile from where the RV had stopped. Fire trucks and police shot past us toward the smoke rising in the sky behind us.

I wrung my hands where I could feel a tingle spreading from the tips of my fingers all the way to my elbows. "Let's not do that again." I said finally.

"Agreed," Harry replied, leading us through a maze of side streets. The sun beat down on us even harder than it had all day, and I could feel fatigue setting in. We walked all the way into downtown Roswell, avoiding most of the major streets.

"As much as I'd like to keep going, I think we need to chill out for a few hours." Harry said. "Wait here. I'm going to go see what we can do to get us a motel room or something."

"Right," I said. He left me at an outdoor café, but after about thirty minutes I was bored to death. I had looked through all the papers Nick had given us a million times and none of it made any more sense now than it did before.

I picked up my bag and started walking, looking in the windows of the shops and businesses.

With not much else to do, I went into a bookstore that had a cartoon alien painted in the window.

The clerk yelled hello from behind a book but didn't look up at me. I shrugged and started looking at the book titles. I had never been much of a reader. That was Jacob's territory. But here we were in Roswell, the city that most everyone in the USA associated with aliens. The guy, Isiro, who was going to make Willow his host--he was an alien. Maybe I could find some information about him.

I looked through book after book, but there was nothing on an alien named Isiro.

"Need help?" The clerk was behind me. I jumped slightly

and grinned.

"Uh, yeah. Would you know where I could find information on an alien named Isiro?"

The clerk rolled his eyes and I swear I heard him mumble the word "tourists" under his breath. "Yeah, yeah, come this way."

He took me to the back of the store where there was a single bookshelf pushed up against the wall. There was an old woman sitting in front of the bookshelf reading.

"Marla, kid's looking for information."

She looked up at me. "On what?"

"Alien named Isiro."

"Huh. Not many come looking for that name."

"Really?" I wondered suddenly if I was making a mistake.

"Hold on." She stood up slowly and groaned as her bones creaked. She disappeared into the back, and the clerk left to go back to his seat behind the cash register.

I stood glued to that spot for what felt like an hour. She finally came back with a very old book in her hands. She smiled at me and handed the book over.

"It's yours. I've had it for fifty years, and you're the first person to ask about him."

"Uh... but..."

"If I may ask, how did you come across that name?" She tilted her head to the side while she talked, watching my face. "It's nowhere else that I can find."

"Uh... My brother told me a bedtime story once," I lied and looked down at the very old book in my hands.

"Ahh..." She smiled. "Once upon a time a man told me that he was real. Is he real?"

I flipped through the book while she watched. I stuttered, "I dunno."

"There are many stories about aliens, many that few believe and many that most believe in, but this is one that I have yet to meet one who knows of him. The book is a bit sad and tragic if you ask me."

"Why's that?"

"Read the book and you'll find out." She patted my arm and went back to her seat in front of the bookshelf.

I returned to the café, but Harry was nowhere to be seen. I sat and began to read.

***

It is said, that many thousands of years ago all of humanity possessed abilities beyond the greatest imaginings. These abilities allowed humans to manipulate, control, and even destroy the world around them. Some even rose to become the gods and goddesses that we read about today in mythology. But humanity lost those abilities in a battle that shook all of the Earth and its people.

In my readings I have gathered together a story of how humanity fell from grace and lost the ability to be more than just a man or woman. Not all the literature that exists about that time agrees, but what follows is what all of the text agrees upon.

One day, probably much like any other day, a star appeared in the sky above the Earth. For months the star moved around the sky like a strange spectre. Some believed that it was one of their respective gods or goddesses and prayed to it.

Then one day it fell from the sky and landed just outside a small village in what most believe is modern day Kenya. The son of the Chieftess was not far away and approached the fallen star (some texts propose it looked like a shiny, silver pomegranate and yet others say it looked like massive sunflower seed). The son, named Hutor, was foolishly curious and touched the star just as it cracked open revealing a creature nearly twice the size of a human.

All of the texts agree on what the creature looked like. It was bipedal, standing on two legs with a huge tail. It was covered in orange and red scales and had a head like a mythological dragon.

Hutor attempted to speak to the creature but they could not understand each other.

The creature reared up and according to most it used some strange power on Hutor in an attempt to possess him.

The boy lived long enough to speak the name of the creature, Isiro, to his tribe as they ran up to see the fallen star. Some of the texts disagree on whether or not the creature intended to kill the boy, only that the attempt to possess him was too much for a human mind to handle.

The Chieftess, by the name of Anyan, in a fit of rage attacked Isiro with her power. Not much is said this early on about what her ability was, but later texts agree that her power was the ability to give or take away the powers of others.

This power, when used on Isiro, ripped his mind, and if such things have souls it ripped that out too. Anyan took her son's favorite necklace, a single green crystal, and encased Isiro's whole essence in it. After her son's funeral she walked to a river and threw the necklace in. She never expected to see the necklace ever again.

A few miles downstream, there lay another village. Who knows for how long the crystal with Isiro in it lay in the river bed, but one day a young girl called Kahya found it and, not knowing the creature that lay within, put it around her neck.

In the months that followed Kahya became aware of another presence speaking to her in the silence of her mind. Isiro had found some way to connect to the young girl's mind and began speaking to her. She was a simple girl with the ability to move the sands and dirt to her will and so when Isiro began to speak to her, he found some way to manipulate her powers into other things.

What the texts all agree on is that no human was born with more than two powers, the ability to speak through the mind and another, personalized power. But with Isiro in her mind, Kahya began to be able to make the wind obey her; the waters of the river listen to her commands; the cookfire dance at a thought. None of the texts can agree on what the next few years held for Kahya and Isiro, but some years later when Kahya was a grown woman she began traveling from village to village gathering people to begin what some say was an army.

Anyan hearing of the name Isiro coming from the lips of traveling tribes knew the worst had happened. She gathered together her tribe and moved them far away from the place where the star had fallen years before.

She was out trading with another tribe when a group of Isiro's people, including Kahya appeared. They spoke of a battle to come, and that as many people who would join would be promised a safe place and the ability to do a great deed.

Anyan left the village without trading and returned to her own, warning the night watchmen to keep out any of these Isiroans.

More stories began to reach the Chieftess about the rise of the army under Isiro's name. She soon found out that the only reason he was raising this army was because of humanity's powers. They were like nothing he had ever seen and wanted to possess them all. The creature was like an incarnation in their fables of a dark being who would tempt them away from the light, and in those fables the being would try to take over the whole of the world for his own.

Anyan knew that she alone saw what Isiro truly was. She knew she was only person who could stop her people from being enslaved. So, she sent her sons and daughters to the distant corners of the world, telling them to recruit as many as they could. For twenty years Isiro's army grew, and for twenty years Anyan's children spread across the world.

When she was sure they had covered all of the land and waters where humans could reside, she reached out and connected with the minds of her sons and daughters and with the people they were connected to. She used her connections to make her ability encompass the whole world, and with the energy reserves of a thousand minds she ripped the powers from the bodies of most of humanity.

***

Harry sat down in the chair across from me, and sighed. "I got us a motel room for the night."

"Oh, good." I closed the book.

CHAPTER 19

"Each night, when I go to sleep, I die. And the next morning, when I wake up, I am reborn." — Mahatma Gandhi

---

The motel wasn't the best, but it wasn't the worst either. I don't know what kind of tricks Harry pulled to make this happen but the room was cool, and it had beds. That's all I wanted. The feverish feeling beginning to overtake me again scared me. The last time this happened I had been with Nick and he knew how to keep my body from burning itself out.

As soon as we got into the room, I laid down on the nearest bed and fell asleep. A couple times I drifted back into consciousness as Harry opened or closed the door, but I didn't hear him watch TV, I didn't hear him leave to get food, I didn't hear him try to wake me up to eat. He would tell me later how dead to the world I had been, running a fever and tossing and turning in my sleep.

Instead I got lost in my dreams. The fog of dreaming was thick and unyielding. I drifted from thoughts that became dreams and dreams that became nightmares. Incarnations of my parents, my brother, my friends, Willow always appeared in front of me. They spoke, but the words were strange and muffled. Images that might have been memories and memories that might have been imagined all struggled in the space between waking and sleep.

But Willow was the most prominent in my dreams. Her voice pushed through thick muffle and I heard her say my name. "Eugene, Eugene... What are you doing?" There was a whimsical lilt to her voice, and when I turned to face her, she was looking down at me from some kind of rock wall. I couldn't see over it.

"I'm going to save you," I said, and reached out for her. She was too far away. The rock wall seemed to inch away as I tried to get closer.

She laughed. "Why do you think I need saving?" Her voice was getting smaller.

"They'll hurt you." I said, my voice was small, and there was little confidence in my words.

She tilted her head down and disintegrated in the wind. Somewhere back in my mind she appeared like an avalanche. Something deep and buried rushed upwards and out of its deep, dark crevasse in my brain. A memory.

Back when Willow had been kidnapped she had passed something to me with her telepathy. I could remember it as just a feeling that she wanted to tell me *something*. Something important. That something appeared before me like giant iron gates and it opened up a thousand thoughts and memories and strange dreamlike images. They were Willow's. All of them were rushing into my mind faster and faster, and I couldn't keep up with them shooting past me.

But then I grasped one and focused in.

I once thought that the world was simple, Eugene. Willow stood on the embankment of a raging river. Her red hair and her white dress sailed in the wind gently. I sat on a wide boulder behind her, watching the river pull trees and silt with its overbearing flow. And even though I could see it, I couldn't feel it.

The world of our childhood consisted of only moments of joy and happiness of friendship and our love of play. Very few times did sadness and anger intercede. We loved it, didn't we? She looked back at me and smiled.

I once dreamed that the world of our childhood was being overtaken by darkness. A darkness that came from above. A darkness that consumed and used without care or consideration the people and places it hurt. It's coming for us now. She raised her eyes to the sky and used her hand to shade them against the sunlight. *Isn't it?*

Dream-Willow turned around to face me and amber

colored eyes met mine. These were not Willow's eyes.

"Eugene, let me out," she said but then she faded away into the darkness.

And then it was over, and I was alone in my dreams again. I couldn't grasp any more of the strings of memory that were trailing through my mind, but I let them go for now just so my mind could find some peace again.

I wandered for what seemed like ages. Part of me knew I was dreaming, but that part of me didn't care and didn't want to experience the waking world. I knew my body was in pain again. I had used fire. I had actually used my power over fire and it was hurting my whole body. What had Nick called it? The EOS? The Energy Overload Syndrome.

I could feel the fire burning through my veins and sleep was the only thing that was keeping it at bay. In a moment of lucidity I was able to think back on the incident with the man in the RV. I hadn't meant to use my powers, but all of a sudden it came out of nowhere. The video Nick had shown me of Joseph Carmichael and I flashed through my mind, but suddenly it wasn't a memory of a video, it was an actual memory. I saw the fire surround me, and I knew full and well that I was in control. The fire was not just a tool or a weapon; it was like the flex of a limb. The fire was not just an extension of me, it *was* me.

But in the fire around me I did not see fear but strength. In the fire I did not see destruction, but utility. In the fire I didn't see my brother killing, I saw myself as... as...

What did I see?

I saw me and only me and I was on fire. But I did not burn. I was not in pain.

Eugene, a voice said.

Eugene. The fire around me began to close in. I felt it, the fear, beginning to take over. The brilliance of the light was blinding and I was scared.

Eugene. The fire became monsters the size of rats, Crawling over my body and biting at my fingers and face.

EUGENE!

I jumped up and slammed my forehead into Harry's

chin. "Ahg!" He cried out and stumbled back. I looked around the room.

The motel, right?

"Sorry, man," I said, rubbing the tender spot on my forehead.

"It's okay. You were having a nightmare or something." Harry shook himself and sat in one of the chairs that were next to my bed. "Are you alright?"

I sat all the way up and swung my legs off the edge of the bed. "I'm okay." My fingers felt hot, like fire was aching to be released. If the dream had gone on any longer, I might have burned the whole motel down.

"What time is it?" I asked, rubbing my hands and arms to release the tension.

"Three thirty a.m.," Harry said, sitting back in the chair and sighing.

"Sorry, I woke you." I said, trying to smile apologetically.

"It's alright. Did you want to talk about it?" Harry smiled back while rubbing at the sleep in his eyes.

"Not really." I shook my head and looked toward the window.

"Ok. Let me know if you do." Harry got up and crawled back into his bed. He pulled the covers over him and disappeared. "Hooverville in the morning?" His muffled voice asked.

"Yeah. Sounds good." I said. But I didn't sleep for the rest of the night.

***

"You're sure?" Jacob asked, almost ashamed that he was in shock.

"It's got their hands all over it." Joe said. He looked at Napoli as he was nodding. "Your brother for one, I swear, he's more and more like you every day."

Jacob chose to ignore that. "The driver?"

"Badly burned, third degree over his whole body. Witnesses said that they saw two boys run from the scene not long before the whole thing and the guy caught fire. I doubt they really know what they did."

Jacob chuckled to himself. His little brother had a soft heart, and if he thought he seriously injured someone, he probably wouldn't live it down.

"Alright, Eugene, showing me something more interesting every day." He laughed and waved at Napoli and Joe to show him the rest of what they found. It was only a matter of time now. He would be seeing his brother in person real soon.

CHAPTER 20

"The gates of Hell are terrible to behold, are they not?"
~ E.A. Bucchianeri, Brushstrokes of a Gadfly

———————————————————

Hooverville was not what I expected. It was a shanty town and not the high end facility I had come to expect out of the Alliance. There were obvious signs of Alliance presence. What few flag poles I had seen had three flags on them, the United States flag, the New Mexico flag, and an Alliance flag. Men and women openly wore the tan and black Alliance uniform in the streets, regularly patrolling the border of town and the few crisscrossed streets.

What little we could see from the outskirts of town was enough to tell us to keep our heads low. If anyone knew my face it would be the Alliance people in Hooverville. The one road in and out of the town was guarded by a tiny building with a gate blocking entrance or exit. There was no fence, but where was there to run? There was nothing for miles around. Harry and I had carefully hitched a ride with an elderly couple close enough to be within walking distance of the town, but other than the tiny collection of buildings, there was nothing but distant hills and deserted land.

Dirty children played in the pockmarked streets, and their parents watched from behind dusty curtains and shredded paper blinds. What few adults we could see walked toward a tall building on the other side of town. The houses inside weren't really houses; they were pieced together from parts of other houses, random assortments of metal sheeting and plywood. I felt like I was not seeing a town in America but a slum from some third-world country.

We wandered the edge of town, trying to gauge what the town was all about, but by nightfall we had little to show for our day in the dust, dry shrubs and bushes.

I took the time then to call up Nick.

"This town is run by the Alliance. Everything that comes in or out is by their order."

"Why would they maintain a town at such a poverty level?" Harry asked. I had the phone on speaker and we both sat down behind an outcropping of rock to listen to Nick.

"I would have to say that the majority of the funding that goes into the Alliance is put into the military. Who cares about some sideshow town where they shove the miscreants and troublemakers who have no societal use?" Nick replied.

"Why doesn't the InfoCon just use their powers to rewrite their memories?" I asked. "They don't seem to have any problems with that."

"They are under the impression that a trouble maker is always a troublemaker no matter what you've done to his or her memory. A first-gen child will continue to make mistakes as his or her powers grow and change, and any one of those mistakes could lead to the outing of our society."

"That seems really strange." Harry said, drawing his knees closer to his chest. A slight breeze was beginning to bring a chill with it.

"It would to an outsider, but it's the way we've done things for centuries."

"That still doesn't make it right." Harry said.

"No," Nick said, and I heard the sigh over the phone. *"No, it doesn't. But to change the infrastructure of such a large organization..."*

"Near impossible." Harry finished the thought.

"Why do you think Marcus brought Willow here?" I asked.

"I don't know." Nick said. *"Nothing I'm coming up with can give me any indication of why the guy was interested in it. It really is just a place where the Alliance keeps it troublemakers. No more, no less."*

"It sounds more like a prison than anything." Harry said.

"You know, you probably wouldn't be far off. I've never been to the place myself but the stories I've heard come from it are less than cozy."

"I'll say." I said, thinking of the little kids who probably had to live in the barely there houses.

"What are you all going to do?" Nick asked.

I glanced at Harry. "I think we're gonna try and look around the town a bit and see if anyone saw Willow... and then I guess we're going to head straight to Laramie."

"Great. Stay out of trouble," Nick said.

"We will." I said. "Bye."

Harry and I had no way to get back to Roswell, but Harry had anticipated a night camping and had brought stuff to make a small tent out of. We set up camp a small distance from the town as the night took over the sky.

The town was pretty quiet, but there was enough activity that next morning we hoped to not go noticed. The sky was unusually dark with bloated rainclouds hugging the western horizon. I crossed my fingers that it would pass us by. We were not equipped to deal with a rainstorm right now.

We entered the town on the farthest corner, out of sight of the one outpost by the road in and far enough away from the tall building on the other corner, that we didn't feel like we could be seen.

This early in the morning, the only Alliance person we saw was a guy who was probably supposed to be watching the street, but instead he was sitting in a chair, chin to chest, eyes closed and feet resting on another chair. We slipped by him easily.

In the middle of the town the sights were even worse. Some of the shacks didn't even have doors. The people in the streets wore dirty and unkempt clothing. We were covered in enough dust and dirt from traveling that, if it weren't for our backpacks, Harry and I would have fit in perfectly.

Harry was about to start speaking to me when he stopped. He was watching something behind me, and I turned to see a girl walking toward us. There was no hesitation in her walk and she came right up to us, letting out a breath that must have been held in too long. "I know who you are." Her eyes glinted.

I stared at her in a state of shock for a few seconds. Her blue eyes flickered back and forth between Harry and me and only stopped on me when I made the first move.

"What do you mean?" I asked, running my tongue around my mouth to try and get rid of the desert that had taken up residence there.

She stared at me, her intense eyes revealing nothing of what she was thinking. But then, I saw a break in her composure. Her face contorted into a distressed expression and she clenched her fists.

"You... you're Eugene. I went to the same high school as you back in Ohio." She said, eyeing Harry, too.

It was only then that it hit me. "Laura?"

"Yes," Laura gasped and grinned. "You're different, like me?"

I blinked. "Uh, I guess so."

"I never thought I would see anyone again from school. I thought I was going to be stuck here forever!" She clapped her hands happily. It was strange, knowing she didn't really leave school on happy terms.

"We're really just passing through." Harry replied.

"Passing through?" She stared at him. "No one just passes through. Unless you're one of them." She pointed to the Alliance guy still asleep in his chair.

The tension in the air was rising. Laura's eyes never deviated from mine. She seemed like she was trying to convey some feeling to me through just her gaze. I felt something crawl through my mind and I stepped back.

"Stay out of my head," I snarled.

She stared me. "What are you doing here?"

I was at a loss for words, shaking my head.

Laura turned her intense stare on Harry, the gaze flickering with an accent of distaste. "You know what it's like. What's it's like to be... like this." She rubbed her arms as if she was cold, and stared up at the sky. "Why are you here if not to be imprisoned like the rest of us?"

"Like we said. Just passing through," Harry said.

"I think what Harry means," I interjected in the hopes of curbing what looked like a wave of hostility between them, "is what you would have us do. Sure, we're 'passing through,' but what do you need from us that you can't get here?" My efforts at being diplomatic had at least a small effect and the tension between the two visibly lessened.

I hid an exhausted sigh and waited for Laura to respond. She seemed like she was having a hard time coming up with a response. Her mouth twitched with words that died before they ever left the confines of her mouth and her body shook with uncertainty.

"I don't—I can't—" she started many times but never finished. But finally a coherent sentence came out so quietly I thought briefly that I had imagined that she had actually spoken. "I want to go with you."

"What?" I asked, even though I understood the request, it seemed so absurd that I didn't know what else to say.

"No," Harry said before Laura had a chance to elaborate.

"Please," she cried suddenly and grabbed my arm, holding on so tight I thought that my blood was being constricted. "I don't want to be here anymore. I don't want to be different."

I opened my mouth to deny her, but something desperate in her eyes tugged at me. I caught Harry's eye, and he gave a microscopic shake of his head. We couldn't take her with us. It was too dangerous for her and most especially for us.

"We can't take you with us," I shook my head and tried to ignore the desperate tears in her eyes.

"I can help you! I... I can use my powers to help you. I can make people do things." Her entire physical being was pleading with me and me alone. Somehow she believed me to be the one to make appeals to because she hardly gave Harry a second glance.

I stopped to consider her offer. Despite the bad consequences of taking her with us, it would mean that we could get to Wyoming even faster, and by way of that, I would be closer to saving Willow.

"Let me talk to him for a moment." Harry stepped between us and pulled me away. Laura watched us walk away, the desperate look in her eyes only increasing with every step we took away from her. She turned abruptly and walked in the opposite direction of us, distance increasing ever more. Harry finally stopped and waited until Laura had disappeared behind a line of shacks to speak.

"I don't like this one bit," he said. He bit his bottom lip so tight that it turned a ghostly white under the pressure.

"But she obviously..."

"A ploy. She's not going help us." Harry growled. "It's just a lie to get us into her confidence. She's just going to use us and then drop us as soon as possible."

"How do you..." I started, but Harry flicked his hand dismissively.

"I can just tell." Harry stared in the direction Laura had disappeared and muttered under his breath.

"I don't think it's a ploy, Harry." I too looked in the direction that Harry stared. "The possible benefits of a third person..."

"Eugene." Harry's eyes glinted with something I couldn't decipher. I stopped talking and stared right back at him into those glinting eyes. "No matter what emotional appeals she's made to you..."

"It's not an emotional appeal," I bit out.

"Then why? Why should we endanger ourselves and this mission on the pining of a lonely girl unable to deal with reality?"

"I do and then again I don't want her to go with us," I said to him, holding up my hand to prevent him from interrupting. "I can't explain it, Harry, but how would you feel if you were totally alone in a world you couldn't understand?"

"I don't think that..." he started to argue but he stopped when his eyes flicked over my shoulder. "Oh sh..." he pushed me behind a set of trashcans.

"What? What?" I tried to peer around the trashcans to see what Harry had seen.

"Oh shit." I said. Walking down the road with a small entourage was my brother, Jacob. He was looking left and right with a slow movement of his head. He was looking for something.

"Did he find us?" I gasped out.

"I dunno." He whispered. "Stay down."

They passed us, Jacob never saw us and only when his whole entourage had disappeared behind some shacks did I let myself relax.

"Why are you hiding?" Laura's voice startled me, and I jumped up.

"We were, uh..." I looked to Harry who was slowly rising to his feet.

"We can't stay here long." Harry said to me. "What do we need to know about this place?"

I looked at Laura. "Is there somewhere we can sit out of sight for a bit?"

Laura looked between us and then nodded. She took us through a maze of buildings and shacks until we got to one that she opened the door to.

"Home sweet home," she said bitterly.

The furnishings of the tiny home were few and far between. There was a tiny table with a wilted flower in a cup resting on it with a basin with water in it up against the wall, and a stack of blankets next to it. The small window on the back wall revealed a joke of a yard with a couple shoddy tents set up next to an unlit fire pit.

"How do you live like this?" I said.

"Can you really call it living?" Laura said, and pulled the blankets out.

"We don't have chairs, so you'll have to sit on these." She shook the dirt loose and laid it out flat on the ground. She sat on a corner of it, and with only a shared glance, we joined her.

"You know it's funny. You're not the first person to just 'pass through' town." She said.

"Oh?" I asked.

"Yeah, Willow... she was here about two or three weeks

ago. Some old guy was showing her around the place. I didn't get to talk to her though. I didn't believe it at first that she was here. Too much of a goody-two-shoes to be in a place like this."

I frowned at her but chose not to say anything about that.

"What was this old guy showing her?" Harry asked instead.

"I'm not sure." She replied.

Harry didn't have time to get out his next question because the door opened and a guy stepped in. Harry stood up abruptly.

"Logan!" Laura stood and greeted the guy. "Uhm, Logan these are my friends. Eugene and..."

"Oliver." Harry said.

She frowned at his name, but shrugged. "Guys, this is my brother, Logan."

"Friends?" Logan said with a smile. "I knew if you just tried you would make some friends. Did they have to be boys?" He said the last in a fake whisper, but turned to us and smiled while he did it.

"Logan, please." Laura blushed and looked at us with a smile.

"Whatever," he laughed, and reached over to pat us each on the shoulders.

Harry, still standing, finally sat back down and I was relieved to see him relax a little. For the next hour Laura and Logan talked to us about this place. They had been shipped here by the InfoCon after Laura's outburst at school. It had apparently been her third incident in a year, and by InfoCon rules, that was enough to punish her, condemning her and her family to this hellish town.

A couple times Laura and Logan's parents came in and out of the little shack, but for the most part they stayed outside in the tents and around the fire pit. It was their day off from work. The non-kinetics in town, mostly the parents of first-generation Kinetics, worked at the tall building on the far edge of town. Laura didn't say much about it, just that they went six days out of the week for some kind work that they weren't supposed to share with anyone outside of the tall building.

Most of the kids and some of the adults here were capable of many powers. They could only redeem their way out of Hooverville if they could become a productive member of the tiny society. A few had been given a clean slate by the InfoCon, and yet others had disappeared without warning.

After we were sure that Jacob and his people were gone we stepped outside to get some "air" as Harry called it, but really he wanted to talk about our next move.

"We need to get out of here without Laura following us and before any of the Alliance finds us. I can't imagine the trouble she'll get us into if she tries and they catch us."

"I guess."

"I know you feel for her, and I do too, but there are more important things than this. You want to save Willow, don't you?"

"Of course."

"Then don't endanger yourself by letting this girl sway you into pitying her. Yes the environment here is bad. It's fucking deplorable, but there is a reason she is here. She's unstable. The nightmares she caused at school... who knows what she could do to people."

"I understand what you mean but..."

Harry pushed me aside just as a hand-painted street sign next to us exploded like a miniature bomb from a direct jolt of brilliant electricity. In the distance I could hear a scream, and before I knew how to respond to the abrupt violence, the slight wooden frame of Laura's shack was being encompassed by flames. The dark rain clouds above our heads gave no relief as distant lightning echoed in the depths of the clouds.

I got up to my feet the quickest and dragged Harry into a safe place behind another shack. I heard another scream and a few indistinguishable shouts--voices I didn't recognize and a few I did sent warning signals off in my head.

I looked out from behind the shack and saw Logan facing off with someone I didn't recognize. The guy had a bright red armband on his jacket. Where had I seen that armband before? The guy pushed Logan over and as electricity danced off his fingers he pointed in the direction where Harry and I were hiding.

"Who is it?" Harry gasped.

"I don't—oh." I had started to say, and then they appeared. Napoli and Joe. They flanked the unknown man and carried on what I could easily tell was a silent telepathic conversation. The unknown man pointed at us again and both Napoli and Joe headed toward us. Napoli was feeding off the power of the other man and was spouting electric bolts that flickered off his hands.

He saw me and I ducked behind the shed just in time for the small building to explode in front of me. Harry pushed me out of the way just in time for the splinters of wood and concrete to pelt my back.

I only had a second to recover before Joe was right next to me and grabbing the nape of my neck. He pulled me back and I fell to the ground. Harry also fell but rolled away right to the feet of Hoodie. Hoodie grunted as he shoved his hands out, and water from a bucket followed the movement, slamming into Joe's chest. He had another one to follow and it collided with a bolt of electricity that was heading right toward me. The water and electricity exploded and water rained down around us.

I pushed myself to my feet and grabbed Harry's arm, dragging him away from our two attackers and Hoodie. We ran past the burning house. I did my best to ignore the fearful sweat that ran down my back and threatened to turn me cold.

Harry tugged on my shirt and pulled me in the direction of a ditch and we rolled through the mud into the nook. Hoodie wasn't far behind. Hoodie put his hands into the part of a drainage pipe that stuck into the ground.

Surprisingly a small trickle of water was beginning to gather at our feet--artillery that Hoodie could use to defend us. In a rare moment of frustration I suddenly wished I could use my powers. He was stuck defending and Harry and I were helpless.

"How did they find us here?" Harry gasped.

Harry's question kicked through the fog entering my brain and I could only shake my head and take in deep breaths. What little there was of the shack was burning to the ground right in front of us.

I heard a shout and saw Laura's mother running with a bucket of water toward one of the tents that had caught fire. She never reached the tent. Out of nowhere a spear of electricity pierced the flames surrounding the house and hit her in the chest. She fell to the ground and I felt my blood run cold.

Her blank eyes stared upwards and the bucket of water pooled around her like clear blood. Her chest was charred and no life-giving breath moved it. She was dead.

"No!" I heard a Laura's dad scream, and he ran to his wife. In seconds he joined his wife on the ground with a fatal electric burn on his chest. Two innocent people were dead. The realization was tearing its way through my brain like a blunted saw.

Lightning flashed in the sky, mocking the burning house and the two dead people at its base, their pale faces gaining no life from the flames ravaging their home. I tasted blood and realized belatedly that my cheek was bleeding from a cut. It seemed trivial in the face of what had just happened.

"What?" Harry started to say and then a great web of trees began to grow around the fire. Hoodie crawled out of the ditch and ran in between a couple shacks across the street. Logan stood in the middle of the street and stared down an Alliance officer. He had his hands out, and as his fingers jerked, the trees and ropelike roots erupted from the ground.

Three men I didn't recognize ran through the wreckage. They stood in front of Napoli and the electrokinesis Kinetic. One of the men, also an electrokinetic, started a fight with the other one. Artificial lightning crackled all around us as they ran at each other.

I heard Harry gasp at something behind me. I didn't have time to see what had shocked him because a truck pulled up beside us blocking the view. Laura was in the driver's seat. Blood was gushing out of a cut along her scalp but she didn't seem to care.

"Get in!" she yelled, her voice cracking.

I took one look back at the destruction behind us before Harry grabbed my arm and pulled me from the ditch into the waiting truck. All around us the flora was coming alive and overtaking the street as if in fast forward motion. Hundreds of years of growth were choking the entire area in seconds. Who was doing this I wasn't sure. All I knew was that the Alliance Kinetics were becoming entangled in it and suffocated along with the flames by the unforgiving growth. Logan stood in the center of it all raising his hands higher and higher, orchestrating the trees in a hostile takeover.

Just as Harry slammed the door on the truck behind us, one of the Alliance officers came up behind Logan and grabbed him around the neck. Logan struggled in his grasp, but he was losing. The trees shot up faster than before, blocking our view.

In moments we were driving away, down the country road, and behind us the smoke piling out of the forest was all too quickly replaced by trees the size of large buildings.

"What was— How was that happening to the forest?" I gasped, staring at Laura across the truck cab.

"Logan," she whispered through a waterfall of tears making tracks across her cheeks. "He's dead. He sacrificed himself for me."

"How do you know he's dead?" Harry asked.

Laura unsteadily tapped her head. "I can't feel him anymore!"

Harry looked shaken and sat back in his seat. I looked back once more at the tall trees in the distance and shuddered when the rain began to fall.

CHAPTER 21

*I never really thought about destiny catching up with me.
I feel though that my destiny was less like a hound making its
way noisily towards me, but like an agile cat, stalking me in the
jungle of my own decisions. I never really thought about it until
destiny tore out my soul's jugular.* – Rei Akito. From her treatise
on being a soldier in the Second Great Kinetic War

We drove until we got to a gas station in Roswell and
Laura stopped to put gas in the truck. She had been crying in
silence the whole way, looking more and more like a shell
shock victim than someone who should be driving.

The fact that a senseless death had just taken place
made me feel like one too, even though I knew I would never
get close to what Laura must be feeling. With her losing her
whole family in the split seconds that she did, I could only cup
my forehead in my hands and listen to the storm that ravaged
the windshield for too short a time. We left the wall of rain and
entered sunlight only a few miles from the interstate. The
small isolated storm behind us looked even more unnatural in
the dawn sunlight. It was no more than seven in the morning
when we stopped for gas, but it felt unfair that such a beautiful
day should meet us now. The storm had come and gone but left
far too much destruction in its path.

Harry was sure the Alliance wouldn't be caught off
guard like that for long. I had few doubts that reinforcements
had come in not long after we had left. And to top it all off,
Laura was stuck with us now. There was little doubt that by
now her brother was most likely dead. She was now alone in
the world. She told us she had no extended family, both of her

parents had been only children and their parents were already long gone from this world.

While she refilled the truck with a tear-streaked stoic mask, Harry and I stepped out, he to call his dad and I to find something to take the edge off the burning headache building between my eyes.

I browsed the aisles in the truck stop where we had stopped and found only overpriced aspirin. I frowned at the fist-sized package and put it back where I had found it. I let loose a curse, startling the sleepy-looking cashier.

"Sorry," I muttered, left the building, and went and sat in the cab of the truck. Laura was done pumping gas and was sitting in the seat quietly gripping the steering wheel with white knuckles. She stared intensely forward, her eyes in some far off place.

I let my gaze travel around to where I could see Harry having a heated conversation on the phone inside. His face was flushed and he was waving his one free hand in dramatic gestures. I had rarely seen Harry angry, but whatever he was talking about on the phone with his Dad was more than making him angry. I closed my eyes and let myself drift into a thoughtless state. It was like meditation in a way, breathing in and out, letting every thought flow out with each exhale. I opened my eyes when Laura shifted in her seat.

"What does it mean to be a Kinetic?" She asked quietly, never moving her eyes from some point in the distance.

"What do you mean?" I glanced at her, surprised that she was being talkative.

"Is it always hard?"

"No... I don't think so. We've just gotten ourselves caught, you know. Rock-and-a-hard-place kinda stuff." I pinched the cloth of my jeans near my knee absently.

"I don't like it." She buried her face in her hands. "It's the worst thing in the world."

"How so?" I can't say that I've had the best experience with Kinetics and powers and stuff. But Willow was worth jumping in head first.

"Did I ever tell you why we moved to Ohio?" She wiped

at her eyes and shook the loose hair out of her eyes.

"No." I searched my memory, but most of what I knew about her before now had been from Willow.

"We used to live in Chicago. We went to this high school out a little past the suburbs. The sort of place where you kinda know everyone. Logan and I were in different classes most of the day except for biology. This one day, he and I were working on a group project when this stupid kid named Henry started teasing Logan about his obsession with plants, and I don't know how but they started fighting with each other and Henry was winning." She grasped the steering wheel again and her eyes glazed over.

"I thought that Henry was going to kill him!" she choked. "I felt his mind. I felt Henry's mind and I saw his nightmares. I did the only thing that I knew to do. I made him... I made him see his nightmares. He was screaming and screaming and no one could make him stop. I couldn't make it stop."

She gulped in air and her eyes welled up. "I didn't want to stop. Logan was bleeding so badly, I wanted revenge. I found out later that Logan had powers too. He was perfectly fine with not defending himself. He was so mad at me for endangering us. Some people came. They called themselves the Informational Control. They wiped all the memories of the people in school about me. My entire existence was purged from my friend's minds. They told us to leave town no matter what it took, or else they would wipe our memories too. I hadn't realized until then that there were more people out there like us. They said I had to wait until I was sixteen to apply for training."

She fell silent.

"What happened to him? The kid you attacked?"

She looked at me with such a haunted look in her eyes. "He died. His brain shut down."

I saw Harry put the phone away and head back toward us. His face was red. I didn't prompt Laura any further.

He opened the driver side door and waved Laura to move over. He saw my gaze and smiled. "Parents, huh?" I smiled back, but let the smile fall the second I remembered Laura and Logan's parents. Laura was now an orphan.

I shuddered on the inside and felt my headache come back full force. I sighed as Harry started the truck and began our journey northward to Albuquerque.

The interstate was not very busy. It seemed odd that a massive causeway would be sparsely populated but I didn't question it because it meant we had little to deal with. Harry quietly drove, and Laura and I sat quietly next him.

Soon, however, Laura seemed to grow uncomfortable with the silence and began talking. Harry didn't respond to anything she said but I tried to at least give some occasional murmur of acknowledgment.

I didn't start really listening until she said something about powers. "—hurt so much. I didn't mean to bring out my powers again. I didn't mean to endanger our lives again. The InfoCon said that if I screwed up again I wouldn't be able to receive training until I was eighteen. That's why we were sent to Hooverville after I... well, you know what happened in Columbus."

I frowned, remembering the nightmare at school. "Yeah."

"Then when we moved, it was like I didn't have..."

I zoned out again after that and considered things. The InfoCon really was scary. I was glad that I never had to deal with them directly. But now, if I did come into contact with them-- well, I hope that didn't ever happen.

"Where are you going, anyway?" She asked out of the blue.

I hesitated. What do I say?

"It's not that I want to go with you, anymore. I'm just curious." Her eyes looked honest, but her tone of voice betrayed far too much insecurity. We had no place to leave her, no one to leave her with. Who's to say she wouldn't follow us anyway?

I had never had much trouble with lying, not that I was an incessant liar, but usually I only lied when I really needed to. Need being a very subjective factor, of course. But lying to someone when they were in an obviously desperate place was something I had always felt uncomfortable with. But if I wanted to get to Wyoming without a hitch, I couldn't have an emotionally unstable person like her the rest of the way.

"We're going into hiding." I started slowly. "We're both actually going to split up once we get to a big city so that we can't be tracked." This seemed to be the best thing to say. She would most likely want to stay with people who were "like her." I should probably call Nick and see if there was a safe place to send her.

Her eyes widened in front of a glint of curiosity. "You're on the run?"

I took in a breath. "Yeah."

"From?"

I really didn't want to get into everything but I had to say something. "From the government of our people. The people who run the InfoCon."

Her gaze became even more curious, even excited. "Our... *our* people?"

I nodded.

"Is it part of the United States Government?"

"No," I shook my head. "Not that I know of anyway. From what I've gathered, it's more of an international alliance than anything else."

"International? Tell me about it? Are there lots of us?" She grabbed my arm and leaned into my shoulder. I cringed a bit and saw Harry rolling his eyes out of the corner of my eye.

I had probably just jumped into a whole other can of worms, but there was no stopping now. I explained to the best of my ability everything that I had learned so far.

She nodded slowly to each thing I said. The curious spark turned to something entirely different that I didn't understand. I definitely didn't like it. It was like a hunger for more. After her remarks about not liking her powers, the need to know more about our people was strange.

"The people who attacked us, *they* were the Alliance?"

I hesitated before nodding. "Yeah."

She stood up and stared at me. "This Lancaster woman

you told me about--she gave the orders to attack?"

I really didn't like where this was going, so I lied. "I don't know." In truth, she probably did give the orders.

Laura's mouth was set in a grim line. She had already made up her mind about who was responsible. "Thank you, Eugene."

Troubled, I looked outside the window and promised myself to talk to Harry when we were alone.

We were on the freeway about halfway between Albuquerque and Trinidad, Colorado when we ran into a rough patch of traffic. From what we could tell the road was backed up for miles.

"What's going on?" I asked.

"An accident, I guess?" Harry said, trying to look between the cars at whatever was holding the traffic in place.

We didn't have much time to sit watching the traffic move at a crawl. Laura leaned forward and gasped. There were people running through the cars from all sides. They were running toward us.

A car in front of us lifted up, defying gravity, and slammed into the front of our truck.

I don't remember what happened after that.

Long ago, I felt the need to run away. Willow leaned against the edge of a tree staring deep into a forest.

It wasn't because I was angry or sad about anything, really. I wanted to explore. I wanted to find out what was missing. She reached her hand into the darkness and smiled sadly.

There's something missing, Eugene. Can you feel it? Her hand and eyes dropped to stare at the forest floor. *I'm missing... something.*

It was becoming a repeating cycle. Losing consciousness and then waking up in a strange place. This time I wasn't in a small room with some old man with cryptic smiles and vague statements. Instead I was in a large room, a warehouse it seemed, and there were no other people that I could see from my tied down state. I was literally tied down. Ropes, or rather a type of metallic cord, bound my arms to my sides and my legs were locked. I squirmed as much as the ropes would allow and turned myself onto my side. The warehouse housed nothing but a tan military Hummer and at least a dozen tall wooden crates. I turned to the other side but there was nothing there either. Just a chair and a ratty, black suitcase. I closed my eyes and tried to not feel the stinging pinpricks behind my eyes. I felt like my entire brain had just been torn up, shredded in a blender and mashed up with a large pile of gravel. A strangled sound escaped my mouth before I could stop it.

The sound in itself was enough to bring someone out. I saw the shoes before I saw the person. But the shoes were enough for me to identify him. Two laceless, black loafers with red lining. I felt the cold concrete floor under me all that much more sinking into my bones.

"Hello, Eugene." My brother smiled down at me in what could at one time have been a happy smile, but the expression never reached his eyes.

PART 3:
BEHIND ENEMY LINES

CHAPTER 22

"...The attitude is not to withdraw from the world when you realize how horrible it is, but to realize that this horror is simply the foreground of a wonder and to come back and participate in it. "All life is sorrowful" is the first Buddhist saying, and it is. It wouldn't be life if there were not temporality involved which is sorrow. Loss, loss, loss."~ Joseph Campbell

Jacob smiled warmly at me. Unfortunately, I knew that warmth was nothing more than a facade. Any niceness or warmth that he had ever put out had always been fake, and a means to an end. I didn't trust this mask of brotherly kindness any more than I trusted that he was going to sit me down and offer me a cup of cocoa.

I was caught. The overwhelming exhaustion eating at my consciousness didn't help the dread from seeping through my skin. I tried to loosen the ropes but they were too tight. I don't know why Jacob had me hogtied and I couldn't see Harry or Laura in the room. I was alone with the one person I didn't want to be around right now.

"Jacob," I coughed. My position on the floor made it hard to breathe right.

"Eugene." He knelt down and touched my arm in a strangely sympathetic move. "I'm sorry we had to have this reunion. But we had to be sure."

"Sure?" I gasped. "Sure of what?"

He sat back on his heels. "Sure that you weren't going to do yourself or anyone else harm."

"How would I do that?" I tried sucking in a deep breath.

Jacob stood and pulled me up with him, un-constricting

my lungs. He pushed me into a straight-backed chair and undid the knots of the ropes around my arms.

"Some believed that you had fully trained powers, despite what I told them." Jacob said quietly and pulled the ropes off, coiling them neatly at his feet.

I glared up at him, my mouth involuntarily twitching into a scowl.

Jacob saw the scowl and grinned. "You always were naive, Eugene."

"What's that supposed to mean," I rasped.

"You're so unaware of what's going on around you. It's irrational the way you've hidden the truth from yourself."

I took a breath, readying myself to argue, but the door opened and a man in a discreet Alliance uniform—a tan blazer with a half-dollar sized Alliance symbol emblazoned on the front breast—hurried across the concrete floor toward my brother. I let my retort die on my lips and listened intently to Jacob's conversation with the Alliance officer.

"They have the spy contained," the man said, glancing at me only briefly.

"Any trouble?" My brother asked, nonchalantly looking at his fingernails.

"None."

"And the extra?" Jacob leaned back on the table and with a disinterested gaze studied the room.

"Contained as well."

"What of abilities?"

"Dr. Faulkner got a report from the InfoCon. He believes that they may be an asset to us."

My brother nodded and waved the officer away and turned back to me with a strange, thoughtful look on his face.

The conversation had made no sense at all. 'Extra?' 'Spy?'

Jacob grabbed my shoulder and squeezed. "Eugene, I want you to know that I didn't want to harm you with any of this."

"That's a bunch of crap, and you know it. If you didn't want to harm me or anyone else why did you sic your friends on us?"

"It wasn't you they were after. It was your spy friend."

Spy friend? Who was he talking about?

"Who?"

"Harry Gleeson."

I shook my head, at a loss for words. That didn't make any sense.

Jacob slammed his palm down on one of the crates, the sound echoing deftly through the building. "You were deceived, Eugene. Harry was a spy! He worked directly for the Isiroans."

"That's a lie." I shook my head again.

"How do you know?" Jacob quirked an eyebrow.

I looked down at my hands. "I...He's my friend! He's not even a Kinetic." I insisted.

"Being your friend didn't stop Willow from switching sides either, did it?" He sneered.

I jolted to my feet and stuck my finger in his face. "Don't you dare! Willow was kidnapped."

He raised an eyebrow. "Was she now?"

I wanted to scream and yell at him but nothing coherent was forming in my mouth. It all halted before I could say it. "She..."

Jacob shrugged and smiled condescendingly. "Whatever you think, Eugene."

"Don't patronize me, Jacob."

"I'm not trying. You're refusing to see logic."

"Logic?" I snorted. "Willow would never join them. That's logic! You didn't know her like I did!"

"No? Eugene she is like many other idealistic girls her age. She's been pulled in by flowery words and the promise of saving millions. She's *weak*. That kind of ignorance is hard to work with, Eugene."

I turned away and leaned into one of the crates. "What do you want with me, Jacob?"

"I want to help you."

I didn't look up but instead took a breath before responding. My parents had always told me I needed to get a handle on my temper. But before now I had never really considered how to control the emotions boiling under the surface of my thoughts. "What do you mean by 'help me'?" I pinched the wood of the crate, forcibly squeezing the wood slivers into my fingers. The pain brought with it a focus. I looked over at Jacob.

"I mean," Jacob crossed his arms over his chest. "I want to help you infiltrate Isiro's base. I was really proud, Eugene. When I heard that you broke into Alliance Headquarters, I knew that you were ready."

I glanced up at him. He was smiling as usual but his eyes finally conveyed something other than that severe coldness that he always had when dealing with people. I felt my chest constrict. It was too good to be true. But his expression was so honest.

My brother was proud of me.

In all the years that I had lived around my brother he had always seemed disappointed with me. Never had he uttered the words "I'm proud" in reference to me; or anyone for that matter. All it took was aggressive actions and he was *proud* of *me*.

"You were deceived, Eugene." Jacob pushed off the table and walked a slow circle around me and the table. "Harry was working for the Isiroans all this time. He's been calling in reports on your location ever since you left Columbus." Jacob spoke in a soft, conciliatory voice.

I started to shake my head to deny his words, but he grabbed my collar and pulled me over to the table. He opened up a laptop laid out on the table and showed me a grainy photo of someone leaving through a set of double doors, the same doors that belonged to my high school.

"How about this..." Jacob pointed to the picture. "Back when Miss Laura Jordan inflicted your whole school with nightmares, he was the only one in your school not accounted for by the InfoCon. If he was a non-Kinetic he would have had his memory wiped like the rest of them. If he was an Alliance Kinetic he would be safely with the others in the auditorium. But no, he was an Isiroan. He didn't want to get caught, so he slipped away before anyone knew the wiser." He showed me another picture, closer in from another angle. It was Harry the day that Laura had brought our school to its knees. He was looking back at the school, hiding behind a parked school bus.

"Or when inexplicably your friend knew how to work his way through highly classified Alliance databases." He clicked to another photo, this one of me and him sitting in front of a computer in the Alliance Headquarters. "What normal 16 year old knows how to do that?"

I shook my head, feeling my chin tremble, and a hot lump in the back of my throat.

"While you traveled his calls to his father were reports on your location and the information he was gathering on you." Jacob pulled a small handheld recording device and hit the play button.

"Hey, Dad." It was Harry's voice.

"Harry. How is the mission?" It was Harry's dad.

"Oh, it's going great. I've been meeting so many new people." Harry's voice stayed conversational.

"Have there been any complications?"

"Not really. We got in a few scuffles with some guys from another camp."

"The Alliance?"

"Yeah. I'll be okay. I've got lots of back up." Laughter.

"You haven't been found out yet?"

"Nope. I've been careful."

"Anything else?"

"Eugene was saying that he might need to go see the doctor, because he has a huge cut on his arm from the wall climbing we were doing."

"We'll send in a team immediately."

"Alright. I'll see you later, Dad. Love you."

The tape clicked off. I didn't understand that conversation at all.

"That was the last conversation we were able to record off his cellphone. This was a strike on Hooverville. A strike that killed over a dozen Alliance men, women, and children."

"That's not possi...." I started to say.

"Also we have video that you need to see." He tapped

the laptop on the table and turned it to show me video from inside the bus station the first day. I could see myself and Napoli. I could also see jets of water attacking Napoli. But there was something missing.

Hoodie wasn't there. I asked Jacob to play it over again, ignoring the smile on his face, and looked again. There was no Hoodie. But I could distinctly remember him being there.

Jacob tapped at the computer again and showed me another video. It was the car chase. Where Hoodie should have been on the roof of the car directing the waves of water there was no one.

"How... who?"

"Harry is a well-trained Isiroan Kinetic. He has been using Isiroan technology to cast an illusion of another person. This "person" has been the one you see using water powers. But really Harry is the one who is in control."

I felt a chill run down my body and all my blood turned to ice. I fell heavily to the chair where I had sat earlier and buried my head in my hands. Harry, the one person I thought I could trust during this whole excursion had turned... had always been one of the enemy.

"I'm sorry it had to turn out like this, Eugene." Jacob said softly. The sudden softness was also something I hadn't seen in... well... ever.

"It changes nothing," I bit out and looked away from Jacob and the repeating video of Harry's betrayal. "No matter what anyone says or does, I'm going to save Willow from that bastard alien. No matter who gets in my way."

It was silent from Jacob's end for a little while, save for the sound of him repacking the recorder and a few other things he had lying out on the table. Then he said this, "Then let me help you. I want Isiro dead just as much as you want to save Willow."

"You really want to help?"

Jacob nodded. He leaned on the table and looked up at the milky skylight above out heads.

"In three weeks' time Isiro will be at his weakest. When the transfer is to take place the minds of himself and Willow will be balanced. And there is where we must strike."

"It won't hurt her, will it?"

"Unlikely. There is a measure of danger involved but Willow hasn't gone through the full five month process like most hosts do. The integration is not as deep."

"Oh."

He leaned forward. "Of course the best possible situation would be to get to her before the process ever starts."

I looked up at him, hope finally filling my chest.

"All you have to do is listen to what I tell you and all with be all right." His lips twitched into a proud smile. Pride rose in my chest alongside that hope and I felt better than I had in weeks.

"What are we going to do?"

"We'll go over specifics later on, but for now we are going to get out of here and find the best way for you to infiltrate the Laramie base."

"'For me?' You're not coming with me?"

"You were going alone before this, weren't you?"

"Yeah, but..."

Jacob grabbed my arm and led me through a pair of double doors and into a long hallway. "Don't worry about it. Everything will be fine."

We walked in silence for a moment and then a thought occurred to me. "How do I know you won't turn me in to Lancaster the next moment you get the chance?"

"Because I wouldn't do that to you. I promise." His voice was sincerely grim. "And you know that I always keep my promises."

I felt a shiver, but my worry was silenced. If there was one good thing about my brother, he did always keep his promises. There was never a time that his dependability ever came into question.

"Okay." I said. "Thanks."

Jacob let go of my arm and we walked side-by-side down the hallway.

"Another thing, Lancaster doesn't have quite the power that most think she does. She is dependent on the Council for all military decisions. I wouldn't depend on her if I could possibly help it, and I certainly wouldn't turn you in to her for a petty promotion. I have my own way of making gains in this world." Jacob grinned.

"Really?" I glanced at him out of the corner of my eye, unsure. Jacob was extremely ambitious. I wasn't sure what he would do to rise in the ranks, but it was sure to be very aggressive.

"You know, sometimes when you want to get something of such importance done, it takes more than just working within the established system. You have to break down everything and start fresh. The old ways just don't work anymore."

Jacob pushed open another set of double doors. I was hit with a wave of hot air and a searing lance of sunlight.

Almost the second my eyes adjusted to the new light I saw Harry flanked by two Alliance officers and being led toward an armored van. Any thoughts or words I had about Jacob's 'new system' were quickly forgotten. He saw me and his eyes widened. "Eugene, help me!"

I flinched at the desperation in his voice and turned away.

"Don't believe anything he says! It's all lies!" He called out again.

I snapped my head up to retort that he'd *lied* to *me*. A rumble like that of a plane flying over tore through the air interrupting me. Then a bolt of lightning speared down from an impossibly clear sky and struck the armored car. The engine of the car exploded sending people and debris flying.

Jacob pulled me out of the way just as another bolt of lightning socked the ground just feet away. I looked around wildly, knowing that this couldn't be natural. It had to be a Kinetic.

Suddenly, one of the Alliance soldiers was clutching his head screaming. "Ahhh! No!"

I could see his eyes. They were glazed and faraway; he swung his hands out as if to protect himself from something that was chasing him. His waving hands released bolts of highly charged electricity.

"Stop!" A gruff voice yelled from around the corner of the warehouse, just in time for me to see Laura bolt out from behind the corner and point toward the Alliance officers who were trying to regain their standing after being thrown yards from where they had been standing. Lighting struck the ground next to them and unfortunately one of them wasn't fast enough to get away. He fell to the ground screaming and burning. Laura was controlling the other Alliance soldier though his nightmares.

Jacob regained his composure the fastest and the moment I saw his hand wave outwards I rolled away from the direction he pointed. A seemingly harmless waist-high rock next to Laura exploded inward then outward and rained dust down onto us, casting everything into shadow.

All were silent for only a second. Laura only just escaped the exploding rock and ran for cover behind a jeep. The only problem was that it would do nothing to help her. Jacob could explode *anything*. I pushed myself to my feet and cradled a bruised arm.

"Jacob, let me talk to her!" I yelled to my brother who looked ready to blow up something again.

He stared at me intensely and then jerked his head toward her. I sprinted as fast as I dared over the uneven ground and skidded to a halt next to the jeep.

"Laura?"

She grabbed my shirt and pulled me behind the jeep. "Quick! I'll distract them and you grab Harry!"

"Wait."

"We can't wait!" Her voice cracked.

"Laura!" I grabbed her arms and forced her to pay attention to me. "He lied."

"Huh?" Her shoulders tensed.

"Harry played us all for fools! He called in the strike that killed your parents."

Her face went impossibly pale and she fell to the ground. "No." She sobbed.

I backed up and waved my brother over. I saw Harry

being pulled toward another armored car not far away.

Suddenly Laura's sobs turned to rage. "I'll kill him!" She scrambled up and ran around the jeep and right toward Harry. I felt the air cracking with energy as Laura's influence called up another bolt of lightning. I had no choice but to run after her. I reached her just as the bolt came down, and made the mistake of grasping her hand to turn her around. The bolt hit so close to my arm that I felt the burn immediately. I hit the ground hard. The skin on my arm was singed and fire red.

Laura gasped but stood mannequin still, staring at her handiwork with horror. Jacob waved over one of the Alliance men. The man touched my arm and the skin tingled and itched incessantly. Seconds later the skin was red only with fresh skin. I mumbled a 'thanks' and looked up to make eye contact with Harry one last time before he disappeared into the armored car.

HARRY GLEESON

The last that I saw of Eugene his face was a mask of hurt and betrayal. I hadn't wanted him to find out like this. Part of me had been prepared the whole way from Ohio for an eventual unmasking. I didn't expect it now, what with us so close to our destination. Jacob Yoshida's men had clamped huge cuffs around my hands and snapped them together behind my back. The metal in the cuffs was something unique to the Alliance. It created an electromagnetic field that negated the powers of the person in close proximity.

They had taken away my Illusionary projector, so even if I did have access to my abilities, I was without any protection or easy escape. Yoshida's men dragged me into the back of a van and pulled a black sack around my head. I heard muffled conversation and the van roared to a start.

The drive could have lasted for minutes or hours, but it felt like an eternity. I was left with the muted sounds of travel and the other occupants of the van didn't talk. My thoughts were louder than anything. I had to start planning. Yoshida was a smart man. And if I had any clue as to what he planned for me, I was in for a world of trouble. Stories always floated in from the teams that came in close contact with Yoshida and his men, stories of torture and week-long interrogations, stories of men and women returning to the Isiroans with their minds shattered and their abilities so out of control that they had to be put under deep anesthesia to prevent them from hurting themselves or others.

I tried to flex my hand, but the shackles kept my fingers from moving out of a clenched fist. He had to think I was weak, that I was worthless to him. Maybe then I would be able to escape with my sanity intact. I had never really lied to anyone, never been in a play or theater production in school, I had little experience with acting. Even with Eugene, while I was playing a ruse, I never really lied to him outright. Misdirected, told partial truths, yes, but what was facing me now was the play, the production, the theater that could save my life. I had to act better than ever. They couldn't believe that I was something weak and nonthreatening.

The men in the van with me started talking again, in low voices. I took a deep breath and started to make crying noises. If they took the bag off my head they would see dry eyes, but I was taking a gamble that they would leave it alone. The men stopped talking as my muffled sobs got louder. They started laughing, and one of them kicked my leg, knocking me forward.

"Oh, now you cry!" One of them said with a laugh. I smiled between loud sobs. This was only the beginning.

CHAPTER 23

"Things fall apart; the center cannot hold; Mere anarchy is loosed upon the world, the blood-dimmed tide is loosed, and everywhere the ceremony of innocence is drowned; the best lack all conviction, while the worst are full of passionate intensity." ~ William Butler Yeats.

EUGENE YOSHIDA

One of the things that I really loved about our neighborhood was all the people. Willow knelt in the grass and picked a dandelion and blew at it, sending the seeds flying. *Different kinds of people, different kinds of ideas and thoughts all bouncing off each other like a thousand pin balls ricocheting around a small game board.* She smiled as the seeds swirled around her head like ethereal fairies. *Isn't it interesting?* She touched one of the floating seeds and bright light consumed the world.

It was a dream. A dream of fire. But no. It wasn't a dream. It was a memory. I was surrounded by bars. The walls were made of roaring flames that chewed at the ceiling and filled the whole room with boiling smoke. I tried to shake the bars loose but they wouldn't budge under my fragile fingers. I screamed wordlessly out to the world beyond the flames for a savior.

A shaft of fire exploded inwards and a figure burst through.

I sat up in my makeshift bed and shakily wiped the sweat from my brow. I kicked away the blanket and sat with

211

my head cradled in trembling fingers. My heart arched its way through my chest rapidly. I closed my eyes against bright sunlight spearing through the window and opened them only to find myself not in the room anymore. I was outside.

The sky was dark but filled to the brim with countless stars arcing across the sky. I sucked in a breath and stumbled backward. "What?"

My voice felt strange and cottony like I wasn't entirely here.

"You're not supposed to be here yet."

I turned sharply and saw a man with a flashlight in hand. The light from his flashlight was so bright under the dark sky I couldn't see his face.

"I... what?" I asked, shielding my eyes from the searing bright light.

"You aren't completely here yet. You're not ready." He said.

"Ready for what?"

I felt something tug at the back of my head. I look back and saw a girl with ratty dreads perched on a rock next to me.

"What is your name?" she asked.

I turned back to the man. Confusion and the odd rumble of my heartbeat jittered my thoughts.

"Where am I?"

"That's not important now. You need to go back," he said.

"Wha?" The man took a huge step forward and touched my forehead. I felt something blossom inside me like a mushroom cloud, filling me with an inner fire.

I closed my eyes, and when his touch on my forehead was gone, I opened them. I was back in the room with my blanket underfoot. I shook away the strange feelings. With little more than a quick glance I remembered all the shit that had gone down yesterday. Harry a betrayer and me alone.

My brother had whisked me away to this tall nearly windowless building with little more than a word and left with even fewer. The room was adorned with a picture of a lotus and a single window that looked out on the cityscape of

Denver, Colorado. A desk and leather loveseat sat up against the wall. I plopped down with a sigh onto the loveseat and shivered at the cold leather. Whatever heat I had left behind before being teleported away was now gone.

As if my life wasn't complicated enough, first there was the dream and then that stupid teleporting thing. I stood next to the window and watched the sun peak over the buildings. Dawn was here, the start of a new day, the continuation of me going after Willow. But instead I was stuck here, waiting for Jacob to get back.

"Wait" he had said. And wait I did like some kind of bozo. I dug my nails into my arm out of self-punishment for even agreeing to halt my progress toward Willow. She was the important thing here, not whatever B.S. that Jacob was playing with.

I paced at the door that led out into the dark hallway. It was empty but for a few fake plants. I growled under my breath, halting profanities before they could emerge into real words. I didn't want to wait here. Wait for my best friend to be taken from my permanently. Turned into some breathing vessel for whatever the hell Isiro really was.

I stopped mid-pace and looked at the door. It would be easy to leave. Easy to find the elevator and enter this unfamiliar city. But would it be easy to get out. Would it be easy to hitchhike across the state to some virtually unknown place? There was only one way to find out.

I gave into the twitching urge to open the door and stepped out into the hallway. It was still dark with only the emergency lights illuminating everything. Just as it had been when Jacob first brought me here.

I looked both ways, expecting for some reason that Jacob would be waiting for me outside. But he wasn't there. I sighed and jogged toward the elevator.

The silver doors remained shut even after jamming my thumb into the down arrow almost a hundred times. I looked around for an answer to the inactive elevators but none were around. At the other end of the hall I saw an Exit sign and a stairwell sign lighting the wall in red and green.

The stairwell was darker than the hallway. The light from the signs above my head only reached so far and the stairs descended into a darker-than-black nothingness. I looked back at the door for a split second before plunging myself in.

Sight became nothing when the door closed behind me, and I could only feel the wall and the stair rail. Fingers touched chilled concrete and cold steel rails, and feet touched rough steps.

You never really understand the concept of blindness until all light is gone. I felt my eyes straining to find light, but there was none and I was literally blind. My sight was now through my hands, the little grooves in the concrete wall and the smooth texture of the rail were huge. My only existence was through those and the vague feeling of the floor though my shoes. I moved quickly, trying to find escape from this unnerving blindness.

I made my way down one whole flight and then felt along the wall. My palm touched the handle of a door and I pushed it open. I hoped this was the ground floor. To be honest I didn't really know how high up the building I was. I didn't know what I was walking into, but I really wanted it to be an easy way out.

I stepped out into a large room. The windows were heavily tinted over and only vague shapes could be seen. The room was as dark as everything else in the whole building that I'd seen. But this room was also different. A dozen or so desks were scattered loosely around the room. Each desk had a computer with a brightly lit monitor.

At first glance most of the monitors held information about things and people I didn't know. There were a few monitors with images casually scrolling across the screen. I walked across the room past little glass doors that lined the wall toward the elevator. Each step I took felt more dangerous than the last. My shoes squeaked loudly on the floor, and I couldn't help but flinch every time I could hear it echo around the room.

The glass doors along the walls led to more dark places.

I couldn't see much from my vantage point, but from what I could tell in the dim light they were only small rooms. Probably offices.

I reached the elevator and punched the down arrow. But the result was the same as the floor above. Nothing and no answer as to why the elevator was down. It's almost like Jacob left me in an abandoned building. I squinted at the little number above the elevator door. It was a three. There wasn't one on the floor above, leaving me with little knowledge about where I was or how far up. Now I knew that there were two more floors below me. I would just have to take the stairs the whole way.

A flash of red caught the corner of my eye. I stopped and stared at the source. One of the monitors was scrolling images of a girl. Willow. My heart quickened and I stumbled over wires to reach the monitor with Willow's face in it. They were pictures of everyday life. I recognized them as the few days leading up to her kidnapping. I was even in a few of them. But the real kicker was pictures of her after her kidnapping. There she was in the towns and places that Harry and I visited not long after her. Even after her kidnapping the Alliance had still been watching her? I know that we had gotten reports of their locations, but these images were close and numerous.

A sigh somewhere in the direction of the offices made me look up, distracting me from the questions rising in my mind.

I saw no one.

"Hello?" I asked cautiously.

A vent on the ceiling started blowing chilled air, and I let out a breath. Just the AC. I shook off the spooked feeling and tapped the keyboard connected to the monitor and computer. The screen flickered and Willow's face disappeared.

Words filled the screen. Reports, statuses, monitoring. I sat down in the chair and began to read. The Alliance had been keeping tabs on Willow for weeks prior to her kidnapping. Did they know that she was going to be taken? I moved, unfamiliar with the layout of the files, through the reports looking for answers.

...targeted by Isiro...matched as a host...is unaware of Isiroan intentions...

I stopped breathing at the next words I saw.

We have made the determination to let her be taken as a host.

I shuddered and stood up, my knees trembling. Some sanity was left so I could see that that last statement had been an order from 'The Council.'

...trying to determine who the Isiroan contact is...not the usual methods at play...no known Isiroans have made contact with the target....

"You're not supposed to be here." A voice rang out in the quiet room.

I jumped back from the computer and slammed into the one behind me. My throat clenched against a cry. Jacob was standing next to me. It took one look at the screen with Willow's information on it and then I felt fury.

"What the FUCK, Jacob! YOU KNEW. You knew they were going to take her and you just let them!" I grasped the screen and chucked it. It didn't go far, but it caused a lot of sparks. I kicked the desk and then fought Jacob's attempts to hold me back.

"Stop."

"Why should I? Huh? WHY SHOULD I!" The next nearest computer got the same fate as the first and then I stopped and sank to the ground in the middle of the chaos I had just caused. "Why should I?" I whispered.

"Look," Jacob began.

"I don't want to. You... everybody, you're all bullshitters." I leaned over my hands and pulled at the strands of hair caught in my fingers. The heel of my palm pushed the unneeded glasses against my face and I tore them off. Nick's fake glasses. I wanted to throw them. I wanted to remove the last of Nick's new image of me from my mind. But I couldn't. I pushed them back onto my face and pinched the bridge of my nose. I couldn't let go of the hope that new image had instilled in me.

"I'm sorry that you had to see that, Eugene." Jacob knelt

next to me and patted my shoulder. "But that wasn't my doing. It was the Alliance. The Alliance Council and Miriam Lancaster."

"You work for them," I accused, glaring at him.

"Yes... and no." He smiled.

"What do you mean?"

"That's for another day, Eugene." He stood and stepped back.

"Not later. Now!" I stood up and challenged the height difference between us. "I'm tired of all this smoke and mirrors shit you all seem way too fond of. I want answers, Jake, not these... these... lies."

"I have never lied to you, Eugene."

"Haven't you?" I refused to look up. I didn't want to see his mocking face, or even a stoic face--whatever incarnation my brother was putting on today.

"No. And it's unfortunate that it has to be now."

"What?" I peered up finally, and saw only concern. Genuine concern.

"That you realize that you can't trust anyone but yourself." He smiled at me, almost sadly.

"What about you? Should I trust you?"

"Yes. Because I am not just anyone, Eugene, I'm your blood. We stick together no matter what. I would only do what's best for you."

I lightly touched a fallen keyboard and looked up at my brother. He offered a hand to me. I clenched my fists and stood up on my own. "If you say so."

"Come on. You should rest some more. You have a long day ahead of you tomorrow."

As we left, I heard a sigh coming from the offices again. I looked back and a trick of the light made it look like a bent-over man peered at us from behind one of the glass doors.

Jacob dropped me off at the room with the lotus flower picture. My blanket was still strewn across the floor. I grabbed it and wrapped it around my shoulders. Jacob placed a folder on the desk and looked down his nose at me.

"Learn these. Don't leave this floor again." He left me

alone then and I sank to the seat of the couch. I was exhausted all over again. I let myself doze off, fitfully dreaming of far off things. I don't think I ever really slept. It was just a feeble escape from reality while my body fought to stave off the rising exhaustion.

It was about mid-day, with the sun so high in the sky I couldn't see it through the window. I shook off the blanket and stared groggily at the wall. The lotus flower picture had faded reflections of the room. I could see my face very vaguely in the after image. My hair stuck out all over the place and my eyes seemed sunken in. I rubbed the crusty seeds out of the corner of my eyes.

I opened the folder that Jacob had left me and found information. A huge map of the Laramie base and a thick stack of papers clipped together. The first page of the papers said: **Classified.**

The papers were a plan. Apparently a failed plan. The first page was a summary of the plan and why it had failed.

... infiltrate the base ... set beacon ... specialized artillery will hit the spot ... take out the emitter.

Plan was a failure ... no safe way to infiltrate ... suicide mission.

I frowned at that. Suicide mission? What the heck was Jacob getting me into?

The map was much bigger than the one Nick had given me and Harry. But most of the major aspects of it were the same. I even saw the place that Harry had pointed out as a good place to get in. A service road.

I dropped my finger from the point on the map and sighed. Harry had given me the idea, so did that mean it was a bad idea? I'm sure he would have tipped someone off that the service road entrance was a possible target. I stared down at the map and traced my finger all around it. I guess I wouldn't know what to really expect until I got there.

I was going to be fine. I knew it. I had to know it. I couldn't go into this place, BY MYSELF, without some kind of confidence. I just had be smart.

I studied the clearly hand-drawn map more and tried to

figure out what everything was. Some things were marked with obvious names but other things, like the five buildings named 'Ar,' pointed at the center of the map where a spiral was at the top of a hill.

Unfortunately, the only entrance was through the service road. And seeing as I was not a teleporter, and from the sound of the failed plan that came with the map I wouldn't have been able to anyway. So my way in was set for me. But the place that Jacob wanted me to go was marked with a star, and the place where I was supposed to find out about Willow-- well I didn't know that. I guess I would have to ask around, but that would raise suspicion.

I dropped the papers to the desk and rubbed my eyes. I would have to ask what Jacob wanted me to do about Willow if he was sending me off on some potential suicide mission.

I read over the plan a few more times over the course of the day, expecting Jacob to come swooping in with some fantastic plans and gear me up to be a superhero. But none of that came, and entertaining silly fantasies was just idle thought to fill the emptiness.

"If you think I'm just going to sit here and wait, then you underestimate me." I said to the door. I imagined my brother's face on the door. But even my imagined brother mocked me. I slapped my palm on the door and looked away. I trailed my hand down the door and grasped the door handle. A tug of the handle and I was squeezing out into the ever dark hallway. Jacob thought he could distract me with papers and plans. Failed plans no less. What kind of magic did he expect to get out of me from all of this?

I was downstairs again. The door on the bottom floor was still locked and the room beyond was inaccessible. No surprise there. I didn't feel entirely comfortable going back onto the third floor. The dark room with dozens of flickering monitors felt wrong somehow. But up there was the only other access to the elevator.

It seemed to me that my brother was less than happy to have found me there. But looking at the locked door now, I couldn't see any other choice but to try the room again. I dragged my feet up the stairs to the point where I was in front of the third floor doorway. I didn't move past it more than to put my hand on the door and listen to the sounds beyond. It felt quieter. I pushed open the door and peeked inside.

The room was empty.

The computers were gone. The lights were all on.

I stepped inside and frowned. The only thing left beyond the glass doors lining the walls were patchy spots on the linoleum where desks used to be and dust never touched. I made my way down to the elevator, passing the glass doors as I walked... and stopped. The door somewhere in the middle of all the others was covered in greenish black grime from the inside. I stopped at a room that wasn't lit up. The florescent lights were broken and the walls...the walls were covered in greenish black grime. It was smeared in angry swaths across the wall. I tapped the glass with my finger and the grime shuddered into sliding further down the glass. I backed up a step.   On the far wall the grime spelled out

M. GREY

...And underneath that was a set of slimy handprints.

"What the hell?" I asked aloud. ? Marcus Grey? Why was that written here?

I gulped and looked around for any explanation. There were none and I didn't want to stay around here anymore. I didn't know what my brother was doing here, and I really didn't want to find out. I jogged the last few feet to the elevator and didn't look back at the gunk covered door. I pressed a finger to the down arrow on the elevator and my heart skipped a few beats as silence resounded.

A ding of the elevator made my heart start beating normally again.

"Hell, yes," I crowed, and jumped into the elevator as the doors skimmed open. The doors closed firmly behind me and I triumphantly pressed the button for the first floor.

Nothing happened.

"PASSWORD?" A huge voice asked through a fist sized speaker above the door.

"A password... to go down?" I asked, incredulous.

"INCORRECT. PLEASE TRY AGAIN. FOUR OF SIX."

"Uh..." I searched all my memories for some kind of password my brother might have used, but I couldn't think of anything. "Alliance?"

"INCORRECT. PLEASE TRY AGAIN. THREE OF SIX."

"Shi..." I closed my mouth not daring to speak. The whatever of six had to be the number of tries I got before it exploded or something. Anything I said the speaker might pick up.

"PLEASE TRY AGAIN."

I wracked my brain but the more and more I thought the more and more I realized that I didn't really know my brother or the people he worked with. There would be no way for me to even think about what the password was.

I pushed the open door button and stepped out in the room. The elevator closed behind me and I kicked the metal door. It buzzed at me angrily and I stepped away. Machine or not I didn't know what would happen if it decided to blow up.

What would I do now? The door wouldn't open below and the elevator needed a flippin' password to go down. I searched the empty room, stepping over dusty runs in the floor. With nothing in the room, other than the creepy slime covered room, I had nothing to go on.

I kicked a pile of dust and it plumed into my face. Coughing, I stumbled toward the window and pushed it open. I sucked in a lung full of clean air and coughed out the bad. And then I saw my way out. A tree that grew alongside the building arched past the windows and a few thick branches reached close. I shook some dust out of my hair and vaulted up to the windowsill. I stood on the precipice and found my target.

I jumped and fell gracelessly onto a hard tree branch. The leaves scattered and trailed to the ground below. It was only then, with my arms and legs wrapped awkwardly around the branch, that I questioned my suicidal decision.

"Bad idea, Eugene." I said to myself and squirmed upwards toward the trunk of the tree. My arm scraped branch shoots, and with every spine scratching through my shirt, I let out a silent curse.

"Really, the things I have to do."

I reached the trunk with an exhale of relief. Sliding down was easier from there and within seconds I was hitting the ground at a sprint. I was out in the dry, warm air of the Denver metropolis before I realized it. I started down a cross street, and then zigzagged from one block to another. I felt like I was probably being followed, so I didn't stop running until I was so confused about where I was that I was sure anyone else would be too. I had to stop only when my lungs protested and I had to halt in the shade of a tree some dozen or so blocks away. I watched behind me, expecting my brother or one of his goons to come after me.

I found a small grassy area in-between two buildings and fell into an exhausted heap. I told myself to not fall asleep, but I was tired. I had done so much running. Running after Willow and running away from others. I closed my eyes against the tart sleepiness behind my eyes.

I felt my body finally shaking. I shook my head against the weariness and pushed myself to my feet. I had to keep moving. Even a few minutes of rest would lead to recapture. My brother's promises of help were not any consolation to me. He seemed no more willing to help than Lancaster had been. No more than Harry turned out to be.

I was on my own and I was not afraid.

HARRY GLEESON

Was it minutes? Or was it hours later? Either way, they dragged me out of the van once we reached their intended destination but didn't take the hood off. It was disorienting and I kept tripping over my feet, but I used that to my advantage and bawled like a baby when I fell to the ground for the fifth time. I had managed to work myself up enough that tears were actually beginning to leak out of my eyes. The men kicked at me and shouted for me to get up, but I curled in on myself and let them drag me to my feet.

"Please don't kill me! I'll tell you whatever you want!" I shouted. The sack around my head got plastered to my face and I had to shake it to get it out of my mouth and nostrils. It was a struggle to breathe through the thick fabric.

"Ha ha, easy pickings!" one of them said. A hand grabbed a whole handful of my shirt and dragged me into a building. The grabbing hand also got part of the hood choking me as my captor dragged me along.

I could only really tell we went from outside to inside because of the ambient noises. Outside there were birds and inside there was the sound of doors opening and closing. I couldn't tell how far or in what directions we went, but eventually they threw me to a cold concrete floor and ripped the hood away, taking a few strands of hair with it. The bright lights seared my eyes for all of a minute, but by then my escorts had shut the door on the cell. The cage stood in the center of a huge room the size of a warehouse. Another cell was connected to mine but separated by bars. There were other cells, double cells scattered throughout the room. But it appeared that I was the only occupant. I let out a deep breath and saw it puff in front of my face. The room was frigid. I shuddered and desperately wanted to wrap my arms around my chest.

I heard my escorts leaving, laughing the whole way out. Once they disappeared through a small door along the wall, I was left with the echoes of my footsteps and the subtle creaks of the structures around me. They had left my hands in shackles, so any hope of using my powers to escape went away in a split second.

Kinetics more advanced than I could pull the moisture out of the air, without the use of hands to direct, but that level of mastery was a little beyond me. I still needed a reservoir and they had probably picked the driest place in the facility. There wasn't a sink or toilet in the cell and no drains nearby either. What little I would be able to pool from my own sweat wouldn't be enough to do the kind of damage I would need to break free, much less to get these shackles off.

I took the following few minutes to study the bars of my cell. There was a bit of frost collected on the bars, but again, it wasn't significant enough to create the kind of water reservoir I would need.

There was a wiring box on one corner of the cell that led me to believe that the cells could be electrified. I didn't like the implications of electrified cells. I had some slim chance of jimmying the locks, but if I screwed that up even once and got caught they could electrify the cell and remove any chance of escape.

It was go big or go home. I sat down in the middle of the room and tried to adjust my shackled hands in such a way that wouldn't hurt. My arms were well past sore from being pulled behind my back for so long. I shivered the first of many and settled in for a long night.

CHAPTER 24

*"I feel as if I were a piece in a game of chess, when my
opponent says of it: That piece cannot be moved."*
— Søren Kierkegaard

EUGENE YOSHIDA

I walked down a main road in the heart of Denver, rubbing at the little scratches on my arms. Cars and buses passed at a dizzying pace. A few of the people I passed stared at me but most went about their business without giving me more than a second glance. I'm pretty sure I looked like some kind of crack addict with my ripped clothes covered in dust and my shoes looking dog-eared.

I peered at myself in the reflection of a window and shook my head. My hair was disheveled and sticking to the sweat on my forehead. The glasses that Nick had given me were blurry and covered with fingerprints. My clothes looked even worse in my reflection than they had when I looked over myself without it. My shirt was torn in a half dozen locations and my jeans had rips up and down my legs. How was I going to get to Laramie now, looking like a dusty street rat?

I shook off some of the dust and tried to make my hair not look like a birds nest. I cleaned the glasses with the corner of my shirt but the cloth was dirty enough that it didn't make the glass any better. I shrugged and put the glasses in my pocket. My reflection looked a little more like me, but not. My eyes were sunken in, and my cheeks looked like they had lost some roundness.

I pressed my hand to the glass and blocked my view. It didn't matter anymore.

I set off at a walk again wandering the streets trying to

figure out what to do. I had been in this position before. But back then I had been wandering the streets of my own city, and I had ended up at the house of one of my friends. Here I had no friends, and my brother was not going to do me any favors.

I watched my feet walk but I didn't really pay attention to where I was going. The streets were filled with people and cars going about routines and fulfilling plans with their friends, family, coworkers. It wasn't enough that I was lost and alone. I was lost and alone surrounded by people with plans and destinations. I had a destination. But how to get there?

Up ahead I saw a man leaning on the hood of a yellow minivan. Thick black letters spelled out "TAXI" on the hood and the doors. The man was chewing on a well-worn cigar and flipping through a magazine. An idea began to form in my mind.

"Hey!" I called out the man.

He looked up and peered at me over his glasses. "Hey, yourself. Need a lift?"

"Yeah. How far north can you take me?"

He glanced at his watch. "I can get you as far as Fort Collins. But the real question is, can you pay?"

"Yup," I lied, and patted my empty back pocket.

He jerked his head at the cab and grinned. "Get in."

I looked around for a moment, feeling the hair rising on the back of my neck. No one was looking at me, but the sudden feeling of being watched didn't go away. I took a deep breath and followed the guy into the cab. We drove through the streets, and I avoided looking at the meter ticking upwards. Whenever we got to Fort Collins, I was going to have to make a run for it, so I had to know where I was going. In the mean time I could rest a bit. It gave me time to plan.

After I was out of the cab, I would probably have to hitchhike the rest of the way into Wyoming. I'd never done anything like it without Harry, but really it couldn't be harder than sticking my thumb out, right? I know I didn't want to repeat the mistake with the RV dude back in Roswell, but without any money it was going to be hard to—

I saw only a single headlight as the truck blindsided the

cab. I wasn't wearing a seatbelt so I hit the other side of the car with a resounding crash. Glass clawed through my arm and a corner of the metal from the top of the cab speared downwards and sliced a huge gash along my temple. I groaned and tried to find my bearings. Everything was upside down, and I could see the cabbie latched in his seatbelt, hanging awkwardly. I saw pavement at the top of the windshield.

"Oh, God," I croaked.

The cab shook and I felt hands pulling me out. My eyes closed and I was left with blackness.

Very few times did I realize that by the time I was 15 I would be part of a world falling apart. Willow walked on the edge of the rhythmic waves from the sea. I walked beside her and felt the grains of sand tickle my toes. *I think I hoped to be part of something beautiful and growing. But things are neglected and I'm uncertain now... can I raise a sapling into a redwood?* She stopped and picked up a small shell in the sand and then put it into my palm. *They say you have to be careful what you wish for.*

I smelled medical alcohol. But the sharp smell was only an annoyance. There was something I wanted to go back to. A dream I wanted to dream. There was softness and warmth that brushed away the pain and the sadness, the fear and the loneliness. The sharp smell stung my nostrils. I felt a resounding ache everywhere, deep into my bones, deeper into my soul. I sucked in a breath and let it out.

"It's about time you woke up, Eugene." a voice said.

I rolled over and opened my eyes to see Jacob sitting on a white wicker chair. "What?" I asked. I was lying in a bed, in a sterile white room with few decorations.

"You were in an accident," Jacob continued. "You should have been wearing a seatbelt. This wouldn't have happened."

It wasn't clicking in my head. "What?"

"I had some of my men wreck the cab you were in. You should know better than to have run off. I was going to help you," he smiled.

"Not fast enough," I whispered. The fog over my mind was lifting. My chest hurt.

"These things require patience." Jacob leaned over his knees and rested his elbows on them.

"I don't have time to be patient." I tried to stretch out my legs but felt a constriction.

"If you don't have time, then you should have stayed home," he grinned, shaking his head.

"Stop it!" I screamed and tried to left hook him in the face. I only fell out of the bed, twisting my wrist in an odd angle.

Jacob sighed and stood up. "You're much too volatile, Eugene. But you're fortunate that I can help you now. If only you would have waited. Involving unnecessary people gets them killed."

I pushed up off the ground. "What do you mean?"

"Your cab driver was killed in the crash." Jacob looked down at me and smiled.

I gulped. "You killed him! You caused the crash!"

"Nope. It was you. Your fault." He stepped over me and out the door.

I slammed my fist into the floor. "Shit...no."

Jacob poked his head back through the door. "By the way, I was on my way to tell you before you pulled a Houdini that you got your wish. You're going to go in. But you go alone."

"Whatever," I said, pushing myself up.

He smiled and twinkled his fingers at me. "Rest up!"

***

Every day I hope that things will get better. That we will recover from this horrible place that we've been placed in. It wasn't us who put us here. It was the ones who came before. The fools of the human race who dared to allow themselves to be drawn in with honey laced words of false promise.

Willow stood on the edge of a boat staring out at an endless sea, the water reflected her amber eyes. The only thing

beside the boat was a barren island. The boat was heading right for it. *Eugene... You must help us...*
Help me...

HARRY GLEESON

The men came for me the next morning. I had expected this. Part of me was ready for whatever torture tactics they might use, even though I had only read about Alliance-specific tactics in my dad's books. But another part was frightened. I latched onto that fear, and for the sake of what little information I had about my people, I was ready to use that fear as a shield.

When the men grabbed me and roughly woke me from sleep, I was disoriented. I couldn't remember where I was, and it took me a second to remember my game plan. My thoughts were slow and chaotic. I knew from the chill in the room that I was probably starting to get hypothermia. I had to make this quick or I would probably die here.

I screamed and shouted, and after a minute of debate with myself while they dragged me kicking and screaming past the empty cells and into a hallway off to the side, I emptied my bladder. My stomach was happy about it, but my dignity in front of my would-be torturers was now at an all-time low. I just gave them ammunition that would have no real effect against me while I diverted attention away the real issue.

I shook my head to try and clear away the leftover grogginess and tried to make sense of the twisting and turning hallways that the two men were dragging me through. Vaguely I heard them already berating me about peeing on myself. I shrugged off their words and tried to concentrate only on my surroundings.

One of the men was looking at me with suspicion in his eyes, so I let out a wail that would probably make a police siren jealous. The guy pulled back his arm and smacked me across the face. The sting resonated through my whole body, shocking me into silence.

"Shut up if you don't want to die!" he said, and pulled me the last few steps into a room that was as hot as the room with cells was cold. They shoved me down on a stool in front of a table and took my hands out of the shackles. They weren't free for long. One of the men took one of my hands and pressed it down to the table. He flicked his fingers and the metal of the table sprang up around my wrist. They left the room. I swallowed and shuddered even though it wasn't cold anymore.

"What do you know about Willow Patterson?" a male voice rang out across the room. I looked around. There was no mirror to indicate a hidden room with a one-way window, and there weren't any cameras. I was at a loss at how they could see me, but I guess that wasn't important.

I let out what I hoped was a convincing sob and through it I said, "She's a classmate."

"What else?" the voice demanded.

I glanced around again, but there was still no way to tell how he could see me. "She was kidnapped!"

"What is she to you?" At first the voice had seemed to come from the front center of the room right in front of me, but now it was off to the left. It then dawned on me that the interrogator was not in another room but in the same room with me.

Invisibility.

Of course.

Something slammed into the table and suddenly I felt a jolt run through my whole body. On the table I could see sparks dancing across the table around the distinct shape of a hand.

Electrokinesis too?

The hand and the jolt disappeared. I could still feel the electricity running through my system. I didn't like where this was going. The two men who dragged me in here came back with what looked like a zombified defibrillator.

I sucked in a breath. "You don't need to do this! I'll talk!"

They laughed and the real torture began. The invisible man didn't speak again, and the other two never spoke. They didn't ask me any questions. Instead they walked in circles around me, ridiculing me on everything from peeing my pants to my appearance to my mother's bedroom activities. And when they didn't get a response from me, the guy with the defibrillator would press it to the table, electrifying the table and me with it.

I don't know when my fake tears turned real. I don't know when I actually started pleading with them that I would tell them everything I knew. I don't know when it finally ended, but forever would not have lasted as long.

They dragged me back through the halls that I didn't pay attention to anymore, back into the super chilled cell room and threw me into a heap on the floor of my cell. They never put the shackles back on, but at this point I didn't care anymore. My game plan to act weak became a reality all too soon. I couldn't even think about escaping anymore. It took too much energy to even blink. An escape would take years with what little I was running on.

How much time has passed? The second day went much like the first. The third like the second. And on and on. They never asked any questions. I was only vaguely aware of the hunger pains in my stomach. When was the last time I ate or drank? They never let me near any water, and even now the cold seeping through my bones in the cell room and the overwhelming heat in the interrogation room was too much to keep up with.

It was just another sensation, I told myself.

CHAPTER 25

"Being deeply loved by someone gives you strength,
while loving someone deeply gives you courage."
— Lao Tzu

EUGENE YOSHIDA

Rest up I did. I had no choice with a broken leg. The room where I had found myself was in an Alliance Hospital, or "Healer's Rest," built into the side of an unassuming office building. In the distance I could see the tall buildings of Denver rising above a line of trees along the horizon line. We were quite a few miles from Jacob's office, but I didn't know the exact location. The Healers were tightlipped about where we were. They barely spoke at all when I saw them.

I was stuck with a cast wrapped around my leg, and told to not leave the little hospital bed. I tried to stand up once but only got as far as the window. I tested the window frame, but it wasn't meant to open. The door was too far away, but I didn't expect that I would get far with a cast hindering my leg.

There was no TV, no books, nothing to keep me entertained in the droning quiet.

I spent a lot of time sleeping, drifting in and out of dreams that made little sense and less connection to reality. Willow floated through my dreams, telling me things with muffled words and foggy images. I always grasped out for her in the dream, but the waking world met my reaching hand instead.

Part of me didn't want to trust that Jacob was going to keep his word, but his three-times daily visits kept me on my toes. He sat with me, bringing my breakfast, lunch and dinner on a little puke-green tray and quietly read from a book.

I didn't want to talk to him, so I didn't.

Even with Jacob or the Healer coming in to check on me periodically, the room was quiet. The walls and windows were soundproofed and besides the AC whispering through the vent, I was alone with the sound of my breathing.

Waiting was painful, and yet I could do nothing now. I was pretty sure Jacob was having the Healers wait until the last moment to heal the break in my shin bone, so that way, even if I did find a way out, there would be little distance to go before my body gave out.

On the third day of my bedridden incarceration, Jacob finally broke the silence between us.

"It's almost time. And I have a few things that I need to talk to you about."

I tilted my head at him. I didn't feel like taking the energy to form words yet.

"In about two days I'm going to have you teleported to just outside the limits of the Isiroan base in Laramie. While there you have the freedom to do whatever you want on one condition."

"Condition?" I ventured.

"Yes. When you have found what you need, I want you to set off this beacon." He held up a small black device no bigger than a cell phone. The little red display on the top read: Inactive.

"Beacon for what?" I held my hand out.

Jacob dropped it into my palm. "This will allow us to zero in on your location and subvert their shield tech. All we need is that secure location to teleport in."

"That it?" I asked, incredulously.

He smiled. "Yes, very easy stuff. Even for you."

I frowned at him.

"I can't give you much else to help you, because if you are caught, then it will lead them to us." Jacob stood up from the wicker chair and started toward the door.

"Why couldn't you guys do this?" I muttered, turning the little device around in my hands.

"I never said that we couldn't." Jacob looked down at me. "This kind of thing is dangerous and if someone gets caught, then it could mean all-out war."

"And what they did, stealing Willow, wasn't?" I snarled, dropping the device to my lap.

"It's politics, Eugene," Jacob shrugged.

"Politics?" I pushed myself up, silently cursing the lump of cast on my leg.

"Accept it for what it is, Eugene. You're not experienced enough to really know what goes on behind the curtain."

"If you say so," I muttered.

He went to the door and talked to someone on the other side, and then retook his seat next to my bed. "I'll have the Healers come in and fix that leg of yours real soon."

"Thanks, you're so generous." I snarked.

"What are brothers for?" He smiled and reopened his book.

True to his word, the Healer came in a half hour later, and with the touch of a hand and some concentration, the break in my leg was gone.

I muttered obscenities under my breath. Jacob really was holding off until the last moment. Well, at least I was getting what I wanted. Willow's location was in sight.

***

We left the Healer's Rest, which turned out to be an office park surrounded by trees and pavement. The only noteworthy thing about it was the man I saw waiting on the curb outside the main doors of the Rest. His hair was stringy and greasy. He was dressed in a clean day-glow orange jumpsuit with silver cuffs around each wrist and ankle.

Even through the curtain of hair over his face I could still see his eyes. They were bright and furious with the men around him. They pushed him into a windowless white van, and as the door closed, he grinned blackish teeth at me. I shuddered but didn't have long to witness the departure of the van when Jacob grasped my shoulder firmly and led me in the opposite direction.

"Who was that?" I asked. He seemed... familiar somehow.

"A volunteer." Jacob replied easily and winked.

"For?"

"It's not time for 20 questions, Eugene. Let it be." He let go of my shoulder and shoved me in the direction of his car.

"Fine," I muttered. I knew little of what Jacob did in the Alliance. Whoever that man was, I didn't believe my brother's easy explanation of him. But really, what did it matter? Only Willow mattered right now.

We took a short drive into the far suburbs of Denver and it occurred to me to ask why we weren't teleporting.

"Because teleporters are in short supply. They are not our personal hover crafts."

"Oh. So..." I decided not to ask the question, but Jacob beat me to it anyway.

"And only the Isiroans have the capability of mimicking the power."

"Really?"

"We're hoping to change that soon. Soon we will all be on equal grounds."

I didn't know what to say after that. The longest conversation with my brother in years ended quietly.

We pulled into the driveway of a three story mansion some twenty minutes later. Jacob pulled the car into an empty garage spot and parked. I reached to undo my seat belt but he stopped me.

"Wait for it."

I looked around and then suddenly the ground shook. The car sunk into the ground, and when I looked out, I saw that we were in some kind of glorified Ferris wheel of cars. The floor dropped a few dozen feet and stopped at a platform.

Jacob led the way out onto the platform and pulled me by my shirtsleeve into a hallway. The featureless hallway led into a room with another platform. This platform was raised, and surrounding it was a circle of men and women at computers. Each of them was talking or tapping away on keyboards.

A slight swoosh of air redirected my attention to the platform where a man and a woman popped into existence.

"Welcome to W.S.389. This is one of many way stations where we are safe to teleport to and from," Jacob said like a proud father.

"Interesting."

"Wait here." Jacob said and left to talk to one of the women at the computers.

Beyond the computers was a set of black windows. I stared at them, trying to see if there were any people behind the glass, but they were far too dark. One way windows.

Jacob came back and waved at me to follow him.

We met up in a different part of the mansion, which really didn't look at all like a mansion on the inside, with a man named Brown. He wore the tan Alliance uniform, very U.S. Navy in color and shape, but unless you knew what you were looking at, you wouldn't know that it wasn't the same.

Brown took one look at me and scoffed. "Are they really sending babies into the field now?"

I opened my mouth to retort, but Jacob took hold of the back of my neck and made me stop.

"He's a special case," Jacob laughed congenially.

"Special? Ha. Gotcha." He grinned at my brother.

Something passed between them, and I think I was the butt of it. I frowned at the both of them.

"Anyway, kid, you know where you're going?" Brown snickered

"Kinda." I looked at Jacob for confirmation. His expression never wavered from muted amusement.

"Well, look here." He pointed out a map of the world on a screen near the back of the room. "Find me the location."

I touched the screen where I thought Wyoming might be and the screen zoomed in toward it. I stepped back, startled, and then growled under my breath at the other two laughing at me.

"Oh, yeah, forgot to mention. Touch screen." Brown gave me a shit-eating grin.

I shook my head and tapped closer to Wyoming. Titles of states and then towns appeared over the terrain. And then as it zoomed closer, I saw names in bright colors, some red, some blue and some green. Some were labeled 'I,' some 'A' and others blank.

I found out fairly quickly that the red spots were Isiroan bases. I found the one and only one in Wyoming, appropriately placed smack dab in the middle of the Laramie Mountains.

"There," I said, pointing to the location.

"Er..." Brown started, but Jacob waved him off.

"Alright. I'll leave you to it, Eugene, Mr. Brown. Eugene? Keep your nose clean."

That was the closest he had ever come to telling me to stay safe. I accepted it, and with a thanks I waved as he walked away.

"You're stupid to go there."

I glanced at Brown.

He shrugged. "Just saying. Come on."

Brown led me back to the huge platform with all the computers around it and directed me to stand in the middle of it. He spoke to a man near the edge of the platform who stood at something like a conductor's platform and tapped at unseen buttons. The man nodded at Brown as he left to join me at the center of the platform.

"Ready?"

I nodded. *More than ready*, I thought.

Within seconds the world around me dematerialized. I felt thin air blowing through me, shattering my being like glass. I didn't have enough time to think about the rest of the odd conflicting sensations before I felt a whole set of new sensations. My body started to congeal and then all of a sudden I felt like a pile of rocks trying to become a boulder. Seconds after that, I was left with nothing more than myself, staring very intimately into the dirt.

"Whoo! First time teleporting?" Brown asked from above my head.

"Guess so," I replied, pushing myself up off the ground.

Brown pointed toward where the sun was falling into a

cup of mountains. "Follow the sun for about 15 minutes and you'll find the base. I highly suggest you wait until after dark to try and get in. But they have a lot of eyes anyway, so you're probably shit caked either way."

"Thanks," I frowned

He shrugged. "Toodles," he said and poofed off in the breeze.

I stared at the spot where he had been and then started walking toward the sun. It felt like only the first step in a journey of a thousand miles.

I took a deep breath and followed the compass and the faraway lights toward the Laramie base. With any luck I would be able to get into the base before dawn.

The trip took me about an hour. It was only a two mile walk, but the dense shrubbery and the uneven ground made the trip about ten times as hard. I stopped just at the two mile mark just inside the line of trees that surrounded the Laramie base. In front of me was a sheer cliff that dropped off into a river.

I sat on the edge of the cliff in a fairly discreet position behind a rock that stuck out of the side like a huge pimple and examined the Isiroan base. All the buildings were made from earthy stucco and looked more like they belonged to a period piece movie on the Aztecs than a modern day city. Even so, a large satellite dish adorned the tops of the highest of the buildings, each pointing in a different direction, breaking the illusion of a trek back in time. At the center was a tall, more modern style building with dark glass windows.

But the strangest part of the town wasn't its Aztec-styled architecture; it was the large structure on the only hill in the middle of the valley. It looked like the monument at Stonehenge, except Stonehenge didn't have triangular overhangs reaching inwardly from each of the pillars. It was too far and too bright out to see any details, but the ground in the center of this Isiroan wonder looked like it was glowing.

Surrounding the base was a large circular levee-type structure, on top of which was a fierce-looking fence with watch towers spaced at regular intervals. The fence climbed up the side of a hill and each end halted at a large building halfway up one of the valley mountains. I pulled out some papers from my pocket and sifted through them for one of the maps.

The building up the mountain was titled 'HEOG,' or 'High Energy Output Generator' Jacob had explained to me that all the titles on this map were not the actual names of the structures but merely notations on certain characteristics. The only one that was properly titled was the Isiroan Teleport Booster. That was the Stonehenge-looking thing on the hill in the middle of the base. I moved my index finger along the line of the roadways and found the supply entrance. It wasn't too far from here.

I crawled to my feet and slipped into the trees to find a sheltered spot to hide out until darkness. If what Jacob said was true, then all I needed to do was to wait for the right moment to strike. And that moment would be at night when there were few awake.

I found a low branched tree and climbed up it to sit in a cradle of tree limbs. I was far enough up that I could see the majority of the base in great detail.

I was confused, however. With all the information that Jacob had given me, they obviously knew quite a bit about the Isiroans. Why then did they never attack? Why was Willow initially abandoned to these people? Could our army be so depleted that we couldn't even pull off a simple rescue?

Then what was I thinking? How could I do this? I am not some super soldier. I couldn't even *use* my powers if I wanted to in the first place. I felt my stomach roil in protest, and a headache pounded at my skull relentlessly. I clutched the bark of the tree branches underneath me, feeling like I was about to fall headfirst into the leaf-covered undergrowth.

I had never been afraid of heights. Willow and I used to climb countless trees in our early childhood, and I never had a problem being inches or yards above the ground. Now, I found myself dreading the distance between tree limb and ground. The jump meant one thing: the continuation of my journey into alien territory. I wanted nothing more than to go home and envelop myself in my thick blankets and forget about the world.

Willow was my only anchor here. The only reason to stay was for her sake. I didn't need to prove anything to my brother. Who cared what he thought was acceptable behavior. I was my own person. And yet, the distance seemed to only get wider. My fate, my future, rested on a successful mission. Willow's safety rested on my successful mission.

I forced myself to look away toward the east and stare at the oncoming darkness. That darkness would be my salvation and my sentence. Soon I closed my eyes and tried to think of things that wouldn't make my heart beat so fast -- things that would make the waiting game easier.

I hadn't been aware that I'd dozed off until I heard something snap and I was startled out of a light doze. I steadied myself on the tree limb and listened intently for any more noise. The only sounds were those that naturally belonged to the forest. I sat rigidly and didn't move a single muscle until I was sure that there was no one around.

It was dark now.

The base was alight with hundreds of shining orbs. I still couldn't see enough detail to make out people, but I was sure I saw movement under the glow of lights.

Looking around once more, unsettled by the sound of that snapped twig, I checked my watch and climbed out of the tree.

CHAPTER 26

"If hiding was something I was good at, I would not be on the front lines facing them. I would be behind them, taking the enemy out with honeyed words and poisoned daggers." –
Karasemmara, Leader of the Isiroan Militia. 1204.

I scaled the small cliff face and dropped to the ground with a huff. The fence of the Isiroan base was about ten times more intimidating from the level ground than from the top of the cliff, rising up over the rest of the earth on a sturdy, but sharply angled hill. It looked like a levee with a tall alien fence crowning its top. From here I could even hear the low hum of the electricity coursing through the entire structure; the sound was unnerving.

I slid down the edge of the river into the ankle high water that flowed through the river bed, which I hadn't realized until now, was made entire of concrete. It looked more like a storm drain than a natural river. The supply road that supported the base lay parallel to the river. A narrow bridge breached the gap of the unnatural river and was hardly wide enough to support much more than a wide SUV. A gate pierced the side of the wall and fence with tall, steel doors that rose all the way up the vertical height of the fence.

I crouched low and looked in every which direction to make sure I wasn't going to be seen running through the water. Ducking into the small cylindrical tunnel that allowed water to pass under the concrete bridge, I waited for any unnatural sounds and continued on my way through it to the other side. Not much further away, I saw a large halved oval cut in the side of the fencing through which the water of the river flowed into the base.

From here it looked like you could enter the base through the ovoid tunnel, but, as Jacob had already warned me, it was guarded by something. It was supposed to be like a laser fence of some sort. I quickly wrote that off as an alternative. My priority was to wait for a supply truck which was usually supposed to come around 1:15 a.m.

I checked my watch. It was only 12:48 a.m. I still had almost a whole half an hour to wait.

"When the truck pulls up," my brother's voice intoned in my head, "that's the best and only time you'll get to sneak into the truck. We know that the driver will get out and open the doors to the cargo and then go back to his seat. You'll have anywhere from between five to fifteen minutes to get into the cargo. Stay hidden. Their sensors will not see you."

I found some secure footing just outside the water flowing through the waterway. The stream was hidden under the shadows cast by the bright floodlights, and then I waited. I don't think I ever liked the idea of waiting here. It made the possibility of changing my mind easier. I didn't want to change my mind. For Willow's sake and for my own.

I rested my head on the cool concrete and breathed in the midnight air. All too soon I would be at the point of no return if I hadn't already reached it. To turn back now would only mean that I would have to walk for miles and miles just to reach normal civilization. Plus I would be overtly abandoning Willow, just like the Alliance had. I would never stand for that.

A loud honk startled my adrenaline into action and my footing turned out to be not as secure as I thought it was. I slipped on some green, mossy slime buildup and fell with a very ungraceful splash into the water. I sat stock still with the chilled water soaking through my clothing and waited for the telltale sounds of discovery.

It never came. Instead I heard another honk. I scrambled to my feet and slid back into the darkest shadows. I saw headlights flare across the side of the steep hill and heard the loud obnoxious rumble of a diesel engine. The truck was early. 15 minutes early. I took a chance and craned my neck and body around the bridge and saw the large semi-truck towering over me. I snapped my head back in just as the driver opened his door. He was whistling tunelessly.

I pressed myself into the wall and waited for a second for my adrenaline to calm down. I didn't wait long because I knew that this was my chance now. If I didn't take it, I'd never see Willow.

Careful to stay in the shadows I crept across the fake river and crawled on my stomach up the side. I would have skinned elbows after this. I saw the driver finish opening the back of the trailer and readied myself to jump out and hide myself in the back of the truck.

The driver whistled his way back to the cab of his truck and closed the door firmly behind him. I hoisted myself up and over the edge of the bridge and under the trailer of the truck. The sound of the entrance gate slowly unbolting itself was all the encouragement I needed to start moving faster. With a deep breath I crawled toward the back of the truck and pulled myself out by the rear bumper.

It was all dark in the back of the trailer and I could hardly see anything inside. I took one more breath and lightly hauled myself up into the back of the trailer. I felt around blindly for one too many seconds trying to find anything I could squeeze between or get under. I started to panic when I heard voices coming closer, talking jovially with the driver. And then-- there! I pushed myself between what could have only been huge sheets of wood. There was a space just big enough between the boards and the side of the trailer for me to fit my entire frame into. I pushed myself in as far as the boards would allow and then fumbled in my pack for the BodyHeat pills that I had been instructed to take as soon as I was in the truck. Apparently they were supposed to lower one's natural body temperature to the same level as the surrounding area. Almost the second that I swallowed the silvery pill, I felt all my extremities going numb. I wasn't sure at first how the pills were supposed to work, but I very quickly realized that the pills were artificially inducing hypothermia.

The boards hardly moved as my body began to shake

violently. What little I could see in front of me was starting to become part of a watery kaleidoscope. I clenched my jaws tight as my breathing became harder and harder to control. Stiffness stilled my shaking limbs and I curled in on myself.

Only a few more seconds.

I turned my eyes out to see through the small opening between the boards and the wall of the trailer. I saw some movement but my swimming vision made focusing an Olympic trial. I tried to interpret the movement that I saw and the faded voices that I heard.

A shadow. "We—nothing—early—"

Light. "—Come? We don't—"

Another shadow. "—Wait for—Ashwater—supplies."

The voices faded off and then I felt a great *bang* as the trailer doors were shut. With trembling fingers I reached back into my pouch and felt around for the second pill, the one that would return me to normal. The truck jumped as it started up and began driving. The sudden movement startled my already weak fingers, and I dropped the inky black pill that would make me warm again. I had no choice. Waiting for the next bump, I intentionally fell over onto my side and groped around in the dark for the pill I couldn't see. My fingers found it and I struggled to get it to my mouth.

Liquid warmth spread out from my very core just as the pill entered my system. I breathed in and out slowly, and with what little room I had, I flexed my sore and still muscles.

I was in.

I laughed to myself through sore vocal chords and pulled out of the space between the boards. The truck pulled to a stop and I heard more voices. Quickly I returned to my hiding spot and waited for the doors to open.

One minute.

Two minutes.

Five minutes.

Ten minutes.

Nothing was happening. The voices disappeared and I was left alone with the eerie noises of the cargo settling into place after its journey.

I waited in a tense silence for almost thirty minutes more. My only indication of passing time was the slow ticking of my watch.

After the pain of the Cold Pill, I wanted to find a bed and sleep. The warmth from the Hot Pill did little for me after it digested into my system, and the real cold of the night and the cramped trailer took hold. I don't know where I would be able to hide around the Isiroan base without attracting unwanted attention, but my main priority now was to get out and assess my next move. I shimmied out of the hiding spot and examined the locking mechanism of the trailer doors. It looked fairly simple enough. The manufacturers had obviously made it in mind with people being trapped on the inside.

I grabbed the rusty pin and pulled up slightly so as to not make any loud noises. The thing screeched loudly anyway. I cringed with every single creak and squeak of the pin and eventually got it all the way out. I had to undo the other one as well because one door wouldn't open without the other being unlocked. After both locking pins had been pulled up, I waited and listened for any sounds of people. Hearing nothing, I pushed open the doors and leapt out.

The truck had been parked behind one of the Aztec-styled buildings and nothing was around to indicate any more people. In the distance I saw a really tall building with lots of lights on.

I shook off all of my stiffness and crept around the truck to inch toward the backside of the Aztec building. The windows lining the side of the building were dark with only a few specks of light to be seen through the void. In one I could see through an open door that illuminated the inside of what looked to be an ordinary office.

The facsimile of normal life hurt like a brand. It was no wonder that they were able to pull so many innocents into their fold. It was also painful to know that all the people, the ones delivering the supplies like that truck driver and the ones who ran this base, were being horribly lied to. I shuddered with the thought that Isiro must be really powerful to have so many bend to his will like that.

Light flashed across the ground and I heard intense voices talking.

"I thought I heard something!" someone shouted.

"What did...? Hey! This thing is open!" another one yelled out.

I cursed under my breath and dove behind a large metal box behind the Aztec building. I had forgotten to close the trailer doors. Stupid! The air conditioning fan hummed loudly, blocking out the sound of my adrenaline-driven breathing. I made myself into the smallest ball that I could and waited.

"Jack probably forgot to close them all the way. It *was* his first time inspecting," one said.

"Yeah, but notify Mr. Nakhimov anyway," the other replied.

"Right."

The doors slammed closed and I heard the pins being pushed back into place.

I didn't let myself breathe normally until I was sure that the two people had left.

I stood up, brushed myself off and began looking for a place to hide out until I had a chance to catch my breath and try to ascertain where they had put Willow. This had been her last known location. For all I knew she could be halfway across the world by now.

The grounds surrounding the tall Aztec buildings were peppered with randomly placed flora. It was like they just built this place around a normal piece of forest and didn't think to remove the surrounding trees. Not that I had a problem with it. It afforded me a bunch more cover than what I had first hoped. I found my resting spot under a thick, thorny bush that grew from two sets of roots around a big enough crevice to squeeze into and see the layout of the base from the eye level of a mouse.

I searched through my pockets and pulled out the wad of papers that had all the information on them about the base. I sifted through the random maps and found a small list of the buildings. The tall one I had seen far off in the distance was unnamed. We didn't know what it was for. The Aztec buildings were all labeled as 'Administration.'

Administration usually meant files. Files meant information. And to me, information meant finding Willow.

I dug out the rest of my pockets and pulled out everything that could identify me as part of the Alliance. The maps for the base were pretty much useless. I could see everything around and everything was labeled with what we thought the purpose of the building or structure was.

I inspected the uniform I was wearing, it was missing many of the sewed on patches that I had seen others wearing. Apparently all Field Ops wore them. I had really only listened with half an ear as Jacob had described its purpose.

Finally I took out the beacon Jacob had given me and shoved it and everything else into a hastily dug hole. I shouldn't have anything on me that could indicate where I was from.

The branches of the bush around me scraped on my face as I wiggled out of the stranglehold of leaves and began making my way toward the Aztec buildings. I figured my best bet would be to infiltrate one of them and see what kinds of files they might have.

I was careful to avoid any of the patrolling guards as I pushed and pulled on every door that I came across. None of them gave way. Every single Aztec building was locked up tighter than a bank vault. Even forcing a window or a door open proved to be impossible.

I found a fairly out-of-the-way place near the furthest of the office buildings and sat in the quiet for a few minutes. My options were getting smaller and smaller.

It was only a matter of time before they discovered me anyway. I had nowhere decent to hide. Light from the flashlights of the Isiroan patrol scanned the ground and I quickly ducked my head behind the side of the building.

There were two of them and they were talking. "...coming in a few hours. It's going to get really busy," one of them said. She didn't sound happy about whatever was coming in.

"Great," the other one said. He didn't sound happy

either.

"I don't know how we are going to contain this breach the boss was talking about if we have to deal with a hundred teenagers wandering around breaking things," the woman scoffed.

"I still say we have nothing to worry abo..." The man's voice faded and I was alone again. I let myself breathe and stealthily made my way back to the bush where I'd buried all my papers.

HARRY GLEESON

I don't know when they stopped coming for me, but I probably went unbothered for almost two days. At some point they stopped feeling the need to shackle my hands so I was free to move about the cell. In that time I slept and tried to not think about the pain my body was in. Some part of my brain that wasn't fried yet was trying to formulate a plan to escape. What little of the facility I had seen wasn't enough to make a full picture of different routes in and out but it was a start.

One morning—or was it afternoon?—I sat up to the guards noisily entering the room with a greasy haired man in tow. He wasn't shackled like I was but held his head low like he was the most beaten and degraded man in the universe.

But under the mop of hair I could see a toothy grin. The guards popped open the cell next to mine and pushed the man inside. He stumbled to a stop and then turned to the men as they hastily closed the cell door and retreated out of the room.

He stood still for the longest time and it was only when I looked away from him did I hear him turn. When I looked back he was staring through the bars at me. The hair around his face was pushed back and I could see his face.

"M—Marcus Grey?" I asked. I had seen the man a few times in person, and of course in the pictures that Eugene and Nick had brought out. But this couldn't be him. The glint in his eye was a terrible thing to behold.

He grinned, black slime filled the tops of his gums making the otherwise white teeth look like they were rotting.

"I am not called Grey anymore. I am called Krino," he laughed and with every name he shouted louder. "I am called Thomas Reddinger, I am called Rainey Grey, I am called Idelfons Heilbronner... And most importantly I will be called Willow Patterson! And I am not my brother." The last he said at nearly a whisper.

As soon as he said that he wasn't his brother, I knew who this Marcus Grey lookalike was. *Matthew* Grey was the twin brother of the man that Eugene and I had been pursuing across the states.

Last I'd heard of his name, though, supposedly he had been killed at the facility where the Alliance Chief Thomas Reddinger had died. Any Kinetic up on their history knew the names of the people involved in that incident. It was the day that peace was supposed to bloom between the Anyan's Alliance and the Isiroan Legion.

But Matthew Grey, Thomas Reddinger and a handful of others had perished that day in a meaningless attack that to this day no one really knew the instigators of. Alliance blamed Isiroan and vice versa. At least, they were supposed to have perished. But here, living and breathing was Matthew Grey, calling himself 'Krino.'

I tried to not stare at him too much, but a realization was dawning on me. Eugene had said that the man who had taken Willow had long greasy hair. But the Marcus Grey I had always known of kept his hair cropped short to his head. I wasn't too sure about what Eugene had seen until now. Eugene hadn't seen Marcus Grey take Willow, he had seen this man, this Matthew Grey. At some point after Willow had been taken by Matthew Grey—Krino—there must have been a hand off or somehow Willow ended up with Marcus Grey.

I frowned as I tried to take in this new information. How did he fit into all this? If *Matthew* Grey took Willow and we've been following *Marcus* Grey across the States— There was more going on here than any of these little clues were letting on and it wasn't adding up.

When I got out of here—If I got out of here, I was going to have to investigate this further. More to satisfy my curiosity than anything. For now, I studied the openings on the bars and the various ways I could get out.

Krino ignored me for the most part and sat in a corner of his cell. He appeared to be counting the wrinkles in his hands.

I shook off the uncanny resemblance to one of the Isiroan Legion's most respected Kinetics and tried to figure out what to do next. Looking at the cell, escape might be easier than I first thought. In fact I could probably use that to my advantage.

It might be time for some reconnaissance.

KINETICS: In Search of Willow

CHAPTER 27

*"To know your Enemy, you must
become your Enemy."*
~ Sun Tzu

EUGENE YOSHIDA
Wrapped up in a tight ball beneath some tall bushes, I barely slept. The place was strange and there were too many noises in the deep shadows cast by the bright lights surrounding the base.

With morning came the inevitable trek across the open grass and concrete walkways to where I could see a large group of people. Even from the vantage point of my hideaway, I could see them milling around in the larger open area of the base grounds. One problem to getting over there was the large open area that spanned between here and there. The other was how I was dressed. This Field Spy uniform was useful at night to help me hide in the shadows, but during the day the black fabric stood out like a flashing beacon in the daylight.

I unzipped the jacket and stuffed it into a crook of roots. I was left with the pants and a plain white T-shirt. I was looking a little less conspicuous, but I wasn't sure if the Isiroans would recognize the make of the pants.

Laughter rang out from the crowd of teenagers, and I took one last breath before pushing myself up out of the bush. I rolled a story around in my head, trying to figure out what to say if someone asked what I was doing.

I was looking around and I got lost.
I was looking for the restroom.
I was looking for my lost pet rock.
Nothing else was coming to mind. My creative skills

weren't helping at all right now, and I didn't want to let my mind fall into a state of absurdity. Pet rock. Right.

I walked through the breezeway between two of the Aztec buildings and paused at the line where the shadow of the building next to me ended and the grass lit by the sun began. None of the people wandering around the middle of the grounds seemed to notice me. Instead they were focused on a man talking to them. He was standing on the edge of a small fountain speaking loudly without the use of a microphone or megaphone.

I used that moment where everyone was focused away from anything but the speaker and moved closer to the edge of the crowd.

"And to close, I would like all of you to follow Rosie," he pointed to a young woman standing next to him. "And she will start the tour of the base. Danny will be counting you as you go, so please line up in a single file." The crowd started a line from Rosie, and I just inserted myself into the line when my first chance came. As I passed Danny I saw him pressing his thumb on a little clicking device for every person that passed him. A counter. That worried me a little. If they had a specific count of the people, then maybe I would be ratted out because they had one extra person.

I kept my eyes open and alert as the long line of people and I were shown the base and each building was described in detail. Any moment now I expected to see the Isiroan operatives heading my way to drag me into a cell. But it never happened.

As we were passing a large building that turned out to be a residence hall for the base occupants, the group disbanded and I silently mingled among the other teens. All of them were happy and excited and ready to learn about being in the Isiroan army. These teens would one day be out on the literal and figurative battlefields in a few years' time. None of them seemed to be fully aware of the horror that would face them out there.

I sucked in a breath of air and wormed my way through the people toward the open grass. When the moment looked right I walked toward the side of the residence hall. It was shady here and much more quiet.

I had to get into one of those Aztec buildings. That was one of the few ways that I could find Willow that I was sure of.

"Excuse me?"

I looked up and there was a woman. Her dark hair was lightly streaked with white near her left eye, framing a lightly tinted cinnamon skin. She held herself evenly and moved like she was a cloud as she walked over to me.

"Yeah?" I said, cautiously.

"Are you feeling unwell?" She sounded very concerned, her mouth moving around the syllables with a lilting accent I didn't quite recognize.

"No," I blinked a couple times in surprise.

"You looked very lost. Are you homesick then?"

I shook my head. "Just... you know, getting used to things."

She smiled and nodded. "Don't worry. Everything will be alright after you settle in. It must be very confusing right now."

Yeah, "settle in." As in, be indoctrinated.

"Mom, could you help me out over here?" A dark skinned boy about my age with wild dreadlocks pushed his way through the crowd and came to stand next to the woman he had called 'mom.'

"Sure." She smiled at me then. "Take care."

The boy stared at me for a longish second and then pulled his mother away with him.

I nodded mutely and watched as they walked away. I shook off the uncomfortable feeling that was rising in my chest and pushed myself to my feet.

I skirted around the edges of the buildings and made my way back to the Aztec buildings. I tried the side door and was rewarded with it opening trouble-free. I glanced around and, seeing no watchful eyes, I slipped inside.

Unfortunately, this building turned out to not have any files whatsoever. It was actually a lab of some kind. There was a glorified chemistry set bubbling with clear liquids in one corner of the first room I looked in and lots of random pieces of broken machinery.

Every room that followed was much like the first with machines in various states of repair or disrepair and chemicals taking up one whole wall.

I growled in frustration and had to take a quick breather in one of the machinery rooms to calm myself down.

What would Willow say?

Anger is not the way.

Anger is only going to cause hurt.

I breathed in and out slowly and calmed myself.

Just move on to the next one, I reasoned with myself.

I checked my exit as I left the first of the Aztec buildings and headed toward the next. I had to back off though, because there was a small group of people crowded around the entrance and were in a heated conversation. I leaned against the edge of the building and waited, staring at the group, silently willing them to go away.

"Hey, you lost?" A voice startled me out of my stare. I whirled around to see the guy with dreadlocks from earlier standing behind me. He grinned and pulled me away from the door of the office building and led me back into the fray of people. "This is hardly the time for sightseeing!"

"I wasn't..." I started to speak.

"Hey, Roy! Found the last one!" he called out. He dragged me all the way to where another dark skinned guy, probably the same age as me and the kid with dreadlocks, was jotting down notes on a clipboard. He looked up with a displeased scowl and made a furious mark on his paper. The intricate crazy swirls of his cornrows seemed to reflect his current mood.

"Power?" the swirly-cornrows guy asked.

"What?" I asked, taken aback.

"Power. Power! What's your power?"

"Uh..." I stuttered.

'Roy,' the other boy had called him, deepened his frown. "Are you dumb or something?"

I glared at him. "No."

"Then answer the question so that I can go home!"

I considered lying for a second, but for all I knew they could test for that sort of thing. "P-pyrokinesis."

"What's your level?"

"Level?"

Roy looked like he was about to blow a gasket. "Proficiency level! What the hell? Have ya been living under a rock? First ya late and then..." His already surfer dude accent got thicker.

"Bro, chill." The kid with dreadlocks grinned and patted his friend's shoulder.

"Jack." Roy's voice was stern.

"Don't say my name that way. Are you my mother?" 'Jack' scoffed and waved dismissively. "Give me that." Jack grabbed the clipboard and grinned at me. "So, do you know your level?"

I shook my head. Jack just shrugged and jotted something down on the clipboard.

"What's your name?"

I considered lying again. It would be more valid than hiding my power. Who knows if they already knew my real name? If they got wind of my travel here, they might be on the lookout for a Eugene Yoshida. "Ah, Toshi. Toshi Yamada." Yamada was about as common a surname as Yoshida. They would have trouble tracking down my family if they went looking.

Jack nodded and clicked the pen so that the business end retracted. "It's kind of late but there's still time to go for the testing."

"Testing?" I asked before I could stop myself.

Jack nodded. "It's for people who don't know their level. That way we can put you in appropriate training."

"Oh, okay." I tried to smile but I couldn't put any feeling into it.

Jack punched Roy companionably in the shoulder and they led me toward one of the buildings that was covered in panes of tinted glass. I didn't speak at all while they bantered between each other.

So far they hadn't acted at all suspicious of me. It appeared that my segue into the base would go smoothly. However, I was somewhat uncertain about this testing thing. What would they do once they found out I was effectively a Vunjika?

I chewed on the inside of my lip and examined everything around me inside the glass paned building. Unlike the other buildings that I'd had a chance to enter, this one didn't have tons of doors lining its halls and it didn't have odd ball things spewing out of every room like the one with all the electronics in it. Instead this one had pastel, peach colored walls and soft lighting everywhere. Tall indoor plants decorated the corners that flanked small, cushy chairs in the lobby area. Not that there was much of a lobby. It was just a big seating area. There was no receptionist to greet us, and the two guys led me into a hallway that bisected the building and turned into a large room with a high ceiling.

The room had nothing in it. The floor was uncarpeted with the concrete base of the floor showing through. The walls were painted an off-white, almost gray color. No natural light breeched the walls into the room. There were no windows at all. All illumination came from the harsh, strict field of florescent lights adorning the ceiling. The air was light and cool, contrasting with the hard lighting and it smelled of freshly fallen rain.

The other two stopped in the center of the room and faced me.

"Just a moment, Toshi." Jack said and looked around the room with the gaze of a predator.

"What do you bet he went home already?" Roy muttered and looked even more displeased with the whole situation.

"Probably." Jack just smiled. "I have an ideeeeea."

"Oh, heck no." Roy seemed to know exactly what Jack's idea was and waved his hands back and forth in front of himself. "No, no, no."

I was completely in the dark.

"I've seen him do it thousands of times." Jack insisted.

Roy's mouth was set in a frown.

"I think not," a deep voice echoed in the large room. All three of us turned to see a tanned man entering the room from the hallway entrance. His long black hair was pulled back into a ponytail and white streaks burst out from his hairline. The thin lines on his face accentuated his harsh features. With his long brown trench coat billowing around him, he was more vulture than man as he zeroed in on us.

"Jack," the vulture man admonished him with his voice. The voice still echoed about the room ominously, but it was full of the warmth that his face didn't convey.

"Hey, Dad," Jack grinned at the man and poked my shoulder. "Was just trying to save you the trouble, that's all."

"Mmm." Jack's father raised his eyebrow and a small smile curled at the tip of his thin mouth softening his features enormously.

I stepped out of the way while the newcomer talked to his son and Roy.

Like his mother whom I'd met not that long ago, Jack's father looked of Indian descent. His voice was distinctly British sounding, unlike that of the woman I assumed was his wife. Jack had neither of their accents but instead had more of a casual northwestern American accent with a few odd nuances mixed in.

"Mr. Ashwater, we jus' had this slowpoke and we wasn't sure what..." Roy started to say, his surfer accent was gone, replaced by a thick southern accent.

Vulture-man waved his hand and then patted Roy on the shoulder. "I'll take it from here." He turned, looked me up and down and asked, "What did they explain to you about this place?"

"Er... something about testing," I shrugged, not sure what else to say.

He nodded as if that was more than enough. "My name is Kouric Ashwater. I am the director of this facility."

"Toshi Yamada," I said.

He stepped a few paces backward and tapped his foot firmly on the ground. A crack appeared in the concrete near his foot and spread out like a growing spider web to surround all four of us. I didn't see the pattern it was making until the cracks opened up, and a large circular device bloomed from the floor and settled into place around us.

I couldn't understand what the device was supposed to do and could only look to Ashwater for instruction.

And all of a sudden it hit me. *Ashwater.* I felt ice take a trip down my veins for a split second. These Ashwaters were probably related to the man who had been in the Alliance prisons with me. That's why the name was so familiar.

"Now," said Ashwater, as he opened up a control panel near his side of the device. "Stand in the middle and demonstrate your powers for us."

Jack and Roy stepped out of the circle made by the device and stood behind a sheet of glass that shielded them from the inside of the circle. Ashwater was already behind a sheet of glass from his spot next to the control panel.

I stared down at the dark circle under my feet and tried to figure out what to do. Even if I wanted to use my powers, I wouldn't be able to. I was a Vunjika.

Despite what Nick had said after my escape from the Alliance headquarters in Ohio, I still didn't believe that I'd used my powers like he had explained. The incident with the man and the RV was another story. I wasn't sure what was going to pop up on their screens.

Ashwater made a noise, and I jerked my head up to stare at him. He looked frustrated.

"Dad?" Jack joined his father at the control panel.

"Something's the matter with this thing. It's not even reading this young man as even being a Kinetic." Ashwater pressed a few buttons and looked confused.

I gulped.

"Maybe it's on the wrong setting?" Jack supplied.

I hoped none of this could identify me as someone from the Alliance. They would lock me up and then interrogate me and find out I was from the Alliance. They would probably kill me then, and I wouldn't ever be able to find Willow.

I felt an intense pressure at the back of my mind, and I

absently rubbed the skin at the back of my neck trying to massage the stress away. Heat flared out from my fingertips, and I was just barely able to get my hand away from my head. I didn't realize that I'd yelled out until I heard the rebounding echo.

I collapsed to my knees.

"Oops," Jack looked shocked.

"Jack, what did you do?" Ashwater stared at his son, shocked and confused expressions swirling across his face.

"I was just trying to see what his power was," Jack said, bewildered.

I rubbed the heat out of my fingers by pressing them to the cool skin of my forearms. A small tingling and heaviness followed after the heat had passed, and my hands felt like sandbags.

"He's a Vunjika!" Jack exclaimed. He looked almost happy at the idea.

I felt the same pressure building at the back of my mind again. But this time I knew what it was. "Get out of my he..." I yelled, but just like before, fire sprawled out of my fingers and I fell all the way to my feet.

I panicked and tried to crab-walk backward away from the fire that was clinging to the concrete. Every nerve in my body was molten fire.

The little flame went out, and I leaned against the side of the device breathing with rasping gasps.

"Not only that. He's afraid," Roy said. He spoke up for the first time. His voice was incredulous. He had been given a view of my face during the second outburst of flame.

Roy laughed in disbelief. "He's a Pyrokinetic who's afraid of *fire.*"

CHAPTER 28

"At the end of the day, it isn't where I came from. Maybe home is somewhere I'm going and never have been before."
~ Warsan Shire

I pushed myself up off the ground and wiped away the layer of sweat that had built up on my forehead. Roy was shaking with the effort of containing his laughter and was pounding on Jack's shoulder. Jack was half smiling, but his eyes were confused.

"How did you make it through the review process as a Vunjika?" Ashwater frowned.

I looked away from them, absently rubbing my hands on my pants. My heart pounded an increasingly frantic beat into my ribcage. If I said that I didn't go through any review process, they might kick me out. If I said that I did, they wouldn't believe me and they would still kick me out. I knew I was looking at them with a very frustrated expression.

A look of comprehension spread across Jack's face and he pointed at me. "You're the one who was sneaking around yesterday! I was wondering why I didn't remember seeing you on the transit bus."

It was then that I had an idea. I looked down at the ground and hunched my shoulders. "M-my parents had me go through the review process and when I didn't make it... they..." I closed my eyes in what I hoped looked shameful. "They wouldn't let me come."

The three of them were quiet for a moment, and then Ashwater cleared his throat and patted the two other guys on the shoulders. "Why don't you two go and see what your mother is making for dinner." The two nodded slowly and walked away, glancing at me out of the corners of their eyes, Jack's with comprehension and Roy's with animosity.

Ashwater crossed his arms across his chest and stared down at me. His dark eyes revealed no emotions and they studied me with great intensity. I looked away from his gaze and stared down at the cold floor.

"It's okay to be a Vunjika. Your journey is just going to be much harder than the rest of our trainees," he finally said.

I nodded but didn't dare to look up. I remembered Nick had said that most Kinetics had a tendency to see people like myself as being disabled in some way. Being a Kinetic but unable to use your powers is like having no limbs for some.

"But, I'm confused. Our machine should show that you are a Kinetic no matter what your level of training." Ashwater walked over to the console of the machine and began tapping at the buttons. "I apologize for my son. He gets overexcited sometimes about people. I don't know what possessed him to use his powers on you."

I didn't have anything to respond, so I stayed quiet and watched Ashwater work. He was different than the old man I had met in prison. He held himself upright and his chin always pointed outward and never in. His expressions and his speech were not nearly as random and incoherent as the elder Ashwater. I would much prefer to be back in that cell than over here where I didn't know what to expect out of any of these strangers.

"I will have to talk to Vernon about this," Ashwater muttered to himself, and continued staring at the buttons and lights blinking on the console. "In the meantime, I think that we should call it a night. This is a mystery for another day." Ashwater flicked a switch and the whole machine geared down.

"Wait here," he said to me, and disappeared out the doorway.

I crossed my arms and glanced around the cavernous room. The walls, despite their chilly and open appearance, were closing in on me. A claustrophobic cocoon.

When Ashwater returned to retrieve me from the

testing room, I was feeling a pounding headache starting at a spot between my eyes. I rubbed at the spot and watched Ashwater shuffle some paperwork on a nearby desk and glance at me on occasion.

"I'm going to see about setting up a training routine for you. It'll be a little different from everyone else's, but I don't want you to feel secluded from all the others because of it." He motioned for me to follow him and we walked out of the room into the hallway where people were leaving offices and other rooms with strange equipment inside.

"I won't," I said, hoping I sounded like the kind of person they thought I was. "I just want to train."

"I normally don't approve of children running off on their own," Ashwater said, crossing his arms and pressing his lips together. "But sometimes exceptions can be made. You need to tell your parents where you are, though. I'll give you access to the communications room and you can call them."

"Ok," I said, but the thought of actually calling my parents frightened me. They knew I was gone, but surely they didn't know where. I could see my gruff father and protective mother showing up on these Isiroan's doorstep demanding my return. There had to be some way to get around it.

I followed him out into the bright light of the day and saw hundreds of people converging on the structure in the middle of the base. On one side some people were constructing a huge projector screen.

Ashwater pointed to the screen as we passed it. "When it gets dark enough we will be getting a broadcast from Isiro himself. You're lucky to be here. Today is a once in a lifetime event."

"What's happening?" I asked.

"Isiro is announcing his new host."

"Oh." I bit my lip because I knew who it was going to be. Willow was his new host. Not if I had anything to do with it. Then a thought occurred to me. "Where are they broadcasting from?"

Ashwater shook his head. "It's a secret even to me. Only four people know its location to protect Isiro in his weakened state."

I quit asking questions after that because we came to another building with a huge satellite dish on top. Ashwater took me inside and pushed me into a room with about a dozen screens along the wall showing only static and a couple phones on a desk in the middle of the room.

"Use one of those phones. I'll be outside." Ashwater closed the door behind me leaving me alone. I looked down at the phone closest to my hand and reached for it. But then I stopped myself. I couldn't really call them, could I? Dad would probably try to send out people to come get me. Worse yet, he might go to Jacob, but Jacob had told me not to contact the outside world until I'd set off the beacon.

I picked the phone up and stared at the numbers. Who could I call? Nick? He was the only other person in on our plan. Nick was about as likely to talk to Jacob as Jacob was about to become a ballerina. I felt my stomach twist and hoped that there was a trash can around if I needed to hurl.

I dialed Nick's number into the phone and waited for him to pick up. I just hoped that he wasn't out of the country. It rang and rang and I was about to give up when...

"Hello?"

"Ah... Nick, hey it's..."

"Eugene! Where have you been, your phone's dead!"

"Yeah, sorry... ran into a bit of trouble."

"What kind of trouble? You've been out of contact a whole week!"

"Uh... Hey Nick, I just wanted to let you know that I made it to Laramie. One of the guys here is letting me use the phone to call you." I hoped he would get that I was trying to avoid talking about the Isiroans like they were the enemy. If there was one thing I had picked up from Nick or every spy movie out there, it was that any phone can be bugged.

"You did? That's great! Are you guys staying safe? Wait... what do you mean 'one of the guys'?"

"Uhm, had a change of plans. Harry was, ah... He didn't come with me. He's... gone Jacob." I hoped he would remember that reference. My brother was notorious for playing both sides of a conflict and then joining the side you least expected him to. We called it "going Jacob" for the longest time.

"What!?"

"Yeah, I didn't see it coming."

"But he's not even a...Is he?"

"Yeah. I'm not sure. Jake said he found some stuff on..."

"Wait, wait. Jake? Jake's there with you?"

"N-no, I'm on my own. But, uh... I got here at the same time one of the training groups showed up. They let me join them. I'm going to get trained." I tried to make it sound happy, but my voice cracked and I shuddered.

"Trained?" His end was silent for a moment, but I could hear the gears working in his head. He was putting the pieces together.

"Be safe, Eugene. No matter what you do, be safe."

"I know." I swallowed a lump in my throat. I was in the lion's den now. I knew it was going to happen, I knew what I was getting into, but now that I was here...

"How... how are Mom and Dad?"

"They're holding up alright. Hey, whenever you see Wil—er your redheaded friend again, let her know that her Mom's pregnant."

"Mrs. Patterson is pregnant?"

"Yeah, three months. She's gonna have a little brother or sister."

"Oh, man."

"Your mom and her have been spending a lot of time together. I think the baby is the only thing that's really keeping them sane since your disappearing act."

I bit my lip and closed my eyes against the heat building up in my tear ducts. "Tell her... tell her I'm ok. Even if I'm not."

"I don't know."

"Please. Tell her I'm okay."

"Alright. But your mom is going to shoot me when she finds out I knew where you went."

"Just don't tell Dad. I don't need him sending out an army after me."

Nick laughed. *"Ok. But I can't promise that your mom*

won't tell him."

"I know," I said, and gave my goodbyes.

The other end clicked and Nick was gone.

I swallowed, my mouth suddenly dry, and placed the phone in the cradle.

I stepped back out into the hallway where Ashwater was standing with his hands clasped behind his back staring out one of the hallway windows. He looked over at me and smiled. "Everything go well?"

I nodded and looked away hoping my face didn't betray any of the anxiety I was feeling.

"Come. I will show you your room assignment and then it will be time for Convocation." He patted my shoulder and led me back out onto the base grounds toward the only tall building in the base. He pointed at it. "That's the dormitory."

Then he chuckled and smiled down at me. "Jack insisted that I place you with him and Roy so that you would have some familiar faces to help you out."

"Thanks... I guess." I adjusted the glasses on my face and tried to memorize the route we were walking.

"Not a problem, but don't let them push you around too much." His grin widened. "Jack's got a lot of passion and Roy is very stubborn, and with the two of them, it can drive just about anyone up a wall."

Ashwater led me up four levels of the dormitory and presented me with a key. The door that he showed me was decorated with pictures of singers and video game characters. Jack and Roy's names were written at the top in spray painted stencil. Next to their names was a blue sticky note with *'and Toshi'* written on it.

I laughed at that and then opened the door at Ashwater's insistence. He smiled, "I think my son is happy to make more friends."

There was a bunk bed pushed up against the wall near the door and a third, single bed to the right of a window just past the bunks. A desk with a laptop sat in between the bunks and the single bed. A couch sat in the middle of the room in front of a TV.

"Homey," I commented.

Ashwater looked me up and down. "Did you bring any luggage?"

I shook my head trying to not think of the beacon buried under a bush.

"I'll see if we can arrange to get you a couple changes of clothes from somewhere. Or we can make a trip into town, if you like."

I nodded and looked around the room awkwardly. I wasn't sure what to do here in a space that was definitely not my own.

HARRY GLEESON

My first "scouting mission" was a failure and so were the next three. But I learned a lot from them. In between torture sessions that continued almost right after they brought in Krino, I learned as much as I could.

Krino and I weren't the only prisoners in the facility.

There were multiple rooms with people in them, some were heavily sedated while others were locked up tight in metal cells, glass cells, and interestingly enough cells made like aquarium tanks. And it was quickly becoming clear what the purpose of this place was.

On my third recon attempt I made it out of my cell and into a conjoining hallway. It led to a place with dozens of computer banks calculating parts of what looked like the human genome. It was strange but when I saw a white dry erase board with the words

POWERS ARE GENETICALLY CONTROLLED?
NATURE vs NURTURE?

I realized they were studying what many had studied over the centuries: The origin of powers. But the way in which they were going about it was brutal and inhumane. I had to return to my cell when some of the guards and a couple people in doctors coats walked through.

The fourth recon attempt got me almost to an exterior exit and I was able the get the fact that I was in a desert somewhere. I had gotten a small glimpse of the outside and saw vast reaches of sagebrush.

My only problem up until now was that I didn't have any source for my powers. They had long ago taken away my Isiroan tech that allowed me to create illusions, so the lack of water anywhere made it hard to really get far without getting blindsided by some Alliance guard.

Krino seemed eternally amused by my attempts. By the time I tried a fifth time to scout for information he was rooting for me, gleefully shouting encouragement through the cell much to my consternation.

I was caught on my sixth time out of the cell. They dragged me back and sealed off the easiest way out of the cell and recuffed my hands.

They might have wised up to some of my tricks, but now I was planning something I hoped none of them could really predict.

I had found multiple rooms, multiple places with the ammunition I would need to really solidify my escape, and the one place I needed to go was the room with the aquarium tank where at least one other person was imprisoned in a watery cage.

But I was also facing a problem. Along with the cuffs, they had electrified the cage. One of my attempts had involved cracking the lock on the cage with a piece of wood I had broken off a drawer on a previous recon. I would have to wait for the guards to take me away for my next shock treatment session. So I waited.

Krino was watching me with interest most of the time now. I had taken to ignoring him. I was more than unsettled by the way he acted and talked. One of the guards, after mentioning Krino's name, had whispered something about all the blood on his hands. He had listed off the names he gave himself, and I think they were names of people he had killed and planned to kill. It was the only explanation.

"He won't hurt us, will he?"

"Naw, man, he's safe right now. Yoshida's the only one who can get him to do anything."

That was enough for me to make assumptions. I hoped I

was wrong, but I couldn't think of any reason why someone that Yoshida controlled would not only be locked up but was eventually targeting Isiroans.

His attention on me didn't waver until the guards came again. But this time they came for Krino and not me. He walked out with them and said loudly, "judge not according to the appearance, but judge righteous judgment!" He laughed maniacally the whole way out.

He returned a few hours later with a stupid grin on his face. The guards looked even less happy to be there than most days and were obviously relieved when Krino was safely behind bars once again.

The guards left and Krino crouched in front of the bars between us. "Fly, little bird." He grinned and three water bottles rolled through the bars and came to a rest at my feet.

CHAPTER 29

"Waiting is torture. Patience is difficult. But too hasty an action, if not carefully thought out, will mar any future that waiting and patience can nurture." ~ Ashanti Diawara. Only known descendant of Anyan in 1985.

EUGENE YOSHIDA

The crowd that had gathered in front of the enormous projector screen was massive. It didn't seem possible that so many people inhabited the base. "Do all these people really live here?" I asked Jack who was standing next to me. He found me in the dormitory just as it was getting dark and dragged me around the dorm showing me the Cliff's Notes version of the tour while we headed back out onto the grounds.

"Nope," Jack replied. "Laramie Base is just a hub for our region so that when big announcements come down, we get representatives from all over."

Some of the people sat in the grass on blankets and others in fold out chairs. The feel in the air was one of a big picnic or what you might see at a 4th of July fireworks show. People were talking and laughing, relatively carefree.

Roy appeared next to us with some lawn chairs under his arm. "Jack, your lack of preparation is getting predictable."

Jack waved his hand dismissively. "It's not lack of preparation! It's freestyle spontaneity."

"Whatever you call it, it's getting annoying." Roy dropped the chairs in front of us made an unhappy face at his friend.

Jack shrugged and reached down to hand me a chair and then popped one open for himself. I sat down next to Jack and half listened to Jack and Roy's bickering. In a way they reminded me of the twins I went to school with back in Ohio. It was a little comforting to know that there were people here my own age, but at the same time it was even scarier. They treated this place like a school. But Jake had said this was a place for them to train their army. I felt like I was in a lion's den and the lion was sleeping. It was only a matter of time before I was someone's lunch.

That was only more reason to get what I needed from this place and get out as soon as possible.

Someone walked up in front of the unlit screen and tapped a microphone. "Hello! My name is Patrice Fabian. Welcome back for another exciting year of schooling! The broadcast will begin in a few minutes, but in the meantime, I would like to introduce you all to our teachers this year. Some are familiar to you all and some are new. Please welcome our faculty!"

A dozen or so men and women came up, waved and bowed. I wasn't really paying attention to the names called out so I almost missed hearing the name "Marcus Grey."

The man the woman indicated was standing off to the edge of the teachers with his arms crossed over his chest. He had a bemused smile on his face as she talked about him.

"Mr. Grey has lived in about fifteen different nations since he was a child and has gathered some of the best training around the globe. This will be his fourth year teaching for us, and any of you taking his classes should feel honored to have such a mind teaching you."

She moved on, but I was still focused on Grey. There he was. The man who had taken Willow from me. The image of that man would forever be branded to my memories, but this man... this man wasn't what I remembered exactly. His hair was different, cut against his head with a splash of grey near his forehead instead of in shaggy dreads. But it was unmistakably him, with dark Asian eyes, with little crowsfeet at the corners and a thin mouth. Other than the hair and the cleaned up clothing, this man was one and the same.

The woman ushered the teachers aside and Grey turned

and left, weaving his way through the crowd. I tried to follow him with my eyes but he was swallowed up by the mass of people.

I was about to get up and follow him when the screen flickered to life and a symbol that I now recognized as the Isiroan seal appeared. Only a few seconds passed before a woman's face appeared. She smiled and began to speak. "Thank you all for attending the start this year's schooling and training. My name is Amelie Delacroix. We have much in store for you to learn and reflect upon. This begins only our thirtieth year of the establishment of the centralized training schools, and we have the honor of celebrating that anniversary with a new face.

"I would like to introduce the person who will host our leader for the foreseeable future." The woman stepped aside and the view zoomed out and there stood Willow.

She was speaking but I wasn't hearing the words anymore. Instead the crowd around me seemed to fade out, and all I heard was a ringing in my ears. All I could see was her. She was not the Willow that I remembered. Her formerly long hair was cut close to her head and she wore an Isiroan style uniform. The lapel was open and loose exposing her collarbone where I could see the faint line of a silver necklace.

She smiled gracefully and nodded back to the woman who took center stage again and continued to talk. Willow stepped back and said something to the elderly man standing next to her.

How could she be standing there so calmly? What did they do to her? Somewhere in the back of my memories I recalled something Miriam Lancaster had said when this had all started. She had said that in a month Willow wouldn't be Willow anymore. I tried to break down how much time had passed since then, but it felt like so much time had passed since I had naively believed began this journey. I watched her eyes when the screen showed her, looking for some sign that she was still Willow, or some sign that she was host to an alien mind. Something seemed off about her, but her mannerisms were the same, the tilt of her mouth in a smile was the same. I shuddered even though it was far from cold out here.

I shook my head and tried to pay attention to what was being said.

"In the coming days we will keep you all updated via the ISTVN, and in the meantime please keep our leader and his new host in your thoughts."

She lowered her head in a bow and the screen faded back to the Isiroan seal.

Patrice Fabian stepped up again. "Thank you all for coming once again. Now we have a showcase in store for you all. Please welcome Gummy To and their dance performance!"

Everyone started clapping as four people dressed in black unitards stepped up on stage. They introduced themselves and began a dance in time with some music. They were all telekinesis users and had a dozen or so props on stage that they moved around with their dance.

The celebration continued, but I broke off from the group and said that I wasn't feeling too well. I walked the length of the base, examining the plaques on the doors, identifying different classrooms, offices, and places like the communications building.

My head was all jumbled. Willow's time was near, and if I didn't act fast, her brain would be some alien's home. I headed back up to the dormitory, but the silence and the lack of anything that I could claim as mine made me feel more like a fish out of water.

I peered out the tinted window in the room assigned to me. I could see the whole Isiroan base from four stories up. The Convocation had ended and the mass of people began disappearing. I pressed my forehead against the glass and watched the last few people milling around disappear into the buildings. I breathed out and the glass misted. I pushed away from the window and turned to stare at the room for the hundredth time since I had had come up from the Convocation speech.

It had all happened so fast. One minute I was sneaking around and the next I was officially an Isiroan trainee. My heart was still sprinting laps in my chest from the shock of it all.

I looked away from the window and into the room. The other two beds were the only problem, not because of their presence but because of the people who occupied them. Jack had insisted that I join him and Roy in their room in the base dormitory. Despite the fact that Jack's father lived on the base in an apartment with his wife, Jack had wanted to stay with his best friend in the dormitory. They had been given a room with three beds because at the time they had another friend with them, but apparently he had ultimately been unable to join them at the base.

I stretched out my stiff muscles and left the room. The hallways in the building were very old fashioned with an odd carpet-like wall covering printed with magnolia flowers and dark mahogany baseboards. I walked along the hallway toward the elevator, running my fingers along the scratchy carpet-walls.

The elevator dinged softly as it descended the four stories.

The lobby of the dormitory was quiet. There was no welcome desk, only two elevators parallel to each other flanking the glass-walled entrance way.

I stepped out and looked around. The moon was high in the sky casting little light on the mountains in the distance and reflecting off the few clouds that scrolled across the stars.

Everyone who stayed on the base had either long gone home or they were in their respective apartments or dormitories. It was amazing to me that not even an hour ago the place had been full to the brim with people, but now it was little more than a ghost town. I wasn't sure where Jack and Roy had gone after the celebration had died down, but for now I wasn't too concerned with it. They weren't keeping an eye on me and that's all that mattered.

There were still four buildings that I had yet to look into, so I started with the nearest one and worked my way through, one by one.

Of course it would be the last building out of the lot that would have what I needed. Apparently they didn't lock anything. One of the first doors that I came across was labeled *Records* and opened with no trouble at all. I pushed my way into the dusty room full of bookshelves that were equally filled with boxes and other unidentifiable computer equipment, quietly closing the door behind me.

On the only desk in the entire room were a small laptop and a few scattered discs. I picked up one of the discs. Its label read '*Video recording. IWR. March 17th*'

I sat down on the solitary chair in front of the laptop and turned it on. The screen remained black but a small line of text asked for a disc to be entered. I tapped my finger lightly on the table then picked up the same disc and popped it in.

Loading...

March 17th. Isiro's weekly report. Feed only.

The screen blinked and the face of an old haggard man appeared. He closed his eyes slowly and then reopened them. *"My friends, I have great news for you. A new host has been found."* He paused as if listening to something. *"I know that many of you feared the worst. But fear no more. While it is true that we have been preparing for the worst in the event that a new host would not be found, I have not stopped in my search. The efforts of your comrades inside the Alliance ranks have discovered a host who will bring a new vitality to our union."* He paused again and then smiled reassuringly. *"Come summer the bond will begin and you shall meet the new face who shall help lead this battle to victory. I tell you now, though, this new host is not one of us. For the second time in my life, I have had to delve into the dangerous ranks of the dread Alliance."* He frowned. *"However, like the last time, I have found a sympathetic soul. There is no danger to us from this one, the same as when there was no danger from the previous. My advisors, and you, my friends, hoped that we would never have to face this kind of risk again, but sadly I have begun to realize that with each passing generation of host, it is becoming harder and harder to find compatible persons."* Pause. *"With this realization, and much deliberation I have come to a decision. It is time, my friends, to step up our efforts to hold back the dread Alliance and achieve that which has eluded us for so long. Time is of the essence."*

The video flickered out and the disc ejected itself.

The old man was Isiro. That is, the old man was Isiro's current host, and he was talking about Willow. It had to be. The disc was labeled only a couple months ago.

I looked around the dark room and spotted a box labeled with the date from about a week ago. Flipping through it, I came across a bright red disc with the words 'New host's introduction.'

Within seconds it was in the laptop and flickering to life on the screen.

The same old man was on the screen, but looked about ten years older from the way he was holding himself. He looked tired and worn down. Two men and a woman stood behind him, their eyes watching him intensely, looking ready to swoop in if he happened to fall.

But the thing that really captured my attention as the camera frame zoomed out slowly was the red-headed girl standing off to the left.

She stood stiffly. Her hair was still long compared to how she looked in the announcement at Convocation. A sheet of sweat covered her tension-marred forehead and her eyes wavered between the old man and somewhere off camera.

I touched the screen and felt only the cold, unyielding surface of the screen instead of the soft skin of her face. It was ridiculous to expect anything else, and yet my heart yearned for the gentle touches of her finger tips—the rare way that she showed affection when she didn't feel like rough-housing—and it yearned for the mockingly-smug smiles she gave whenever she knew something I didn't.

I swallowed, trying to ease the lump rising in my throat, and pushed the small laptop away. I buried my head in my arms, breathing in and out slowly. Slowly, that little part of my psyche that had been empty with her gone filled up a little. But, it wasn't nearly enough to smother the rising ache that took hold of my chest.

HARRY GLEESON

The cuffs on my hands kept me from using my fingers to direct the water, but all I needed was to get the water between the cuffs and my hands and I could freeze the damn things off.

I fumbled with the cuffs and managed to get one of the water bottles open with my teeth. I coaxed the water out and let them fill the crevasses between the cuffs and my hands. Once the content of one bottle was sloshing in the cuffs I closed my eyes and concentrated. Molecules are funny things. The speed at which they move determines if they are solid, a liquid, or a gas. It's one of the things that any Aquakinetic worth his or her weight in water had to know, because by knowing that, you knew exactly how to change and affect the water you were using. The water in my cuffs was cool, but not nearly as cool as I needed it to be. I wiggled my fingers and started to pull the latent heat out of the water, visualizing the molecules slowing down to a near stop.

The water was turning to ice.

And right before the water was completely frozen, I clenched my fists and the icy water spiked outwards, drilling holes through the metal. I heated the water up and then froze it back into spikes again, turning the cuffs into Swiss cheese with hundreds of holes. Eventually I got the clasps that held the cuffs in place and they fell away. I shook my hands free and stretched them to ease the cramping that had started because of my power wielding.

I opened the other water bottles and set them on the cell floor in front of me. The water would not be enough to subdue the large amount of people between me and the outside, but it would be enough to get me out of the cell and into the tank room.

I looked at Krino who was sitting back watching me with half lidded eyes. I nodded to him. I didn't know why he was helping me but at this point I'd rather not ask. "Thanks, man."

I drew my hand upwards, drawing the water out of the bottles and off the floor at the same time. I struck the lock on the gate with the water and froze it. The electrified bars crackled angrily.

I punched the lock, spiking the ice through the lock. It slammed open and I was out. I rolled the leftover water, whatever hadn't been turned to gas by the electrified bars, around my arm like a gauntlet and sped out of the room. Behind me Matthew Grey began to laugh. And I hoped that I hadn't just signed my death warrant.

I sprinted through the halls slamming bolts of water into any guard I saw. The tank room was not that far away, but it felt like it took a whole hour to get through the sudden mass of Alliance guards.

They were coming out of every room and door like cockroaches, and an alarm began to scream around me.

I punched past one guy who thought he could come up beside me and turn the floor under my feet into marbles. The Alter power was far too temporary to keep up with me. An experienced Alter user could maintain a transformation for about thirty minutes, but because I was moving he had to change the location of the transformation to follow. I slipped past him and used a small wave of water to scoop up the marbles under my feet and catapult them into the guy's face.

He was soon followed by a trio who were using their powers in tandem with each other to teleport one from either side of me to create a slowly growing net of metal. The two metal wielders and the one teleporter worked around me, but I grabbed the nearest metal wielder and used a bit of my water to lock her arm into a wall with a staple made of ice.

I spun around and kicked at the teleporter who showed up behind me and chopped him in the neck with a blunt ice club. I was not going to have this water forever. The more I fought the more I was going to run out. I had to blast through another two fighters before I made it to the tank room and by then I was almost out of water.

The tank had one person floating inside. If I could crack open the tank, it would throw the one guy in there out on the floor. I didn't want to hurt the guy inside. There was no telling who he was, but more than likely he was another victim of these creep's experiments.

I slammed the door to the tank room behind and froze

the lock, this time to keep me in, and didn't wait around to hear the scuffles on the other side as they tried to break their way in. It was only a matter of time before they got the door open.

I quickly scaled the metal stairs going up one side of the tank and stood on the top where there were a few large buttons that opened and closed the gate that covered the whole tank. I pressed the green one and the gate rumbled and began to retract. As soon as the water was exposed I pulled a small wave of it out and threw it at the door freezing a cap on the door. It wasn't much, but it was enough to keep them from getting in any easier. The guy inside the tank began to wake at the movement and struggled. I started pulling more and more water out of the tank, creating a vortex on the floor at the base of the tank. The guy inside saw me, and when we made eye contact he calmed down. I kept the vortex spinning and pushed one more button that pulled the guy's harness out of the water. As soon as his head was above the waterline, he ripped the breather out of his mouth and coughed.

"Oliver!" he shouted as soon as he stopped coughing.

I did a double take and it was only then that I realized who he was. "Logan?"

It was Laura's brother, the brother who had supposedly been killed back at Hooverville. But here he was alive and well... as well as could be, trapped in a water tank.

"What are you doing here?" he asked. I grabbed his hand and pulled him the rest of the way out of the tank.

"Captured, just like you apparently," I said, and looked at the door. Something was going on outside, and I was disturbed by the fact that they had yet to come in. They had to have had a wide variety of Kinetics here. At least one of them should have been able to chop through that door by now.

Logan peered over the side of the tank and saw the vortex. "Water user?"

"Yeah, but we need to get out of here. Are you good to run?"

Logan shook his arms and legs free of the protective bodysuit he was in and nodded. "My legs are a little wobbly but that's okay."

I quickly explained my plan and Logan worked out how he could help with his Florakinesis. I threw more water on the floor and the vortex grew bigger. Logan carefully ran down the stairs and pressed his hands to the floor, trying to find a root system.

And just as if it were planned, the door blasted inwards, hitting the vortex and ricocheting into the tank. It cracked it, spilling water out onto the floor. I stood on the part of the tank that wasn't collapsing and worked the vortex into a water spout over 18 feet tall. The top was pointed sharp like a cone. Logan shouted in triumph just as a handful of Alliance Kinetics poured into the room and started blasting us with all manner of powers. I punched upwards, and the vortex of water blasted upwards boring a hole in the ceiling.

Over the roar of the water drilling through the ceiling, Logan's vines and roots blasted through the floor, spinning tangles around the other Kinetics' legs and arms. I pressed further and further, feeding the water drill with the water from the tank until it punched through the ceiling into the room above.

"Logan, now!" I shouted. I pressed the reservoir of water up into the room and Logan quickly constructed a root ladder up to the next floor. I jumped from the edge of the tank to the roots and scrambled up it to the next floor. Logan wasn't far behind. I started boring the next hole while Logan ran for the windows and pried them open.

The water drill punched through again, spilling sunlight through the room. There were no more floors but just the sky. Instead of going out the hole in the ceiling Logan and I jumped through the window out on the lower part of the room and spun around into another room. The room was a little storage area and Logan and I settled in behind a wall of boxes. Let them think that we had escaped out the roof, while we were really still under their noses.

We sat in silence for almost thirty minutes before we couldn't hear any more shouts or loud voices from inside the building. At one point I felt brave enough to look out the window and see that they were scouring the surrounding desert.

"Are we safe, Oliver?" Logan asked.

"For now," I replied. "Also, my name is actually Harry."

Logan's eyebrows creased. "Harry?"

We had plenty of time while we waiting for an escape window so I proceeded to explain the deception and my part in it.

"Can you tell me what happened to my sister?" Logan finally asked.

"I don't know. Yoshida, that's Eugene's brother, seems to have gotten her under his thumb." The last I had seen of her had been when I had been captured and she had tried to save me and Eugene until Eugene had been taken in by Jacob Yoshida's lies.

He nodded and buried his face in his hands. I left him alone after that. I felt he needed time to grieve and to think.

Once night fell, we felt safe enough to escape the facility. Logan and I slipped out under the cover of darkness, and it was only then that I found out where we really were: a large warehouse district in the deserted Colorado wilderness. There was almost nothing for miles around. We walked for close to fourteen hours before we found a tiny gas station with a phone.

The first person I was going to call was my father to tell him about the facility and then I was going to call my friends at Laramie and find out if Eugene made it.

The phone rang and my dad answered, "hello?"

"They're experimenting on people, Dad."

***

Internal Memo
To: J. Yoshida
From: T. Blair

Facility HEB3 has been compromised. Subject AK-773 escaped from holding cell and released Subject FK-642. Included with this memo is security footage of the incident. Subject EK-Prime apparently assisted AK-773 with the escape. He is now in lock down with extra protections.

Subjects AK-773 and FK-642 have disappeared from the facility. A cursory search of the surroundings has come up with nothing on their whereabouts.

We have released a missing person's report to the local police and surrounding counties. However it is the conclusion of the facility management that they will have been picked up by Isiroans by now.

We are relocating the remaining subjects to HEB2 and HEB4.

Subject EK-Prime may no longer be an asset. Please advise.

CHAPTER 30

"Discovery is a beautiful thing. Knowledge is the silver lining on all things." ~ Nhu Trang. Kinetic Poet and Author.

EUGENE YOSHIDA

I opened the door to the Records room and peered out. I paused to wait for any sound or shift in air that would indicate that someone else was in the building with me.

Nothing.

I slipped out the door and nearly jogged down the hall toward the window where I had entered the building. A door slammed somewhere in the building and I stopped in my tracks. My heart was running a triathlon in my chest. Footsteps echoed in the otherwise quiet hallway and I looked around frantically for a place to hide. The only dark enough space was under a small row of benches flanked by a couple of fake potted plants. I hit the ground and rolled under the bench, pushing myself against the cold wall. The footsteps tapped closer and I saw dress shoes and the hem of a coat stroll past only a minute later.

I held myself rigid against the wall for a few dreadfully long minutes. A door somewhere far off closed and the building became dead again. I glanced around the corner of the wall into the long reaching hallway and checked to make sure the coast was clear.

I counted to three and then stepped into the hall. The eerie quiet followed me through the rest of the building until I reached the room where I had initially entered it. I slid into the room and closed the door behind me as quietly as humanly possible. I felt my adrenaline start rising as my escape from here got closer and closer.

Cool air greeted me on the other side of the open window. I breathed a sigh of relief when my feet were firmly planted on the other side of the building and I was well on my way back to the dormitory.

I saw a couple people wandering the grounds, but they were too far off for me to see the details of their faces. I hoped it would be the same for me. I walked away from the tall dormitory structure at first and wandered to the far edge of the base not far from where the supply entrance was where I had first entered.

The air was oddly cooler on the far edge of the base. I breathed into my hands, but the heat lingered only a few seconds in the chilly air. I quickened my pace and made an uneven turn in the path toward the dormitory.

"Hey!"

I jumped slightly at the voice, but stopped myself from panicking. It was only Jack. He trotted up beside me and grinned. "What are you doing out this late?"

I shrugged. "Walking."

Jack seemed to consider that phrase a moment before nodding his head and fell into step with me. "Are you worried?"

Worried? I glanced at him out of the corner of my eye. I could still clearly remember the feeling of him trying to invade my mind with his powers. What could he know? What *did* he know?

Better to play it safe. Steer the conversation in the direction that I want it to go. "About the training, yeah."

His chin lifted slightly and I saw an odd glint in his eye, as if something had been confirmed for him other than what I had answered. His words, however, revealed nothing of what might have been confirmed in his mind. "It'll be okay. It's always hard at first. But we have some of the best wielders in the world at our fingertips. In no time you'll be out there with the rest of us."

Fighting a war with a people that have taken so much from everyone, including me? Not likely. I breathed in the cold night air and buried my fingers in my armpits. "Yeah, I can't wait."

"But first we have to train you. Dad says that he'll talk to the Educational Minister later and find out where we should start with you. Until then he said I could introduce you to some of the theoretical concepts behind our powers. Also gonna take you to see our best Pyrokinetic."

I gulped. I already knew where this was going. "Marcus Grey?"

"Yeah. The guy from Convocation." Jack patted me on the back. "I'll drop some books off with you tomorrow, and when I get back from my internship, we can go see Mr. Grey."

I nodded and followed Jack. The rest of the trip back to the dormitory was quiet. Jack seemed to feel uncomfortable with silence and would occasionally start humming or singing lyrics that I didn't recognize.

Fortunately we reached the hall quickly, and I settled in to bed with the covers enveloping my entire body so that I wouldn't have to hear the low conversation between Jack and Roy. Sleep claimed me faster than I could ever remember.

You know the time that we ran across the fields as children? We were carefree and full of joy. I can't say that we aren't like that now, but back then, didn't things seem lighter? Willow danced in a circle around an old well. *I know I keep talking about the past... but for some reason it's hard to look forward anymore.*

She stopped and looked into the well.

Eugene... I'm afraid.

***

Jack dropped a stack of books on top of the bed I was sitting on. I looked up from a sports magazine that I had found lying in the room. Jack grinned.

"Hoooomewooooork!" He said in a sing-song voice.

"What is it?" I closed the article on the rise in tennis fans among preteens and picked up the nearest book. It looked like it had been read through one too many times and then rebound sloppily.

"These are just a few of the books on Kinetic Power Theory." Jack waggled his eyebrows. "This is everything you'd ever want to know about powers, how they work, why they work, etcetera, etcetera."

The book I held, *Fundamental Theories of Pyrokinetic Energies*, was the smallest of the bunch and it was well over 200 pages.

"Erm, where do I start?"

Jack shrugged. "Choose something! Though personally I would pick the *General Practices of Kinetic Combat.* That one was always a good read." Jack grabbed a small box out of his closet and waved. "I'll see you later. If you get hungry, the cafeteria on the second floor is open till ten tonight."

He slipped out of the room, saying hello to someone he saw in the hall.

I put down the book I was holding and grabbed the one that Jack had suggested. It had a ton of pictures in it that looked like a cross between martial arts and dance moves. Some of the figures wielded weapons like swords and bows. I read the caption of one. *"Through the weapon, the powers are directed toward the intended target, increasing accuracy."*

My mind and my eyes drifted from there and I spent the next hour flipping through the books.

One of them talked about how powers were oftentimes based on a wielder's environmental and psychological surroundings. Powers were also often need based. In some places where droughts were common there was usually an increase in Aquakinetics.

Another spoke of ways of utilizing words in conjunction with powers in order to make those powers more effective for users.

And finally, one of the most interesting, called *Upajigratiosus Mythos,* discussed old mythologies and how Kinetics of old had taken it upon themselves to become gods to non-Kinetics and had forever marked the history and mythology of non-Kinetic literature.

Unfortunately, none of the books could hold my interest for very long, and I fell asleep with *Upajigratiosus Mythos* splayed across my chest. I fell asleep thinking of Willow. Her vibrant green eyes telling stories to me in my dreams.

I woke up staring into a pair of angry brown eyes. I nearly jumped out of my skin. Roy was standing over my bed and glaring down at me. I sat up slowly and eyed the other guy warily. "Hey," I said softly.

"Watch yourself." Roy's eyes narrowed and he took a few steps backward before leaving the room talking all his electrified hostility with him.

A shiver coursed through my arms and into my back. More and more Roy was disturbing me. He had to know me than I had told them. Jack didn't seem at all bothered by me, but Roy--he was outright mean. He glared at me more than anything. Something didn't quite seem right in the way he watched me.

But if they truly knew who I really was, why hadn't I been imprisoned? Why had I been welcomed with open arms? I chewed the inside of my mouth and shook off the unwarranted paranoia. These Isiroans would never accept an Alliance member into their ranks like this. So unless I was part of some elaborate double-cross game played by all of these Isiroans, I should be safe.

I shook off the last of the shivers and picked up one of the books still sprawled all over my bed. The random choice was able to keep my attention, and it oddly felt good to think of other things.

The book, entitled *Fire in the Mountain, Fire in the Sky*, was a treatise on Pyrokinetic powers. It read:

Pyrokinesis is the direct manipulation of energy in anything, including the air, people and physical inanimate objects. Energy flows through everything and everyone. A typical wielder of Pyrokinesis is usually only able to create and manipulate fire on a small scale. As opposed to setting on fire an entire building, they can only set fire to a small object and merely help it along. This means coaxing the energy in the direction the wielder wants it to go. If a wielder is able to receive the right training, he or she can expand the sphere of influence he or she can have. This means that the wielder is able to not only control the energy in the immediate area but also to control the energy in an increasingly wider area. One of the benefits of this teaching is not only gaining a wider influence over ones environment but also on a more microscopic level.

Jack returned an hour later and dragged me out of the room to go visit the training field. I watched as nearly fifty new recruits tested out their powers and were oriented to the training regimens that would dictate the rest of their lives.

Jack stopped in front of three girls and four boys starting and stopping small flames. They were in a semi-circle passing a small fireball back and forth, laughing and talking. I looked away from the glimmering flames and watched an almost identical display between a dozen Aquakinetics playing with water. Other, less flashy powers were worked on in the fringes.

I allowed myself to be dragged from one display of powers to the next for the rest of the day, and when Jack was finally worn out with talking and pointing out everything that he thought was interesting, we had an early dinner at the cafeteria with Roy and a couple other people who I didn't know yet.

Finally, Jack took me to see Marcus Grey.

Most of the adults on base lived in a small area just off the side of the base. There were small houses and a couple strips of apartments. Grey lived in one of the apartments by himself.

Jack knocked on his door, and we could hear Grey shout from inside for us to enter.

He sat at his table with some papers in front of him and waved us in. Jack took a seat right across from Grey, which left me with the seat in between them. I sat and dared not look up at him.

"Kouric tells me that you are a Vunjika," Grey said without looking up. He reached out for a cup sitting on the table and took a drink.

"Uh, yeah."

It was only then that Grey looked at me. He really was nothing like how I had remembered him. He looked far less rough around the edges, less haggard. The image of the man that had stolen away Willow was burned into my mind, but this man barely fit the image. His hair was close cropped, with that little gray streak. The man from my memory had long, disheveled hair. "But you want training," he said.

"Yeah." I said, but it came out quieter than I had intended.

"Do you know just how difficult it would be to get to the level of your peers?"

I looked down at my hands. "Not easy."

"Not at all. You would have been better off staying home. You're opening a box that shouldn't be opened by the weak hearted."

"I can do it," I said, trying to inject strength into the words.

"Can you?" Grey sighed and sat back, crossing his arms. "You very likely aren't prepared for the pain and the agony of first few months of training you will have to undergo. Have you heard of the EOS? It is one of the worst conditions any Kinetic can go through and still come out alive. There are even a few who haven't survived and have been killed in the mere effort of breaking free from the bounds of the Vunjika."

"I'm ready," I said, biting my lip against the anger that was bubbling up. "I've already had the EOS once."

"You have?" Jack stared at me.

"Yeah, I had an incident before I headed out here."

Grey was looking at me with curiosity. "How long did the fever last?"

I tried to think back, it was so long ago. "A few days I think."

Grey's eyes narrowed and then he nodded. "Good, then you've already taken the first step of many. Do you know what caused your condition?"

"You mean, why did I become a Vunjika?"

"Yes."

"I don't really know. My parents said it happened when I was a kid."

Grey's hand shot out, grabbing my arm and I felt a tingle

shoot through my body. He frowned. "Hmm, it's more than just Vunjika. Something is acting on your abilities--something not natural."

He let go and sat back again. "Come see me tomorrow and we will look into this further."

We left and Jack gushed about how awesome it will be to be personally trained by Marcus Grey. "He does a lot of theoretical classes and stuff, but he doesn't really do a lot of Pyro stuff anymore. He'll do a lecture every now and then but that's it."

"That's great," I said, not even trying to sound interested.

The Records room where I had seen Willow's video was calling to me again. I didn't know for a fact that I would find Willow's current location there, but I would at least be able to start tracking her. I had seen at least the past three months' worth of records. Something had to tell me where she was.

Once we got back to the dorm, I curled under the blankets of my bed and waited until both Jack and Roy's breathing from their own beds was level and quiet. I slipped out of the covers fully dressed and escaped out of the room as quietly as possible.

The journey to the Records room was much easier than it had been the night before. I started where I left off the previous night and began fast forwarding thorough all of the video reports. Eventually, I had to delve into the written records, which, fortunately, were all digitized back at least four years. I only needed the last month.

I was starting to doze off when I hit gold.

Host transference...

I scrambled to sit up and reread the entire sentence of what appeared to be an outline of security duties.

Those participating in the security for the host transference will be required to arrive at the Aconcagua Base three days prior to the actual transference. A list of these arrival times will be provided in your weekly info-packet provided by the Isiroan Affairs sector of the Security Offices.

Isiroan Affairs? I looked around the Records room

scanning any of the shelves for the name. If this was as concise a records room as it had been, then they should have those info-packets as well. I left the comfort of the chair and rifled through the shelves looking for the Isiroan Affairs shelf.

I found financial transcripts and just about ignored them except that they listed off important members of the Isiroan ranks and detailed spending audits for each of them. One of the people on the list was Marcus Grey. I started reading through the records and laughed when I found the date just before Willow's kidnapping.

Through the records I was able to follow his stay in Ohio and then his departure from Ohio across the States. He bought gas, food and lodging the whole way and it was apparently on the Isiroan payroll.

Once he got into Laramie the records stopped. I rifled through them more and more, but there were only other people and no more of Grey. Laramie was a dead end once again. Where had they gone from here? Where was she now?

I was about to give up when I saw a page from the financials with no name listed. But it still gave the locations of things that had been bought. I looked for one with dates close to Grey's arrival at Laramie.

Then I saw it. But my discovery was cut short. A light shined through the window and I heard voices coming closer. I ducked down out of the view of the window and half-crawled, half-ran toward the exit. That turned out the be a stupid move, because only seconds before I would have been in sight of the door, it banged open and four men with offensively bright flashlights burst into the room. The lights scanned the room, coming closer and closer. Sweat trickled down my temple cooling even more the ice water that was replacing my blood.

I quieted my breathing as much I could while at the same time attempting to stuff myself into an empty section of the shelf. I paused for a moment, and, hearing the men get closer, I moved some boxes to obscure their view of me and then wrapped my arms around my head and buried my face into my scrunched up knees. I was thankful, then, that I had the foresight to wear a black turtleneck. The dark fabric would hide the damning paleness of my skin against the darkness of the shelves.

"You're sure it came from here?" one of the men said.

"Yeah. Positive. That security light has been going off for a whole day." A second man replied.

"And no one noticed it until now?"

"That was an oversight."

"Enough," a third man interjected. "Find the intruder."

"Look, these boxes have been opened."

"Carl's much neater than this. That's proof enough for me that someone was here."

The four men began shoving aside boxes and were poking their lights into every dark corner and shelf. My heart pumped faster with every step that they got closer. They were a couple feet away when I heard a shout from yet another man.

"This way! There are alarms going off in the next building!" The four men sprinted out of the room.

I jumped out from the cramped shelf space and peered out into the hallway. Three people in the hallway were right in the way of my exit.

I cursed under my breath and looked back in the room. The window was sealed shut. It was one of the few windows in this building that weren't meant to open. I tapped the glass. It wasn't all that thick.

The table in the middle of the room was made out of thick steel. I doubted that I could actually pick it up. The chairs were the same, but much smaller. I grabbed the seat of the nearest chair and chucked it at the window.

The glass shattered into trillions of sand to hand-sized shards. I didn't wait around to see if anyone heard. I had no doubt that they did. I vaulted over the window sill and sprinted into the darkness of the base grounds.

CHAPTER 31

"Anger, if not restrained, is frequently more hurtful to us than the injury that provokes it." ~ Seneca. Roman philosopher.

The bleeding wasn't stopping. My vault over the window sill of the Records room had dug toothpick-sized glass shards into my hands. If I went to healer on the base then, they would know it was me who was in the building just now. I ran all the way back to the dormitory and sat in the shared bathroom with my hands wrapped up in towels. Jack and Roy were still asleep and it was abnormally quiet in the room. I wished that they would start snoring to hide the noise made by my clumsy attempts to stop the profuse bleeding.

I clenched and unclenched my fists. My left hand was stiff and wouldn't move as well as the right hand. I winced as I pulled the towels tight around my hands. A knock on the bathroom door startled me out of my pain for a moment, and I knocked a haphazard toothbrush off the edge of the sink.

"Hey, Genie, what's the hold up?" Jack's tired voice flitted through the door. I frowned at the odd nickname but said nothing about it.

"Not feeling too good," I said.

"You need anything?" Jack's voice was suddenly laced with concern.

I started to answer no when the towel around my hand slipped a bit and blood splattered onto the floor. That would be hard to explain. My heart took a running leap and I began taking deep breaths.

"Eugene?"

The door handle shook as Jack tried to open the door.

"Wait," I started to say, but Jack did something to the

door and it snapped open.

It was over. I was dead. Jack would see me, sitting on the edge of the bathtub, with my blood pooling on the floor. He would report me and all would be lost.

But Jack didn't run off to report me. He just stood in the door staring at the blood. His eyes were wide and stricken. He backed out and disappeared into the darkened room. I heard murmurings--Jack talking to Roy.

Roy, groggy from sleep, stepped into the threshold of the bathroom door, turned around and grabbed a white box out of the cabinet just outside of the bathroom. He knelt on the floor in the middle of my splattered blood, and with the ease and deftness of a professional, took the slivers of glass out of my palms, wrapped my hands in white gauze and didn't speak a single word all the while.

"Move." It was the only thing that he said. Once I was out of the way, he turned on the bathtub and filled a bucket he got from under the sink with water. He spilled the water on the floor and the water took the blood on the floor with it down the drain in the middle of the bathroom floor.

I backed up a few steps while he turned off the tub and threw the shard of glass into the trashcan beside the toilet. He pushed past me and moved next to Jack's bed.

"You going to be okay?" Roy asked in a low voice to Jack.

Jack nodded, voiceless, as he stared into the dark room almost sightlessly. His gaze was far off, and I suddenly felt bad, but I was unsure as to why. The blood had shaken him up somehow.

Roy glared his token look at me and then shoved his blanket over himself and went silent in a cocoon of cotton.

I went to my own bed quietly. Exhaustion was taking over now that my adrenaline rush was fading, and the pain of the tightly wrapped gauze quieted to a dull throb.

"We'll go see the Healer later," Jack said, not averting his gaze in the slightest.

I almost protested. But the realization hit that I was already caught. When everyone awoke it would come out that a break in had occurred and I, being inexplicably injured in the

course of the evening, would be implicated right away. I was
doomed. But I nodded into the dark and curled up under my
own blankets, cradling my hands close to my chest. The least I
could do would be to be healed in preparation for the hell that
was sure to come. As much as I tried though, sleep eluded me
for a long time. Something niggled at the back of my mind, but I
couldn't grasp it. I fell asleep an hour later still worried about
something, just not knowing *what.*

*Oh, something has gone terribly wrong! Eugene, we may
not make it! I'm afraid the world as we know it is falling apart
around us.* She clutched my arms and looked deeply into my
eyes. I could only stare back.

I woke to Jack and Roy talking in low voices on the other
side of the room. Roy was nearly yelling his whispers. His tone
was so harsh that it grated my nerves. I shifted under the
blanket. The voices cut out and it was quiet. I pushed myself up
and saw Jack and Roy sitting at the table near the door. Papers
were spread out on the table, but Roy very quickly gathered
them up and stuffed them in a backpack under his bed.
"Ready to go to the Healer?"
I nodded and threw on a change of clothes that I hoped
was clean and followed the other two out.
The base was again bustling with activity in the form of
training the new recruits. Fortunately, we went in the opposite
direction of the fire wielders. Roy led the way through the
grounds to a two story building. Inside looked exactly like a
doctor's office in any normal city. The waiting room was empty
and the receptionist was chewing on the end of her pen while
reading some novel with a scantily clad couple on the cover.
Roy spoke to the receptionist and pointed to me. She
blinked at me for a few seconds and then picked up her phone
and chatted with someone on the other end. We three sat down
and five minutes later the Healer came out and beckoned me
into a smaller room.
"You boys are always getting into trouble." The Healer's
gaze was reproving, but she did not hesitate while stripping off

the now bloody fabric and examined my hand with the eye of a hawk. She turned my hand back and forth, asked me to flex my fingers a couple times and then she began to rub tiny circles at the heel of my right hand. She worked her way up the palm and I felt a chilly surge in icy pinpricks flowing down my arm into my hand. I watched as the broken skin squirmed in a revolting way and began closing in on the wound. My hand then heated up and the newly formed skin reshaped a bit to the miniscule patterns on my palm and then stilled.

The Healer took up my other hand and the process was repeated.

"There you go. Your name is Eugene, is it not?"

I nodded, and then paused. How did she know that?

My worries from earlier suddenly bloomed again. *Jack knew my real name.*

The Healer frowned. "You must have lost a lot of blood. You look very pale." She touched my forehead with her fingertips and her frown deepened.

"I'm just tired." I moved away from her touch.

She paused at that but nodded and didn't argue. "If you start feeling weak, sit down. I want you to go home and rest now. You need to let your body regenerate that lost blood. Eat something, too."

The Healer shuffled me out and I entered the reception area alone. Adrenaline started to course through my veins and I knew that my end was here. Our next destination was the jail or whatever they used to lock up people around here.

"My dad needs to get some stuff from one of our other bases. We need an extra hand to carry things. Want to come?" Jack asked, leading the way out of the Healer's.

That wasn't what I was expecting to hear. So in my shock, I just nodded my head.

"Great! We'll just stop by the room real quick and then head on out."

Roy said nothing the whole way back. The moment we got back to the dorm, Jack rooted through the closet and pulled out three heavy winter coats.

"Here's a coat."

"Isn't it too hot for these?" I murmured, still in shock that I wasn't locked behind a set of bars by now.

"Trust me, you'll need it." Jack nodded knowingly.

I frowned at the coat and took it despite my misgivings but didn't put it on.

Jack and Roy put their coats on right away. Confused I followed them out.

Jack spearheaded the way through the base and then up the hill toward the monstrosity of a teleporter. I wasn't that far behind him and Roy was only a few steps behind me. I felt a little uncomfortable having Roy walking behind me. I could almost feel the pupil-sized holes being gouged out of the back of my skull. Jack acted like he didn't know who I was, but Roy treated me like he knew exactly who I was.

I looked back once at the base which was becoming evenly viewable as we got up higher. The teleporter was nearly in the very center of the base, and, other than the building powering the large fence, it was the highest single-story man-made structure on the base. The dormitory was the tallest of the buildings, even overshadowing us in the falling sun, despite our vantage point.

I nearly bumped into Jack when he stopped on the threshold between two of the columns of the teleporter. The columns were not made of stone as I had previously thought but of a rough looking metal. I couldn't identify it off hand.

That's when I noticed the veins. Small, spidering veins were etched into the metal flooring and columns in intricate designs that all started—or ended—at the very center where they all spiraled around a waist high pillar in the very center. All that the little pillar had on it was a silver ball on which were two imprints, a pair of hands.

Jack went to one of the columns and opened up a barely visible panel and began flipping switches, typing something into a little keyboard. He read the equally small display and closed the panel with a grin.

"Ready when you are," he gestured toward the hand pillar.

Roy shoved past me and took up a position in front of

the little pillar. "My turn." He gave Jack one of the first grins I think I'd actually seen him display.

Jack huffed and crossed his arms. "You and your stupid bet."

Roy's playful grin turned smug. "Told ya I was the awesomest."

Jack rolled his eyes and waved me over. I hadn't followed any of what the two guys had just bantered about. I mentally shrugged and stepped into place beside Jack, choosing to ignore it.

Roy gave me one last glare before placing his hands in the imprints and pressed the silver ball. It shifted under his hands and a yellowish glow spread out from the ball and enveloped us until yellow light was all that I saw. I then felt Deconstitution take hold. It was a little different from what I remembered when I was first teleported to the Laramie Mountains. It was less like I was being torn apart atom by atom and more like I was being inflated with air. The bloated feeling dissipated slowly, and then abruptly the yellow light was gone like a light switch turned off, and I was now looking at a whole different set of mountains. These were covered in snow and I now realized why Jack had given me a coat in the middle of summer.

"Where are we?" I yelled over the wind that was screaming through the columns of an identical, if not larger, teleporter.

"Argentina!" I heard Jack yell back. It took a moment to process that information, and then I was pulled by my jacket sleeve by Jack toward a dark opening in the side of the cliff face nearest to the teleporter. "Come on! We need to get inside!"

Roy was leading the way this time and greeted someone so bundled up that it was hard to tell the sex of the person. I couldn't clearly hear what they were saying to each other as the bundled person led us into the square opening, but I was having trouble hearing anything over the bellowing winds.

Once we were inside, the new person smacked a red button on the wall, and the opening was shut by a huge metal door. The person shook off the snow that had collected all over the thick coat and then untied the hood and cotton facemask.

The dark-haired woman who came out of the hood gave all three of us appraising looks and then jerked her chin in the direction of the dark depths of the tunnel before us.

"Follow me, *niños.*"

The tunnel was sporadically lit with thin panels at the tops and bottoms of the stone and metal stretch. Doorways opened to the left and right of the tunnel leading to other hallways or rooms.

The woman and Roy struck up a conversation in Spanish, but I couldn't understand what was said at all. My choice in high school for foreign language had been Japanese. What could I say? It was supposed to be an easy A. Jack didn't look like he understood what was being said either, but at the moment I couldn't think of anything to strike up for conversation.

The need for conversation ended when we reached the end of the tunnel and came out into a wide open dome full of computers, large screens and other high-tech equipment.

The most startling thing however was Willow's face on the largest of the screens.

Her mouth was moving but I heard nothing but the scattered conversations of the people in the dome. Willow's eyes kept looking down like she was reading something while she was talking. Her forehead was creased with deep thought lines. The lines smoothed out every time she finished a sentence and started another one.

The screen cut away to black and showed only the Isiroan symbol. The conversation in the room seemed to increase after the screen cut out.

"Ooh, nifty," Jack said to Roy.

Roy nodded as if he was responsible for the hundreds of computer screens and consoles.

We were led into a corridor off to the side, away from all the consoles by the woman, and taken to a large room. It was not as large as the dome, but large by normal standards. The ceiling was pockmarked with square florescent bulbs and thick streams of wiring strung back and forth. The room itself was full of boxes and crates with labeling in Spanish. The woman led us to a small conclave of the room and pointed out three boxes. They were different from the other boxes and crates. The sides of them were painted in blue in contrast to the pale brown of cardboard and wood. The writing on the side was painted over by the blue, so even if I could read Spanish, I wouldn't have been able to see the writing.

The woman and Roy continued to converse in Spanish for a few minutes more while Jack cracked open the boxes with a pocket knife. I sidled up between Jack and Roy and examined the contents of the boxes over their shoulders.

A fragile-looking glass-encased diode the size of a baseball was at the center of a large silver disc. The surface of the disc had deep grooves giving it the appearance of a vinyl record. I hadn't a clue what it was. I was the only one, however. Jack looked at the thing like it was made of diamonds. He muttered "good design" under his breath over and over. Roy was still talking to the woman but now they were looking at a clipboard with a list of items on it. I backed off a bit and tried to use my limited Spanish language abilities to read the other boxes. I had no luck, of course.

This place was actually bigger than I had first thought. The mass of boxes and crates made it look cramped, but the walls created by them hid the depth of the room. I turned one of the corners made by a stack of crates and saw something that I recognized.

Willow's bike.

My heart leapt up into my throat and I stopped in place. I would recognize the silver and blue frame anywhere. Now it wasn't all that hard to think that someone else would have had the same kind of bike somewhere, but few would have the wrestling stickers and the initials *W. A. P.* etched into the handlebars. Willow Andrea Patterson.

Willow cherished that bike. It was the first thing she ever bought with the money she earned at her summer job. She wouldn't even let anyone ride it without signing away their first born in the event of damage. And now here it was in a glorified cave in Argentina leaning against a wall of cardboard.

She couldn't be far off.

My heart left my throat and stampeded into my chest. Excitement coursed through my veins on the backs of a thousand wild horses. My first impulse to start running through the halls screaming her name was shut down the moment Jack rested his hand on my shoulder.

"Hey, buddy, it's time to go."

I hesitated. I could easily run past him. But then my cover would be blown. I had no idea if Willow was actually here or not. She'd been kidnapped and the bike must have been stored here.

"Right," I said instead and followed after Jack, Roy and the woman. I didn't dare look back at the bike.

The woman held her hand out delicately, physically holding nothing, but telekinetically leading two large crates after us. I stayed as far away from the crates as I could and still be walking with the other three.

We made quick progress through the base, back through the dome room with the screens and consoles where only a few people still milled about and finally back out into the cold. The woman left the floating box in the center of the teleportation device and we traveled back through the Argentinean transporter to the base in Wyoming.

CHAPTER 32

*"We live in a pretty bleak time. I feel that in the air.
Everything is uncertain. Everything feels like it's on the precipice
of some major transformation, whether we like it or not."*
~ Sean Lennon

"The disc goes here." Jack pointed to an empty case on the base of the teleporter. Roy and I both put our backs to the box, pushing it—carefully—across the spiral portion close to the edge of the teleporter where Jack was standing. Jack reached inside and pulled out a thick cable. The cable had a four pronged connector on the end, glinting gold in the noon-day light. Jack opened the box and clicked the connector into the diode. The diode's lights blinked and some mechanism on the disc started spinning around and around. Jack smiled as if this was the best thing that could happen.

"Great!" Jack exclaimed and tugged the connector out of the diode, promptly stopping the light and the spinning. "We'll just leave this here for the technicians to install."

Jack closed up the box and patted it like a father would a favorite child, pushing it into a snug position between one of the support pillars and the base of the teleporter.

"We're going to have dinner with my folks tonight. You're welcome to join us," Jack hollered over his shoulder as we walked down the side of the hill off the paved path.

I looked at my hands where faint white lines of new skin marked where the glass had cut through my hands. I wasn't quite ready to go back to the video room. No doubt they would have the place under heavy surveillance and I would be caught the second that I stepped a toe into the building.

"Sure," I shrugged and followed behind Jack and Roy all the way to the dormitory.

Jack left the dormitory not long after we returned, saying he had to work an hour or so at the security office. Roy didn't seen any more pleased to be left in the room alone with me with than I was. I chose to make the first move and buried my nose in one of the books Jack had given me.

Roy on the other hand opened up his laptop and typed away on it like crazy. His fingers hitting the keyboard frantically distracted me in the dead afternoon quiet of the room. I opened one of the books Jack had left me and tried to ignore him.

I stopped examining the book the second I heard the typing of Roy's laptop cease. He was staring into space, his eyes wandering about the room, unfocused. He eyes traveled into contact with mine and I looked away.

"Where are you from, originally?" Roy's voice seared a startling hole in the dead silence.

I considered a fib, but thought better of it at the last second. "Ohio."

He nodded knowingly. "You accent doesn't sound local."

I hadn't thought about my accent since I had been with Harry at her aunt and uncle's place. I had long dropped the act of a Japanese transplant. I thought for a moment and tried to place Roy's accent. He sometimes sounded like a stereotypical California surfer dude, but sometimes he sounded like any normal Midwesterner. Right now his accent was the neutral Midwestern.

"You?" I prompted, somewhat amazed we were actually having a conversation.

"Nowhere." Roy snarled and slammed his laptop closed.

Well, there went the conversation.

I opened the book again and looked at it without reading. "Well, okay, then."

Roy stormed out of the room and slammed the door behind him.

I had yet to gain any inkling of understanding of Roy. His emotional outbursts were random and inconsistent. He set off an internal alarm bell in the back of my mind and I knew, even without the use of instinct, that he was a loose cannon.

I returned to reading about the various methods to Kinetic power conservation and expansion. It was a dry, boring text, but I could see the value in it. I had no intention of actually putting into practice any of the suggested exercises at the moment. Maybe in the future I would, as unlikely as it seemed.

Roy reentered the room about a half an hour later. He was talking on a cell phone in what sounded like German. That was surprising. Not only was he able to converse in Spanish with the lady in Argentina but he also was now speaking with someone in German. How many languages did he know?

He wrapped up his conversation quickly and then stared me down with a hard look. "Are you still coming to dinner with the Ashwaters?"

I nodded.

"Then let's go," he said, barging out the door without as much as a by-your-leave.

I dropped the book on the bed and scrambled after him as he gained ground with his sprinter's legs and fast pace. He passed the elevator and made a beeline for the stairs taking two or three of the steps with each bound of his feet.

I was a flight of stairs behind him the whole way down and then I was trailing a good forty feet behind him when we finally reached ground level. He didn't slow down or let me catch up at any point as we traversed the length of the base grounds toward the little residential area, the same area where Marcus Grey had his apartment.

Roy spearheaded the way through the cobblestone pathways between the townhouses, not reacting at all to me slowing down in surprise. The house we stopped in front of was like the others except that it had a colorful elephant ornament sitting cross-legged in the lawn surrounded by white rocks. Roy went right up the concrete walkway and opened the door without knocking.

"Hey, we're here," he called into the living room. I stepped in and copied Roy's action of taking off his shoes and padding further into the room. Roy waved me toward the semi-circle couch that faced a large-screen TV.

I melted into the overly soft cushions and listened to the low tones of Roy speaking to some woman in the kitchen that was further back into the house. I couldn't hear what they were saying but quickly stopped caring when I heard Jack and his father conversing as they came down the stairs.

"They should be starting the broadcast in the next few minutes or so," Ashwater was saying to his son.

"When did they get it?" Jack asked.

"About an hour ago. They've decided to revise tonight's broadcast to address it directly."

Jack plopped down into the couch beside me. His mouth was set in a pressed line and his eyebrows were knitted together. Ashwater rested his hand on Jack's shoulder for an inexplicably short moment, but that moment was good enough to make his tightly fused brows to ease apart.

Jack gave me a short smile and reached between the cushions of the couch. He pulled out a thin black remote and flipped on the TV.

"—recorded and will be broadcast on this station for all members of the Legion to see. Following the Alliance speech we will continue with our weekly reports." A woman was speaking on the TV. She was sitting across from another woman and two men around a glass table.

"Is it true that George will not be speaking tonight?" one of the men asked.

"So we've heard. Apparently his condition has been deteriorating drastically in the past few days. Because of that and now this message from the Alliance, they've decided to finish the transfer process well in advance of their previously planned date," the second woman said.

"What's this?" I said without thinking.

Jack looked at me in surprise. "You've never watched the ISTVN?"

"The what?"

"I. S. T. V. N. ISiroan Television Network."

I cringed internally for my ignorance of Isiroan culture. "No. Never heard of it."

Jack just nodded. "It's our news network. Like CNN. Except you have to have a special receiver in order to pick it up." He pointed to the silver box that was stacked with a DVD player under the TV. A green light blinked on it. "Each major language region has one."

Ashwater was still standing beside his son and looked between us with an odd look on his face. I tried not to pay attention to him and focused on the TV.

"Without further ado, we bring you the message sent to our global network from the Anyan's Alliance."

The screen flickered and Miriam Lancaster appeared standing behind a podium emblazoned with the Alliance insignia. Roy and Ashwater's wife came into the living room and took up places in the living room. Roy sat beside Jack opposite me and Ashwater's wife stood with her arms around her husband's waist.

"Six thousand years ago, humanity began the great fight against the Isiroan Legion in the hopes of retaining our freedom and personal prosperity and safety. In the past decade of my leadership we have not pursued you, but merely defended ourselves against your unlawful enslavement of our people. For years we have tried to make peace with you, for years we have tried to negotiate, and for years we have tried to find a median. But never have you met us half way. Always you have stolen, killed and destroyed our families, property and sense of well-being.

"Three weeks ago, the Isiroan Legion carried out the kidnapping of a young healer by the name of Willow Patterson. The Legion's intentions are clear. This child, a promising entrant in the Healer Corps, was taken for the sole purpose of infesting her mind and soul with the alien parasite Isiro. She is not the first. The Legion has kidnapped many of our number.

"Thirty-four years ago the Isiroan Legion supported and condoned the actions of war criminal Reginald Cook."

"Nearly twenty years ago, one of our leading scientists and advocates for peace was taken and used as a host for Isiro.

"Ten years ago our Chief Minister, my predecessor, was brutally murdered along with his wife and child."

"Liar!" Jack suddenly yelled, but his father's hand back on his shoulder quieted him down.

"...the past few weeks, multiple kidnappings of two of our children have taken place."

"These acts are unconscionable." Lancaster looked up from her podium and stared right at us through whatever camera they had used to film this. *"But no more."*

"We, the Anyan's Alliance, through the consensus of our Council and this administration's executive authority, hereby declare war on the Isiroan Legion. Any and all who oppose this declaration will be found in contempt of our authority and will be dealt with under a new zero tolerance policy."

"You who dwell within the protection and wing of the Isiroan Legion will be freely welcomed to the Alliance should you desire to surrender. Any and all who do not surrender within the next 72 hours will be treated as enemy combatants and will be dealt with accordingly."

The video cut out and the four people who were talking before the broadcast were back. They all seemed shaken. They started talking about the implications of open war and the effect on society.

"That bitch," Jack snarled.

"Jack," Ashwater's voice was heavy with warning.

Jack's fist clenched tight and he looked ready to punch the next thing that moved. "I hate her." His words hissed through his teeth.

I kept my mouth shut and didn't participate in the conversation between the others. Jack didn't participate either but stared down at his clenched fists with a furious look on his face.

"And now we present tonight's regularly scheduled live broadcast from Isiro's inner circle," one of the women said. The screen again flickered and another podium appeared, but this time it had the Isiroan Legion's insignia on it. But the person behind the podium wasn't Lancaster's opposite, Isiro. It was some woman whom I had never seen before. Text appeared under the screen showing the woman's name.

Mercedes Gentry – Acting Prime Minister.

"We had hoped," the woman began, *"to use tonight's broadcast to celebrate the decision to finally pass the torch from our beloved host George to our new host Willow. But this broadcast from the Anyan's Alliance has made us pause. Soon, my brothers and sisters, the time will come for our battle to end. We will come out victorious, that we know. But this new threat from the Alliance endangers our mission. It is true that we have struggled against them for thousands of years but the last decade has brought a level of peace and prosperity. Or so we had thought."*

Gentry looked up from the papers on her podium.

"In recent weeks the health of George has been deteriorating out of the control of our best Healers. His time is quickly coming to an end.

"The stress and strain of managing a war with his health in such a bad state would not be advisable. Therefore, we will be performing the transfer tomorrow. Our new host, Willow Patterson, will be one with Isiro in three days' time."

CHAPTER 33

"He who exercises no forethought but makes light of his opponents is sure to be captured by them." ~Sun Tzu.

"Our new host, Willow Patterson, will be one with Isiro in three days' time."
The Bonding was going to take place in three days! I felt my blood turn to ice water. The next hour at the Ashwater's passed in a blur. I didn't pay attention to Roy's unveiled hostility toward me or any of the three Ashwater's attempts to engage me in conversation.

After I had mechanically eaten dinner and only half listened to the conversation around the dinner table, I made a quick excuse and left the townhouse.

I was running.

I sprinted into the Records room and found the papers that had all the financial information on it. Within seconds I had found the papers with the unknown names. The paper with the date closest to when Willow and Grey would have been at Laramie showed that the next transactions had taken place in none other than Buenos Aires, Argentina. I stuffed the paper in my pocket and ran out, not caring if anyone saw me leaving.

I found myself scanning the scraggly bushes that inhabited the outer edges of the base for the one that looked like a flame, the place where I had hidden all the papers and maps and, most importantly, the beacon that would allow Jacob to know where I was and infiltrate the base. He would zero in on my location and be here within only a few minutes.

I dug under said bush and pulled out the small beacon

that would transmit my location to my brother and the Alliance. They had to come now. The bonding was soon. I couldn't let it happen, but I couldn't do it on my own this time.

I pressed the button and reburied it under a light coating of dirt. I breathed in and out slowly so that I would be prepared mentally when Jacob appeared.

Any minute now.

A small whoosh of air behind me signaled a Teleport Kinetic was behind me. I turned to greet the Alliance person, somewhat surprised that Jacob had yet to contact me. My mouth opened half way and then shut when I realized that the uniform in front of me wasn't an Alliance one, but that of an Isiroan guard.

"You!" He snarled.

I stepped back but miscalculated the distance from the bush and tripped into it. With the cracking branches clinging to my clothes, I struggled to regain my footing.

Two more whooshes of air followed after the first and suddenly there were four men in front of me. One of them grabbed my arm roughly and pulled me up.

"It was about time you slipped up, spy," one of the men growled. He jerked his head at the others. "Take him to the secure holding cell and contact Doctor Ashwater."

'This should transmit your location to us securely, Eugene. They'll never know that it was on.' Jacob had chuckled a low laugh and had smiled almost smugly.

How did they find out?

One of the men grabbed my arm and I was teleported quickly into a cement room with only a table and two chairs in the middle. The man who teleported me was gone in a whoosh of air and I had little time to protest. The walls were bare except for a singular camera in one of the top corners and an air vent in the opposite corner noisily pushing air into the room.

My heart started to beat harder and harder. I could hear my blood thrumming though my veins and my heart beat into every bone. There was no door. There were no windows. I ran my hands along the concrete walls hoping that I would find a door hidden in the immaculately smooth walls.

I pounded my fists into the wall and screamed voicelessly in frustration. No one answered and no one came.

"Let me out!" I screamed at the camera which followed my every movement around the tiny room.

"Impossible." A voice behind me breathed.

I whipped around and saw Ashwater and three men, including the one who had teleported me into the room, all standing on the other side of the table.

"We found him on the southwestern corner of the base. Further investigation found these as well." The Teleporter handed Ashwater my bundle of papers. Ashwater glanced over the items and then locked gazes with me, staring hard.

"Not too smart, using a beacon signature that we've already cracked." Ashwater didn't move an inch and continued to stare at me. He never blinked.

I stared back and resolved to say nothing.

"I supposed you are the one who's responsible for the break in at the Archive Center." He narrowed his eyes and threw the papers onto the table.

"I was right to be doubtful of you. My son believed you to be safe and therefore convinced me to look over your suspicious origins for the time being. I don't know what you've said to him..." Ashwater glanced at one of the men behind him and jerked his chin upward. The man nodded and he and the Teleporter whisked away.

"What were you trying to accomplish? What possessed you, or your handlers to send in a child? You're fifteen!" Ashwater slammed his fists down on the table knocking some of the papers to the floor.

I gritted my teeth and crossed my arms over my chest, resolving again to say nothing.

"Gabriel," Ashwater growled.

The other man in the room stepped forward and stared at me hard. I could feel a buzz in my head getting louder and louder. I spun away and clutched my head in my hands but the buzzing only got louder. I felt something else then like a cool trickle of water slipping through the increasingly painful buzz, chilling whatever it touched. Dazed by the battle waging in my brain, I fell to my knees. Heat rippled through my veins taking over the chilly trickle of before. Now my blood was on fire. The tips of my fingers began to glow red hot and I knew what was coming next. Flame burst from my fingers, enveloping me.

I pushed back away from the fire which was clinging to the concrete and singeing the gray wall. The fire was still coming out of my fingers in bursts and waves burning everything it touched. Panicked, I rolled away.

The buzzing in my head got louder and louder, drowning out the scream of the blaze around me. I heard myself yelling, "No, no, no, no!" over and over again. Ashwater was also yelling, but I didn't hear any of what he was saying. The fire was building around me higher and higher. I couldn't see anything but the red and orange flames. I curled in on myself and waited for the fire to consume me.

The buzzing ceased. The heat around me chilled.

I opened my eyes.

The concrete was charred. The table was burnt to a crisp.

I was alone.

***

Hours passed.

The camera that sat in the corner was melted into an amorphous blob. The only sound, other than the shuffling of my feet or the low wheeze of my breath, was the constant flow of air coming in from the air vent.

I pushed myself into the unburned corner of the room and stared into the wall trying to ignore the maddening silence. The first hour after my fire had burst, I screamed and yelled at the walls until I realized they probably couldn't hear my anymore. If the camera was any sign, they couldn't see me either.

The second hour I tried to make my fire on my own and failed. The third and fourth hours I went back to trying to find some kind of hidden door. Other than the burnt portions of the walls I found few anomalies in the concrete.

The fifth hour was under way. I had spent most of it curled in the corner feeling my sapped energy finally taking its toll.

I must have dozed off without realizing it because when I woke I didn't immediately realize where I was. When the knowledge hit me I moaned and hit the wall. My knuckles burned with the impact and I found every muscle in my body beginning to burn with unimaginable pain.

It was like the time I had blacked out in the Alliance hallway because of Joseph Carmichael. I was going through hyperthermia again. I could feel it all twisting through my body like a disease. I crawled to the center of the room and pushed the charred pieces of table around until I found the remains of the beacon that Jacob had given me. It was cracked in half with its little mechanical circuit board hanging out pitifully.

I tried to push the little board back in and push the halves together but the beacon didn't take to the action of pushing it's broken parts back together and shattered even more in my fingers. I dropped the thing and covered my face with my hands, getting soot on my face. I didn't care. I screamed and grabbed the nearest charred bit of table and threw it at the wall where it exploded into a burst of blackened wood.

I curled up into the fetal position and held my head in my hands.

I fell into a fitful sleep.

I woke up to my arms being pulled up. I struggled for the first second before I realized what was happening. I saw the Teleporter for a split moment and then I felt Deconstitution and Reconstitution faster than ever before.

My new surroundings were just as depressing as the previous. Instead of four walls of concrete there were three. But the fourth wasn't much better. It was a wall of thick metal bars.

The man Teleported to the other side of the bars and took up a position against the far wall. He watched me with a keen eye.

The hallway which enclosed my new cell went down a long ways to the left but turned a corner to the right. My cell was one of many in the hall. I didn't see anyone else in any of the other cells. I pushed myself to my feet and looked at my surroundings.

There was a toilet open and for all to see, a sink, a table and a thin mattress. The former three were all made out of concrete. The mattress was enclosed in a concrete bed frame which was more of a box than anything.

"Welcome to your new home." Ashwater was now standing outside of the bars. His arms were crossed over his chest and he stared at me hard. "Eugene Yoshida. Son of the Chief Minister of Security in the Anyan's Alliance. Brother to the most brutal member of the Military High Command. Clever, really. Who would have expected the son of such a high ranking member of the Anyan Corps to be here? You won't be going anywhere for quite a while. This place is equipped to handle your Fire powers so don't even think of trying to escape. It will be pointless." He snarled out his last sentence.

I didn't even think of what I was doing, but I slammed my body into the bars and tried to grab Ashwater. "You mother..." I felt a searing electrical shock blast through my body from the bars. I stumbled back and fell to the ground.

Ashwater sniffed, unaffected and turned away. He and the Teleporter walked down the hall and turned the corner to the right.

"You can't keep me here!" I yelled through bars of the cell. No one responded. The near-silent whispers of the footsteps faded down the hallway and I was left strikingly alone. The dead silence of the hall rang in my ears more loudly than if someone was yelling at me.

I sank to the floor with my palms pressing against the cold face of the door. I let my hands soak up the coldness before I rested my over-heated forehead between my fingers and breathed in and out to calm myself.

A sore on my arm throbbed with angry beats and my fingers shook from the adrenaline coursing through my veins.

I closed my eyes and tried to find that little place in my

mind where I knew my powers sat. I pushed and pulled at my mind trying to find it. The knowledge, the skill that I should have had, was somewhere in there.

My fists clenched, and my nails dug into my palms, but the pain did little to coax the latent powers from their hidden place in my mind and body.

I slammed my fists into the floor. "No!"

CHAPTER 34

"For every action there is an equal and opposite reaction." ~ Newton's Third Law of Motion

---

More time passed with little to do, and even less to see. The walls continued to be blank and the bars were still electrified. Every so often I would pour water over my hands and flick droplets at the bars, relishing in the noisy hiss created by the contact. Eventually I hoped to find the bars turned off, but so far it seemed that they were going to keep the bars electrified. Was I really that dangerous, or were they just that cruel?

I didn't have a good grasp of the time passing by. My watch had been killed by the contact with the electrical bars earlier. It was stuck on 10:43. I habitually checked it even though I knew it was broken. I knew I probably perceived time as passing slower than it really was because I had nothing to do but think, but so much time had passed. I slept for a little bit, but it didn't do anything to relieve the tiredness that was weighing on my brain and body.

Ashwater had said that they had already cracked the beacon signal. I had waited too long to contact Jacob. I had failed not only him but Willow. Soon, she would be infested with Isiro's soul. All that I had worked for was over now. All that I had loved would be lost.

I couldn't see where I would go from here. These Isiroans might kill me, or they might leave me to rot in this mind numbing cell for the rest of my life. How long would I live in a place like this without going completely batty?

I curled up into a loose fetal position on the lumpy

mattress and stared at the sink across the cell from me. The faucet dripped a steady tune into the bowl and beckoned me to close my eyes and sleep again. I conceded and closed my eyes but I did not sleep. Instead I felt in my mind for my telepathic powers. I could feel the dormant telepathic link, stiff and unused for too long.

I opened the link and reached out for Willow's mind. It was nowhere to be found. Oddly enough, I could sense the minds of others. This strange new sensation of sensing the little mental signatures was new. Willow hadn't said anything to me about this before. Was it possible to search for a mind like searching for something in Google?

I danced around the mind of the others I could feel, not quite touching their minds but flirting with the energy that their telepathic links gave off. I don't know why I had never noticed this before. The more time I spent reaching out, the more I began to actually visualize what I was feeling out there.

The mental world that I "saw" was purple. White lines drifted unhinged and touched with others only briefly, creating bursts of light that faded like food coloring in water. Unintelligible whispers tuned in and out, echoing eerily. Telepathic signatures stood out like miniature suns. The white lines came out of them like solar flares. In my limited exposure to Kinetic powers I had never heard of anything like this before. To actually "see" the psychic world that connected all Kinetics was beyond anything I had ever even conceived. It must be an effect of the EOS, right? It wasn't natural to be cut off from the powers, so to do so must have just made me aware of what was already out there. At least that's what I could come up with anyway.

I played with the images in my mind for an undeterminable amount of time until I heard something. I pushed myself up into a seating position on the bed and the imagined world of telepathic links flitted away.

Someone was singing far off down the hall, an unrecognizable tune echoing off the pasty white walls. I stood close to the bars and looked out at the hallway. I saw no one, but the singing was getting closer. It was a woman from what I could tell.

Finally I saw her. An elderly woman walked down the hallway, running her hands across the walls as she walked. Behind her the walls glowed with an unnatural light. The walls behind her were cleaner than the walls in front of her. The pitch of her voice rose higher and she passed by my cell. Her words were in Spanish. Whatever her power was doing to the walls it set off the electrical element to the bars. I felt the tingle of electricity and backed up a few steps.

She passed on by and disappeared down the hall. Her voice faded and I was alone again.

I didn't return to my meditations in the odd world of Kinetic psyches but instead began pacing. There had to be some way out of this place. Eventually they'd have to turn off the bars. They couldn't keep me locked down forever.

More time passed and my stomach, which had been rumbling protestations to the abuse I'd been putting my body through, started to growl in hunger. I hadn't eaten anything since dinner at the Ashwater's before they had captured me. How many hours had it really been?

I waited longer, unable to feed myself. I finally tested the water in the tap and found it to taste okay. I drank my fill of water, and finally fell into a dreamless sleep.

***

When I woke, I was confused. I looked at my watch again, but it still said 10:43. I tried to stand, but my legs turned to jelly under me and I fell to the concrete floor in a heap. I laid still and breathed in and out, trying to regain my bearings. The cell wobbled around me and I clung to the floor for dear life.

My water filled stomach flipped uncomfortably and nausea set in. I groaned and pulled myself back up onto the mattress. Maybe drinking a ton of water wasn't such a good idea. Good thing there was a toilet in here. Otherwise, I'd really be in trouble.

I had just gotten done relieving myself when I heard the elderly lady from earlier singing again as she came down the hall. I zipped up and stumbled to the middle of the cell just as she turned the corner and came to stand in front of the bars.

"*Comida.*" She pushed a tray through a thin, but wide gap in the bars near the floor. Then she left.

I kneeled down next to the tray and examined what had been brought. A bowl of thick beef stew and a bread roll. There were no utensils. I sighed in frustration, but pulled the tray up and sat on the mattress and sipped from the edge of the bowl. I used the bread roll to scour the rest of the stew from the bottom of the bowl. I didn't know how wise it was to trust the food from the Isiroans, but I was hungry enough to not care.

I was so involved in eating that I didn't notice that I had gained a visitor.

"Eugene."

I turned around so fast that my neck creaked in protest. "Harry?"

I stood up in the middle of the room and eyed my former friend. "What are you...?" I stopped. He was one of them! I was at the bars before I realized what I was doing and grabbed his shirt collar through the bars. I got a nasty shock from the bars and was thrown to the ground.

"This is your fault!" I shouted through my pain.

He stepped out of out of my reach and frowned back at me. "Nice to see you, too."

I slammed my fists on the ground and then turned away from him. "What are you doing here?" I couldn't stop the weariness from peppering my tone.

"I escaped your brother and I've come to join my friends here."

"Your friends?"

He smiled grimly. "You've been living with them."

Jack and Roy.

Harry was the third member of Jack's group of friends. I had heard enough third party stuff about him but it had never really clicked that it was Harry. I hadn't seen it at all and the knowledge slapped me in the face.

This explained why Jack was so perceptive about me and probably why Roy was so hostile. Harry must have been sharing information. This explained why he never seemed surprised by anything about me. He knew things he shouldn't have known.

I wanted to run but the walls around me mocked the very idea. I was trapped, always trapped.

"I was almost surprised when they told me you were here," he smiled. "I really didn't expect you to get this far."

"I'm not stupid." I frowned at him, turning around to add a glare.

"I never said you were." Harry stepped a few more feet back and leaned into the wall. He crossed his arms over his chest and watched me with his eyes half-lidded.

"Why are you here?" I asked in a low voice.

"I wanted to see how you were. I'm sorry about what happened, Eugene. I promise that my intentions were never to harm you or Willow. I wasn't sure what was going to happen when I returned, but it seems that you've outed yourself to the whole place. Saves me the trouble, I suppose." He grinned, but his eyes were sad.

I turned away again and stared at the wall opposite the bars, opposite Harry. "You won't win; evil like this can't go on." I said to the wall.

"This is not some childish battle between good and evil, Eugene. I thought you of all people would realize that." His voice was angry.

"Realize what? Realize that enslavement of Kinetics is not a bad thing? That taking over our planet is just another way of saying 'oh, hey, let's be friends'? Bull. "

"One of these days, Eugene, you're going to realize that the world is not so black and white." I heard him move away from the wall and walk away. I slipped to my knees onto the floor and buried my head in my hands. It took all my will to not try and rip my hair from the roots.

CHAPTER 35

"We may be brothers and sisters in the eyes of God, but we are not brothers and sisters in the eyes of Man. Brotherhood requires too much of him, for it requires him to trust." ~ Reginald Cook. Kinetic who attempted to take control of the Alliance. 1983.

The next time the old lady came by with food. I didn't eat. I ignored the tray. The smell of the food made my stomach roil, and I felt that if I ate anything I would just hurl it up. I curled up in a tight ball and for the first time in my life truly wished I could use my powers. I strained my mind and my body while curled up in that ball, but no flame manifested. I didn't understand how it was that my powers came to life only when my mind was under attack.

I meditated on the psychic world trying to seek out a mind that I could try and attack to hopefully receive an attack back from, but my search was fruitless. It seemed the more I tried to grasp onto my newfound vision of the Kinetic psyche, the more it faded and blackened. I was losing even that.

My sense of time was gone completely. Hours, days, I couldn't tell the difference even if I wanted to. Time was now a meaningless dimension. I slipped in and out of sleep, drifting to the point where, at times, I couldn't tell the difference between reality and dream. I saw things and people, the world shuddered and shifted with sounds, and my body seemed to take on the consistency of Jell-O. I thought then that I could see through my hands as they turned into pure fire, but I never felt a burn.

Thoughts of Willow twisted sinuously through my

weird visions, and I dreamed that she was standing outside my cell speaking comforting words. But I knew that, of all things, was a dream. Willow was lost to me. Willow was becoming one of *them.* She was never going to be the same. She was never going to know. Never going to see.

I mourned her loss. She was as good as dead now. Would she survive the process of taking on Isiro?

Eugene

Where was the line between the two?

Eugene... wake up

Where would her fiery personality go? Surely an old mind like Isiro's wouldn't leave anything behind.

EUGENE

I shot up out of my dazed dream state and gasped as if I had been underwater. Sweat poured down my face and my shirt was soaked.

I blinked, clearing the blur that made my vision wobble. "Jacob," I breathed.

My brother stood triumphantly outside the bars of my cell, grinning like a man who had just conquered the world.

"Jacob, you came!" I stumbled off the bed and staggered toward the bars. I had the foresight, even through my fevered brain, not to touch the bars again.

"I have to thank you, Eugene. This couldn't have happened better." He nodded in approval.

"What do you mean?" I grinned.

"This place is the perfect spot to bring in our troops. I wasn't sure if they were going to bring you here, or worse, to an open cell."

I felt my grin falter. "What?"

"It seems that you've either royally pissed them off, or you actually worry them. I think I'm quite proud of you, little brother." He laughed. "I'm sorry that I had to give you a bad beacon. We were presented with an opportunity through you to get us an access into this place. No one in his right mind would dare send any of our operatives into this place. It's too heavily guarded, too much of a risk to send in valuable troops. You have done a great service to the Alliance by doing this

Eugene, even if you didn't realize it."

"I don't understand." I whispered.

Jacob smiled indulgently. "You've been the unwitting martyr to the Alliance cause, my brother. I gave you a bad beacon on purpose. The code for that has been broken by the Legion for a good five years now. They could tell it was one of ours the moment you set it off. All it took was a day or so and I knew they would have you in a cell of some kind while they tried to figure out what to do with you. We've used you as a focal point for teleportation."

"We...?" It was then that I noticed the others in the hallway next to my brother. They wore the uniforms of the Alliance.

I felt my blood run cold. Jacob hadn't cared a whit about Willow. What was I thinking? Why would anyone believe that a fifteen-year-old boy could do anything to a well-established organization like the Isiroan Legion?

My brother had used me. I was his Trojan horse. The Laramie base was his Troy.

"Why? When..." It was the only thing that I could think of to say at this point.

"Unfortunately, Eugene, this is war. Sacrifices must be made." Jacob waved to one of his men and he nodded curtly before teleporting away.

All of a sudden more and more troops were being teleported in. They filled the hallway and spread out like a wave in either direction.

Wait. Something Jacob had said earlier.

"How many days? How many days has it been since the beacon?"

Jacob paused in the middle of direction some of his troops, "About 46 hours. Not long. "

Two days. Willow couldn't have bonded yet. There was still time.

Jacob began to leave... without me.

"You can't leave me here! I've got to at least try to save Willow!"

"Don't worry. You should be quite safe down here.

You'll be out of the way of any major fighting. I'll be sure to come get you when we've taken the base. As for Willow, she's a lost cause, Eugene. By now the bonding has already begun. It began well over a week ago, about the time you got here."

"That's impossible. The transfer..."

"Is the last step in the bonding *process*. At this point I would say that she's only a shell of her former self. She's a vessel, and that's all."

"No." I moaned. "You said..."

"I lied."

Jacob smirked and jerked his head at the last of his troops. They filtered away as Jacob lingered only a few moments more.

"I'm truly sorry, Eugene. But we've all had to make sacrifices in this war. It will be over soon."

And then he was gone.

CHAPTER 36

*"Nobody ever did, or ever will, escape the consequences of
his choices."* ~Alfred A. Montapert

I yelled. I shouted. I cursed. I nearly screamed. Nothing brought Jacob back. I hurled the mattress at the bars but it only resulted in singeing the mattress and filling the air with the smell of burnt polyester.

There was nothing else I could throw. I walked the perimeter of the cell trying to find some way out. There had to be a way. If they didn't have teleporter Kinetics, how else could they get people in and out of these cells? I kicked and punched the walls. I felt every minor bump in the concrete and explored every crevasse. This place was sealed tighter than a spaceship. I dragged the mattress out of the way and, without touching it, I examined the bars with a meticulous eye. The electrified bars hummed quietly. I put my hand up to one of the bars but didn't let my hand come in contact with the metal. The energy put out by the bars tickled my hand.

I raised both my hands up to the bars and clamped my hands down on them. Energy shot through my arms and I could feel all my nerves exploding with fire. I felt blood trickle from my nose, but I refused to let go. Each and every time my powers acted out, it was when I was under attack.

I closed my eyes, and held onto the bars tighter and tighter. I could feel my skin burning on my hands. I could smell it. And then... I felt it...

Fire blossomed from my fingers and swirled around me. I was the center of the firestorm. I was the eye of the storm. My raging fire screamed out and began melting the metal bars. In seconds the bars were reduced to nothing but hot white puddles of molten metal. The concrete around me was black. The mattress was a roiling bonfire. I took a breath to suppress the pain everywhere in my body. Soon, it would all be over.

With one last intake of congested air, I ran through the mess of cooling metal and sprinted around the corner of the hallway. I had no clue where I was going. For the first few minutes I ran blindly, turning corners in what seemed to lead outwards. The prison was a labyrinth.

I could feel hyperthermia setting in again, and my thoughts began to get muddled. I stumbled and ran, at the same time searching for the way out. The walls were blending together with the floor and ceiling so it was getting harder and hard to walk straight. I found myself in an open room with a huge pool of water in the middle of it. The water was pouring out of a huge hole in the ceiling where electrical wires were hanging down, spurting sparks.

I ran right through a cascade of water and felt my body release some of the heat that was building. The water was ice cold. I moved out of it as quickly as I had entered it and searched for the clarity of mind that had begun to escape me. The hyperthermia would set in again. I had to move quickly. I reached out with my telepathy and tried to find the source with the most Kinetic minds attached to it. Far off I sensed hundreds of minds broadcasting an array of emotions, everything from shattering fear to unbridled glee. Confused, but certain that that was the way I needed to go, I waded through the water flooding the halls. The further I went, the more sounds I heard. Gone was the bone white silence and quickly coming was the sound of terror.

Screams and shouts twisted through the hallway toward me. I found my way out.

A ramp in the hallway made a sharp incline upward leading toward the sounds of fighting, but also to the light. Bright orange light shone down onto the ramp heralding the way. I ran the last few feet up the ramp and burst out into a world on fire. The Isiroan base that, only a couple days ago, had seemed a serene place despite the people who occupied it was now burning from the ground up. Every building was either on fire, crashing to the ground or somewhere in between.

There were Alliance and Legion fighters battling it out on every square inch of the base. Light from various powers flashed everywhere, returned by the rumbles and sounds of other powers. The sky was filled with ominous clouds that struck lightning onto the ground and base. Wind howled through what few trees were left standing and rattled the wreckage. I looked around and tried to find my brother among the pandemonium.

A woman was thrown to the side by a Telekinetic. Her ragdoll body flopped and she was still.

A man was torn limb from limb by a rock spearing up from the ground.

Another man was screaming as his skin was being burned off.

Blood was everywhere.

The screams were getting louder and louder. I couldn't tell who was who. Blood, mud, dirt and sweat obscured the insignias and the identities of the fighters. Brother could be fighting brother at this point, not knowing that he was killing his own kin.

Some of them were resorting to fighting with fists and whatever blunt objects were available. Anarchy ruled. This war wasn't a war. War was supposed to be organized. One side fights the other, with clear lines and discernible borders. But this... this was mayhem. This was chaos.

I ran through the fighters, trying to recognize *anyone*. I had to find out where Willow was. I had to make sure, if anything before I die, that she was safe. I didn't care what Jacob said. There had to be a way to save her. There had to be a way to make it all okay.

A young woman stood over a fallen man and pulled a bloody knife out of his chest. She turned as I was running past and I stopped in my tracks.

"Laura!" I called to her.

She looked at me, confused. "Eugene?"

"Laura, what are you doing?"

"Eugene," Laura smiled, calm, at ease with herself. "Jacob has given me the way."

"What way?"

"The way to take revenge for my family." Her smile got wider and she looked to her left where a small contingent of Isiroan soldiers was fighting an even smaller group of Alliance soldiers. Suddenly the Isiroan soldiers stopped and all of them began screaming and clutching their heads.

Laura raised her hand gracefully toward them and then clenched her fist. All of the Isiroans fell to the ground and an odd purplish light seeped from their ears, eyes and mouths. The Alliance soldiers took that chance and within seconds all of the Isiroans were dead.

"I have the power now," she laughed, and a wild light entered her eyes. "My parents will be avenged!"

"Laura..."

"Eugene, your brother will be happy to see you." Laura closed her eyes and tilted her head upwards. "Go toward the center of this place and you will find him."

I backed up a few steps and, feeling a cold wind flow through my body, ran straight toward the center of the base. I became lost in the fire, blood and falling bodies. People on all sides were falling to the ground, dried leaves falling from dead trees.

"Eugene!" Jacob's voice speared through the other sounds of chaos.

I whirled around and stared at him. "Jacob!" I hissed.

He grinned, brotherly-like, "You escaped. Good for you. I'm proud."

I felt a rebellious trickle of hope at that, but it was dashed when I remembered. "You betrayed me! You lied to me!"

"Oh, Eugene, you're not still stuck on that. It's in the past!" Before he had finished his sentence an Isiroan had run at Jacob with a wave of ice daggers. Jacob had flicked his wrist and the man seized up and exploded. No blood, no gore. Complete combustion. I had never seen my brother's power so up close before. It wasn't nearly as bloody as I had thought. But it was oddly more brutal. There was no humanity at all in that Isiroan's death. I felt an odd rumble in my chest as my brother clapped his hand on my shoulder.

"You really have proven yourself. I don't know how you managed to get out of that cell."

I shoved his hand away. "Don't patronize me."

Jacob grinned and held his hands up. "You'll thank me later, Eugene. This will make you strong."

I growled deep in my throat and spun around. I had to find out where Willow was. My brother called to me, but I ignored him. I ran toward the dormitory. Jack would know, and if he didn't, then Harry would. I knew it. They had been in on this the whole time.

The elevators were destroyed in the dormitory. Scorch marks and large blackened spots marred the once pretty entryway. The roof was slightly caved in at the back and wiring and water was leaking from a couple holes in the ceiling.

I ran toward the stairs and sprinted up them. When I reached the floor of the dormitory where I had lived for a couple days I found all the doors ripped from their hinges and laying in sad heaps through the hallway. Half of the lights were off or flickering. Far off I heard screams and shouts and the noises of battle. The rooms that I passed were ransacked. It seemed impossible to me that the Alliance could have caused so much destruction in so little time.

Jack and Roy's room was a duplicate of the other rooms, ransacked, with items thrown everywhere. I kicked some of the shirts and books out of the way as I stepped further into the room.

Voices coming closer made me stop and I shoved myself into the closet and closed the door only enough so that I could peek out.

Roy, Jack, Harry...and *Logan,* Laura's allegedly dead brother, all entered the room. I hardly had a chance to register that he was standing there, alive when they started talking to each other.

"I can't believe it." Jack sighed and looked around the room.

"Nothing is surviving." Harry whispered.

"We should go, quickly. Your dad is waiting for us." Roy looked out the broken door and frowned. Logan picked up a charred pillow off the floor and let it drop to the bed into a sad heap.

"Right." Jack picked up a few books off the floor and stuffed them in a messenger bag. He was about to join Harry, Logan and Roy who were standing at the door when I decided to make my presence known. I pushed open the closet door, visibly startling the three others.

"You've all been working together, haven't you? This has just been some sick joke, hasn't it?" I yelled out.

"You!" Roy was at my neck in a split second. He pushed me up against the wall and I felt my breath leaving me. I dug my fingernails into his arm, drawing blood.

He squeezed harder and I kicked out, hitting him in the groin. He flinched and retaliated with a punch to my face. I fell to the ground and rolled away just before his foot came down where my stomach was. I jolted to my feet and tackled him.

Roy grabbed my hair and shoved my face into the wall. My vision went black for a second and then I regained my balance and punched his jaw.

Roy was off balance for only a second before he returned with three successive punches, two to my stomach and one to my face. I fell to the ground but he didn't let up. He kicked at my chest and I felt the air in my lungs leave me.

I tried to roll away and was only half successful as his foot came down again and caught my arm. I staggered to my feet and lashed out at him with my fists. He ducked and grabbed my neck again.

"Roy!" Jack and Harry finally pulled him away and I fell to the floor coughing and gasping.

"Wh—where—is—she?" I heaved out.

"Who?" Jack asked.

"Willow." Harry supplied, answering for me.

"Where?" I pushed myself to me feet and glared at all three of them.

Jack's fingers clenched. He looked about ready to do

what Roy had just tried to do. "What makes you think that we will tell you?"

"Where is she!" I took a step toward Jack but both Roy and Harry stepped in front of me. Logan appeared bewildered and actually backed up.

Jack and Roy looked at Harry in surprise. I was confused for a moment, and then realized that Harry must have sent them a telepathic message.

Jack glanced at me with a new look in his eyes. The gleam wasn't one I was comfortable with. He looked like he was planning something.

"She's on her way here with Isiro's entourage and a mass of troops. They have to stop here before transferring to the Argentina base anyway," Jack supplied.

"Jack, you shouldn't..." Roy started, but Jack touched his friend's shoulder and held eye contact with him for a few significant seconds. Roy nodded. Were they passing a telepathic message?

"They'll be here any minute."

I took in a deep breath, still feeling the pain from being choked by Roy. I rubbed my throat and then sprinted around the four, making my way down the stairs.

There. There he was. The second I saw him, I was in an all-out sprint. I jumped off the bridge and stumbled to stop right behind him. He turned just in time for me to see the whites of his eyes. My fist connected with the back of his head. Grey stumbled only for a split second before whirling around and grabbing my wrist.

"How did you get out?" he said.

"Guess!" I shouted and spun to untwist my arm from his grasp. He let go and I fell back and hit the ground with a *whumph.*

"Now is not the time." He murmured and started to walk away.

I lunged after him and grabbed his legs mid-step. He stumbled and fell to the ground, groaning in pain. He spun on his butt and kicked out, the heel of his shoe connecting with my forehead. I rolled away, but remembering my escape, I latched onto the pain coursing from the growing bump on my forehead. I felt the fire licking the back of my mind steady with a thrum. Just as in the cell I grabbed it and used my outstretched hand to channel the fury and pain into a shooting star of fire. The bolt lanced from my open palm and right toward Grey's weather-beaten face.

In one swift move with his arm the bolt exploded mid-air in a shower of fireworks. His eyes glimmered in the light and the fire in my mind was iced over with his cold stare. "Don't, boy. You have no idea what you are doing."

"I know perfectly well what I am doing!" I shot off a second bolt, weaker this time as the pain subsided.

He deflected it again, but this time the cold stare was replaced by something I couldn't read. Curiosity? Anger? I stopped looking at him for something I could use to fire up my powers again. A power pole a few hundred feet away had been knocked over and its wires were sparking with live electricity.

I vaulted off the ground and ran for the sparking wire, I didn't even hesitate to grab the wire and within seconds the energy coursed through my body. My hand was in severe pain and my heart hurt in so many ways. The wire still in hand, I turned toward Grey who was staring at me like I had sprouted extra limbs. The energy and pain coursing through my body built more and more and I held out my free hand toward Grey. His eyes only just registered what was about to happen when a shot like a flamethrower burst out straight toward him crossing the gulf between us in a matter of split seconds.

He stepped toward me, and when the flame was about to connect, a shield formed around him as he walked closer to me.

"Where is she?" I screamed over the roar of fire.

His brow twisted into confusion. "Who?"

"The girl you kidnapped! Willow!" I dropped the live wire and the fire shunted to a stop.

He stopped in his tracks and stared at me. Recognition passed over his features. "You're the guy she spoke of."

"She knew I was going to save her."

"She knew no such thing. She just said you would be

great one day if you learned to control your powers. How did you manage that?" He glanced down at the live wire cracking at my feet.

I grabbed the wire again and shot off another bolt. He quickly and easily deflected it just like the last ones. I stopped thinking and stared rapid fire bolts, hoping to catch him by surprise. Every bolt I fired he deflected, walking closer to me.

"You are mistaken" -- *Deflect.* "—if you think I am the cause for your-" *Deflect.* "—friend's arrival here."

"If you aren't-" *Bolt.* "-then who is?"

"Why don't you-" *Deflect.* "-ask her?"

"WHERE IS SHE, THEN!"

The arm that he had used to deflect my bolts rose up and pointed in the direction of the Spiral. There the light from the teleportation wave illuminated a dozen or so people arriving from parts unknown. Standing next to an elderly man was a redheaded girl of 15. Willow. She had an ear tilted toward the old man as he talked and pointed to the destruction. Far off I heard the shouts of Jacob's men ordering every building searched. From the Spiral more and more Isiroans appeared to confront the invading Alliance. Willow and the old man stood in place. Willow surveyed with a slow look until she was looking right at me. Our eyes met and I stumbled forward toward her. She spoke to the old man, then traversed the hill toward me. Grey followed after me and the old man followed after Willow. She stopped on the other side of the walkway. I moved toward her, but her strong voice stopped me. "Did you cause this?"

"I did it for you! To save you! Quick we can get out of here!"

She shook her head, looking like someone who was about to scold a child. "Eugene, what you have done here is unforgivable. People have DIED."

"But..."

"Why are you here?"

"I came to save you."

"I thought I left enough reassurance with you to tell you I was going to be okay."

"They told me that he was going to hurt you."

"Who? Isiro? NO. Isiro saved me from the Alliance. The Alliance is the one who tried to harm me."

"But..." I barely got the word out, but the thought was already forming. She was brainwashed. Jacob said as much.

"Go home, Eugene! You are NOT needed." She spun on her heel and walked back toward the Spiral. The old man stayed a moment more and evaluated me. Around his neck glimmered a small, green crystal. Isiro.

Rage. Rage was the pain. Without knowing what I was doing I lunged forward and sent a blast bigger than anything I could have imagined possible. The ground itself seemed to set on fire in front of me. In seconds I was on the ground, Grey had tackled me and the fire I had produced was raging out of control. My clothes were setting on fire as were the clothes of Grey. I struggled under his scarily strong grip and the fire continued to rage.

Grey was unaffected by the fire I was blasting out. It was out of control now. I didn't have any more control over it than an ant has over the weather. I started to get scared. I couldn't stop it. Grey seemed to realize the same thing and slammed his hand into my head.

Stop. I felt his voice in every crevasse of my brain. His telepathic voice shuddered all the way down my spine.

My muscles locked, and I stared wide eyed into his face. But something else was happening to me in my chest. Tears started flowing out of my eyes and the pain in my chest started to grow. I curled in on myself and clenched my chest. I felt a fire like none other burning a hole. I looked down and saw a bright light coming from where my heart was. And suddenly everything went dark.

All I felt was an indescribable feeling of being stretched.

My body became colder and colder, and what should have been the pain of having my body ripped to shreds in the teleportation wake was dashed by the feeling of warm water flowing through my body and

I was

Light.

Unfortunately, everything has changed.
Willow melted like food coloring into water.

An image of Willow stood in front of me. Somewhere in the recesses of my mind a dozen dreams and memories came flooding back. They were all of Willow, speaking to me in between moments of unconsciousness, somehow telling me something that I should have known from the start. I could almost remember them all now. But something was wrong. The Willow in front of me--

"You... you're not Willow," I said to her. She stood out like a single spot of paint on the black canvas that surrounded us.

She looked at me and smiled. Her eyes were the color of polished amber and not the soft green of Willow's. "No. I am not. Welcome to the space between thoughts."

CHAPTER 37

*"War does not end strife - it sows it. War does not end
hatred. It feeds it. For those who argue war is a necessary evil, I
say you are half right. War is evil. But it is not necessary. War
cannot be a necessary evil, because non-violence is a necessary
good. The two cannot co-exist."* ~ US Congressman John Lewis

HARRY GLEESON

Eugene went limp and Mr. Grey grabbed him. But I
didn't have time to see what was going on. The Alliance
insurgents were coming around for another wave of attacks.
Right behind us, one of the Isiroan generals was forming up a
defense line between the insurgents and the Spiral. More
troops were coming in through the Spiral, filling the base with
caustic light and sound from over a hundred battles.

We were in a dangerous position. What little formation
there was in the Alliance was coming up to meet the Isiroan
defense line with an offensive line of their own. Jacob Yoshida
himself was at the front shouting orders. I turned to tell Jack
and Roy that we needed to leave and saw Eugene getting to his
feet. He pushed away from Mr. Grey and looked at the Alliance.
But something was wrong. His eyes were glowing white.

Eugene stepped forward and reached out his hands. A
ring of fire at his feet began to spin and swirl around him
getting bigger and bigger, turning into a hurricane of fire. His
hands became engulfed in flames as he appeared to gather the
latent energy in his body.

Jacob Yoshida looked at his brother and shouted at him
to stop. But his younger brother wasn't listening anymore.
Eugene spread-eagled his arms and a wall of fire shot out,

separating the Isiroans from the Alliance. The wall of fire roared and where Eugene was standing the fire was turning blue and white.

I grabbed Jack's shoulder. "We need to use this opportunity to get out of here."

"But we can't leave him." Jack said, pointing at Eugene. The fire wall was even bigger now and beginning to encapsulate the Alliance insurgents. Most of the Isiroans were free. Someone in the distance shouted for us to evacuate to the teleporter.

Minus the defensive line, a massive wave of people were running toward the Spiral. Jack didn't move an inch and because of that Roy didn't either. And surprisingly enough Grey was still standing next to us too.

"Mr. Grey?" I shouted over the roar of Eugene's firewall. "Aren't you going to leave?"

He shook his head and shouted back, "No. That boy has more going on in his head than he's letting on. A Vunjika shouldn't be able to do what he's doing right now." Mr. Grey came to stand right next to us.

"What do you mean?" Jack asked.

"There's something acting on his powers. A foreign power source." He narrowed his eyes. "I can't tell what though."

The firewall reached up and over the heads of the Alliance and created a dome around them. The Isiroans were almost gone now, leaving only us, the defensive line, Eugene, and the Alliance insurgents inside Eugene's fire dome.

What little I could see past the fire, the Alliance was attacking Eugene. I saw all sorts of powers thrown at him. But they deflected or he burned them away like leaves to a torch.

"We have to go!" An Isiroan troop waved at us to follow her. The Isiroan troops were starting to disperse, heading back to the Spiral now that Eugene pretty much had them under control.

"You kids go," Mr. Grey said.

"But," Jack started to say but Mr. Grey ignored him and ran up to Eugene.

He wrapped one arm around Eugene's neck and the other around his waist. Eugene burned hotter but Grey was unaffected. Grey with his arms still around Eugene reached up and tapped a device on his wrist. I recognized it as one of the few technologist teleporters. The two of them glowed and then disappeared with a swirl of fire in their place. We ducked when the firewall exploded outwards and the Alliance insurgents were all that was left in the base besides us and the last few remaining Isiroan troops.

Roy grabbed my arm and dragged me up the hill after Jack. We were pressed and pushed into the center of the Spiral when one of the Isiroan generals activated the teleporter. We Deconstituted in seconds.

None of us had any time to prepare for the teleportation to the snowy mountains of Argentina. As soon as we reconstituted on the other side, harsh winds and frozen snow chilled us to the bones. Fortunately the gate to the base was already wide open and they were letting everyone through.

I had never seen the inside of the Argentinian base so packed with people. "Let's get to the monitors." I said to Jack and Roy.

They followed after me as I pushed and squeezed through the masses that were all shouting and crying and demanding answers. Of course no one could have seen this coming. No one could have known that the Vunjika named Eugene could have caused so much harm and danger. A whole base had been brought to its knees by the simple fact that Eugene loved Willow too much to let her go.

"Harry!" Willow's voice called out over the crowd.

I looked over and saw her working her way through the crowd. She grabbed my arm and pulled herself through the last of the people between us. "What happened to Eugene?"

I shook my head. "Mr. Grey took him somewhere."

"Is he safe?"

I nodded. "If he's with Mr. Grey he's probably really safe."

"Thank you. I love that boy, but he's an idiot sometimes." There were tears in her eyes. She had been

337

incredibly strong since joining the Isiroans, especially knowing that her whole life was changing drastically, especially knowing that she was abandoning everything she knew.

I chuckled. "I know the feeling."

She hugged me and said, "Thank you for looking after him."

"I did what I could." I hugged her back and looked up to see the monitors on a far wall showing the security footage from Laramie. The whole base was overrun and crumbling to ashes.

"Miss Patterson." One of Isiro's guards squeezed through the crowd and came up next to us.

"Tom, what is it?" Willow broke free and faced the newcomer.

Tom swallowed and looked around apprehensively at the people pushed together like sardines. He seemed worried that one of them would attack at any moment. "It's time. We have to go now. Isiro is ready to be transferred."

***

EUGENE YOSHIDA

"You're not Willow." I said again. The feeling of losing something bit at my heart.

She shook her head. "Ever since your Willow was kidnapped, she left something in your mind. It is a message that you have slowly been unpacking, and at the same time you have been letting me see."

"I've been dreaming about..." I tried to remember all the things that I had dreamt about. I could see Willow's face, but the words were hard to recall.

"Let me assist you," she said.

Like a gardener pulling roots I felt parts of my mind wake up to dreams I'd been having for weeks.

I once thought that the world was simple, Eugene. Willow stood on the embankment of a raging river.

Long ago, I felt the need to run away. Willow leaned against the edge of a tree--

One of the things that I really loved about our

neighborhood was all the people. Willow knelt in the grass and picked a dandelion--

Very few times did I realize that by the time I was 15 I would be part of a world falling apart. Willow walked on the edge of the rhythmic waves from the sea.

Every day I hope that things will get better.

You know the time that we ran across the fields as children?

Oh, something has gone terribly wrong!

Unfortunately, everything has changed.

Willow melted like food coloring into water.

And then I saw it. The thought she was trying to leave me. **I L O V E Y O U.** I could sense it in the words and the thoughts, spread out through a million shades of emotions.

"The memories were hers." The Not Willow cocked her head. The more I looked at her the more the difference between her and the real Willow stood out. "The thoughts, the emotions were hers, but I was using them to facilitate a connection with you."

"Who are you?"

"My designation, my name if you will, cannot be pronounced with human language or understanding. Ben Ashwater called me Sarasvati."

"Sarasvati?" I looked around at the darkness. It looked like we were floating in a black void. "What's happening?"

"You were in danger, and therefore I was in a danger. I have taken over your body for the meantime until the danger has passed." Sarasvati smiled.

"Taken over? Wait..." Something had taken over when I had lost control at the Laramie base. Was it her?

I remembered more moments. I could remember back at Roswell with the man who had tried to kill me and Harry. I remembered the voice that shouted *NO* while the fire exploded from my hands. I could remember sitting under the overpass listening to Willow's voicemail message and feeling her rush up from the bottom of my mind trying to get out. I could remember standing in front of Joseph Carmichael and feeling his mind invade mine, but only it was stopped by the presence of this Sarasvati who not only stopped it but took over everything.

She nodded as my realizations unfolded, as if she was watching them flow out of my brain.

"Through less than fortunate circumstances, Ben Ashwater put my AI into you when you were little more than a baby. I have been tied to you since then and as my primary programming objective is to protect myself I must take matters into my own. You will wake in due time, but for now I am in control of your body."

"Why me?" I asked. Now that I wasn't standing in Laramie anymore I could think clearly. I had lost control over my powers and she had taken over. But that meant that the battle raging elsewhere... Where was it? Where was Willow? Where was *my* Willow.

"I do not know why I have been placed with you, a child with no means and few abilities." She shook her head and appeared to think about it.

"Can you not... can you not look like Willow?" I asked.

"Is this form not pleasing?" She looked down at herself and frowned.

"N—no it's not that, it's just... never mind." I looked away, wondering if my face was turning red.

The image of Willow shimmered and a different, taller woman with long dark hair, cinnamon skin and a red sari appeared. "This was the form of Ben Ashwater's mother, Priya Kapoor. She will work?"

I nodded, amazed at the shift. "What are you?"

"I was created almost a millennia ago by our people to begin archiving all the knowledge that we encountered."

"What people? Kinetics?"

Sarasvati shook her head. "The people from which Isiro was born. The Sho'da."

I think I would have choked if I was breathing real air. "Isiro? You're Isiroan?"

She looked to the side and patted her forehead. "Ahh, why Ben Ashwater, this one? You are not too bright. I was put in you by an Isiroan. Surely it makes sense."

"I guess. How do I get you out?"

Sarasvati clasped her hands together and began to walk. I followed after her instinctively, trying to not pay attention to the fact that I was not really walking on anything at all. "Only Ben Ashwater can get me out. Fear not, I mean you no harm. In my many forms, I travelled far and I have gained the knowledge of a thousand rulers and beggars. I am only a gatherer of knowledge and I only strike when I must protect myself and through that I will protect you, because you protect me."

Suddenly she stopped and stared up. I felt something, my real body perhaps, being teleported. "What's going on?"

She didn't have time to answer because I was kicked back into my body and found myself staring up at a starry night sky. Beside me I heard conversation but the words made no sense. It took a moment before I realized that the people talking were doing so in Chinese.

I looked over and saw Marcus Grey talking to a young girl.

I didn't have the energy to think much more than that, because as soon as I realized it, the pain of the EOS struck and everything that I had done to pull my powers out of my body rebounded and I was in immense pain.

I screamed and screamed and screamed.

And little did I know thousands of miles away Willow was well on her way to becoming the next host of Isiro.

HARRY GLEESON

I followed Willow into the Healer's rest where Willow would become the next host of Isiro.

There were two cots in the middle of the room laid head to head. George Lancaster, Isiro's current host, already lay in one.

I had never seen our leader this close before. It was strange. In George's body he wasn't nearly as intimidating as he could have been. George had become old and wizened. He

341

had been Isiro's host since his mid-thirties, and now well into his sixties he looked so much older than he should have been. I had heard that in some ways being host to Isiro could extend life for some, but George hadn't been one of the lucky ones. He had aged well beyond his years under the weight of Isiro's mind.

"Harry?" Willow pinched my shirtsleeve.

"Yeah?" I looked down at her. Her stance was strong, but her eyes were worried.

"Will you hold my hand... when... you know." She glanced to the side, she was nervous and it showed.

"Of course!" I said and wrapped my arm around her shoulders and squeezed.

The Healer monitoring the transference came over to us. "George and Isiro have gone into a deep sleep," she said. "We have to put you under now too, Miss Willow."

"Stay with me until I wake?" she asked me.

"Yes," I smiled.

Willow nodded and sat on the second cot. She looked around at the small gathering of people who had come to witness the transference. "I keep forgetting," she whispered to me, "that this is almost a once in a lifetime experience for some."

"It is for me, too." I said.

The Healer came over and patted Willow's shoulder. She lay down and closed her eyes. I reached out and grabbed her hand. It shook in mine.

The Healer touched Willow's head and Willow's hand and entire body stilled. I swallowed and tried to shake the feeling that she was dead. I could still see the light rise and fall of her chest as she breathed.

Another Healer came over and stood between the two cots. He placed a hand on George's forehead and a hand on Willow's and began to breathe in and out deeply.

"What's he doing?" I asked the first Healer who was now standing next to me, watching the other Healer work.

"He is regulating their internal energies. They need to be on the same wavelength for the transference to complete itself. They are already in tune with each other because of their meditations this past month, but the extra help while they sleep will make the transference go smoothly."

I nodded and squeezed Willow's hand, even though I knew she was in too deep a sleep to get anything from it.

"Transfer," the second Healer said. The first Healer left my side and placed her right hand on George's arm and scooped the green crystal lying on his chest into her left hand.

I had momentarily forgotten the others that were in the room. But when the Healer picked up the crystal there was a collective gasp from the onlookers. The Healer reached over and placed the crystal on Willow's chest and then placed her left hand on Willow's arm. The crystal glowed brightly and I could hear an electric hum coming from the two Healers and the two hosts, old and new.

The air crackled and I felt more than saw a massive amount of energy flow from George and into Willow.

The shoulders of the two Healers slumped and there was a sigh from the onlookers.

The transfer was complete.

END OF BOOK 1
TO BE CONTINUED IN BOOK 2
FORCES: IN SEARCH OF POWER

SUPPLEMENTALS
Glossary of Terms

Anyan's Decision (AD): An experimental drug that suppresses a wielder's powers for a short time.

BodyHeat pills: A set of two pills, the silver one lowers the body temperature, the black one returns it to normal.

Combine Power: Combine powers are powers that join two other powers to make a unique power.

Isiro: An alien of indeterminable age and purpose. He has no physical body and has lived via human hosts for generations. What remains of his 'soul' is in a green crystal pendant through which he can connect to hosts.

IsiroanTech: Because of Isiro's alien origin, Isiroans are well versed in highly advanced tech. Most of their modern tech is combined with traits from powers. Anyan's Alliance has little access or understanding of this tech.

Kinetic: Term for a person who can utilize powers. The term was coined via a translation error made in a speech by former chief minister of the Anyan's Alliance Ashraf bin Saqib Al-Fulani. The term stuck and has become widely used in modern day.

Omni-powers: Powers that have access to all variations of powers. Included are Omnipotence and Mirror.

Primary Power: The Primary Power is always Telepathy.

The Prime: A point of time when a Kinetic is young where the volatility of their powers is most extreme. This is the point where children begin to fully manifest and settle on one unique power.

Secondary Power: The Secondary Power is any other power, it changes from person to person, but not exclusive to anyone.

Sphere: A general term for a sphere of influence. This is how far a Kinetic can use their powers from their person. It can grow with the skill of the person.

Telepathy: Telepathy is distance restricted. The further the 'Pathers the more skilled they must be.

Tertiary Power: The Tertiary Power is like the secondary power but is much less developed and very rarely does anyone gain more than a fundamental control over it.

Kinetic Weaponry: Weapons that certain kinetics can imbue with their powers. These weapons are not specific to any power; the imbuement occurs with the Kinetic not the weapon. Rather, weapons can act as a sort of centering device. The powers do not stay in the weapons after use.

Vunjika: A Vunjika Block is what a kinetic has when he or she goes untrained in their powers after the age of 7. With a Block it becomes increasingly hard to remove as the years progress. Blocks often occur automatically with extreme psychological trauma. Blocks can only be broken with intensive work and training. A kinetic with a Block is called a Vunjika.

Wielder: Any person who uses Kinetic powers

KINETIC POWERS AND SOME THEORY

***

- The following abilities are only the *known* powers. There are still powers out there with no class or specification of use. Also due to the nature of the human mind, powers are subject to extensive variation. Combine powers for one have led researchers to the conclusion that powers are not set in stone. A person like Laura Jordan has a Combine power that melds together the two Psychic Class powers of Mind Read and Illusionary and because of how she uses it causes her targets to experience nightmares. She can also cause them to enter a sleep walking state where they can interact with the world around them while still seeing some form of nightmare.

- Powers are not determined at birth. A Kinetic spends the first five years of their life in a state of uncertainty, their bodies and minds are constantly trying out new powers and trying to make one fit in with the child's environment, personality, upbringing, and so on. At five they enter the Prime. The Prime is the primary influential environment for the development of powers. By the age of 7 the mind begins to acclimate to a particular pattern and the environment in which the wielder resides. At 8 or 9 the power settles and becomes permanent.

- If a Kinetic goes untrained throughout his or her life they become inflicted with a Vunjika Block that often times cannot be broken without serious work and pain on part of the wielder. Use of powers as a Vunjika, as Eugene did, causes Energy Overload Syndrome, a malfunction of certain circuits in the brain that become overloaded with Kinetic energy. EOS then causes the body to try and expend the energy via fever or, ironically, continued use of powers.

- The tendency for the mind to acclimate to its wielder's surroundings is oftentimes the cause of new and unusual abilities to arise. There is no limit to what the mind can come up with within reason.

- A wielder's power works on a sub-molecular level. For example, when a Breather is breathing in a poison gas the gas itself is being sub-molecularly changed into oxygen. Fire and like powers are especially potent powers because the wielder is effectively tapping into the energy of atoms themselves.

- The first conscious ability that any Kinetic learns is that the human body contains only so much energy. There is energy all around us so they must learn how to draw energy from any sources around them. As a Kinetic trains his or her reservoir of energy in their body grows.

- As a Kinetic grows in power, her abilities and control over her environment will expand. For example: initially a Pyrokinetic will only have control over fire itself, as she trains she will be able to temper and control the smaller aspects of energy. Some powers and persons are able to branch out to other similarly constructed powers at advanced levels. This particular ability is not easy and many have coveted the training required to do it.

POWERS

PHYSICAL CLASS
Alter: Transforms any inanimate object into another object
Teleport: Teleports the wielder and anything he or she wishes to a specified location.
Telekinesis: Gives the wielder the ability to move and manipulate physical objects.
Transform: Changes the form of the wielder to another human

or animal.

Healing: Heals wounds, highly advanced Healers can occasionally heal or cure various ailments, but the ability to do so is beyond many wielders proficiency.

Invisibility: Turns an object or the wielder invisible via reflective light.

Fission: Obliterates an object. Effect is like an atomic bomb on a significantly smaller scale.

Solid Shifter: Allows wielder to become part of a physical object, chameleon-like, but the effect is that the person is separating the molecules in their body to enter another object.

PSYCHIC CLASS

Mind Control: Gives the wielder the ability to control and enter another's mind.

Mind Read: Gives the ability to read only the mind.

Mirror: Mirrors an opponent's power.

Sensory Sphere: Kinetic radar or sonar

Illusionary: Allows wielder to create illusions.

Clairvoyance: Ability to locate anyone

Tracer/tracker: Ability to read or trace another wielders power signature.

Timer: Ability to manipulate a person or persons' perception of time.

Altermind: Wielder has the ability to see through the eyes of another person or animal.

ELEMENTAL CLASS

Pyrokinesis: Ability to manipulate and create fire.

Electrokinesis: Ability to create and manipulate electrical currents

Aquakinesis: Allows wielder to create and manipulate water.

Terrakinesis: Ability to manipulate the earth and minerals.

Florakinesis: Ability to rapidly generate plants and to manipulate them.

Ayrkinesis: Ability to manipulate air molecules.

UNCLASSED POWERS
Mechanical: Allows wielder to control and manipulate
        machinery
Animality: Rare power. Wielder can communicate with
        animals, wielder is usually feral or almost feral.
Spiritor: Ability to encase other metaphysical things in to other
        objects. Only known wielder of this is Anyan.
Omnikinetic: The wielder has the ability to learn all powers
        with little to no difficulty. Unlike Mirror, the effect is
        permanent. Only known wielder is Ben Ashwater.
Wallwalker: Ability to climb any physical object.
Breather: ability to breath in any environment, gaseous or
        liquid.
Lingua: Ability to understand and speak any language.
Weather wielder: A combine power that allows the wielder to
        control small pockets of the weather. This is a mix of
        powers between Air and Water

Levels of control
Level One - Basic – Manipulation, Range limited to personal
space
Level Two - Median – Molecular manipulation, Range
amplified.
Level Three - Advanced – Limited molecular change, limited
power branching, Extreme range

The Tiers
Tier One - Most Destructive (i.e. Fission)
Tier Two - Less destructive, can be used to create destruction
but also not (i.e. telekinesis)
Tier Three - Non Destructive. (i.e. Healing)

ACKNOWLEDGMENTS

This book would not be possible without the assistance and encouragement of sixteen-years-worth of friends, family, and random strangers upon whom I foisted my excitement about writing a book. To those of you who read about a dozen versions of this book, I'm sorry and thank you. To those of you who have read any version of this book, thank you. To those of you who said you would read it but couldn't when you were busy, thanks anyway, love ya.

In writing this book I have learned more about writing then any class could have taught, and while I still have a million words and a million miles to go before I am the kind of writer I'm meant to be, this is an important first step. Thank you, thank you, thank you!

And finally, the editing on this book was partially crowd-sourced by my friends and compatriots and most diligently by the wonderful primary editors Sara McManamy Johnson and Paul Barrow. Without them all would be lost. Any and all remaining errors are mine alone.

ABOUT THE AUTHOR

I hate talking about myself in the third person.
I live in Tennessee.
I have a cat named Dragon and a snake named Stella and no I don't
let them play with each other.
I enjoy movies, books, music, sunsets and long walks on the beach.
My favorite Beatles song is All You Need Is Love.
My favorite flavor of ice cream is strawberry.

On a more serious note, I've wanted to be a writer since before I can
really remember, and I've been determined to make that dream a
reality. I never wanted to be one of those people perpetually "writing
a book" and never let it see the light of day or a reader. I wanted to
write something that I could be happy to share. So with this humble
submission to the world I give myself over to you the reader.

I can be reached through various social media.
Feel free to find me on Facebook:
Author page: https://www.facebook.com/arborwinterbarrow
Personal page: https://www.facebook.com/arbor.barrow
I sometimes post pictures to Instagram: @magnetrose
I happily accept any and all emails including recipes I should try:
magnetrose@gmail.com

37530611R00212

Made in the USA
Charleston, SC
09 January 2015